A REASON
FOR
ROMANCE

Books by Rachel Knowles

Published by Sandsfoot Publishing
The Merry Romances
A Perfect Match (Book 1)

Published by Pen & Sword History
What Regency Women Did For Us

A Reason for Romance

THE MERRY ROMANCES BOOK 2

Rachel A. Knowles

Rachel Knowles

Sandsfoot Publishing

Published by Sandsfoot Publishing 2021

A catalogue record for this book
is available from the British Library

ISBN 978-1-910883-02-0

Sandsfoot Publishing is an imprint of
Writecombination Ltd
28, Sunnyside Road,
Weymouth, Dorset. DT4 9BL

To Andrew,
the love of my life

*All at once, I knew it was you I was in love
with. I felt that if you went out of my life,
the sun would never shine so brightly again.*

GEORGIANA MERRY'S FAMILY TREE

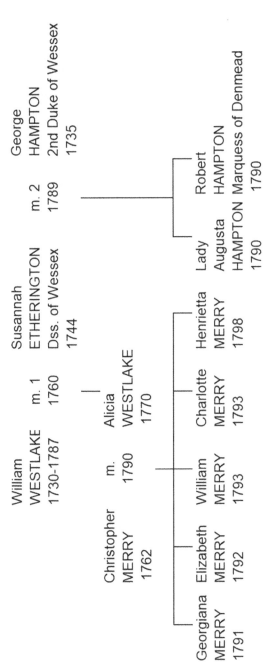

William WESTLAKE 1730-1787 m. 1 1760 Susannah ETHERINGTON Dss. of Wessex 1744 m. 2 1789 George HAMPTON 2nd Duke of Wessex 1735

Christopher MERRY 1762 m. 1790 Alicia WESTLAKE 1770

Georgiana MERRY 1791 Elizabeth MERRY 1792 William MERRY 1793 Charlotte MERRY 1793 Henrietta MERRY 1798

Lady Augusta HAMPTON 1790 Robert HAMPTON Marquess of Denmead 1790

Key: m. = married
     Dss. = Duchess

CHRISTOPHER MERRY'S FAMILY TREE

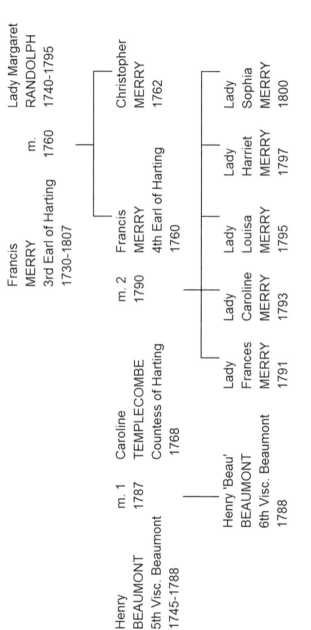

Francis MERRY, 3rd Earl of Harting, 1730-1807 m. 1760 Lady Margaret RANDOLPH, 1740-1795

Children of Francis MERRY and Lady Margaret RANDOLPH:
- Francis MERRY, 4th Earl of Harting, 1760
- Christopher MERRY, 1762

Henry BEAUMONT, 5th Visc. Beaumont, 1745-1788 m. 1 1787 Caroline TEMPLECOMBE, Countess of Harting, 1768

Francis MERRY, 4th Earl of Harting, 1760 m. 2 1790 Caroline TEMPLECOMBE, Countess of Harting, 1768

Child of Henry BEAUMONT and Caroline TEMPLECOMBE:
- Henry 'Beau' BEAUMONT, 6th Visc. Beaumont, 1788

Children of Francis MERRY and Caroline TEMPLECOMBE:
- Lady Frances MERRY, 1791
- Lady Caroline MERRY, 1793
- Lady Louisa MERRY, 1795
- Lady Harriet MERRY, 1797
- Lady Sophia MERRY, 1800

Key: m.   = married
       Visc. = Viscount

CHAPTER 1

Georgiana Merry slipped out of the house into the moonlight. She cast a guilty look back at the parsonage. For a moment she hesitated. Was she doing the right thing?

Deep down, she knew there was no other way. Gulping hard, she closed the door behind her. It banged shut, and the sound resonated for miles in the darkness. She stood still, not daring to move, nervously biting her bottom lip as she held her breath, listening, waiting to hear if there was any movement within.

All was silent. With a sigh of relief, she hurried down the garden path and into the woods beyond, fastening the buttons of her pelisse with one hand as she went. The other hand was clinging to a pair of bandboxes. Moonlight only penetrated the branches here and there, but it was enough for Georgiana. The path was so familiar that she could have walked it with her eyes closed.

A little way ahead, the copse opened into a clearing. She was relieved to see a solitary figure standing there, waiting.

"Beau!" she called out, rushing toward the Viscount, her deep blue eyes glistening with admiration at the romantic picture he presented.

His short, dark hair was somewhat unruly, falling over his forehead and giving his classically handsome features a more saturnine look. His broad shoulders set his greatcoat off to excellent advantage. Though Georgiana did not share his passion for sport, she suspected that it accounted for his magnificent physique. He was no doubt destined to be a member of the Corinthian set. And he was tall. Not as tall as her father, but well above average height, and despite her own lack of inches, she had a decided preference for tall gentlemen.

Lord Beaumont's eyes lit up with pleasure and he reached out his hands toward her. Dropping her bandboxes on the ground, she walked into his arms. She turned her face up to his, peeking up at him through her eyelashes, anticipating the long-awaited kiss. Beau lowered his head and pressed his lips to hers in a lingering embrace.

At length, he pulled away. "We must go now, Georgie," he said huskily.

"Oh yes," she mumbled, as the colour rushed into her cheeks. "I was forgetting." The kiss had put everything else out of her mind. It had stirred up feelings she had not known were there, and she was not altogether sure she liked it. She did not feel quite as in control as she had done before.

Beau picked up the discarded bandboxes with one hand and took Georgiana's hand with the other. He led the way out of the wood and onto the road behind to where Beau's groom was standing with a magnificent pair of matched bays harnessed to a travelling chariot. She recognised Beau's horses and smiled, relieved that he had taken her advice and was using his own equipage.

With a quick word to the loyal Jem, Beau handed Georgiana into the carriage and climbed in after her. Jem folded up the steps and shut the door on them before mounting the nearside horse.

As they pulled away, Beau glanced at his pocket watch and frowned. "I don't like it," he muttered. "A pair of horses – even *my* horses – will not take us anywhere fast enough."

"But if you had hired a post-chaise and four from the George as you suggested, news of it would have reached my father."

Beau grunted. "I suppose, but don't think I'm going to ruin my horses pushing them beyond their limits. We'll change at Alton."

"Then you might as well resign yourself to being caught," Georgiana snapped. "The ostlers at the Swan know you even better than those at the George. Can't we go a different way?"

He looked at her as though she were mad. "Leave the post road? Don't be so daft! Then we wouldn't be able to change horses at all."

Georgiana took a deep breath. This was not how a romantic elopement was supposed to be. They had only been in the carriage together for five minutes, and already they were arguing. Too late, she recollected that Beau needed to feel as if he were in charge.

"I'm sorry. Don't be cross with me," she pleaded. "I'm sure you are right. If we change at Alton like you said, you could say that you are going straight up to London and want your horses stabled at home. If I stay hidden in the chaise, no one will think anything of it."

Her apology worked.

"Good girl," he said with a lopsided grin.

The change at Alton passed without a hitch. No one came to the carriage window. Beau left his precious horses with Jem and a new team was soon hitched to the chariot, driven by one of the Swan's postilions. Georgiana suspected that the ostlers, knowing Lady Harting's exacting personality, would not be surprised that the Viscount was heading off to visit friends without stopping to see his mother.

As the carriage continued along the post road, Beau slumped in the corner of his seat and fell fast asleep. Georgiana was aghast to discover that he snored. She cleared her throat noisily until he opened one eye.

"We should talk about where we're going to live," she said, giving him a dazzling smile. "Will it be hard to find somewhere suitable in Cambridge?"

"Cambridge?" he said, with a blank look. "Are you all about in the head, Georgie? My estates are in Surrey, not Cambridgeshire, and I've already got a perfectly good house there."

"I know that, but we'll need a place to live when you go up to Cambridge, and Michaelmas term is only six weeks away."

He stared at her, screwing up his face in disgust. "I'm not going to university."

"Not going? What do you mean you're not going?"

"I'm not bookish. I never was. Just thinking about more study brings me out in a cold sweat. I thought you knew I didn't want to go."

She shook her head slowly. "That piece of information seems to have passed me by. I suppose that I expected you to go up to Cambridge and then take your seat in the House of Lords when you came of age." She saw the look of revulsion on Beau's face and realised that she had assumed incorrectly.

"What will you do then?"

"Don't you know?" he said, a curious smile on his lips. "I intend to breed racehorses."

"Racehorses?" She could not believe what she was hearing. Did he think she was marrying him so he could breed racehorses instead of going to university? All the men in her family went up to Cambridge.

It was what they did. If she had ever thought about it, she had always envisaged marrying a university man. Besides, she didn't even like horses that much.

"Yes. Like the Earl of Derby and Lord Egremont and countless others."

"Why haven't you set up your stud already if you are so taken with the idea?" she asked, trying, rather feebly, to mask her irritation.

"I have started in a small way, but I can't build up a stud on my paltry allowance, and my mother holds the purse strings tightly when she does not approve. You know that by the terms of my father's will, my fortune is tied up until I'm an old man unless I get married. That's why this elopement seemed such a good idea."

Georgiana's face clouded over. "I thought it was a good idea because you wanted to marry me," she said in a small voice.

"I do, I do," he reassured her, giving her a quick peck on the cheek. "We rub along very well together."

Her bottom lip quivered. These were not the words of love that she had hoped to hear. Her vision of a romantic elopement was disintegrating. The more she thought about it, the more it hurt. She gulped hard and blinked away a tear, not wanting him to see how much he had upset her.

Beau must have seen her struggle and guessed that he had said the wrong thing. He tried to make amends, drawing her close and putting his arm around her, but the damage was done. She closed her eyes, trying to block out his words, but it was no good. A seed of doubt had been planted in her mind.

For the first time in their rapid courtship, she questioned whether Beau loved her at all. She had known him all her life, his widowed mother having married her uncle when he was a small boy. It had only been this summer that things had changed between them, and they had fallen in love. At least, she thought they had.

If he did not love her, what was she doing here? It was an enormous step they were taking, and it went much against her principles. She loved her parents and hated to hurt them, but an elopement had seemed the only way for them to be together. Her mother had told her not to be so particular in her attentions toward Beau. What other proof did she need that her parents did not approve of her choice?

Her mother's disapproval had come as no great surprise. Lady Harting never visited the parsonage, and Georgiana had concluded long ago that her aunt and her mother must loathe each other. After reading *Romeo and Juliet* and taking it to heart, she knew that the path of true love did not run smoothly.

Perhaps the two families did not hate each other as much as the Montagues and the Capulets, but she did not think it was so very different. It had convinced her that the feelings she had for Beau must be genuine love and not just a passing fancy.

She felt a lowering sensation in the pit of her stomach. It had been so easy to persuade Beau to elope. Perhaps she had been a little too good at pointing out the advantages of taking control of his fortune. What if he did not love her and had only agreed to this runaway marriage to fulfil his dream of breeding racehorses?

At length, she fell into an uneasy sleep from which she was woken abruptly.

"Wretched post horses!" Beau said, banging his fist against the side of the carriage in frustration.

She realised they had slowed to a walking pace.

"Sorry, Georgie. We've got a lame one. At this rate, it'll be daylight before we reach Reading."

She gazed up at him, examining his features, searching for the signs of affection that she had seen there before. Beau saw her upturned face as an invitation, and he started to lower his lips to hers, his eyes alight with desire. Georgiana felt suddenly out of her depth and panicked.

"I must stop and stretch my legs at the next change," she said, sitting up abruptly.

"We could always stay for the rest of the night," he whispered in her ear. The husky voice that had seemed so exciting just a few hours before now made her feel uncomfortable.

"A cup of hot chocolate would be nice," she continued as if he had not spoken.

He leaned back into the corner of the carriage, a wide grin on his face. She suspected he was laughing at her prudishness, but at least the dangerous gleam had gone out of his eyes.

When the chaise reached The Sun inn, it was nearly four o'clock and the first signs of dawn were lighting up the sky. Beau handed her down from the carriage and led her into the inn. The taproom was empty, but a sleepy landlord came to meet them.

Georgiana did not like the way he looked them up and down, as if deciding whether he would serve them. She wished Bessie were with her. Her maid would have put him in his place. But she had not risked telling her maid about the elopement, as she would have felt duty bound to inform her father.

Shrugging off the heavy feeling that was threatening to overwhelm her, she demanded refreshments in her most imperious voice. This seemed to impress the landlord as he scuttled off to fetch what she had asked.

She had never been treated with such wariness in her life and did not care for the sensation. With a weary sigh, she sat down at a table and stared out of the window, trying hard not to wish she had stayed at home.

*　*　*

Lord Castleford helped his mother descend the stairs and led her to the door of the taproom. He glanced inside to see if it was occupied. It was quite by chance that he and his mother were at The Sun inn at all. They had not intended to spend the night on the road, but the Countess had been too unwell to complete their journey the previous day. Despite her indisposition, she had, however, insisted on being woken before sunrise that morning. She was eager for the ordeal of travelling to be over and longed to be home again.

The moment the landlord caught sight of them, he abandoned what he was doing and hurried across to the doorway.

"Do come in your lordship, your ladyship. I must apologise that I have no private parlour to offer you, but as you can see, you may almost call the taproom your own. I am sure my wife can find something to tempt your appetite. Some toast, and perhaps an egg, for her ladyship?"

"What do you say, Mother? Would you care for a morsel to eat before we set out?"

The Countess nodded, and hobbled toward the table nearest the door, leaning heavily on her son's arm. He helped her into a chair with its back to the wall and sat down beside her. Having ordered a light meal, he allowed his gaze to scan the room. It appeared to be clean but had nothing else to recommend it. The landlord disappeared into the kitchen to prepare their food, leaving only two other people in the taproom – a young lady and gentleman, sitting by the window.

He turned back to his mother to find that she was gazing at the youthful couple. She looked from one to the other and frowned. There was something about the lady that arrested her attention.

"Frederick – that girl. Who is she?" she whispered.

Castleford took another look at the lady. She was slight, with fair, almost white hair, and a pretty face. And she was young. Sixteen or seventeen, he reckoned. There was no glimmer of recognition. He was sure he had never seen her before in his life.

"I don't know. Why do you ask?"

"She puts me in mind of someone I once knew. A gentleman who was kind to me when I was…when your father was…" Her voice trailed away. He squeezed his mother's hand in silent understanding. Neither of them wanted to remember those dark days when his father had been alive, when every drop of kindness had been an oasis in an emotional desert.

"What are two young people doing alone at a posting house at such an early hour?" she asked in a low voice as she continued to watch them. "If I had not been so eager to reach home, we would not be setting out at this time. Isn't it rather unusual?"

Before Castleford could think of a suitable reply, his mother twisted to face him, her eyes open wide, but whether with excitement or horror, he could not tell.

"I have an idea," she whispered. "You don't suppose they could be eloping, do you?"

"I fear your imagination is running away with you, Mother. She is just some dab of a girl on her way to London accompanied by her brother."

"In August, Frederick? I don't think so."

At that moment, the gentleman they were observing reached out across the table and lifted the girl's hand to his lips, kissing it in a most unbrotherly way. Lady Castleford gave her son a satisfied smile as if to say, "I told you so."

The young gentleman downed his tankard of beer and urged his companion to hurry. "I have no wish to face your father until we've tied the knot. Or my mother, for that matter."

Although he talked in an undertone, his words floated across the empty taproom.

Lady Castleford glared at her son. "Do something."

"I have no right to interfere," he retorted.

15

"Pray, do not take that tone with me. It is always the duty of a Christian to intervene when an evil may be prevented. Ask her if her father's name is Merry."

He gave a wry smile. His mother knew that pulling out the card of Christian duty worked on him every time. He took a deep breath and walked across the room to where the young lady was still sitting, sipping her chocolate.

"Pray forgive the intrusion, madam, but my mother believes she knows your father."

The girl looked up at him. Her big blue eyes met his own for a moment, but she lowered them quickly, as if something in his gaze made her feel too uncomfortable to continue.

He stood his ground and waited. After a minute, she looked up again, but not at him. She glanced across at his mother, who nodded her head in acknowledgement.

Still she said nothing. He tried again. "Perhaps you could satisfy my mother's curiosity. Is your name Merry?"

She cast a furtive glance up at him, but dropped her eyes almost at once, blinking rapidly to keep back her tears. She did not seem to know what to say.

He hated to cause such distress but felt compelled to continue. He had glimpsed the horror in her eyes and pressed home his advantage. "Does your father know you are here?"

He watched as his words sunk in. Her face turned ashen, and he thought he had won his point. Then, suddenly, the colour flooded back into her cheeks and she rose from her seat and turned toward him, her eyes clouded with unshed tears.

"Thank you kindly for your interest, sir," she said in a tone that would have frozen the Thames, "but I cannot see what possible concern it is of yours." Giving her arm to her companion who had risen beside her, she walked out of the taproom without a backward glance.

Castleford watched their retreating forms and strolled back across the room. He would have admired her courage if it had not been contrary to his wishes.

"I tried, Mother," he said with an apologetic shrug of his shoulders, "but she would have none of it. She would not even admit her name."

"Go after them," Lady Castleford said, as if it were the obvious thing to do.

He looked up at the ceiling and sighed with exasperation. What did his mother think he could do to stop them if they were intent on continuing their journey?

"I don't see..." he began, lowering his gaze to his mother's face, but he got no further. She was looking at him expectantly, her eyebrows raised as if asking why he was still there.

He saw the look of trust in her eyes and knew in a moment he would do what she asked. He would not let her down as his father had done. Shaking his head in mock despair, a reluctant grin on his lips, he held his hands up in surrender and went out into the stable yard.

Looking around in the early morning light, he spotted a single carriage on the verge of leaving. As he walked toward it, the vehicle pulled away, but not before he had heard raised voices coming from within.

The horses had not taken more than a few strides when they stopped again, and the carriage door was thrown open by the eloping gentleman. He spoke with the postilion, and then retreated inside the carriage, slamming the door behind him before they set off a second time.

Castleford followed them out of the yard and smiled to himself as he watched the travelling chariot take the turnpike road south, in the opposite direction to Gretna Green. He had succeeded in stopping the elopement after all.

CHAPTER 2

"It is no matter," Georgiana said, wincing as her partner trod on her toe for the second time. The large young gentleman she was dancing with grew red in the face as he stammered his apologies. Forcing her lips into a smile, she hastened to reassure him that she was not hurt.

She could not be cross with poor Thomas Philby. It was not his fault he danced as if his feet were made of lead. Unfortunately, he was becoming rather particular in his attentions. She did not want to give him false hopes, but it was difficult to avoid dancing with him when there were so few gentlemen to choose from.

Georgiana had hoped that she might meet someone new in the Winchester Assembly Rooms tonight, but it had always been a faint hope. As it was, she had known every gentleman present from when she was a girl.

It was hard not to feel disheartened. Ever since that dreadful night when she had tried to elope with Beau, she had longed to recapture that feeling of being in love which had ended so abruptly when she discovered he was more in love with his horses than with her. But it had not happened. During the past two years, she had not met a single gentleman who had provoked the slightest flutter of her heart.

Further down the dance, she spotted her cousin dancing with Mr Cox. Lady Frances was looking down her nose at her partner in a way that made Georgiana fume. It annoyed her to see Frances sneering at such a learned gentleman who was old enough to be her father.

She was not jealous of the fact that Frances was the daughter of an earl and her father was only a rector, but she confessed that she was a trifle envious that her cousin was going to London for the season.

If only she could go to London. If she stayed in Hampshire, she supposed she would end up an old maid as she refused to marry Thomas Philby. Or Mr Patterson, she thought, her eyes resting on her father's curate who was dancing with her sister Eliza. At least Mr Patterson could dance, but his laugh sounded as though he had the whooping cough, and she could not live with that.

She feared her toes would not survive another dance with Thomas, so when the music stopped, she begged him to fetch her some lemonade and made her way across to where her mother was standing. Unfortunately, her aunt reached her at the same moment.

"My dear sister," Lady Harting oozed, greeting Mrs Merry as if they were close friends.

Georgiana stood beside her mother in well-bred silence, but inwardly she felt sickened by her aunt's hypocrisy. She may have exaggerated the dislike that the two women had for each other in the past, but to suggest that they were on an intimate footing was absurd.

"Tell me, is there to be an announcement soon?" her aunt continued.

"An announcement? To what are you referring?" her mother said.

"No? Pardon me, but I assumed it must be settled. It is obvious that Mr Philby is smitten with Georgiana, and I quite thought you would grasp at such an eligible match for your daughter. A nice little estate and so near to your home. Not what I would want for Frances or one of my other girls, but Georgiana has not the same advantages."

Georgiana felt the colour rising in her cheeks. Her mother reached out and gave her hand a warning squeeze. A quick glance showed that her mother's eyes were blazing as brightly as her own.

"I feel for you," Lady Harting whispered, but not so quietly that Georgiana could not hear. "It must be hard to have a husband so dead to worldly considerations that his daughters' prospects are so limited. If Georgiana were to be presented at court like Frances, maybe she could do better for herself, especially if your mother were to give her the benefit of her influence. The Duchess is, after all, an expert in achieving a good match. She landed a duke. If Georgiana went to London, who is to say she could not do the same for her? As it is, I recommend you settle for the squire's son."

"Thank you for your interest, but I do not foresee an announcement in that direction," Mrs Merry said, her polite tone belied by the thinness of her smile and the dangerous sparkle in her eyes.

"No? Well, do not delay too long, my dear. With three other daughters to marry off, you cannot afford to wait."

"It is good of you to be so concerned, but our situation is not desperate. You will no doubt think me unnatural, but I am in no hurry to see my girls married. Indeed, there is no urgency as Charlotte and Henrietta are still in the schoolroom. But I must thank you for putting me on my guard regarding young Philby. I have been too lax in allowing his infatuation to run on. I am sure you agree it is a hard thing for us mothers to hold our daughters' admirers in check."

Georgiana's mouth twitched, and she kept her eyes fixed on the floor, trying not to smile. Lady Harting clearly brought out the worst in her mother. She had never heard her speak like that before. If she were honest, it was not kind. Her cousin Frances was rather plain, and that, coupled with her superior attitude, meant that she was not exactly besieged by admirers.

Lady Harting muttered her agreement and gave a hollow smile before moving away.

Georgiana's father had been talking to one of his parishioners, but he must have seen her aunt descend on them because as soon as Lady Harting left her mother's side, Mr Merry strode across the ballroom toward them.

He gave her mother a searching look. "Now what has my dear sister-in-law been saying to get you riled, Alicia?"

"I need some air, Kit. Take me away before I say something I should not," she said through gritted teeth, her eyes blazing.

Georgiana knew she should not applaud her mother's loss of temper, but it convinced her of two things. First, the relationship between her mother and Lady Harting was every bit as strained as she had imagined. And second, her mother was as appalled as she was at the thought of her marrying Thomas Philby.

* * *

Later that evening, Georgiana and Eliza climbed into the carriage after their parents for the drive back home to West Meon. No sooner had the door shut, then Mrs Merry could contain herself no longer.

"Lady Harting had the gall to congratulate me on Georgiana's forthcoming engagement."

Mr Merry turned to Georgiana, a quirky smile on his lips. "Who's the lucky man?"

"It is no laughing matter, Kit," Mrs Merry said, glaring at her husband, but the effect was spoiled as she failed to keep her mouth from twitching in response to her husband's banter. "She told me she expected our daughter to marry Thomas Philby."

Georgiana watched her father's expression change in a flash. He was now frowning as much as her mother. "No."

"No?" Mrs Merry repeated as if she were surprised, her eyes gleaming with amusement.

"No. He's a solid young man and will doubtless be as good an estate manager as his father, but he's not the man for one of our daughters. He's no man of learning."

"Did you have someone else in mind? Were you thinking of Mr Bridgeman? I am sure he would be delighted to marry Georgiana, but I cannot say I am in favour of the match. It is too much to expect a girl of eighteen to become a mother overnight, and his boys have become somewhat unruly since dear Mrs Bridgeman died."

Georgiana tried not to laugh. Her mother might sound as if she were suggesting an alternative husband for her, but she knew she was not serious. She exchanged a glance with Eliza, who grinned back at her. Their father pulled a face of mock horror, causing both girls to giggle.

"I see we agree about Mr Bridgeman," Mrs Merry said, "so maybe it is Mr Cox you are considering. He is the cleverest man of our acquaintance and has never made a secret of his admiration for Georgiana, but his age is somewhat against him as he's even older than you."

Mr Merry stuck his tongue out at his wife.

"Then it must be John Patterson. I confess I did not think you had noticed that your curate was besotted with Georgiana and thought you would not quite like it, but if he has your blessing…"

The funning disappeared in an instant. "Patterson is in love with Georgiana? You must be mistaken."

Mrs Merry shook her head. "Georgiana asked me what she should do weeks ago as she did not want to offend your curate but suggested it might be better if she spent less time visiting the poor in his company. I have to warn you that she says she won't have him if he asks."

Her father frowned. "I see what you're driving at, Alicia."

Her mother did not reply but sat and waited.

"I will not let Georgiana go to London," he said.

Georgiana's heart sank.

"At least, not alone," he added with a grin, causing the three female occupants of the coach to exclaim. "We will all go after Christmas, and you can present Georgiana and Eliza to the Queen. The twins and Hetta can come too. William can have a bit of fun before preparing for Cambridge. Charlotte and Hetta can see the sights. I'm sure that Patterson can be trusted to manage things here for a month or so, and it would be no bad thing if he got over his infatuation," he said, rolling his eyes in Georgiana's direction, "before it becomes obvious to the whole parish."

"My mother has invited us to visit," Mrs Merry said. "It would save me the cost of a court dress if she presented the girls, and they could remain with her for the rest of the season after we return home."

Georgiana waited to see what her father would say. She knew he did not altogether approve of her grandmother, the Duchess of Wessex. From what she had gleaned over the years, he took exception to the rather dubious means by which her grandmother had secured the Duke as her second husband and thought she overindulged their twin children, Robert, Marquess of Denmead, and Lady Augusta.

"I know it's not what you'd like but think how wasteful it would be to rent a house when my mother has so much unused space." She paused. "The truth is, Mother is finding the twins rather difficult. She never expected to have more children. It seems bizarre that I have a half-brother and sister who are almost the same age as Georgiana. She despairs of Augusta settling her affections on any of her admirers, and Denmead will talk of nothing but going into the army."

Her father shook his head. "I'm sorry for the boy. The Duke will never let him join up. He won't jeopardise the succession, not when the next in line is that scoundrel of a nephew who tried to kill off his duchess and," he added, reaching up and stroking his wife's face, "my most beloved wife. It is a shame that the Duke's middle brother died childless. Maybe the Duke would feel different about it then."

"I doubt it," Mrs Merry said. "He dotes on the boy. But you're distracting me, Kit. May I write and tell my mother we'll stay with her?"

"Very well," he said with a reluctant smile. "I can see you've set your heart on it. But she had better keep her matchmaking to Augusta. I've no wish for any match of her making for either of our girls."

Georgiana sank back into the corner of the coach and closed her eyes. She was going to London at last. London was the place for romance. It was where her parents had met and fallen in love. Maybe she would not dwindle into being an old maid after all.

CHAPTER 3

LONDON
JANUARY 1810

"I can't believe we have to wear such dreadful clothes to see the Queen," Eliza moaned as Bessie helped her into her court dress, careful not to disturb her hair. "This bodice is so tight I can hardly breathe, and the skirt is so full, it looks ridiculous. I feel more like a balloon than a lady. If we get caught in a gust of wind, I am sure we will blow away."

"I think my gown is beautiful," Georgiana said, looking down with satisfaction at her white satin dress that matched her sister's. The petticoat and drapery were embroidered with silver and trimmed with white satin ribbon and bunches of pink roses.

"And the headdress is magnificent," she added, admiring the white ostrich feather and pearl creation in the mirror.

She still could not quite believe that she was here in London at last. They had arrived in the first week of January, less than two weeks before Queen Charlotte's birthday drawing room. The Duchess was to present her and Eliza to the Queen at this special reception at St James's Palace.

Georgiana had wondered how they could be ready in time, but she had reckoned without her grandmother's skill and influence. The Duchess was an expert in all matters of fashion and had an unerring eye for colour. She seemed to know instinctively what would suit each of them and commanded instant attention from any mantua-maker or milliner whom they chose to patronise. Her presence had ensured their orders were completed much faster than they would otherwise have been.

Georgiana could not believe the number of gowns that their grandmother had bespoken for them. Morning gowns, walking dresses, opera dresses and ball gowns besides the all-important court dresses. They had new pelisses, new spencer jackets and several new pairs of shoes, as well as a new pair of half-boots and huge fur muffs.

They had returned home with a carriage full of bandboxes and packages containing such indispensable necessities as silk stockings and gloves, besides numerous hat boxes protecting some of the most expensive creations from Mrs Wardle's millinery shop.

Georgiana twirled around and almost lost her balance, earning a scold from Bessie.

"I wouldn't want to wear a hoop every day," she said, "but for a special occasion, it is most fitting. I feel like a fairy princess."

Eliza gave an unladylike snort. "I'm sure we can find you a wand."

The Duchess wafted into the room in her court dress as if she had been born into royalty, resplendent in blue velvet and diamonds. Georgiana was transfixed as she took in the full magnificence of her grandmother's attire. The body and train were trimmed with fine point lace and gold braiding, and the draperies were drawn aside and fastened with bunches of gold flowers to reveal the petticoat of the same colour velvet, richly embroidered with gold.

On her head was a stunning array of diamonds and ostrich feathers which had been dyed the exact shade of blue to match her dress. More diamonds hung from her ears and around her neck, so she glistened whichever way she turned.

"Only speak if the Queen addresses you directly," the Duchess reminded them, "and try to converse in sentences. Queen Charlotte has a poor opinion of one-word answers. Do everything within your power to avoid coughing or sneezing. And please, Georgiana, do not fall over. It would make your presentation memorable, but not for the right reason."

Georgiana felt the heat flood her cheeks. She wished she found it as easy as Eliza, who had no difficulty curtseying or walking backwards. The Duchess herself had instructed them in deportment to prepare for their big day at court and had frequently lost patience with her. She had rarely kept the small book of prayers balanced on her head for more than a few moments and was rather inclined to wobble. She hoped that she would not let her grandmother down.

* * *

When they arrived at St James's, the courtyard was already swarming with people. They had only taken a few steps before the Duchess stopped to talk to an acquaintance. Despite the cold, Georgiana was glad of the opportunity to look around her without having to worry that she might miss her footing. She wanted to etch the entire scene in her memory so she would not forget a thing.

Her eyes flitted this way and that, taking it all in. Officers resplendent in their uniforms; peers in their robes; other aristocrats in their richly embroidered velvet coats. The ladies were dressed in velvet and satin in a myriad of colours with embroidery and lace in abundance, but she did not think any of them looked as magnificent as her grandmother. Most wore ostrich feathers in their hair, and she glanced from one to another, working out whose headdress was tallest.

Eliza nudged her. "Why is that gentleman staring at us?"

"I don't suppose anyone is staring at *us*," Georgiana replied, without taking her eyes off the height of the feathers she was trying to compare. "I expect they are ogling Grandmama's diamonds!"

"No – that gentleman over there is definitely gazing at us. At least, he's looking at you. Perhaps it is someone you know. He must be a lord because of his robes – an earl, I think. He looks as if he recognises you but can't quite place where he has seen you before."

Her interest piqued at last, Georgiana turned her eyes in the direction of Eliza's nod. But she was too late. The gentleman had disappeared.

"Tell me if you see him again," Georgiana said.

When the Duchess had finished her conversation, they resumed their progress across the courtyard. They walked sedately behind their grandmother, up the stairs and into a chamber whose walls were covered with exquisite tapestry. The Duchess handed cards with their names on to the person in attendance and they were ushered into the drawing room where they lined up with the rest of the company.

Whilst they stood, waiting for the Queen to appear, Georgiana scanned the sea of faces. As she had expected, she saw no one she knew apart from Lady Frances and her parents. How strange that a gentleman – no, a nobleman – should think he recognised her. He must have been mistaken.

* * *

No one could have guessed at the rebellious thoughts behind Lord Castleford's smile as he arrived at St James's Palace that afternoon. Since becoming earl, he had done his duty, appearing at court and taking part in the round of balls and concerts and other sundry events that composed the London season, with the hope – the slim and seemingly vain hope – that he might find his 'one woman'.

From the day he learned that his father was not faithful to his mother, he had vowed that there would only ever be one woman for him. It still made his stomach knot with pain when he remembered how his father had flaunted his mistress in front of him and laughed at his confusion. He had seen the hurt his mother had borne and resolved never to cause his wife the same grief.

His father had thought him weak not to take a mistress, but he knew that was a lie. It was not easy to wait, especially since finding a wife was proving more difficult than he had expected. Was it too much to ask that he might find a godly woman like his mother to love?

Here he was, at the start of another year, and his search for a wife continued. He resented parading himself as a prize on the marriage mart, a prey to every ambitious debutante, but saw it as unavoidable. Fortunately, he was blessed with great patience and a rather dry sense of humour that enabled him to view the schemes of matchmaking mothers with cynical detachment.

He was in no hurry to make his way up to the state rooms. The less time he spent in that stifling atmosphere waiting for the Queen, the better. He thought he would linger a little longer in the courtyard, where at least the air was cold and fresh. A moment later, he was regretting his decision.

"Castleford," a familiar voice drawled in his ear. Involuntarily, he stiffened. He turned to greet Lord Harting with every appearance of civility, but he could not like the older man. His political opinion oscillated, sometimes this way, sometimes that. How could you trust a man who changed his mind on a whim?

"Harting. I hope you are well?"

"Yes, yes. Quite well, I thank you. Lady Harting has gone ahead of me with our daughter – our very dear eldest daughter, Frances – who she is presenting to the Queen. Such a sweet girl, and so nervous about appearing before royalty. I have told her she will get used to it. A most accomplished young lady, and one who is dying to meet you. Simply dying."

Castleford knew the required response. "I shall be delighted to make her acquaintance." He had no wish to prolong the conversation. "Shall we go up?"

Lord Harting gave a satisfied smile, his job done, and together they walked across to the stairs that led up to the state rooms. Without a second thought, Castleford gave precedence to the older man and his eyes roamed around the courtyard as he stood waiting to mount the steps behind him.

He saw with some dismay that the Duchess of Wessex was at no great distance, half-way across the courtyard. Thankfully, she was so intent on her conversation with the Dowager Duchess of Leeds that he did not think she had noticed him. Of all the matchmaking mothers he had faced, she was the most persistent. Although Lady Augusta was as disinterested in the match as he was, the Duchess had pursued him throughout the last season and as her daughter remained unwed, he did not doubt that she would resume her pursuit as soon as the opportunity arose. He determined to avoid her if he could and put off the inevitable to another day.

He glanced at the two young ladies standing behind her and wondered who they were. Poor relations whom the Duchess had agreed to present? Not that he believed for one moment that the Duchess could be persuaded into doing anything she did not want to do. Perhaps she had wanted more scope for her matchmaking talents, he thought, shuddering.

He looked more closely at the girls. They were an attractive pair, very fair, and so alike that he guessed they must be sisters. One was elegantly tall, but the other was lamentably lacking in inches – a mere dab of a girl. Something about that turn of phrase brought back a dim recollection. Had he met the shorter girl before?

He gazed at her white-blond hair and big doe-like blue eyes, and all at once it came to him. She was the eloping girl. Two years had not changed her much. They had certainly not added anything to her height. Her face was a little thinner than he remembered, but no less attractive. The face of a beautiful woman rather than a pretty girl.

But who was she? A distant connection of the Duchess? Was her name Merry, as his mother had believed?

He had been staring for some moments before he realised his gaze had caught the taller girl's attention. He immediately turned away and headed up the stairs, annoyed with himself for showing such poor manners. His curiosity would have to wait.

He joined the waiting throng in the drawing room, exchanging a few words here and there, but all the time, watching the doorway, so he could see the Duchess of Wessex and her party arrive. From where he was standing, he saw them enter without being observed. His mouth twisted into a smile. The Duchess looked perfectly at home in the state rooms. He had to give her credit. She was splendid.

The two girls following in her wake appeared somewhat over-whelmed at the magnificence of the occasion. He supposed it *was* magnificent, but having been to court so often, it had long since ceased to amaze him. As his eyes lingered on the eloping girl's face, he could see that she was nervously biting her bottom lip and he felt a burst of compassion. He wished he could reassure her that the Queen did not bite.

The thought took him by surprise. Why was he even thinking about this girl? Judging by their previous encounter, she was lacking in principles. Not the kind of lady he wanted for a wife. He blinked hard, as if the action would clear his head, and turned away, determined not to fuel his misdirected interest. It did not work. His eyes kept drifting back to the girls with the Duchess.

Just after two o'clock, the centre door was thrown open and Her Majesty Queen Charlotte entered, followed by the princesses and a whole bevy of servants. Although the Queen looked magnificent in dark green velvet and gold embroidery, Castleford could not help thinking, with an inner chuckle, that the Duchess of Wessex looked more regal. He was glad to see that the Princess Charlotte of Wales was present. It was important that they saw their future queen more often.

His Majesty's band performed the Ode for the New Year, and the Queen received the congratulations of the company. Then the presentations began. He watched intently as the Duchess presented her charges. Unfortunately, he was not close enough to hear the Lord Chamberlain announce their names.

The eloping girl was presented first. She must be the elder sister, despite being the shorter of the two. The Lord Chamberlain named her to the Queen, and she stepped forward and sank into a low curtsey, taking the Queen's hand and kissing it, before rising. If he had not been watching so closely, he would not have noticed her wobble. It was only the slightest tremor, but he found himself holding his breath, praying that she would not fall over.

As she reached her feet safely, he let out a tremendous sigh of relief. He frowned. He was doing it again. Why did he care what happened to the eloping girl?

CHAPTER 4

A walk in Hyde Park was a welcome change after the ordeal of the presentation. Although it was bitterly cold, Georgiana was glad to see somewhere that vaguely resembled the countryside. Except that the countryside was not this crowded. She thought the entire population of London must have emptied itself into the park.

They had all attended the church service at St George's Hanover Square, but in the afternoon, the Duchess wanted to be left in peace. She shooed them out of the house so she could put the finishing touches to her arrangements for the magnificent ball which she was giving to launch her granddaughters into society.

Augusta had been quick to suggest that they visit Hyde Park, and it soon became clear why. It was so cold that the Serpentine had frozen solid and people were skating all over it.

Leaving Mr and Mrs Merry strolling along the path, watching them from a distance, the younger members of the party made their way down to the lake. The boys ran ahead, followed by Augusta, with the four Merry girls bringing up the rear, ambling along, observing the skaters as they went.

Lord Denmead had come prepared, and he and William were soon strapping skates to their boots, ready to join in the fun on the ice.

When Georgiana and her sisters reached the Serpentine, Augusta was waiting for them. She stood with her back to the water, her hands behind her, and her eyes bright with mischief.

"Do you skate?" she asked Georgiana.

"No! I tried once when the lake in the village froze, but I decided after that embarrassing episode that I would never do so again. I could not seem to grasp the ability of keeping upright and my body aches just remembering the bruises I got that day."

Augusta laughed. "And you, Eliza?"

"I love to skate," she said, looking longingly at the lake.

Augusta brought her hands out from behind her back, revealing two pairs of skates. "Good. Would you care to join me?"

Eliza's eyes lit up, and she nodded, a big smile spreading across her face.

"It's quite the thing in Paris," Augusta said, handing one pair of skates to Eliza, "but you will not find that many ladies attempt it here in London. Mama doesn't approve, but she hasn't tried to stop me, and I haven't come to any harm yet."

Charlotte scowled at them. "Why would you want to do something so dangerous? Just imagine what would happen if the ice broke. If you did not drown, you would be sure to die from the cold."

"It does sometimes break, but there is rarely a nasty accident." Augusta pointed to two men standing outside a hut on the other side of the lake. "They're on the lookout to rescue anyone who falls through, and to warm them up if they get a soaking."

"Humph!" said Charlotte. "You're making a big mistake."

Eliza pulled a face. "You are so inclined to imagine danger everywhere that it amazes me you ever find the courage to walk out the front door."

Charlotte glowered at her sister. "You will be sorry when I am proved right," she said, folding her arms and plonking herself down on a nearby bench.

Ignoring Charlotte, Georgiana went to stand at the edge of the frozen lake with Hetta. There were so many people to look at, skating round and round, some with graceful movements whilst others looked as if they were going to fall over at any moment.

She spotted two small boys, looking as if they were out on the ice for the first time, clinging to their father's hands as they wobbled along, close to the edge. As Augusta and Eliza glided into the middle of the lake, Georgiana realised they were the only ladies on the ice.

Linking arms with William, Eliza skated around to the admiring looks of the crowd. Not content with this, they were soon attempting more intricate moves, twirling round and round, skating backwards and drawing patterns in the ice with their skates. They were by far the most proficient skaters on display, and Georgiana felt rather proud of them.

"Where is Gusta going?" Hetta asked, pulling on her sister's sleeve.

"Making sure she doesn't get knocked over," Georgiana said without taking her eyes off Eliza and William. "She is more interested in looking elegant than in performing intricate manoeuvres on the ice. I don't suppose she wants to risk being caught up in the others' antics."

With the obstinacy that she had come to expect from her twelve-year-old sister, Hetta refused to let it rest. "But look, Georgie," she said, continuing to pull on her sister's sleeve until she had her full attention. "She's talking to a man. He was waiting for her on the other side of the lake. Do you think she knew he was going to be there?"

"A man? Where?"

Hetta pointed to a tall figure on the far edge of the ice, near to where Augusta was standing. Georgiana's eyes narrowed as she watched her exchange a few words with the gentleman. At least, she assumed he was a gentleman if Augusta was talking to him. Had she had an assignation to meet him? Was that why she had been so keen to come to Hyde Park this afternoon?

Her consternation grew as they skated off down the lake together. She did not know what to say. Surely Augusta should not be going off alone with a gentleman – but perhaps people behaved differently in town. She looked at Hetta and shrugged her shoulders.

Their attention was soon drawn back to the other three who had stopped on the ice in front of them. Denmead was challenging William to a race, and Eliza was claiming she could beat them both.

They agreed on a starting point and set off. Whilst the boys had the strength, Eliza had the advantage in agility. Georgiana hoped her sister would win.

* * *

Lord Castleford was amongst the spectators in Hyde Park that afternoon. He had ridden out to exercise his horse and stopped to admire the performances of the skaters. It was not a pastime he had pursued since he was a boy, but he knew his brother sometimes skated and wondered whether he would spot Anthony on the ice today.

There was no sign of his brother, but his eye was drawn by the sight of a lady, skating gracefully on the arm of her partner. It was not the first time he had seen a woman on the ice, but it was unusual. He admired the proficiency and elegance of her skating, but he was not sure he approved of her being there. Whilst he did not find the exercise itself unsuitable, he questioned whether it was appropriate for a lady to put herself on public display like that.

It was then that he noticed the distinctive white-blond hair peeping out from under her bonnet. For a moment, he thought it was the eloping girl, behaving recklessly again, but then he realised it was not her, but her sister.

He transferred his gaze to the edge of the lake and, sure enough, there stood the eloping girl, observing the skating. As he watched, a small boy, skating free from his father's hand, fell over on the ice just in front of her.

Even from where he sat, on the back of his horse, he could hear the eloping girl let out a squeal. Castleford frowned, thinking she had over-reacted to the child taking a tumble. It was, after all, to be expected when learning to skate. Then his eye caught sight of her sister who was speeding round the ice with her head down, intent on beating the two young gentlemen who were chasing her.

He saw the danger at once. If they carried on at that speed, they would crash into the boy before he found his feet again. He looked on hopelessly. There was nothing he could do. Even if he galloped down to the water's edge, he could not possibly reach the child in time to get him out of the racers' path. Neither could he warn them. He could never make himself heard above the chatter of the crowd. All he could do was pray that they would look ahead and see the child and be able to avoid him.

Castleford's eyes darted back to the boy who was lying in a heap, crying, and making no attempt to stand up again. His expression grew grim. The boy was not going to get out of the way in time.

As he watched, unable to draw his gaze away from the child, he saw the eloping girl crouch down on her hands and knees and reach out her hand to the boy. When he did not take it, heedless to the risk to herself, she crawled across the ice, as fast as she could, hampered as she was by her dress. The boy was only a few feet from the edge, and she was soon able to grab his hand, pulling him toward her, just as the other girl reached them.

Too late, her sister saw the danger. She swerved to avoid hitting them and collided with the second racer with such force that he went flying into the third and all three of them landed in a heap on the ice.

34

The two men quickly got to their feet again, but not the girl. When one of them helped her to her feet, she gave a little yelp and fell back onto the ice. She must have hurt herself in the fall. The man tried again to pull her to her feet and this time he succeeded, though the girl could not put any weight on her left foot. With an arm slung over the shoulder of each man, the shorter of whom he could now see was Lord Denmead, the injured girl made her slow and torturous way to the edge.

A man skated over to claim the rescued child who had started to cry again. Castleford hoped he would keep a closer eye on his son in the future. There was no doubt in his mind that the man had the eloping girl to thank for saving the boy from harm.

He looked on the girl with a new respect. She had acted instinctively, with no thought to the danger to herself. She was brave and compassionate, though perhaps not very wise.

Judging by her intimacy with Denmead, he expected she would be at the Duchess of Wessex's ball. Would she be embarrassed when they were formally introduced? Or perhaps she would not remember him as clearly as he remembered her.

He watched as the injured girl finally made it back to solid ground where she was met by her sister and another girl who helped pull off her boots. Castleford predicted she would not be skating again for a while. Nor, he thought, would she be dancing at the Duchess of Wessex's ball.

* * *

It was a sad end to the afternoon's excitement. Eliza struggled to hold back the tears, and Georgiana could not dismiss her fear that perhaps her sister had broken her ankle.

Their parents hurried to meet them as soon as they saw what had happened. Mr Merry frowned as he scooped Eliza up in his arms.

"I was not aware that I had given you permission to skate," he said, shaking his head. "No doubt following Augusta's excellent example."

Mrs Merry glared at her husband. "This is hardly the time," she said in an undertone. She reached out and gave Eliza's hand a comforting squeeze. "It was an accident."

She looked around, frowning. "But talking of Augusta, where is she? We must get Eliza home to see the doctor."

At that moment, Augusta skated across the ice toward them. There was no sign of the gentleman she had skated off with. Georgiana hurried to explain to her what had happened. Despite her concern for Eliza, Georgiana noticed that Augusta's face was flushed a deep red. Could there be a connection between her heightened colour and the gentleman?

"Who was that man you were skating with, Gusta?" she asked innocently. "Will I meet him at our ball?"

"Dear me, no," she replied dismissively as they followed the others back to the carriage. "An amusing rattle – nothing more. Poor Eliza," she continued, changing the subject so pointedly that Georgiana did not dare pursue it. "How unfortunate that she should fall over. I shall buy her a present to cheer her up. What would she like? Some sweetmeats or a novel or perhaps a necklace?"

"That's generous of you to offer, but I am surprised you have any of your allowance left. You always seem to go through it so quickly."

"Think of it as a gift from Lady Buckinghamshire."

Georgiana looked at the glee on Augusta's face and frowned. "I don't understand."

"I won it. At cards."

Her frown deepened. "How much did you win?"

"One hundred pounds," she said with a wide smile.

Georgiana's mouth dropped open.

"Don't look so shocked," Augusta said.

"But it's dreadful."

"What is so dreadful about winning money?"

"The gambling. You must have gambled more than a few shillings to have won so much."

Augusta tutted loudly. "Don't lecture me about the evils of gambling. Everyone gambles."

"Not everyone," Georgiana said without the glimmer of a smile, hurrying to catch up with the others.

Charlotte was very smug. "I told you skating was dangerous," she said. "You should have listened to me."

"Thank you, Charlotte," snapped Mrs Merry. "That is hardly helpful. If you can find nothing better to say, I suggest you keep your mouth shut."

As soon as they arrived back at Wessex House, Eliza was carried upstairs and tucked into bed.

Georgiana sat beside her sister, holding her hand, and murmuring how brave she was. "We must be grateful that it was only you who was hurt. Just imagine if you had hit that poor child."

She continued chattering until dismissed from the room by her mother when the doctor arrived. When she returned to her sister's side, the tears were streaming down Eliza's face.

"The doctor said my ankle is badly sprained, not broken, but that I must rest it. It will be weeks before I can dance."

"I'm so sorry. It would have been fun to be brought out together, but there's always next year."

"You don't understand," Eliza said, wiping away her tears with a handkerchief. "I don't care about missing the season. That is not why I am upset."

Georgiana looked at her blankly. "You're not crying because you will miss the season?"

"I just wanted to see him again."

"Who? We don't know anybody in London."

Eliza fell silent, suddenly very interested in the pattern on her bedcover.

Georgiana screwed up her face in confusion. Her sister was not normally shy with her. Who could her sister possibly want to see? They didn't know anyone in London apart from Lord and Lady Harting and their cousin. And Beau. Her mouth fell open at the thought.

"Surely you don't mean Beau?"

"There is no need to sound so surprised. You liked him well enough not so long ago."

She shrugged her shoulders. "Why do you want to see *him*?"

Eliza's eyes glazed over as she looked up, and a shy smile crept onto her lips. "I love him."

"Love him?"

"It was not just you who fell in love with Beau that summer. When you confessed your love for him, I thought it perfectly natural. Why wouldn't you fall in love with him? I had. You raved about his perfections until that day you eloped, never guessing that I was in love with him too."

Georgiana took both her sister's hands in her own. "Oh, Eliza. I'm so sorry. I didn't realise."

"Don't think I blamed you for wanting to marry Beau, any more than I blamed him for choosing you. I was just a tiresome schoolgirl who begged for rides on his horse. But I wasn't sorry when you changed your mind," she said, with a lopsided smile. "I never was so glad to see you as when you returned, unwed. If *I* had eloped with Beau, I would not have come back."

"But how can you still be in love with him? You don't even know him. Neither of us has seen him for over two years and he's turned out very wild, I believe."

"Do you think I mind that? Frances writes and tells me what he is doing. Not because she thinks I have any particular interest, I hasten to add, but because she can't resist exclaiming about his latest exploits. It is indirect boasting, I suppose. I can't work out if she genuinely deplores his behaviour, or she's secretly proud of his notoriety."

She paused, looking up uncertainly into her sister's eyes. "You're not still in love with him, are you Georgie? I was sure that you weren't, even though you used to talk so fondly of him."

Georgiana shook her head and smiled wistfully. "I think I stopped being in love with Beau when I realised he wanted to breed racehorses. It suddenly dawned on me that we didn't want the same things from life. You should have seen the look on his face when I suggested he should still go up to Cambridge."

"That was cruel of you. You know he's not bookish."

"Poor Beau. His mother forced him to go after all." Georgiana hesitated for a moment before she continued. "Eliza, are you sure you are in love with Beau and not with some dim memory of what you think he is like?"

"That is what I want to find out. Next season might be too late. Frances says her mother is keen to see him established. If I don't make my debut this year, I won't stand a chance." She stifled a sob. "I won't ever know."

Georgiana did her best to comfort her sister, but although she sympathised, she was far from understanding the depth of her emotion. She had once believed herself in love with Beau, but the thought of losing him had not driven her to distraction.

It was very romantic that Eliza had carried around this secret passion with her for years. Georgiana wondered whether she would ever feel that much in love. Brushing aside her fears that Beau was not worthy of such devotion, she promised to do her best for her sister. But what could she do to prevent Beau from becoming engaged to someone else?

CHAPTER 5

Georgiana discovered to her surprise that she was rather nervous about the ball that would launch her into society. It would be the first time she had seen Beau for over two years, and though she had assured Eliza she was not still in love with him, she wondered how she would feel when they met again.

Lord and Lady Harting and their daughter Frances were some of the earliest guests to arrive at Wessex House. Georgiana was not impressed when her cousin latched onto her and fell into conversation as though they were the best of friends. She was a poor substitute for Eliza.

"I intend to find a rich husband and have a house like this," Frances said, looking around the Duchess's ballroom with admiration. She pointed discreetly to an elegantly dressed gentleman with short, wavy hair, and an aquiline nose.

"*That* is the Marquess of Hartington, the most eligible bachelor on the marriage mart. He'll become duke when his father dies and inherit a fortune and seven or eight houses at least. I am sure he will ask you to dance before me, for you are much prettier. Though I am an earl's daughter," she said with an irritating titter, "which may tip the balance back in my favour."

Her cousin's snickering grated on Georgiana's ear, and she could not think of a suitable retort.

Frances, however, needed no encouragement to continue. "I would try to secure him despite his deafness, but I do not hold out a great deal of hope as Mama says he is still heartsick over Lady Caro marrying Lady Melbourne's son, William Lamb. I believe I stand a far better chance setting my cap at Lord Castleford, and he is nearly as wealthy."

"Is that all that matters to you? How much money a gentleman has?" Georgiana said, finally goaded into replying. "Don't you wish to marry for love?"

Frances wrinkled up her nose. "As long as he is rich and titled and not positively grotesque, I am sure I will love him well enough. Mama does not think Castleford will be easily caught, but we shall see," she said, gleaming like a cat about to pounce on its prey.

Georgiana thought how vulgar her cousin sounded and pitied the unknown lord. She was thankful when Frances moved on to plague someone else, but her heart sank when she saw her aunt approaching with Beau in tow. She realised she had been bracing herself for this meeting. Inevitably, there would be some awkwardness, especially as they were being forced to meet under the watchful eye of his mother.

Lady Harting gave a rather weak smile as she looked at her niece. "You are looking well tonight, Georgiana."

"Thank you, Aunt."

"I am sure you remember Lord Beaumont, though it is some years since the two of you met. As you can see, my son has turned into a fine young gentleman. Beaumont, where are your manners?" Her soft tone was accompanied by such a piercing look that it was clear Beau's reticence annoyed her.

"I am pleased to meet you again, Miss Merry," Beau said, in a somewhat constrained voice.

"Beaumont is a delightful dancer. Probably the best dancer in the room. But you must be the judge of that." Lady Harting looked expectantly at Beau and waited.

"Would you care to dance the next two with me?" he said, forcing a smile as he obeyed his mother's unspoken command.

"Thank you, Lord Beaumont. It would be a pleasure," Georgiana said, hastening to accept. What, after all, was the point of a ball if you did not dance? And she did not need Lady Harting's reassurance. She knew he was an excellent dancer and not one who was going to tread on her toes.

He led her away to join the dance that was forming. "Fiend take the woman," he muttered under his breath.

Georgiana bit back a smile. That sounded more like the Beau she knew. Perhaps she should pretend not to have heard, but they had always been on good terms before they had eloped together, and she could not endure this distant formality.

"Who? My aunt?" she asked.

Beau shot her a sheepish glance, colouring slightly as he realised she had heard his words, but when she cast him a sympathetic smile in response, his eyes brightened, and he nodded.

Georgiana felt nothing but pity for her former sweetheart. She could not understand why he let his mother bully him.

"How does she do it?" she said, always one to speak her mind and consider the propriety of it afterwards.

Beau did not reply. He was glaring at his mother's retreating form and did not appear to have heard her. The resentment in his eyes showed a vulnerability that she had not noticed before. It was clear that he hated the way his mother treated him, but she suspected he despised himself for allowing it.

"I beg your pardon," he said, as if waking from a dream.

"How does she do it? You are a grown man. How does she bully you into doing what she wants, Lord Beaumont?"

"Lord Beaumont?" he said in disgust. "That makes me feel positively middle-aged. You always used to call me Beau."

"And you used to call me Georgie – but that was a long time ago."

A big grin spread across his face. He puffed out his cheeks and let out a huge breath. "Heavens, yes. What trouble you caused me. It was a good thing we didn't marry. I discovered I enjoy my freedom. Just imagine if we had a nursery full of little brats by now." He shuddered. "What a revolting prospect."

"Then you have no wish to get married?" she said, thinking that Eliza had nothing to fear.

"None – though I daresay I might be forced into it. My mother is always pushing me at some eligible lady or other. If she has her way, I will be married before the season is over."

"She looks delighted to see us dancing together."

"I think you may be the latest eligible lady," he said, grimacing apologetically.

Georgiana hesitated. "Did you...did you tell her about what happened when...you know..."

"Goodness, no. There you were, convincing me she would have hated the match, but it appears it was the only reason she sent me to stay with you. Your grandmother's rank and the generous dowries she has settled on you and your sisters outweigh all other considerations.

Mother hoped something would come of my visits and would only say I had botched it up if she ever found out."

"Why don't you just tell her you don't want to get married?"

"Dash it, Georgie. It's not that easy," he said, trying to justify himself. "You've no idea what it's like. My mother can be most unpleasant if I don't toe the line."

Georgiana shook her head in despair. It seemed unlikely that Beau would be able to hold out against his mother's ambitions, which did not bode well for Eliza.

* * *

As was his habit, Lord Castleford arrived at Wessex House not long after the appointed hour. It was polite to be on time, even when he expected an evening of boredom. He refused to allow his feelings to overcome his innate good manners and shorten the ordeal by turning up late.

On this occasion, he was not spurred on by politeness alone. Ever since witnessing the accident in the park, he had not been able to stop thinking about the eloping girl. Was she the daughter of his mother's old friend Mr Merry or not? And what was her connection with the Duchess? He hated unanswered questions. Tonight, he meant to find out. At least he would be able to give her a name. He could not keep thinking of her as the eloping girl forever.

The Duchess of Wessex greeted him effusively, tapping his arm playfully with her fan. It was no more than he had expected.

"My dear Castleford – what an age it has been since I last saw you. Where have you been hiding?" Without giving him time to reply, she answered her own question. "Up in the wilds of Yorkshire, no doubt. I do not know how you cope with living so far away from civilisation."

"Then it is as well it falls to my lot and not yours," he replied with a practised smile.

"Indeed, it is. Such fortitude," the Duchess continued, undeterred. "I am so glad to see you have flown south for the season. We would be bereft without you. I am sure you want to ask dear Augusta to dance as she is such a favourite with you, but you will have to engage her for later in the evening as I know she has promised the first to a more exalted person than yourself."

Castleford did not like to be manipulated, but he had to admire her tactics. There was no roundaboutness with the Duchess; it was a straightforward attack. She would have made a fabulous general, he thought to himself with a smile.

"I am sure she will delight her partner as much as she would have delighted me."

After exchanging a few words with the Duke, he moved into the ballroom, pleased that good manners had not obliged him to promise to dance with Lady Augusta. He was still congratulating himself on his success when he faced an attack from a different quarter.

Lady Harting had been on the watch, and the moment he entered the room, she bore down on him with her daughter in tow.

"Castleford. How fortuitous. Harting said you were eager to meet our daughter, and here she is. Frances, allow me to present Lord Castleford. Castleford, our eldest daughter, Lady Frances Merry."

As was clearly expected, he expressed his delight at making Lady Frances's acquaintance and obligingly invited her to dance, but his mind was elsewhere. He had forgotten that the Hartings' family name was Merry. Were they related to the eloping girl?

Mechanically, he led Lady Frances into the dance and with a supreme effort, he drew his thoughts back to his partner before his lack of attention showed.

She was a tall young woman, with as much elegance in manner and grace in movement as he hoped his future countess would possess. She had fine high cheek bones and an aristocratic nose, and her chestnut-coloured hair was becomingly arranged around a rather long face. He thought, however, that her mouth was a tad too large and her brown eyes decidedly dull.

He supposed she might be described as handsome by those who had an eye to her dowry, but he was not tempted to call her beautiful, and most definitely not pretty.

But it was not Lady Frances's lack of beauty that repelled him. What was inside a person was far more important to him than their appearance. He did not like the self-satisfied look on her face. It gave him the distinct feeling that she was aware of her own worth and looked down on others as vastly inferior beings. And when she smiled up at him, he could not help noticing that her smile did not reach her eyes.

He did not care for frivolous talk, but he knew his duty and duly started a conversation.

"How do you like London, Lady Frances?"

"Very well, thank you."

"Have you been here long?"

"A little over three weeks."

Silence.

"The weather has turned cold, hasn't it? At least the skaters are happy. Have you seen them gliding up and down the Serpentine? It is a fine prospect."

"Yes indeed."

After three attempts, he gave up. Lady Frances was doing all that was proper, but it was not a stimulating conversation. Feeling acutely bored, he counted the minutes until he could relinquish his partner.

His gaze drifted around the room. Lady Augusta danced with Hart. Lord Granville Leveson-Gower and his wife had just arrived and were talking to the Duchess of Wessex. The man looked smitten with the woman at his side, but Castleford wondered how long it would last. With a reputation like his, he didn't hold out much hope for Lord Granville's faithfulness to his new bride.

Then he saw her. The eloping girl. She was with Lord Beaumont, a man he barely knew except as a rather wild crony of his brother's. Seeing them together, he realised Beaumont was the man she had been eloping with two years earlier. Had he failed to prevent the elopement after all?

And yet here they were, in the bosom of society, all scandal forgotten. He felt a sharp pain somewhere deep inside, but he dismissed it without a second thought. What difference did it make to him whether she was married?

But something did not add up. He was sure Beaumont was still a bachelor like his brother. What was more, he had watched the Duchess of Wessex present the young lady to the Queen. Even the Duchess would not have dared present a girl with scandal attached to her name.

It was a relief when the dance ended. He dutifully handed Lady Frances back to her mother and made his escape. His head was full of questions, but he knew who could answer them. The eloping girl had been with the Duchess of Wessex at St James's, and so to the Duchess he would go.

CHAPTER 6

By the time Georgiana finished dancing with Beau, she was sure of two things. She was not the slightest bit in love with him and Eliza's case was desperate, as he seemed to lack the resolution to resist his mother's plans to see him wed.

Lady Harting was waiting for them, a thin smile on her lips. She took Georgiana to one side.

"I know you have not been in London society before, my dear, and so you must not take it amiss if I offer you a hint now and then. Gentlemen do not care for chatterboxes. You will give your partner an earache. You cannot do better than make your cousin Frances the model for your behaviour. I only hope you have not given Lord Beaumont a distaste for your company."

Georgiana wanted to retort that Lady Frances was a poor example to follow as she only kept her mouth shut when she was trying to impress, but she refrained. It was a shame she could not have a decent conversation without her aunt accusing her of talking too much.

She was relieved to be rescued by Lady Augusta, followed some little way behind by her mother and grandmother. With a significant look at Beau, Lady Harting moved away. Georgiana thought with a flicker of amusement that her aunt was no match for the combined forces of the Duchess of Wessex and her daughters.

Beau immediately stepped forward to ask Lady Augusta to dance, but she forestalled him, asking if he could fetch her some lemonade instead. When he started to complain that she was abusing his devotion, she interrupted him.

"Oh, go away, Beau. I am not one of your flirts, so there is no use trying to persuade me you are in any way devastated by my lack of interest. I want to talk to Georgie."

Beau gave a mock bow to both ladies and went off in search of the required refreshments.

"You seem to be mighty thick with Beau," Augusta exclaimed. "I feel I should warn you he is hopelessly unsteady."

"There is no need to warn me, Gusta. You forget I've known him all my life. We were just reminiscing about old times."

"Oh goodness," Augusta muttered, spotting the approach of a tall, fair gentleman over Georgiana's shoulder. "Here comes Castleford. He's tremendously rich, but the most dreadful bore."

Georgiana's ears pricked up at the mention of Lord Castleford's name. Then this was the poor gentleman whom Frances intended to ensnare. She turned so she could look at him as he approached. He was as tall as her father and his hair almost as fair. His features were pleasant, with a firm chin and bright eyes, but there was no smile to lighten the guarded expression on his face.

"He looks rather serious, but he is certainly handsome," she said.

"Well yes, I suppose so, if you admire the angelic look. Mother says he gives hundreds of pounds away to charity each year. Maybe that is why he looks so...so virtuous. Castleford is the epitome of good breeding – the delight of every hostess. He arrives early, can always be relied upon to dance with the most unprepossessing wallflower, and never disappears into the card room half-way through the evening. What is more, he never dances with the same lady twice and so cannot be accused of raising false hopes in any maiden's breast. I wonder whether he will ever find a woman who meets his high standards."

"Then he doesn't want to marry you?"

"No! Mother, however, thinks he would make me an excellent husband, and she takes a great deal of convincing once she has set her heart on something. The truth is, Castleford acts like a middle-aged man who has sown his wild oats, though there never *were* any indiscretions, or so his brother says. He is always sensible, always polite. And he never flirts. In short, he is perfect, but you cannot get away from the fact that perfection is rather dull. His brother Anthony is much more entertaining."

"And yet, he comes to ask you to dance."

"He usually asks me first, not because he wishes to, but because of my rank. Alas, the trials of being the daughter of a duke. Tonight, however, he was usurped by Hart."

"Hart?"

"The Marquess of Hartington – the Duke of Devonshire's son and heir."

Georgiana remembered the gentleman Frances had pointed out to her. "The most eligible bachelor here according to my cousin."

"That being so, you might well ask why Mama is not trying to push me in that direction, especially since she tried so hard to secure a match between Den and Hart's sister Harriet. The truth is, she cannot stand the new Duchess, and does not want to have anything more to do with the family than necessary. But, as I was saying, Castleford could not dance with me first tonight, and had to endure dancing with Frances instead, even though she is only the daughter of an earl and has the face of a horse."

"Quiet, Gusta. Someone might hear you," Georgiana said.

Lady Augusta pouted prettily. "What if they do? Anyone can learn my opinion of your cousin if they want. I could almost feel sorry for Castleford for having to dance with her. Almost. I wish he would leave me alone. Lord Helston is moving this way and I would much prefer to partner him."

"Perhaps I can persuade Lord Castleford to dance with me instead," Georgiana said, her eyes sparkling at the challenge. It would not be too much of a hardship to dance with him. After all, she thought, recalling Frances's words and struggling to suppress a giggle, he was not positively grotesque.

* * *

It did not take Lord Castleford long to spot the Duchess across the ballroom. As he had expected, she was on the lookout for him, hoping to catch his eye. He sighed with exasperation. He wished she would stop trying to marry him off to her daughter, but he needed answers and so did not hesitate to obey her unspoken summons.

"My dear Castleford, how kind of you to come and talk to an old lady, but do not let me keep you from dancing. Pray secure yourself a partner," she said, indicating where Lady Augusta and the eloping girl stood, a short distance away, deep in conversation. "I warrant you will not find two such pretty girls elsewhere in the room."

He muttered something complimentary and allowed the Duchess to lead him across to where the ladies were standing. They could not have looked more different from each other. The Duchess's daughter was a raven-haired beauty, tall and elegant, and, he had to admit, stunning. The sort of looks he had always admired.

Her fair-haired companion was as petite as he remembered. He judged that her head would not even reach his shoulder. Half an hour of attempting to converse with her would leave him with a neck ache.

He was taken aback to observe stifled amusement on the eloping girl's face. The nasty suspicion crossed his mind that he was the butt of some private joke. Unused to being laughed at, he stiffened, silently labelling the girl as ill-mannered, though his smile did not waver.

"Georgiana, the Earl of Castleford. Castleford, my eldest grand-daughter, Miss Georgiana Merry."

So that was it. She was the Duchess's granddaughter and still unwed. His intervention had succeeded. The elopement had been averted and her reputation saved. His mother had been able to return the kindness shown her by Miss Merry's father after all.

Miss Merry curtseyed prettily and met his eyes with a degree of confidence he would not have expected to see in a debutante, but there was no glimmer of recognition. She clearly had no idea that this was not their first meeting.

He now knew who the eloping girl was, but his curiosity was not entirely satisfied. It did not explain why she had been dancing with Beaumont. Were they still attached to one another and courting in the regular way?

He considered asking her to dance. No doubt, she would be able to answer his questions, but the ballroom was not the place to confront her about their previous meeting – a meeting which she did not appear to remember and had probably done her best to forget. Besides, he was in no humour to honour her with a dance when she had presumed to laugh at him. He decided to ask Lady Augusta instead and deal with Miss Merry another time.

"I shall not be offended if you do not ask me to dance," Miss Merry whispered, looking boldly up at him with a roguish twinkle in her eye as the Duchess moved away. "You had better ask Lady Augusta. It will please her mother."

Castleford was momentarily discomposed. Was she suggesting that the Duchess controlled his actions? For some reason, it rankled that

Miss Merry thought him capable of such weakness. He was seized with the desire to do the opposite to what she expected.

"Lady Augusta and I are old friends, Miss Merry, and I am sure she would be more than happy to yield her claim to a dance to allow me to better acquaint myself with her charming relation," he said, offering her his hand.

He did not feel quite so pleased with his decision when he caught his partner casting a speaking glance at Lady Augusta, her eyes alight with something akin to triumph. He concluded that Miss Merry had fully intended him to ask her to dance rather than Lady Augusta. The thought of being manoeuvred irritated him. Was she as manipulative as her grandmother?

Miss Merry needed to have that smug look wiped off her face. Or did she just need to be soundly kissed? Castleford inwardly froze. What was he thinking? He was far too sensible to be seduced by a pretty face. He was not even sure he liked her. What, after all, did he know of Miss Merry?

He determined to endure the dance and then rid himself of her company as quickly as possible. She was having a most unnerving effect on him.

Attempting to recover his customary equanimity, he was about to ask her how she was enjoying her visit to London when, to his surprise, Miss Merry addressed him.

"This is almost as scary as being presented," she confided. "Why do people stare so?"

"Perhaps they like what they see."

"Do you think so? I must admit that I'm pleased with this dress, though it is quite distressingly plain. White is *not* my best colour. I do hope that I don't look hideous in this one."

"Not *very* hideous," he replied solemnly, his eyes aglow with mischief. The desire to tease her, just a little, was irresistible.

She glanced up at him in alarm, but when their eyes met, her face relaxed. "Oh dear," she said, giving him a dazzling smile. "That must have sounded as if I were fishing for a compliment. It was most kind of you not to snub me."

"Forgive me," he replied with a grin. "You look charming."

"At least I am not likely to fall over here. Oh yes – it was a real possibility at St James's, but I am thankful to say that I didn't. I dread to think what my grandmother would have said if I had toppled over in front of the Queen."

Castleford was intrigued. He well remembered her wobble, but any other debutante would have wished to forget how close they had come to disaster, whereas Miss Merry was openly laughing at herself and inviting him to join in. It felt good to share the joke. There had not been enough laughter at home when he was growing up.

The ingenuousness of Miss Merry's conversation was at complete odds with her managing behaviour. She might have cornered him into asking her to dance, but he had to admit that she was refreshingly different.

By the time their dances ended, all thought of escape was forgotten, and he dutifully offered to accompany his partner in search of refreshments.

"How do you like London, Miss Merry?" he asked as he acquired her a glass of lemonade. Inwardly, he groaned. How had such a humdrum question popped out of his mouth?

She considered for a moment. "It is huge," she replied seriously. "And loud. But I expect you get used to that in the same way you get used to a rooster welcoming in the morning in the country. The noises here are unfamiliar, and I jump several times a night when the watchman does his round."

She looked up at him with an impish grin. "I wonder whether he stops below my window on purpose, for I am certain he stands there to shout his call."

He found himself smiling back at her. "As you say, Miss Merry. You will get used to it."

"I am sure I will," she replied gaily, but then her face clouded over, as if her next thought was less pleasant. She hesitated, suddenly unsure of herself.

"Do go on," he said.

"There are some things in London that I will never get used to, and I wouldn't want to. Like the number of half-starved children that I have seen begging on the streets."

Castleford was not expecting that. Few young ladies of his acquaintance had ever shown a thought for those less fortunate than themselves, and none of them would have dreamed of broaching the subject in a ballroom. It was acceptable – even fashionable – to give money to charity, but it was rarely motivated by such compassion as he heard in her voice.

"The problem is so big. I want to help, but what can one person do?"

"We work together," he said. "We cannot eradicate poverty overnight, but we strive to protect the vulnerable and aid those in distress through ill-health and want. By our generosity and compassion, we can help transform lives, one life at a time."

He watched as she digested his words. Her brow cleared and she gave a little nod.

"You are right. That is the sort of thing my father would say. The sheer number of people in need seemed overwhelming and made me feel that the situation was hopeless, but it is never a waste to help the one."

They stood in companionable silence for what seemed like an age. Castleford was strangely unwilling to bring it to an end.

The Duchess passed close by them and gave her granddaughter a significant look. Miss Merry appeared to recollect where she was and started talking about the variety of entertainments to be found in London.

"You cannot conceive how excited I am to have the opportunity to visit the theatre," she said. "I confess, it is a passion of mine. Particularly Shakespeare. I do hope that I get the chance to see the great Mrs Siddons whilst I am in town. We had planned to go to Covent Garden last Saturday for *The Merchant of Venice*, but it was not to be thought of after my sister Eliza's skating accident."

"Ah yes. I saw it happen."

"You did?"

"I was riding in the park that afternoon and your sister's skating drew my attention. It was a nasty fall, but your bravery averted a worse accident. Is your sister much hurt?"

Miss Merry blushed rosily at the mention of her courage and kept her head bowed until her normal colour returned. "Eliza sprained her ankle badly. She can hardly walk and certainly not dance and cannot take part in the season until next year. I wish she were here with me, but I can't help feeling just a little disappointed that I missed the play. You probably go to the theatre all the time and are quite used to it."

Castleford thought he probably was. It had all seemed jaded not an hour before, but it was impossible not to be infected by Miss Merry's enthusiasm. Without giving the matter his usual careful consideration, he offered to accompany her to the play. It was, he told himself, the chivalrous thing to do.

"I believe that *The Merchant of Venice* is being performed at Covent Garden again tomorrow evening, if you would care to go."

If he wanted any reward for his impulsive offer, the expression of pure delight on Miss Merry's face was more than enough. Her eyes shone as she accepted, provided her mother did not object, and begged that he would take her to Mrs Merry immediately so she could get permission.

They walked across the ballroom to where her mother was standing with the Duchess. The look of delight on her grandmother's face made him feel uneasy. Why was she looking so pleased with herself?

An unpleasant thought occurred to him. Was this all part of a plan to ensnare him? Was Miss Merry all she appeared to be, or had he been duped? Had she talked about the poor just to capture his interest? Was he being pressured to take her to the play in the same way that he had been coerced into asking her to dance?

He was suddenly not so sure he wanted to see her again. Maybe his earlier impression was right, and she was a pert, bold, managing female after all. Probably lacking in principles too, given the circumstances of their first meeting. A good sort of woman for someone happy to be ruled by his wife, but he was not that man.

Alternatively, perhaps she just needed a strong hand to guide her. He wanted to believe that she had spoken from the heart and was as innocent and compassionate as she appeared.

Either way, there was no question of retracting his offer. He would not stoop to such ungentlemanlike behaviour. Besides, the theatre trip would give him the opportunity to get to know her better and to quiz her about their first unfortunate meeting – a meeting which Miss Merry did not seem to recall.

With the Duchess standing by, he felt obliged to extend his invitation to Lady Augusta to join them. He hoped he could turn it to his advantage by inviting Helston to make a fourth. Though he questioned the wisdom of his friend's infatuation, if he could persuade the Duchess that Lord Helston was a desirable candidate for her daughter's hand, then maybe she would stop trying to forward a match with him.

He exchanged a few words with Mrs Merry before dutifully asking another lady to dance – a forlorn lady who had been forced to sit and watch the dancing all evening. The conversation was as insipid as with Lady Frances, but at least he had the virtue of knowing he was doing his duty and he was free to wonder what he really thought about Georgiana Merry.

CHAPTER 7

"I believe I have finally persuaded Mama that Castleford and I do not suit," Augusta said to Georgiana as they walked up the stairs to the drawing room to receive morning calls the next day. "But I am afraid that you are to be the sacrificial lamb. The only way I could reconcile her to relinquishing the pursuit was to plant in her mind the thought that you were more likely to ensnare him than me."

Georgiana frowned. She did not care for Augusta's turn of expression. "I hope that your mother does not expect me to *ensnare* Lord Castleford or anyone else. I have no wish to receive an offer of marriage from any gentleman until I am assured of our mutual affection for each other. Lord Castleford is a sensible man and I look forward to knowing him better, but I'm not in love with him. We've only just met."

"Heavens, Georgie. I don't expect you to marry the man, but he invited you to the theatre first and Mama thinks it is all very promising. If you could send him a few smiles, it will keep him away from me. I swear those blue eyes of his are so penetrating that he could get me to confess all my sins with a single look." She shuddered. "When I marry, it will be to a man who adores me as much as my father does. Someone who is prepared to overlook my faults, not one who will try to change me."

Georgiana tried not to allow Augusta's words to unsettle her. A wave of annoyance bubbled up inside her at the thought of being catapulted into one of her grandmother's matchmaking schemes. She had enjoyed her conversation with Lord Castleford at the ball. Apart from

Beau, he was the only partner with whom she had exchanged more than a few commonplaces.

It was certainly to his credit that he had invited her to the theatre, but she felt so rebellious toward her grandmother's designs, that she almost wished he had not.

She had just taken her seat next to her mother when the first visitor was announced.

"The Right Honourable, The Earl of Castleford."

Lord Castleford walked into the room and bowed to the ladies. Georgiana could find no fault with the way he looked. He was smartly turned out in buff pantaloons and a dark blue jacket with tails. His neckcloth was neatly tied but without the slightest hint of showiness, his boots clean, but no one could accuse them of being excessively shiny. If she had been in any doubt about it before, his appearance today showed that though well-dressed, he had no aspirations to dandyism.

Her grandmother was so effusive in her greeting that Georgiana did not know where to look. Lady Augusta seemed perfectly used to it.

"I hope you are not too tired this morning, Miss Merry," he said, taking the seat offered to him.

She was quick to disclaim. "Not at all. I woke feeling completely refreshed and not as if I had been dancing all night."

"I am delighted to hear it. And did you enjoy your first London ball?"

"Yes, I did. I think it was a great success – the most glittering social occasion I have ever attended. But as you say, it was my first, and maybe it was nothing out of the ordinary."

"The Duchess's entertainments are rarely surpassed."

Georgiana expected him to say more, but he sank into silence. She could not help but compare his current reticence with the previous evening. They had not struggled to converse at the ball. She could not believe he was shy, so why did he have so little to say for himself today?

Before she could think of a suitable question to ask him, her grandmother launched into one of the anecdotes for which she was famous, and neither she nor Lord Castleford had any option but to listen.

As she finished, The Right Honourable, The Viscount Beaumont was announced. The Duchess's eyes flashed with annoyance. As Beau entered the room, Lord Castleford rose to leave, and nothing that her grandmother said could persuade him to change his mind.

"I look forward to seeing you again this evening, Miss Merry," he said in an expressionless voice.

Georgiana did not think he sounded as though he meant it and wondered whether he regretted the impulse of asking her to the play. She hoped she was wrong and tried not to dwell on such a melancholy idea. The important thing was that she was going to see a play, and she determined not to let anything spoil the enjoyment of her first experience of the London theatre.

As the door shut behind Lord Castleford, her thoughts turned to her other visitor. Poor Beau would never shine in the drawing room. The setting was too formal for him. He sat on the edge of his seat looking thoroughly miserable, speaking as seldom as Lord Castleford had done.

Fearing her grandmother would hear what she said, Georgiana did not dare to resume the bantering tone they had adopted the day before. She made a few polite comments about the ball, but Beau struggled to contribute to the discussion.

Thankfully, her mother took pity on him and asked after Lady Harting and his sisters, and with a grateful smile, Beau gave a much fuller answer than necessary. After fifteen minutes of strained conversation, he rose to take his leave. Unsurprisingly, the Duchess did not try to stop him.

When he had gone, Georgiana wondered which of her two visitors had disliked the experience more.

* * *

Lord Castleford set out for the theatre that evening without his customary calm, unable to get Miss Merry out of his mind. He had spent a restless night after the ball trying to decide whether she was a designing minx or an innocent in need of protection, and he was still no nearer an answer.

The morning call had been a disaster. He was no good at small talk. He never had been. Exchanging inane comments about nothing of any import seemed to him a complete waste of time. Once they had talked of the ball, his conversation with Miss Merry had dried up. He had been all too aware that her grandmother was listening to their every word. Perhaps he had misjudged her, but he did not think the Duchess would have approved of him debating the state of the London poor in her drawing room.

What he really wanted to discuss was Miss Merry's elopement, but it was not a subject he could broach with her grandmother listening. He was not even sure it was widely known amongst her family and he had no wish to embarrass her before the Duchess. It could wait until later.

Castleford ensured they arrived at the Theatre Royal Covent Garden in plenty of time for the start of the play. He invited Miss Merry to sit at the front of the box and was about to offer the seat next to her to Lady Augusta when Lord Helston asked her to sit by him. When she agreed, he raised his eyebrows at his friend, a barely concealed look of amusement on his face, and sat down beside Miss Merry himself.

She was full of questions and he was more than happy to answer them. She wanted to know the identity of the occupants of the other boxes, whether the people in the pit could see, and how the new theatre compared with the one that had burned down. It did not take long for her natural chatter to convince him that his fear of being duped had been unfounded. She was without guile – as innocent and passionate for life as he had thought before his doubts had got the better of him.

The same could not be said for Lady Augusta. She was flirting with Helston in the most determined manner and showed no signs of letting up her conversation when the play began.

Miss Merry turned around and scowled at her.

"It's not as if I am making as much noise as those horrid price riots," Lady Augusta said. "Mother brought us when the new theatre opened in October and we could scarcely hear a word poor Mrs Siddons said. It was exciting at first, the booing and hissing and loud complaints about the increase in prices, but the performances were disrupted for weeks and it became quite tedious."

"Shh."

Lady Augusta pulled a face at Miss Merry and lapsed into silence at last, leaving them to enjoy *The Merchant of Venice* in peace.

During the interval, Helston begged Augusta to accompany him to visit his mother's box. She agreed, causing Castleford to raise his eyebrows at his friend for the second time that evening. Helston merely grinned and followed her out into the corridor. Perhaps he had a better chance of succeeding in his suit than Castleford had supposed.

The door shut behind them and he was left alone with Miss Merry. This was the moment he had been waiting for. In the privacy of the box, with no one nearby to eavesdrop, he could ask her about the elopement.

"You don't remember me, do you?"

Miss Merry did not answer. She did not even look at him. He realised that she had not heard. Leaning over the front of the box to get a better view, her eyes flitted this way and that, absorbed in the activities of the crowd in the pit. He did not hurry to repeat his words. It seemed a shame to drag her attention away from sights that she found so interesting.

Instead, he sat watching her. He watched her eyes, already bright with innocent enjoyment of the play, grow wider as she noticed two men having an altercation in the pit. His gaze was drawn to her bottom lip, which she was nervously biting while she watched the argument progress. He thought how adorable she looked, wrapped up in the concerns of people she did not know.

He caught his breath. Where had that come from? He was still trying to figure it out when an even more unexpected thought popped into his mind.

"She's the one."

Castleford sat in stunned silence. He felt as if he had been struck by lightning. It was as if heaven had opened and God himself had pointed at Miss Merry and told him she was the woman he was to marry. He was rarely overcome by his emotions, but this was a unique moment. His throat felt constricted, and he struggled to breathe. He had been searching for so long that he hardly dared to hope.

While he was still gazing at her, trying to recover his wits, Miss Merry let out a sigh of relief as the men in the pit shook hands. She turned and looked up into his face, her eyes wide open and full of apology.

"I'm sorry. I was distracted. Did you say something?"

Castleford did not know how to respond. He no longer wanted to talk about the elopement he had helped prevent. Thank God he had prevented it, or Miss Merry would now be a married woman. Bringing up the past would only embarrass her and minister to his own vanity. He needed time. Time to think.

"Lord Castleford?"

"How is your sister's ankle? Is she making a good recovery?" He knew it was feeble, but it was the best he could come up with.

Thankfully, Miss Merry saw nothing amiss. She smiled her appreciation at his thoughtfulness and launched into a comprehensive account of Eliza's progress. With a little encouragement, she chattered on about the rest of her family until the others returned to the box.

Castleford struggled through the rest of the play, desperately trying to make sense of the new thoughts and feelings that were bubbling up inside him. Fortunately, he knew *The Merchant of Venice* well enough to respond to Miss Merry's raptures without giving away the fact that he had scarcely heard a word.

Though he would not normally have stayed for the pantomime, he determined not to deprive her of a single moment's enjoyment. He was well rewarded. Although the *Harlequin Pedlar* failed to hold his attention, watching Miss Merry was entrancing. He took in every nuance of emotion as it passed over her countenance.

He expected another barrage of questions in the carriage going home, but it did not come. She fell silent, and in a matter of moments, she was asleep. Gazing, transfixed, at her sleeping face, he was aware of something stirring inside of him that he had never experienced before. He had an overwhelming desire to cherish and protect her. Was this how it felt to be in love?

CHAPTER 8

The evening at the theatre left Lord Castleford feeling more restless than ever. He could not stop thinking about Miss Merry – Georgiana – wondering whether he was mad or if she really was the right woman for him. He felt confused. It was such a strong conviction and his feelings seemed to grow deeper by the minute, but it was not rational to rely on emotion alone.

It was against his character to act on impulse. He needed to get to know her better, to make sure he was not mistaken. This presented him with a challenge. How could he court her without raising expectations that he might later decide he could not fulfil? If the Duchess got wind of his interest, he had the nasty suspicion that she would try to push him to the altar before he was certain of his own mind. It was a danger, but a risk he had to take.

Hoping to see Georgiana, he chose to worship at St George's Hanover Square, where the Duchess usually attended the church service. As it turned out, he did little more than that – see her. He was not able to exchange more than a few pleasantries with her before her grandmother wanted to leave.

As they parted, he expressed a wish that he would see her again soon, but even in his own ears, his words sounded shallow.

On the following day, Castleford called at Wessex House as early as he deemed acceptable, only to discover that he was not the first visitor. With some difficulty, he brushed off his annoyance that Lord Beaumont had arrived before him. Beaumont was deep in conversation with Mrs Merry, but of her eldest daughter, there was no sign.

Hoping she would join them if he stayed long enough, Castleford decided to wait. He was more than a little chagrined to discover that

Beaumont was determined to wait too. It surprised him that he was still received by Georgiana's parents after trying to elope with their daughter, but supposed it was ignored because of family ties.

They had not come face to face before, and he wondered whether Beaumont would recognise him as the man who had stopped his elopement. Castleford studied his countenance, but he could see no glimmer of recognition. He felt all the awkwardness of the situation, but his rival was as oblivious as Georgiana to their previous meeting.

After the interruption caused by his arrival, Beaumont resumed his conversation with Mrs Merry. Castleford observed that it was rather one-sided as Beaumont was deep in the throes of describing his new curricle. His respect for Mrs Merry grew when he saw how graciously she responded to Beaumont's enthusiasm. She admired the cleverness of the design of the perch he had just described, before drawing Castleford into the conversation.

Castleford uttered a few encouraging words, and Beaumont continued to describe his equipage in minute detail until Georgiana entered the room. She was wearing a smart purple velvet pelisse and Persian cottage bonnet and carrying a huge swansdown muff in her hand. Castleford thought she looked beautiful, but his heart sank. There could be no doubt about it. She was dressed to go out.

As soon as she saw him, Georgiana launched into an apology. "Pray forgive me, Lord Castleford. It is inexcusable, I know, to be deserting you when I have not had the chance to exchange five words with you, especially when I am so grateful to you for taking me to the play on Saturday. But Lord Beaumont and I are old friends and have much to talk about. I do hope we will meet again before long."

Castleford forced himself to utter a few graceful words to accept her excuses, fighting hard not to let his feelings show. They may be old friends, but he was concerned to see her encouraging the very man she had once tried to elope with. How could such a man be trusted? A pang of jealousy coursed through him as she disappeared through the open doorway with Lord Beaumont. It felt as if the light had suddenly gone out of the room.

Good manners dictated that he should not leave immediately, even though Georgiana had gone, and he refused to allow his disappointment to affect his behaviour. Putting thoughts of Georgiana to one side, he sat and talked politely to Mrs Merry. He was pleasantly surprised to find she was well informed, although she and her husband rarely came to London, and her manner was gentle – so very different from her mother.

As he rose to take his leave, he was about to congratulate himself on having avoided both Lady Augusta and her mother when the Duchess swept into the room. Her eyes flashed with annoyance as she noted the absence of both the young ladies who might have been expected to be entertaining him.

Mrs Merry confessed, a little guiltily, he thought, that she had given her daughter permission to go out for a drive with Lord Beaumont.

A second wave of displeasure flitted over the Duchess's face, but it was gone in an instant. The frown was replaced by an approving smile, directed at him. Without preamble, she invited him to dinner with a warmth that would have been embarrassing from anyone else.

He was under no illusions about the Duchess of Wessex's ambitions. He had heard about her rise to the peerage when he was a small boy. His father had told him the story as an example of what could be achieved by ruthless ambition and urged him to emulate it. He supposed that if he were ruled by such considerations, he would have made a push for Lady Augusta. It would have done no harm to his position or his pocket if he had married the wealthy Duke's daughter. But he had never had any wish to follow his father's advice or imitate his behaviour.

The dinner invitation was rather pointed. He suspected the Duchess would still secure him for her daughter if she could, and he was loath to give her any encouragement. However, the opportunity to forward his acquaintance with Georgiana was too tempting to ignore.

He accepted gracefully and tried not to squirm when the Duchess oozed her approval.

"Excellent. It will just be *en famille*, but I know you won't mind."

Castleford felt as though the ground had just been cut from beneath his feet. The Duchess would be sure to make the most of the intimacy suggested by his dining with the family alone. His concern must have shown on his face.

"I am sure my mother is not suggesting you will be the only guest, Lord Castleford," Mrs Merry said with a speaking look at her mother.

"Castleford does not need your reassurance, Alicia. He is always asking me for money, so that must make me one of his intimate friends."

"Asking you for money?"

A reluctant smile crept onto his face. The Duchess was impossible. "For my charities, Mrs Merry, not for myself."

Mrs Merry met his smile and laughed.

"Why? What did you think I meant?" the Duchess said, her eyes dancing with amusement. "Castleford is always asking me to subscribe to some good cause or other. I am sure that your husband will find plenty to talk about with him."

Much as Castleford desired to meet Mr Merry, he wished he had refused the invitation. If he were not careful, she would bully him into raising expectations before he was ready. He was determined to move at his own pace and refused to be lured into dancing to the Duchess's tune.

*   *   *

"It's mighty good of you to come out for a drive with me, Georgie," Beau said, pulling a thick blanket out from under the seat and spreading it over her knees. He took the reins from his groom and gave him a nod of dismissal. With skilful ease, he manoeuvred his carriage along the crowded street, heading for Hyde Park.

"My mother was mad with me for not joining her at the theatre on Saturday and insisted that I call on you today. Now I can tell her I've taken you out driving, and it will no doubt give her added satisfaction to know that I cut Castleford out in the process."

Georgiana shook her head. "How can you talk so? Why do you let your mother cow you into submission? Do you still want to breed racehorses?"

He let out a long sigh. "If only."

"Then why don't you?"

"Money."

"Oh dear. Have you run through your inheritance already?"

"My inheritance?"

"I'm sorry. Did it prove to be less than you expected?"

"Dash it, Georgie. I thought you knew. My father served me a bad turn. I don't come into my property until I'm twenty-five. Twenty-five. Another four years – unless I get married. I didn't discover it until I came of age. Suppose I never paid attention to the details of the will before. My mother thinks she will marry me off this season because I'm short of funds, but I'm not that desperate yet. I'll think of some-

63

thing. She may hold the purse strings, but I'm not her puppet, though I daresay it looks like that. It's easier to keep her happy where I can, as it keeps the money flowing. Some battles are not worth fighting."

Georgiana did not place much confidence in Beau's ability to withstand the constant pressure of his mother's wishes. Lady Harting would not let up until she saw him married, or at least making progress toward being wed.

She thought of Eliza. Would she still want to marry Beau when she saw what sort of man he was – a man who could not even stand up to his own mother? Would he even make her happy if they did marry? Georgiana realised that was not for her to decide.

For Eliza's sake, she must try to keep Beau unmarried if she could. Only then would her sister have a chance to win his heart and discover whether her own was truly engaged.

A plan began to form in Georgiana's mind. Perhaps there was a way.

"You are certain you don't want to marry me, aren't you?"

"Quite certain," Beau said without even pausing for thought.

Georgiana had no wish for his affection, but it was lowering that he was so very set against her.

Having answered abruptly, he tried to make amends. He glanced sheepishly at her.

"I like you Georgie, but I couldn't live with you. You make me feel uncomfortable. All that romantic twaddle and references to things I feel I ought to remember but somehow can't recall, to say nothing of the things I never knew. A man doesn't want a wife who makes him feel stupid. Besides," he added sulkily, "I don't want to marry anyone. If I could just lay my hands on my inheritance, I would be perfectly happy to remain single forever."

"Forever, Beau? I didn't think you were the monkish type."

He grinned wickedly. "I never said I was."

"Oh, you mean…" Georgiana stopped, realising she was in danger of displaying an unbecoming knowledge of the world. Her cheeks turned a deep shade of red.

"How could you set me up like that, especially since I intend to be your salvation?"

The laughter drained out of Beau's face. "I meant it, Georgie. I don't want to get married – to you or anyone else. If only my mother would just accept the fact and stop trying to marry me off to some eligible female, I could wait until I come into my inheritance to fulfil my dreams."

"I am not talking about marrying you," she said with a touch of impatience, "but what if it looked as if you were making headway with me? Would that buy you a little peace and prevent your mother from pushing other potential brides in your direction?"

Beau thought for a few moments and then nodded. "It might just work. But what of your plans? Won't it put off other suitors if you pretend to be in love with me?"

She screwed up her face in disgust. "I'm not *that* good an actress," she said, dismissing his concerns without a second thought. Eliza's needs were paramount; her sister was the one in love.

"There's no need to overdo it," he complained. "You liked me well enough a few years ago. You make it sound impossible that anyone could love me."

"Don't be silly," Georgiana said, thinking of Eliza. "I am sure there is a lady, somewhere in the world, who loves you. But it's not me."

CHAPTER 9

Georgiana was pleased that Lord Castleford had been invited to dine with them that evening. She thought it would gratify her father to discover that there were some gentlemen of fashion with a heart for the poor. She was not quite so pleased to find that the other guests were more of an age with the Duke than with Lord Castleford.

The only exception was Lord Helston, but as he was only interested in Augusta, it was clear to Georgiana that her grandmother was pushing Lord Castleford toward herself. She found her grandmother's manoeuvres rather embarrassing and hoped that they were not as obvious to him as they were to her.

The Duchess invited Lord Castleford to sit beside her at the top of the table and urged Georgiana to take the seat on his other side, whilst her father sat opposite.

It might be more polite only to speak to those on either side of you, but her grandmother was bent on drawing them all into conversation.

"Did you hear the story of Mr Brown of Ark Hall's lucky escape?" she asked.

The two gentlemen admitted they had not. Georgiana's ears perked up. She liked to listen to her grandmother's stories. You never knew what she would come out with, as there was less restraint here than in her father's house. She was glad that the elderly gentleman seated on her far side was more interested in his dinner than in making conversation, allowing her to listen without interruption.

"It is important for you to know that Mr Brown is a good, upright gentleman, like yourselves, who readily responds to those in need," said the Duchess. "One day, it so happened that he was walking in his

66

own grounds and came across a woman in great distress because she had lost her way and had no money to buy food or lodging. Mr Brown, being the good, kind man that he was, took her inside his home and bade his servants give her something to eat and a bed to sleep in. He also asked them to sort out a bundle of clothes for her.

"A servant was diligently complying with his orders after the rest of the household had retired for the night when she heard a noise on the stairs. She hid in a closet and watched while the stranger – for it was the poor woman – laid a knife and two pistols on the table and went to the doorway to hail her accomplices. The brave girl sprang from her hiding place and shut the door and roused the household, and the man – for it was a man in disguise – ran off into the darkness. Now what do you think of that? Is that the way to repay kindness?"

"Goodness," Georgiana exclaimed impulsively. "How courageous of that girl to raise the alarm. I wonder whether she took one of the pistols and aimed it at the thief. What a foolish thing to do, to take someone into your home when you don't know who they are."

Lord Castleford had spoken little during the meal, but her words provoked a response. "Helping people is always a risk. Would you deprive the poor of help for fear that they might be less deserving than you believed?"

Georgiana's face fell. The kindness of his tone did not hide the fact that he was rebuking her. He must think she was overly ready to judge others.

"No, I suppose not. I hadn't considered." Perhaps she was not as merciful as she liked to believe. She hoped that he would see the contrition in her eyes, but he did not meet her gaze again, perhaps aware that he had upset her. He fell silent, not seeming to know how to continue.

Her father stepped into the awkward pause. "Georgiana has got a good point, Castleford. I am familiar with my parishioners and their circumstances. Some men come begging for money for food and yet if I were to give them what they ask for, they would spend it all on drink whilst their family starved. They are to be pitied, but their families more so. I offer them food, not money. What puzzles me is, with the number of people living in London, how do you sort out those who genuinely need your aid from those who are trying to milk you for anything they can get?"

"You can't," he replied. "I am a governor at the Magdalen, and it is a constant challenge to decide who to help."

Georgiana tilted her face toward Lord Castleford. "What's the Magdalen?"

"The Magdalen Hospital is a home for fallen women. A safe place where they may stay to escape their way of life."

"Oh!" she said as the colour rushed to her cheeks.

Her father did not seem to notice her embarrassment. "Is it successful?"

"For the most part," Lord Castleford said. "There are always a few who accept our help and then drift back to their previous existence. That is why our rules stipulate that a woman may only be admitted once. That helps us to direct our aid to those who sincerely mean to reform."

"Can you accommodate all the poor creatures that need your support?" asked Mr Merry.

Lord Castleford's shoulders drooped. "No. Our resources are not boundless. We have limited room in the hospital and try to discern which are the most deserving cases. Those we cannot find a place for, we are sometimes able to reconcile with family or friends."

"How do you decide which women to help?" Georgiana asked.

"With difficulty," Lord Castleford replied. "It is a hard decision and not made lightly. We always try to give refuge to those in danger of taking to prostitution to put bread in their mouths." He paused, and his eyes glazed over, as if remembering the faces of some of those who had come to the Magdalen for help. "These are the most heart-breaking cases. Women – often girls of your age or even younger – who have been deceived by promises of marriage and then abandoned by their seducers. Many in our society choose to adopt an immoral lifestyle, but these women feel as if they have no choice. A single, impetuous step can lead them on a pathway to ruin."

Georgiana thought of her elopement. When she had run away with Beau, she had not doubted that he would marry her. And when she had changed her mind, she had not doubted that he would take her home. Not for a moment had she considered the vulnerable position she had put herself in.

"How dreadful," she said, in little more than a whisper. "I did not think things like that actually happened. I thought such wickedness only occurred in Gothic novels."

"Unfortunately, I have witnessed it occurring and have seen the distress of those who have left the safety of their father's home only to be deserted by those who professed to love them."

He paused before continuing in a more cheerful voice. "But there is a bright side to this work. Reputations cannot be repaired by repentance, but relationships can. One of my chief roles for the charity is to mediate on behalf of these women and, where possible, to facilitate reconciliation with their families. They are often more foolish than wicked, but sadly, it is folly with a huge cost."

"You scare me," said Georgiana. "My father will tell you I am too inclined to act first and think later. It has, on more than one occasion, got me into a great deal of trouble."

"You are fortunate, Miss Merry, in having friends and family around you. People whom you love and trust. People who can protect you."

"True, but my family is not always here. I need someone looking out for me all the time, advising me and reminding me about what is right. Despite my best intentions, I so often forget. What I desire is my very own Sylph."

"A sylph?" Lord Castleford said.

"Georgiana is, I regret to say, addicted to novels," her father said, with a wry smile that matched his tone. "I believe my daughter is referring to a novel written, so I have been told, by the dear late Duchess of Devonshire."

"I am still in the dark," Lord Castleford said.

"It is a love story," Georgiana explained. "A man falls in love with a lady and goes off to make his fortune, so he can marry her. He returns to claim his bride, only to discover that she has just married someone else. Her husband is evil – a fashionable gentleman, addicted to gambling. The first man is devastated but loves the lady so much that he seeks to protect her from the ruinous influence of her husband and the fashionable world in which they live. He assumes the identity of the Sylph – a guardian angel – who writes to her, giving her advice on how she should behave and warning her when she is at risk of doing something wrong."

Lord Castleford's brows drew together in a deep frown. "How is that a love story?" he said in a stern tone. "Did she know that the Sylph was a gentleman who was in love with her? I hope you are not advocating finding happiness outside of marriage?"

Georgiana's mouth dropped open. "Absolutely not," she hastened to assure him. "The wicked husband kills himself and so, at the end of the book, the lady is free to marry the Sylph."

"A cautionary tale indeed. Weren't you appalled that he met with such a demise, or are you of a violent disposition that you approve of such things?" Lord Castleford asked.

"Not generally, but he was very wicked, and it is only just that the wicked should perish."

"But if someone is dead, there is no chance of repentance."

"Agreed, but the heroine could not marry her true love if she were still married to him."

"Real life does not always work out so smoothly, Miss Merry," he said without a smile.

Georgiana made no reply. It appeared that Lord Castleford was *not* of a romantic turn of mind.

* * *

Lord Castleford's eyes glazed over as the Duchess launched into another anecdote. The practised smile returned to his lips, masking his inner turmoil. How had he got it so wrong? He had tried to encourage Georgiana to think a little more deeply in what he thought was a gentle manner, but their conversation had ended in stony silence. She had taken his words as a reprimand and no doubt resented his interference. He regretted not having more experience with the fairer sex. Maybe then he would know how to make his advice more acceptable.

But that was not the worst of it. He had seen the way she looked when he talked about the Magdalen. He should have realised it would turn her thoughts to her elopement and she would wonder what would have happened if Beaumont had not returned her to her parents. For the first time, he questioned whether his behaviour that night had been as honourable as he liked to think it was.

To please his mother, he had intervened, challenged Georgiana's actions, and dissuaded her from eloping, but he was not proud of the fact he had done nothing more. He had not offered her a means of escape. Although he had watched the carriage turn south, he had not known that her companion could be trusted to take her back home or that her family would receive her. Until a few days ago, he had given the matter little thought at all. He was thoroughly ashamed of himself.

The ladies soon rose from the table, leaving the gentlemen to drink alone. The port did nothing to lighten his mood, and he was relieved when the Duke suggested that they adjourn to the drawing room.

He hoped he would have the opportunity to talk to Georgiana again and repair the damage he had so unwittingly done. As he followed his host through the doorway, he could hear music. A plaintive melody was being played on the piano with a depth of feeling that arrested his attention. He glanced toward the instrument to see who was playing, but his gaze did not linger when he saw that it was not Georgiana but another girl with the same tell-tale white-blond hair – presumably one of her sisters who was not yet out.

A young gentleman was propping up the wall near the piano and, judging from his rapid eye movements and the pencil in his hand, he was sketching the pianist. Castleford assumed that the fair-haired youth was Georgiana's brother. Eliza, he knew, had a sprained ankle and would not be present, which left, if he remembered correctly what Georgiana had told him, one sister unaccounted for.

He had not taken more than a few steps into the room when he was accosted by a girl with chestnut brown hair whom he guessed from her features to be the missing sister, and the youngest member of Georgiana's family.

"Please say you play chess, my lord. I feel sure you do," she said without ceremony.

Castleford was taken aback. "I beg your pardon?"

"Do you play chess, my lord?"

"Yes, I do."

"Please would you oblige me by playing a game with me? By the way, I'm Hetta."

Georgiana had seen her sister pounce on him and hurried over to his rescue. "You are supposed to wait for a gentleman to be introduced to you before conversing with him, Hetta. Surely you know that?"

"I am sure Lord Castleford does not care for all that stuff, do you my lord?" the girl said, shooting him a challenging look.

He repressed a smile and turned to Georgiana. "Pray introduce me to your fair companion, Miss Merry."

"Hetta, this is Lord Castleford."

"I know," Hetta retorted.

"And this," Georgiana said, addressing Lord Castleford and continuing to speak as if the interruption had not occurred, "is my youngest sister, Miss Henrietta Merry."

"I am delighted to make your acquaintance, Miss Henrietta Merry," he said, making his most formal bow.

Hetta stifled a giggle and bobbed a curtsey. "You can call me Hetta. Everyone does."

"You must not bully Lord Castleford into playing chess with you," Georgiana said.

Hetta glared at her. "I am not bullying. I'm asking." She turned her big green eyes up toward his face. "You would like to play with me, wouldn't you, my lord?"

"I cannot think of anything that I would rather do," he replied promptly, winning himself a dazzling smile.

"See!" Hetta said, her eyes shining with triumph.

Castleford could not complain about how things worked out. Moved by compassion, Georgiana refused to abandon him to her sister's mercy and gallantly took up her position to watch the game.

"Are you just learning to play?" he asked Hetta as they set up the pieces on the board.

"Oh no," she said. "I've been playing for years, but unfortunately, I have grown rather good at it."

"Why unfortunately?"

"No one cares to play with me when they know they'll get beaten. Except Father. He is the only one who can do so."

"Unfortunate indeed. Are you fond of the game?"

"Yes, very. I enjoy planning my moves. It is a challenge to figure out how to make the pieces work for me."

"I must warn you I am accounted something of a skilful player myself."

Hetta smiled up at him with confidence. "I am not afraid. Please don't make concessions for me because I'm only twelve. I like a strong opponent and you need not fear an excess show of emotion if I lose, because I don't cry."

"What, never?"

Hetta thought for a moment. "I may have shed a tear or two when Grandfather Harting died, but we had a special relationship. We were comfortable with each other."

By this time, Hetta had set up the board and she fell silent as she concentrated on her moves. He was impressed. There were few people who pushed him to the utmost of his ability, but Hetta did. He won, but it was a close game.

"Checkmate," he declared.

Hetta held out her hand. "Oh well done. I should have seen that coming. Perhaps you will allow me to challenge you to a rematch next time you visit?"

"Certainly, Miss Hetta," he said, taking her hand and shaking it.

Hetta seemed determined not to lose his attention now that their match was finished. She launched into what he assumed was a favourite subject of hers.

"Have you ever been to Paris?"

"Yes. I was there eight years ago, during the Peace of Amiens."

Her eyes glazed over. "I would love to go to Paris, but Father says we can't travel to Europe until the war is over, and the war has been going on and on as long as I can remember. Sometimes I wonder if Napoleon will ever be beaten. Did you happen to meet him whilst you were in Paris?"

"I didn't meet him, but I saw him at a review."

Hetta's eyes lit up with excitement.

Even Georgiana seemed impressed. "What was he like?" she asked.

"He was a little man with a pale face, riding a white horse."

"Little, but brilliant," Hetta declared.

"My father thought so," he said. "He was presented to the great man and exchanged a few words with him. Why do you want to go to Paris so badly?"

"I want to visit Versailles where the poor Queen lived, and the Place de la Concorde where she died. I have deep sympathy with those who have suffered at the hands of tyrants."

"A noble sentiment," he said.

"Is Paris as beautiful as they say?" asked Georgiana. "Does it compare to London?"

Castleford thought of his visit to Paris and a bitter taste invaded his mouth. His father had wanted to educate him into the mysteries of Parisian women. He had refused, and his debauched parent had never forgiven him.

"There is as much beauty and vice in Paris as there is in London."

Georgiana wrinkled her brow. "You do not sound as though you enjoyed your visit there."

"Why ever not?" interrupted Hetta, objecting to the conversation carrying on without her.

"Because I did not have such delightful company as I am enjoying tonight," he said, casting off his unpleasant memories. "But why dwell on the miseries of the poor French Queen when our own good Queen Bess was locked up not far from here?"

"I suppose you mean at the Tower of London," Hetta said, immediately guessing what he was talking about.

"Yes, I did. Have you visited yet?"

"No. Perhaps you could take me to see it?"

Her request took Castleford by surprise. He was unused to being asked out by a lady, albeit a very young one. He felt pushed into a corner. Maybe it was a habit with these Merry girls. It would be unkind to give Miss Hetta a set-down, but did he really want to take a schoolgirl, even a very engaging schoolgirl, to visit the Tower of London?

His good manners and natural kindness tipped the scales in Hetta's favour. He would be amply rewarded if he could secure Georgiana's company too.

"I would be delighted."

"Georgie can come too, can't she?"

"I'm rather depending on it. She can be your chaperon."

Hetta laughed. "I don't need a chaperon, but I am sure Georgie would like to come with us."

"It is not polite to ask a gentleman to take you out, Hetta," Georgiana said.

"But he told me he wanted to," she said, pouting. "You heard him. If he didn't want to, he shouldn't have said so." She looked up at him again, her eyes wide and mournful. "You do *want* to take us to the Tower, don't you, my lord?" she asked in a pathetic voice, with just a hint of a challenge that he would not dare change his mind.

"I look forward to it," he said. "And when you have tired of dwelling on the miseries of those once incarcerated in the Tower, we can visit the menagerie. There are lions and leopards and even a big white bear from Greenland."

"Then you need not worry about asking Charlotte," Hetta said, rolling her eyes toward the girl at the piano. "She is afraid of lions. And leopards. And bears."

He felt relieved that Hetta did not require him to escort the entire family.

"Shall we say Thursday?"

"That would be lovely." He followed her across the room to where her father was standing. With her chin in the air, she informed him that he need not trouble himself to take her to the Tower after all, as she had a better companion to go with.

"Have you asked your mother's permission?" Mr Merry said.

"Oh no. Do you think I ought?"

He nodded and Hetta went scampering off across the room to beg her mother's consent.

"You are under no obligation to give in to my daughter's bullying," he said to Castleford, giving him a sympathetic look. "And I feel sure that some bullying was involved."

"Indeed, you are mistaken. Miss Merry has already chastised her sister for cajoling me into taking her to visit the Tower, but Hetta checked with me that I genuinely wanted to go, and it would be shabby of me to cry off after assuring her that I did. She also told me I need not include Charlotte in the invitation because she did not like lions."

He paused. "Hetta is a very engaging child."

"Precocious!" her father said with feeling.

CHAPTER 10

It had been an eventful day. Georgiana wondered what she had let herself in for. It was not the romantic beginning to the season she had wanted. Pretending an attachment to Beau had seemed inspirational, but on reflection, perhaps it was unwise. Although she told herself she was merely acting a part to help her sister, she felt that she would be living a lie. Her father would not approve of Beau renewing his attentions. But he would be even less impressed if he discovered that it was a sham.

Playing chaperon to Hetta with Lord Castleford was little better. She dismissed the lowering sensation in her stomach that recurred if she thought of the disapproving look that he had given her at dinner. He had been more agreeable in the drawing room, but he had said nothing to change her opinion that he was not of a romantic turn of mind.

There had been no chance to speak to Eliza, so it was not until the following morning that she could share her plan to protect Beau from his mother's matchmaking. Straight after breakfast, she made her way to the Blue Room, which the Duchess had given over to Eliza's use. The time had come for her to share her strategy, but Georgiana found she was reluctant to begin, nervous about how her sister would react. Whilst confident that she would approve of anything that kept Beau unmarried, she feared Eliza might be upset that such subterfuge was necessary.

Georgiana despised Beau's lack of resolution in standing up to his mother. It did not reflect well on his character, and although it was in Eliza's interests that he should fall in with a plan of her devising, she felt that he had agreed rather too readily. It was a painful reminder of persuading him to elope with her. She hoped that this plan would not have such an unfortunate ending.

"Well?" she asked when she had finished relating her conversation with Beau and told Eliza of the fake courtship they were proposing.

"Thank you. I knew you'd come up with something."

Eliza's ready acceptance of the ruse made Georgiana question whether she was doing the right thing trying to keep Beau single. Eliza seemed blind to the weakness in his character, but could such a man really make her sister happy?

Her eyes clouded over with uncertainty. "Doesn't it bother you that Beau needs help to stand up for himself? That he seems incapable of making his own decisions? Would you truly risk trusting your happiness to a man who is ruled by his mother?"

Eliza's face hardened. "I believe he is a better man than you think he is. He has good reason to submit to his mother. Lady Harting has left him little choice. He must have money for his horses. I understand that, even if you don't. Beau will be strong when he needs to be. You'll see."

Georgiana hoped she was right. She failed to see the inner strength that Eliza believed he had, but maybe such unwavering faith could bring out the best in him.

"But are you certain you don't mind?" Eliza continued, the hard look gone from her face. "I would hate to see you sacrificing yourself for me."

Georgiana dismissed her concerns with a laugh. "It is no sacrifice having a handsome gentleman flirting with me. Provided Father doesn't get to hear of it, all will be well. My only fear is that you'll become jealous."

Eliza smiled at her sister. "Not now. Not when I know it's only make-believe."

Georgiana smiled back, but she felt rather hollow inside. She hoped that not every gentleman who courted her would be pretending. She took a deep breath, taking herself to task for being so melancholy, and told Eliza about the conversation at dinner, and Hetta's outrageous behaviour in the drawing room.

"I cannot believe you have agreed to go to the Tower," Eliza said when she had finished. "Since when have you been interested in suits of armour and weapons and instruments of torture?"

"But you have forgotten the menagerie. How could I pass up the opportunity of seeing a huge white bear?"

Eliza shook her head and grinned. "There must be more to it than that. You're not fond of animals either."

Georgiana laughed. "You're right, but it is my duty to protect Lord Castleford from Hetta. I don't think he has ever met her like before and she wound him around her little finger before he was aware of what she was doing. It would not be fair to leave the poor man at her mercy when he had been so good-natured as to succumb to her persuasions rather than giving her a heavy set-down."

"How noble of you, but perhaps you are not so self-sacrificial. Maybe you are hoping to persuade him to take you to the theatre again."

Georgiana peeked at her sister through her eyelashes, a slight pink-ness in her cheeks. "He's already promised to accompany me to the Lyceum on Saturday."

Eliza shook her head, a mischievous smile hovering over her lips.

"Don't look at me like that," said Georgiana. "There is nothing romantic about my relationship with Lord Castleford. I enjoy talking to him – that is all. He is well informed and does not shy away from difficult topics. No one else I've met seems to speak about anything of any importance – at least, not to me."

Their conversation was interrupted by a knock at the door. A foot-man entered and held out a silver salver to Georgiana. It bore a letter with her name on. She picked it up, dismissing the footman with a word of thanks before turning to her sister, her eyes alight with curiosity.

"What is it?" Eliza asked.

"A letter for me that came in the two-penny post." She examined the address. "I don't recognise the handwriting. I wonder who it's from."

She broke open the seal and spread the single sheet of paper in front of her. As she read, a broad smile spread over her face and her eyes twinkled with delight.

"Whoever is your letter from to merit such a response?"

"It is from the Sylph."

"What!"

"Let me read it to you:

My dearest G,
    You have expressed a wish for a guardian angel to watch over you and guide your actions. As one who has your best interests at heart, I humbly offer myself for the task. If you agree to accept my advice, I will try to guide you through the quagmire of fashionable society and keep the narrow road firm beneath your feet. Should I see you acting rashly, I will warn you, lest you be dragged down to that point from which there is no return. If you have questions, ask, and I will endeavour to answer them. A note to the White Horse, Fetter Lane, will find me.
    Your devoted Sylph.

What do you make of that?"

"Who do you think it's from?" Eliza asked. "It must be from someone who knows you well, but you said the handwriting wasn't familiar."

"No, but I assume the Sylph has disguised his writing. I think it's Father, for who else but our family appreciates my fascination with that book. He's trying to appeal to my romantic nature and offer me advice in a form he thinks I'll listen to."

"Or it might be our dearest brother making fun of you."

"William would not go to so much trouble. It must be Father."

"But what advice could you possibly need?"

Georgiana looked sheepishly at Eliza. "Mother must have told him I went out driving with Beau. Father never thought he was the right husband for me, and I don't suppose he has changed his mind." She remembered how angry her father had been after the elopement. He had accused Beau of lacking strength of character and judging by the way Beau still cowered before his mother, she was forced to agree with him. Tactfully, she did not repeat this to her sister.

"Why make a game of it, though? Why doesn't he just stop you from seeing Beau?"

"I suppose I have been somewhat contrary in the past. He might be afraid that if I were forbidden, I should do just the opposite."

"Perhaps you're right. Are you going to answer the letter?"

"Of course," she replied, moving to her grandmother's writing desk in search of pen and ink. She found what she was looking for and taking a sheet of notepaper, she sat down to write a reply.

"What shall I say?

Dear Sylph,

How often I have longed for my own personal Sylph to help me remain on the right path. I accept the offer of your advice with gratitude. Though I promise always to listen, I dare not promise always to obey, for I don't know who you are, so how can I be sure how wise your words will prove to be? I would not like to make a promise that I might not be able to keep.

G.

Brief and to the point. I'll send it by the two-penny post and if I'm lucky, I shall not have to wait too long for an answer."

Georgiana was not disappointed. The next day another letter arrived. She hurried off to the Blue Room where, fortunately, Eliza was alone.

She waved the letter at her sister. "Look what's just arrived in the two-penny post."

Eliza begged her sister to hurry and open it. Georgiana broke the seal and glanced through the letter.

"It doesn't say much," she said, "but I'll read it anyway:

My dearest G,

I am honoured by your confidence and pray that my words might guard you from harm. There may come a time when I reveal my identity to you, but let it remain a mystery for now. It will allow me to be more direct, and I am confident it will make my advice more palatable. All I would say to you now is this: do not be in a hurry to plight your troth.

Your devoted Sylph."

"Wise words," Eliza said, "but hardly necessary. As I'm confined to this room, I may be missing something, but I wasn't aware you were thinking of becoming engaged."

"I'm not, but I suspect that Father is wary of our grandmother's matchmaking and is hoping to put me on my guard. She can be very persuasive."

"I wonder how long Father will keep up writing letters as the Sylph."

Georgiana shrugged her shoulders. "Who knows? While he feels it's working, I suppose. Let's not tell anyone about the letters, Eliza. If we talk openly about my Sylph, Father might stop writing and that would be a shame. I feel like I'm inside my favourite novel."

* * *

On Thursday, Lord Castleford came as promised to take Georgiana and Hetta to the Tower of London. His carriage was drawn by a beautiful pair of greys. Georgiana made a point of noticing because although she was not interested in horses, she knew that Eliza was, and she wanted to be able to tell her about them later.

As they drove to the Tower, Hetta pressed her nose up against the window, her eyes taking in everything she saw. Her questions were endless. She wished to know the names of the churches, the purposes of various buildings, and the identities of the people whose statues they passed. Georgiana was impressed with Lord Castleford's patience. He answered all Hetta's questions and occasionally pointed out something that she had missed.

Leaving the carriage at the top of Tower Hill, they crossed the moat and walked through the impressive gateway into the fortress. It surprised Georgiana to find that it was not a single castle as she had expected, but a maze of buildings and walkways within the outer wall.

"Their clothes are rather old-fashioned, aren't they?" Hetta whispered, eyeing with amusement the full sleeves and flowing skirts of the warders' scarlet coats as they walked past.

Georgiana glared at her sister, afraid that one of the guards would overhear. Her lack of tact was lamentable but, in this case, somewhat justified. The uniforms were antiquated, but Georgiana did not think this detracted from their magnificence. It also made them distinctive; you would have no difficulty in recognising who the warders were.

In the centre of the fortress was a large square building with white-washed walls.

"I suppose this is the White Tower," Hetta said, taking a copy of *The Picture of London* out of her reticule. "It says in my guidebook that 'the models of all new-invented engines of destruction, which have been presented to the government, are preserved in this tower.' I should like to see them, please."

Lord Castleford handed over the three shillings required for their entrance and allowed Hetta to lead the way inside.

"Is your sister of a particularly gruesome inclination?" he whispered to Georgiana.

For a moment, Georgiana thought he was genuinely concerned about her sister's passion for violence, but a quick glance revealed the laughter in his eyes.

"I think it is her age," she replied in the most serious tone she could muster. "She should grow out of it, but then again," she added, a mischievous grin on her face, "as you know, I am passionate about a book where the villain meets a violent end, so maybe she won't. Perhaps it is a family failing."

"Perhaps it is," Lord Castleford said, returning her smile.

There were enough suits of armour and weapons of warfare to satisfy even Hetta. After looking at the Artillery, the Volunteer Armoury and the Sea Armoury, Georgiana's attention was flagging. She trailed behind her sister and Lord Castleford as they made their way to the Horse Armoury, but here her interest rose. Georgiana had to admit that the line of kings on horseback, from William the Conqueror to George II, was impressive.

"Why is the crown hung over this one's head?" she asked. "It says he was Edward V."

"Don't you remember your kings, Georgie?" Hetta scoffed. "This is the poor king who was killed by his wicked uncle before he had the chance to be crowned."

"Oh yes. I remember."

"You know that it was here that the king and his brother were imprisoned, don't you?" Lord Castleford said. "It is believed that the two boys were murdered in their sleep and their bodies buried at the foot of the tower where they had been imprisoned."

"How could it have happened?" Georgiana demanded. "Why didn't anyone take care of the boys? It is wicked when people take advantage of those who are too young to protect themselves, and worse still to be maltreated by those who are supposed to be looking after you."

Lord Castleford squeezed his lips together, a stern expression in his eyes. "It is wicked when *anyone* is mistreated by those who should have cared for them."

The strength of his reaction surprised Georgiana, and she wondered what had provoked it. She was about to ask him in her impetuous way when Hetta interrupted.

"Where's Queen Elizabeth?"

"It is a line of kings, silly, not queens."

"That doesn't seem fair."

"I think you will find a model of Queen Elizabeth in the Spanish Armoury," Lord Castleford replied.

He was right. Hetta's face lit up with pleasure at the sight of the Queen with her horse, wearing armour like the kings.

"This is the armour the Queen actually wore in 1588 at Tilbury when she spoke to her brave army," she said, consulting her guidebook.

Georgiana liked the model of Queen Elizabeth, but she did not care for the instruments of torture on display. The thumbscrews made her feel queasy.

"Aha!" exclaimed Hetta. "The axe which beheaded Anne Boleyn."

"How horrid," Georgiana said. "It was wicked of Henry VIII to have his wife killed. Perhaps he had reason to divorce her, it is hard to tell, but wasn't that enough? I cannot see why she was guilty of treason and deserving of death. I'm so glad that we don't behave like that today. Just imagine what it would be like if the Princess of Wales were put on trial for her life because she could not get on with her husband and gave him a daughter instead of a son?"

"There have always been men who mistreat their wives," Lord Castleford said. "Henry had two of his wives executed, but I believe there is a kind of living death that some wives endure for the sake of their children." A wave of sadness passed over his face, as if the thought had dragged up a painful memory. "It is tragic when any woman suffers cruelty from the hand of the husband who vowed to love her, and the law does nothing to protect her."

He spoke with such conviction that Georgiana did not doubt he was speaking from experience. She suddenly felt young and naïve, and lapsed into silence, uncertain how to respond.

By the time they had toured the Small Armoury, she was feeling weary beyond words. She had seen enough armour to last a lifetime and debated how to hint that it was time to go home without sounding rude.

The offer of seeing the crown jewels, however, revived her flagging interest. She wondered whether they would rival her grandmother's jewel collection. Lord Castleford duly handed over three more shillings and they were shown into the Jewel Office.

There was gold and silver everywhere. Georgiana was enthralled with the size of some of the gemstones, especially one or two of the diamonds, which she thought were the largest she had ever seen. The most dazzling item was the imperial crown, embedded with diamonds, rubies, emeralds, sapphires and pearls. Not even her grandmother wore quite so many different jewels in a single piece. Georgiana admired the amethyst on the top of the golden globe, but Hetta seemed more taken with the silver font.

"Just think of all the royal babies who were baptised in this," she said in wonder, "though if I were the Queen, I would have made it of gold. Silver seems rather shabby in comparison."

Lord Castleford gave a slow nod as if agreeing with Hetta's opinion. "I will have to mention it to Her Majesty next time I see her," he said in a serious voice.

Hetta looked terrified at the thought, but Georgiana knew better. She tried not to laugh as she assured her sister that he was only teasing.

"Would you like to see the animals before we go home, Miss Hetta?" Lord Castleford asked.

"But what about the chapel and the mint?"

Georgiana glared at her sister. Surely there couldn't be any more places to see. Lord Castleford took one look at her weary face and, to her great relief, swiftly denounced the chapel as uninteresting. "And I am afraid that even my rank will not get you into the mint as visitors are not allowed."

Hetta let out a heavy sigh. Georgiana could tell that she was disappointed, but Lord Castleford came to the rescue, managing to distract Hetta from her woes by launching into a dramatic explanation of the Traitor's Gate which they happened to be walking past.

Georgiana had to admit that the menagerie was worth visiting. She had never seen such creatures before. The lions impressed her with their size and ferocity, but the large white bear from Greenland was her favourite.

"I wish they still had monkeys here," Hetta said. "I would have liked to see one."

"It is perhaps as well they do not," Lord Castleford replied, his eyes twinkling, "unless you can spare a leg. They banned monkeys from the Tower after a nasty accident here some years ago. One of them attacked a boy."

Hetta shuddered. "No, I would not like to lose a leg. I expect they thought the monkeys were harmless and let them wander about in the yard. You should never underestimate animals."

Georgiana smiled. It always amused her when Hetta started making pronouncements as if she were a wise old woman instead of a girl of twelve.

"I would still like to see a monkey," Hetta said. "Wouldn't you?"

Lord Castleford admitted that he had seen the monkeys at the Tower before they were removed.

"Oh, I see," Hetta said, with a downcast face.

"There is a baboon at Pidcock's Museum," he said. "It is a large monkey that may be even taller than you."

Hetta's face lit up. "I don't suppose you would like to take us to see it, would you? I know that Father would take me if I asked, but he doesn't care for anything that's alive. He prefers looking at old things. Especially ancient manuscripts and statues like those they have at the British Museum. So, would you?"

Georgiana glowered at her sister, embarrassed at her forwardness. Did she have no scruples at all about asking for what she wanted? Lord Castleford would be quite within his rights to give her a set-down.

It seemed, however, that she had underestimated the depths of his kindness. He shot her a sympathetic look, as if he understood her sentiments, and then looked down into Hetta's face, which was turned up expectantly toward him

"I'd like nothing better," he replied with a grin.

CHAPTER 11

It was the first Sunday afternoon in February and by the time they arrived, Kensington Gardens were already busy with visitors. The Duchess had rallied the whole family to walk with her, except the Duke who stayed playing backgammon with Eliza. She had pounced on Lord Helston and secured his company as soon as the morning service at St George's had ended. Georgiana was not surprised to discover that she had invited Lord Castleford too.

Leaving their carriages at the gate, they entered the gardens from the north. Her grandmother took Denmead's arm and started along the path by the Long Water.

Hetta seemed rather reluctant to follow her lead. "I would like to see the palace."

"It is a long walk to the palace, Henrietta," the Duchess said, with more feeling than truth, a touch of annoyance in her voice.

"I cannot walk far in these boots, Mother," Charlotte exclaimed in alarm. "I would be sure to get a blister."

Hetta scowled at Charlotte, and Georgiana could see that a family row was brewing.

"I'll go toward the palace with Hetta," she said, trying to diffuse the situation. "But perhaps someone should come with us, as I frequently lose my way and I've no wish to be stranded in Kensington Gardens all night."

"I'm happy to come," Augusta said. "I want to see if anything is growing in the flower garden yet."

The Duchess turned toward Lord Helston, a wide smile on her face. "Perhaps you would be so good as to accompany the young ladies to the palace, Helston?"

Georgiana knew her grandmother was inclined to matchmaking, but she had never heard her being quite so direct before. She held her breath, her eyes fixed on Lord Helston, wondering how he would respond. His expression hardened, making it obvious that he was aware of the Duchess's scheming and did not like it. She caught him exchanging a fierce look with Lord Castleford before his gaze fell on Augusta and then suddenly, the grimness vanished.

"It would be my pleasure," he said with a smile. Georgiana let out her breath as he walked over to Augusta and offered her his arm.

Hetta immediately attached herself to Lord Castleford. "You will come too, won't you?" she asked, looking up at him with her big green eyes.

"I should be delighted, Miss Hetta," he replied with the twinkle in his gaze that her sister often provoked.

Offering one arm to Hetta and the other to her, he led the way down the path toward the palace. Georgiana stole a quick glance up into his face and stifled a chuckle. He looked content with his lot, answering Hetta's questions about the gardens as if she were not a tiresome schoolgirl. She thought, not for the first time, how good-natured he was to accept the role of honorary uncle that Hetta appeared to have given him.

As promised, he had taken them to Pidcock's Museum to see the baboon and then Hetta had persuaded him to take them to Barker's Egyptian Panorama, and most surprisingly, to Miss Linwood's Exhibition of Pictures in Needlework.

By the time they reached the Round Pond in front of the palace, Lord Helston and Lady Augusta had fallen a considerable distance behind. Without waiting for them to catch up, the others walked around the water to admire the outside of the palace and inspect the flower beds which were showing signs of life now that the freezing weather had passed.

Hetta glanced back. "I wonder where Gusta and Lord Helston have got to? Shall we go and find them?"

"Perhaps they do not want to be found," Georgiana said, making no effort to slow her pace.

Hetta opened her mouth to speak, but shut it again without saying a word, thinking better of asking any more questions, for now at least.

They walked on to the kitchen garden and Hetta exclaimed at the size of the magnificent greenhouse that stood to one side. She wanted to look around and had little difficulty in persuading Lord Castleford to join her.

Georgiana's shoulders drooped. She supposed she would have to go too and was about to enter the greenhouse when she saw Lord Denmead hurrying down the path toward them. With a sigh of relief, she encouraged the others to carry on without her. She had seen little of Lady Augusta's twin brother since arriving in London, and she would much prefer talking to him than looking at plants.

Whilst she waited for Denmead to reach her, she amused herself by watching Lord Castleford trailing after Hetta, examining every plant, and extracting information from the gardeners to satisfy his young charge's curiosity.

As he approached, Georgiana could see that Denmead was extremely agitated.

"Whatever is the matter, Den?"

For the first few moments, his only response was to clasp her hands in a firm grip and shake them up and down.

"You're always good to me, Georgie. I've wanted to talk to you all afternoon, but I've only just got away from Mother."

She waited whilst Denmead struggled to find his words.

"I have discovered something today that I believe will change my life. My father must let me join up now."

Georgiana looked at him in astonishment.

"Just before we drove out this afternoon, Father told me he had received a letter – an extraordinary letter. If it is to be believed – and there is no reason to doubt it – I have a cousin – two, in fact. And one of them is a boy."

She shrugged her shoulders. "I do not see that there is anything so extraordinary in that. It was to be expected that your cousin Joshua would marry and have children. I don't know the full story, but he went abroad after behaving atrociously toward your mother and mine. It would have been awkward if you had not been born, leaving your disgraced cousin and his offspring as your father's heirs."

"No, no, no. It has nothing to do with him. Are you aware that my father had *another* brother?"

"Yes, of course. Lord Edward died abroad in some battle or other, didn't he?"

"At the Battle of Valencia de Alcántara in 1762," Denmead replied, his eyes sparkling. "How glorious to die fighting for your country."

Georgiana marvelled at the way Den could spout dates if they related to war. She thought, not for the first time, that his enthusiasm for the army bordered on madness. She could not see how the Duke was going to keep him at home forever.

Denmead continued. "The letter is from a Mr Bruce. He claims to have married Edward's widow and is bringing up Edward's grandchildren. Their father was killed at the Battle of Tournay in '94."

"Can it be true?"

"Mr Bruce says his solicitor has all the documents to prove what he is saying."

"I still don't understand. I thought Lord Edward died unwed."

"We all did, but we were wrong. He married before he went to war but told no one he had a wife. I suppose he thought his parents would not approve of the match. His son was born posthumously, and his widow married this Mr Bruce who has written to Father."

"But why write now? How old are the grandchildren?"

"Of an age with us. Mr Bruce is dying and wants them to take their rightful place in the world. He has begged Father to look after them for him. It was always his intention, he says, but he was reluctant to do so before as he has brought up the children as if they were his own."

He paused, his face alight with excitement. "Isn't this wonderful news?"

"It is certainly interesting, but I cannot see why you are so excited about it. I suppose we will get to meet these cousins of yours, but if they have been living in obscurity all their lives, they may be shockingly vulgar."

Denmead shook his head, his face contorted with frustration. "You don't understand, do you? I am no longer the only heir that my father has. If he knows that he has a respectable heir through his brother Edward's line, he must let me join up."

"I would not place any confidence on it, Den," Georgiana said gently.

These were not the words of encouragement he had hoped to hear. He started pacing up and down, disturbed by his thoughts.

"Georgie, if I stay here, I will only disappoint my father. He expects me to marry and produce a son to inherit the dukedom. I can't do that."

"You only say that because you haven't met a girl you like enough to marry."

Denmead stopped his pacing and looked into her eyes, his face a picture of agony. As he continued, his voice became more and more agitated.

"Believe me, I am not. I *cannot* do what my family expects of me. It would be better by far if my father would just allow me to go and serve my country."

Unable to contain his emotions any longer, he stormed off down the nearest path, muttering to himself that she didn't understand. Georgiana stood and looked after his retreating form with a growing conviction that somehow, she had let Den down.

* * *

Lord Castleford watched Denmead's abrupt departure and wondered what could have caused it. Georgiana looked troubled and he decided that he had spent long enough listening to facts about plants that did not interest him in the slightest.

With a word of thanks to the gardener, he made his way out of the greenhouse giving Hetta no choice but to follow. That did not mean she was going to be quick about it. She continued to bombard the gardener with questions as she trailed slowly behind Castleford until long after he had reached Georgiana.

"Has Denmead gone?" he asked, though he already knew the answer. "I hope all is well."

Georgiana shrugged her shoulders. "I'm not sure," she said, relating what Denmead had told her. "He seems so relieved that the responsibility for the succession does not rest with him alone anymore. He sounded as though he meant it when he said he would never marry. Can you understand it?"

Castleford feared that Denmead's aversion to marriage might be more deep-rooted than a simple reluctance to settle down, but he kept his thoughts to himself. There were some things Georgiana did not need to understand.

He endeavoured to divert her attention by giving her a vivid description of how Hetta had gained the devotion of the head gardener. As he talked, he noticed that she did not take her eyes off her sister, who was slowly making her way toward them. By the time Hetta emerged from the greenhouse, Georgiana looked decidedly irritated with her tardiness. Hetta, on the other hand, was oblivious to the fact that she had kept them waiting. They started walking in the direction of the wilderness beyond the formal gardens.

"Was Den complaining about not being able to join the army again?" Hetta asked.

"Something like that," Georgiana said.

Hetta tilted her head to one side, lost in thought. "He would be as happy in the ranks as if he were an officer, but I shouldn't. I would want to be a general so that I could plan campaigns rather than fight them. Or maybe an admiral. Which would I choose? The army or the navy? The army, I think, as I prefer horses to ships, but I do admire Lord Nelson. Did you ever happen to meet him?"

"No, but I saw him once," Castleford said. He kept his tone serious but could not keep the laughter out of his eyes. Georgiana cast him a quizzical look and he gave her a conspiratorial smile.

Hetta's face lit up. "Did you?" she asked. "What was he like?"

"Dead! My father took me to see his body when it lay in the Painted Hall at the Greenwich Hospital."

"Oh – how horrid," said Georgiana, laughing, but Hetta was impressed.

"It must have been an awesome sight. I should have liked to have seen it."

Castleford was not surprised by her reaction. Miss Henrietta Merry was a very unusual girl.

As the path took a sharp turn, he spotted Helston and Lady Augusta under some trees a little way off to the right, locked in a passionate embrace. His response was not what he expected. He was pleased for his friend, but his pleasure was overshadowed by another emotion. Envy. Helston had secured the hand of the woman he was in love with, and Castleford felt all the uncertainty of his own position. He was aware of a deep longing to sweep Georgiana into his arms and kiss her in the same ardent manner.

Georgiana had seen them too.

"Oh my," she said with a big smile. "I suppose Gusta said yes."

Castleford was unable to give her an answering smile. He felt stunned by the intensity of his emotions. He could not help imagining how he would feel if he were standing in his friend's shoes, kissing the woman he loved, and how little he would relish being interrupted. It made him reluctant to intrude on such a private moment.

91

He turned away awkwardly and steered Georgiana and Hetta down a path that led to the Serpentine. He gulped hard. He should not have thought about kissing Georgiana. These feelings were so new to him that he had not learned to control them, and he was sure his embarrassment at thinking such a thought must show all over his face.

As they walked away, he glanced across at Georgiana and was disconcerted by the strange look she gave him. It vanished in a moment, but he could not forget it. What was it he saw in her eyes? Disapproval? Disappointment? He wasn't sure. She must have seen the confusion in his face, but she could not have known he was thinking of her.

But if that was so, what had he done to make her look at him like that? Did she imagine his embarrassment sprung from seeing his friend kissing Lady Augusta? If that was so, she must think him a passionless creature indeed.

It was not long before they came upon the Duchess and the rest of the party. Hetta once more demanded his attention.

"I think Lord Nelson was a brave man," she said, "but Father says he was very ambitious and behaved badly toward his wife. Do you suppose Lady Hamilton still misses him?"

"Hetta!" Georgiana exclaimed.

Castleford looked grim and was unusually severe in his response. "Lady Hamilton would have done well to keep her marriage vows, as would Lord Nelson," he snapped.

Seeing Hetta's stricken look, he continued in a lighter tone. "There is no doubt, however, that he was a brave man and gave his life in service of his country. They are going to construct a superb memorial in his honour in St Paul's Cathedral."

Hetta looked confused. "But Lord Nelson died years ago. Why haven't they built it yet?"

"That is a good question, Miss Hetta," he replied, "and one to which I do not have an answer. However, if you want to see where they have laid his bones to rest in St Paul's Cathedral, I am sure I could arrange it."

"Yes please," Hetta said. "Do you want to come, Georgie?"

"I would not object to visiting Lord Nelson's final resting place," she admitted, "though I don't suppose there is much to see if they haven't built the monument yet. He is every schoolgirl's hero."

"Can we climb all the way to the top of the cathedral?" Hetta said. "I'd like to see across the city."

"We could if your sister agrees," Castleford said.

"I suppose there are a great many steps," Georgiana said with a sigh.

"Yes, but it is worth the effort. On a clear day, the view is magnificent. Besides, you would not want to miss the Whispering Gallery and the outside viewing area is not many steps further."

He was pleased to discover that he had successfully piqued her curiosity.

"The Whispering Gallery? Why is it called that?" she asked.

"Come to St Paul's and find out."

"Very well, Lord Castleford, I'll come. I love a mystery."

"I expect it will tell us in *The Picture of London*," said Hetta. "Do you want me to look when we get home?"

"What would be the fun in that?" Georgiana replied in disgust. "I am happy to wait until our visit so we can discover the secret of the Whispering Gallery ourselves."

At that moment, Helston and Lady Augusta reappeared and started talking to the Duchess. Castleford guessed that they must have given her the news of their betrothal as the Duchess's face was wreathed in smiles and she was fawning over Helston as if he were the prodigal son come home.

Georgiana hurried across to offer them her congratulations, leaving him alone with Hetta.

"I wish that I could live in London," she said in a melancholy voice. "Then I could visit all these wonderful places whenever I chose. I shall miss them when I go home."

"But you're not going just yet, are you? Why concern yourself with something that is so far off?"

"I suppose five weeks is a long time, but so many places I want to visit do not open until April or May, and I shall not get to see them."

"You won't be in London in April?" he asked, his smile fading, hoping that he had misunderstood.

Hetta shook her head. "We go back to West Meon in the middle of March. Father says that he cannot leave Mr Patterson to care for the parish forever and plans to return in time for Easter."

He slowly digested her words. There was no misunderstanding. They were going home in little more than a month. With a sinking heart, he looked across to where Georgiana stood. He had supposed she would be here all season.

Hetta followed his gaze and smiled. "Oh, you think Georgie is leaving too. She isn't. She is staying with our grandmother after we've gone. It is all arranged. Grandmama says she will have her married by the end of the summer. If I'm quiet," she confided, "they sometimes forget I'm there and say things."

Castleford did not doubt Hetta's words for a moment. He would be foolish not to admit that the Duchess was weaving her web around him, trying to ensnare him for her granddaughter. What the Duchess did not know was that he was already well and truly caught.

But what of Georgiana? He refused to let her be pushed into a marriage that she did not want. She needed time. Time to know her own heart.

Hetta had been watching him in silence. "You like Georgie, don't you?"

He gave a wry smile. She was amazingly perceptive for a child of her age. "How discerning of you."

"I like you," Hetta said. "It would be fun having you for a brother. I do hope she marries you."

"I hope so too."

Hetta's eyes grew wide in wonder. "Do you? I'm not sure she knows. You had better tell her before someone else asks her. After all, I won't be here to look after you all season."

Castleford smiled ruefully. If his future was in the hands of a twelve-year-old girl, he was lost.

CHAPTER 12

Gossip spread quickly, and the next day, Wessex House was inundated with callers eager to discover if the rumours of Augusta's betrothal were true. It did not surprise Georgiana that her grandmother could talk of little else. With almost regal condescension, she confirmed their suspicions and invited her visitors to congratulate her on securing such an eligible match for her daughter.

Georgiana thought she would go mad if she had to listen to the enumeration of Lord Helston's perfections for much longer and was relieved to hear Beau's name announced. He, at least, would not want to talk about Augusta's betrothal, and she greeted him with genuine warmth.

Wilting under the Duchess's obvious disapproval, Beau perched awkwardly on the edge of a chair and issued the invitation he had come to bring.

"I thought maybe you'd like to go to the theatre tonight, Geor...Miss Merry. I've hired a box and got a party together, and I would be delighted if you could join me."

Georgiana thought he looked anything but delighted. In fact, he looked so desperate that it was almost funny. She wondered what Lady Harting had said to him this time to send him scurrying to her door. Having assured herself that her mother and grandmother were too deep in conversation to pay them any attention, she gave him an enquiring look.

"Mother was standing behind Castleford when your grandmother invited him to walk out with your family yesterday," he said miserably. "It suddenly dawned on her that I had competition and she berated me for being half-hearted in my courtship. She told me I needed to press my suit before it was too late. Please say you'll come to the play with me tonight. It might keep her off my back for a little longer."

"I was supposed to be going to a concert," she replied in an undertone, "but I will ask Mother whether I can go with you instead. She knows how I love the theatre."

Beau shot her a grateful smile. "You're a real gem of a girl."

At that exact moment, there was a lull in the conversation and his words floated across the room. Georgiana saw the look of concern on her mother's face and wished she could reassure her that there was nothing romantic between them now. But how could she? Whatever Mother felt about Lady Harting, she would not approve of them trying to deceive her. When you spelt it out like that, it sounded rather wicked.

Pushing her guilt behind her, she asked for permission to accept Beau's invitation. Her mother looked solemn but agreed without asking any questions. Georgiana hoped she would not have to confess that things were not as they seemed.

*　*　*

The evening did not start well. Lady Harting had insisted that Beau include his sister Frances in the party, and she took so long to get ready that his carriage was late in calling for her. By the time they arrived at Covent Garden, the entrance hall was already full of people. When she went to the play with Lord Castleford, the crowds seemed to part before him, and she reached his box without feeling at all crumpled.

This was not the case today. She was pushed and jostled on every side as they made their way to their box, and Beau did not attempt to protect her. She had not appreciated before how well Lord Castleford looked after her.

By the time they arrived at their seats, the play had already started, and she sank into a chair, wishing she had not come. She was cross with Beau for failing to take care of her, and the party's composition did not set her at ease. Frances was probably there to spy on them and would give her mother a full report on the evening. The other two members of the group were gentlemen, neither of whom she knew. One was a rather odd-looking gentleman called Mr Whitlow, and the other was Beau's cousin, Mr Templecombe.

Mr Whitlow attached himself to Frances and sat down next to her at the back of the box. Georgiana observed with some surprise that her cousin was flirting excessively with him. She knew that it was wrong to place too much emphasis on appearance, but she struggled to see what Frances could find to admire in Mr Whitlow. The poor man had one of the most unprepossessing countenances she had ever seen. His nose seemed too large for his face and he had a wide, soft mouth that looked as if it would drool.

She hoped Frances would be so occupied with her companion that she would not observe the lack of loverlike behaviour between her and Beau.

Mr Templecombe sat down next to Georgiana and drew his chair so close to hers that he could have whispered in her ear if such had been his desire. He fixed his gaze on her instead of watching the play, which she found both rude and distracting.

Beau did not hide the fact that his cousin was annoying him and pulled up his chair equally close on her other side, making her feel rather squashed. She resolved to make the best of the situation and pulling her chair forward to the front of the box, she gained a little more room to breathe. She ignored both gentlemen and concentrated her attention on the performance of *Othello*.

At the end of the first act, Mr Templecombe turned to her and asked how she was enjoying the play.

"Very well, thank you, though I found it hard to grasp what was happening to begin with as we were so unfortunate as to miss the start. Iago is most convincing. I would not like to have him for my enemy, would you?"

His face looked blank. It dawned on Georgiana that he had not expected such a full response. He had made a polite enquiry which most ladies would have answered with a simple, undemanding reply.

"I can't say that I have ever thought about it," he said at length.

She was disappointed. Lord Castleford had spoiled her. After visiting the theatre with him, she had rashly supposed that every gentleman would be willing and able to discuss the play with her.

"I know that Beau remembers little of what he learned at school, but surely you are familiar with your Shakespeare, Mr Templecombe? This is the most heart-breaking love story of all, but perhaps you do not care for the tragedies. Which is your favourite?"

Mr Templecombe was getting more confused by the minute. "My favourite what?"

"Play, Templecombe," Beau said, enjoying his cousin's discomfort. "Miss Merry wants to know which is your favourite Shakespeare play. Mine is *Romeo and Juliet.*"

Georgiana suspected that it was the only other play he could think of, but his assurance discomposed his cousin. It was too bad of him, but she had to admit, it was rather funny. She gave Beau what she hoped was an admonishing look, but as she could barely repress her amusement, it was likely to serve only to encourage him.

Poor Mr Templecombe appeared most put out. Glancing from her to Beau and back again, he seemed to reach the conclusion that they had an understanding. He shoved his chair away, and, with a mumbled excuse, he left the box.

Once he had gone, Beau stood up and looked around the auditorium, no longer feeling it necessary to entertain her. He scanned the theatre for his acquaintances, whom he recognised with a slight bow, and allowed his gaze to linger when he caught sight of a pretty girl.

Georgiana soon saw that he was not alone in this occupation. Everywhere she looked, gentlemen were surveying the crowd, acknowledging their friends, whilst others were more intent on ogling any young lady who took their fancy.

As her eyes drifted around the theatre, they were attracted to a box on the other side of the auditorium. A gentleman was standing in it, staring right at her. They held each other's gaze for a moment, and then Georgiana pulled back from the edge of the box, blushing to find herself the object of a stranger's attention.

Once the play restarted, she was oblivious to all else, but at the end of the act, she found her attention straying to the box again, to see if the stranger was still gazing at her. The harder she tried to stop looking across the auditorium, the more her eyes were drawn to the unknown gentleman's box. Each time she peeked, he was staring in her direction. Each time she took herself to task, determined not to let it happen again.

When the next act ended, she self-sacrificially started a conversation with Beau by asking him a question about horses. This served two purposes. Not only should it convince Frances of their affection for each other, should she be spying on them for her mother, but it also occupied her attention. In this way, she reached the end of the interval without having once raised her eyes to the box containing the unknown gentleman who had stared at her so intently.

When *Othello* ended, Beau suggested they leave without staying for the pantomime. As Georgiana had already seen the *Harlequin Pedlar*, she was happy to fall in with his plans, but Frances had other ideas. She was determined to remain, and it was clear she was going to make things difficult for him if he insisted that they go.

Beau shrugged his shoulders and gave Georgiana an apologetic look. This was not a battle he was prepared to fight. He opted for the quiet life, and they stayed.

As they waited for the pantomime to begin, she could not resist glancing once more at the unknown gentleman's box. He was still standing there, looking across at her, as if that were all he had come to do. He nodded his head toward her, acknowledging her attention, and she guiltily pulled back from the front of the box, wondering if any of her companions had noticed the exchange.

Against all reason, she found her heart fluttering because of a few long looks from a stranger.

*   *   *

Despite the company, and despite arriving late, Georgiana was glad she had come. She was unwilling to admit, even to herself, that any part of her enjoyment derived from the distant admiration of an unknown gentleman.

As they made their way out through the crowds, she remembered how inept Beau had been at clearing a path for her on their arrival and predicted with a sigh that he would prove equally unable to secure a comfortable exit. She clutched her reticule to her body as she was swept along by the throng of theatregoers trying to leave and became separated from the rest of her party.

Jostled by people on every side, she put out her hands to stop herself from falling. Seeing his opportunity as she stumbled, a boy darted out of the crowd and grabbed her reticule.

"Oh!" she cried, as the boy dived back through the crowd and headed for the door. "Stop! Thief!"

The same throng that had separated her from the others also impeded her efforts to reach the boy. No one seemed to take any notice of her cries.

She was about to despair of ever seeing her reticule again when the gentleman who had stared at her so intently during the play stepped forward out of the crowd.

"Oh please, sir – stop that boy. He has taken my purse," she pleaded.

"Make way, make way!" he cried in a deep voice, full of authority.

Perhaps thinking that royalty was approaching, the crowds parted miraculously. The gentleman darted after the thief, finally pinning him down on the theatre steps. Having retrieved her reticule, he held it up in triumph. The boy wriggled loose from his grip and disappeared into the night, and the gentleman returned to the entrance hall where Georgiana was waiting.

"Thank you, sir," she said with a grateful smile, her cheeks pink with pleasure. "That was well done of you indeed. I thought I had lost my reticule forever."

The gentleman bowed. "Sir James Maxwell, at your service, madam. Providence has certainly smiled on me tonight to bring me to the notice of the beauty I have been admiring all evening. How lucky that I should be on hand to rescue you in your distress."

"Thank you again, Sir James. I am truly grateful."

Looking up into his face, she now had full opportunity to observe him. She liked what she saw. He was a little over average height, fashionably dressed in a close-fitting black coat with such an intricately tied neckcloth that she wondered whether he belonged to the dandy set. There was no weakness in his features – a strong, square jaw line, an aristocratic nose, and a firm mouth, with a pair of deep brown eyes that seemed inclined to look at her as much from this distance as they had from across the auditorium.

His rather rugged face was softened by long sideburns and several locks of his dark, curly and somewhat wild hair which fell across his forehead. He might not be the most classically handsome gentleman that she had ever met, but he certainly presented a romantic figure.

"But why is such beauty here alone? Where is your protector?"

"Somewhere in this crowd," she said, looking around.

A moment longer and she would have defied convention and introduced herself, but before she could get the words out, Beau reappeared by her side.

"Whatever happened to you?" he asked grumpily.

"We were separated by the crowd. A boy snatched my reticule, but this gentleman was so kind as to recover it for me."

"What gentleman?"

Georgiana realised that Sir James had disappeared into the crowd.

"No matter. He's gone. He said his name was Sir James Maxwell. Do you know him?"

Beau ignored her question and frowned. "You shouldn't talk to gentlemen you don't know, Georgie."

"If you had looked after me better, it wouldn't have been necessary."

He shepherded her outside to the waiting carriage, muttering an apology.

Georgiana barely heard him. She was thinking of Sir James and how grateful she was that he had come to her rescue. Such a man would be much more capable of looking after her than Beau.

* * *

When Georgiana awoke the next morning, her first thought was of Sir James. How exciting his dramatic rescue of her reticule had been. She wondered when she would see him again. Soon, she hoped. What a shame it was that they had not been introduced as he would not be able to call on her. Still, she was bound to meet him somewhere. She was sure of it.

As soon as she had breakfasted, she hurried up to the Blue Room to talk to Eliza. She could not wait to tell her what had happened. As she was about to open the door, a footman handed her a letter. She glanced at the handwriting and grinned. Another message from her Sylph. Now she was twice as keen to see her sister.

Eliza had not had a good night. "I cannot believe how long this stupid ankle is taking to get better," she said, thumping the book she had been reading down on the table. "One little walk around the garden and I turned my foot over again, and this morning, it hurts worse than ever."

Georgiana commiserated with her, but then dangled the letter in front of her eyes. "Maybe this will cheer you up."

Eliza's frown vanished. "Another letter from the Sylph. What does he say this time?"

"I don't know as I haven't opened it yet. And there's more. I met someone."

"Who was he? For I'm sure the someone was a gentleman."

Georgiana pictured Sir James in her mind. "Yes, he was. But I shall keep you in suspense a little longer."

She broke open the seal on the letter. "Let's see what my Sylph has to say first:

My dearest G,

I urge you once more not to rush into marriage. To get to know someone takes time. It is tempting to judge by outward appearance, but the Lord looks at the heart and I encourage you to do the same. How can you know what is in someone's heart? By their actions. 'A good man out of the good treasure of the heart bringeth forth good things: and an evil man out of the evil treasure bringeth forth evil things.' Wait, watch and learn.
Your devoted servant
Sylph. "

"Why would he write that?" Eliza asked.

"Perhaps the fake courtship with Beau is working a little too well."

"I find that hard to believe. You have been with Lord Castleford just as often."

"I suppose so – though frequently with Hetta in tow. Still, if we had any lingering doubts about the identity of the Sylph, this letter must dispel them. Trust Father to add a verse of Scripture to give more weight to what he is saying."

"I think he only wants you to take your time and make the right choice."

"And that has to be excellent advice as I did not even know that Sir James existed before yesterday."

"And who is Sir James?"

"Well you might ask," Georgiana said, her eyes sparkling as she recounted the events of the previous evening to a spellbound Eliza.

"I didn't think I would ever see my reticule again, but then *he* stepped out of nowhere. He went after the thief and retrieved my purse."

"How romantic!"

"I know."

"I'm sure you will meet him again," Eliza said.

Georgiana sighed heavily. "I'm depending on it."

CHAPTER 13

When more than a week passed without so much as a glimpse of Sir James, Georgiana's confidence began to wane. Perhaps this romantic episode in her life was just that – an episode which would never amount to anything.

At least she had the visit to St Paul's with Lord Castleford to look forward to. It would come as a welcome distraction, but judging by the weather on the appointed morning, even that was going to be denied her.

"Lord Castleford hasn't sent a note round yet," Hetta said hopefully, "so perhaps he is waiting to see if the rain will clear."

They were still sitting at the breakfast table when the footman came in bearing a silver salver with a letter on it. He held out the tray to Georgiana.

"Thank you," she said, taking the note.

There was no address on it – just her name, written in a rather florid hand. Georgiana frowned. The handwriting did not match what she knew of Lord Castleford's character. She had expected his style to be simpler. She broke open the seal and looked for the signature. It was not the letter she had expected.

"Is it from Castleford?" her father asked.

"No. I don't know who it is from. It's not signed."

"Then you had better read the contents aloud."

> *"O, my love's like a red, red rose,*
> *That's newly sprung in June;*
> *O, my love's like the melody,*
> *That's sweetly play'd in tune.*

As fair art thou, my bonnie lass,
So deep in love am I;
And I will love thee still, my dear,
Till a' the seas gang dry."

"Why has someone sent you a poem?" Hetta said. "It's not even their own work. Everyone knows it's by Robert Burns. And they've forgotten the last two verses."

Georgiana knew the words by heart, but despite their familiarity, the fact that they had been sent to her gave them an intimate new meaning that brought the colour to her cheeks. Who would write to her like that?

"I believe you have in your hand a Valentine, Georgiana," her father said with a look that made her blush even more. "Today is February the fourteenth – Saint Valentine's Day – and it is traditional for lovers to send anonymous love poems to their sweethearts. Now who would send my daughter a Valentine?"

She shook her head. "I don't know."

"I see no harm in you keeping it," Mr Merry said. "It is, after all, just a few lines by Burns."

She put the letter away in her reticule, but she could not put her thoughts away so easily. Who could the Valentine be from?

Beau? Why would he have sent her a love letter unless his mother had been watching? She chuckled to herself. He would have had to look up the lines to have written them down.

Lord Castleford? She was sure he would know the words, but she could not imagine him doing anything so romantic. He would be more likely to dismiss a Valentine as a silly waste of time than write her an anonymous love letter.

Her mind drifted back to the night at the theatre. Could it be from Sir James? She had not given him her name, but she supposed it would have been possible for him to learn it if he had been so inclined. *Had* he been so inclined?

She was still wondering when a second letter arrived. For a moment, Georgiana thought it might be another Valentine, but it was not. The address was written in a firm, business-like hand and she was not at all surprised to discover that it was the expected note from Lord Castleford postponing their visit to St Paul's to a later date.

Hetta was disappointed, but as the rain was followed by snow, even she was thankful that they had deferred their trip.

*　*　*

It was not until the following week that the weather had cleared sufficiently for them to venture out to St Paul's. Lord Castleford apologised to his young friend for the delay.

"I hope you were not too disappointed, Miss Hetta, but some things are beyond my control. It was a foul day. I felt guilty even sending my man out with the note in that weather."

"I wonder whether the other man felt guilty," Hetta said.

"Shh," Georgiana said, flushing with embarrassment. But it was too late. The words had been said.

"The other man?"

"Yours was not the only letter Georgie received that morning," Hetta continued, oblivious to her sister's discomfort. "Someone sent her a Valentine. I wondered whether he was sorry to send his man out in that rain, or perhaps he delivered it himself."

Castleford's eyes clouded over, and he fought against a surge of jealousy that made his next words sound harsher than he had intended. "A Valentine? You mean a love-letter?"

"Does it surprise you that someone should want to send me a love-letter?" Georgiana snapped.

"Not at all," he said in what he hoped was a soothing tone. "I am only surprised that your father let you receive it."

"He was with me when I opened it and as it was only a few verses from Burns's poem *A Red, Red Rose*, he said I might keep it."

"Who was it from?" he asked before he could stop himself.

Georgiana glared at him, her nostrils flaring. "I fail to see why that is any of your business."

"She couldn't tell you even if she wanted to," Hetta said in a matter-of-fact tone. "She doesn't know because it didn't say. I've been wondering, Georgie. Perhaps it was from the gentleman who came to your rescue at the theatre."

Georgiana looked as if she would like to throttle her sister. What mystery was she trying to hide?

"I was not aware that you needed to be rescued at the theatre. Was the performance too emotional for you?"

105

"Of course not," Hetta said, speaking for Georgiana who seemed reluctant to answer. "She was robbed."

"Robbed? How so, Miss Merry?"

Georgiana scowled at Hetta. "A boy snatched my reticule, but a gentleman was kind enough to run after him and retrieve it for me."

Castleford was aware of a second surge of jealousy, even stronger than the first, toward this unknown man.

"How fortunate," he said, unable to keep the cynicism out of his voice. "Did he secure himself an introduction out of the episode?"

"He did not," Georgiana said, her eyes blazing, "though I should have liked to be introduced to a gentleman who had performed such a great service to me. He gave me his name but did not ask for mine."

Castleford did not pursue the subject. It would not help him to discover the mysterious gentleman's identity. The tell-tale blush on Georgiana's cheek convinced him that the incident could not be forgotten too soon. He regretted hinting that the meeting was not such a coincidence as it looked. She did not believe him and had been too ready to defend her romantic hero for his peace of mind.

* * *

St Paul's was enormous. She had seen it often enough as she had travelled past, but it was not until she was standing on the marble pavement of the cathedral, staring up at the ceiling, that Georgiana realised just how big it was. Big and empty. She had imagined that the inside would be as impressive as the outside, but the only thing she had found impressive about it so far was its size.

As she had expected, Hetta wanted to see everything she possibly could. With a flash of her beguiling smile, she persuaded Lord Castleford to take them to explore the library, a model of the cathedral, the insides of the clock and the great bell which, when it was struck on the hour, could be heard from miles away.

"Where is the Whispering Gallery you promised me?" Georgiana asked before Hetta could find any more obscure parts of the cathedral to visit.

Castleford smiled. "Ah, the mysterious Whispering Gallery. This way." They followed him up a spiral staircase and through a doorway that led into the gallery. A stone seat ran all around the inside of the dome and in the centre, surrounded by a balustrade, it was open to the body of the cathedral below.

"What a long way down," Georgiana exclaimed, peering over the edge. "If Charlotte were here, she would be suffering from spasms by now."

"Then it is just as well she is not here," Lord Castleford said, letting out an exaggerated sigh of relief. "Let me show you the secret of the gallery."

He led them to the far side of the dome where there were several yards of matting covering the stone seat. "Sit here and wait until I have walked back to the entrance. When you see me wave, put your ear to the wall and listen."

Georgiana and Hetta exchanged a bemused look. It was a strange request to make, but they did as they were told and sat down and waited. When he reached the other side, he waved and then turned away from them. Obedient to her instructions, Hetta placed her ear against the wall and listened.

After a few moments, she pulled away. "Oh, how clever," she said, a big smile on her face. "I could hear what Lord Castleford was saying as if he were standing right next to me."

"What did he say?"

"I'm not sure I should repeat it," she said. "It might sound rather boastful."

"Go on. Tell me."

"Well, if you must know, he said 'Miss Henrietta Merry is a very clever girl.'"

"As if you needed any encouragement!"

"You try, Georgie."

Georgiana put her ear to the wall and waited. She wondered what he would say to her. Hetta waved to Lord Castleford to show that they were ready, and he turned and whispered to the wall.

"My love's like a red, red rose."

Georgiana pulled away, a puzzled look on her face. She must have misheard. Those weren't the sort of words she had expected to hear.

"I don't think I can have heard right."

Hetta waved across the gallery, and Lord Castleford turned his face to the wall and spoke again.

"My love's like a red, red rose."

There could be no doubt about it. He was speaking to her in poetry. It surprised her how embarrassed she felt. She was getting used to gentlemen paying her compliments to her face, and the anonymous love-letter had made her blush, but the same words whispered in her ear seemed even more intimate.

But what did it mean? Was he admitting that he had sent her the Valentine? Did he wish that he had?

Then a less pleasant possibility occurred to her. He was laughing at her. It was silly, romantic nonsense to him, and he was teasing her about it.

"Don't mock me," she whispered back.

Georgiana glared across the gallery to where Lord Castleford stood. He stepped away from the wall as if she had slapped him in the face. Seeing the look of hurt surprise, she wondered, for a moment, whether she had misjudged him.

She was still staring, still wondering, when she heard a cannon fire. She jumped up, alarmed, but soon realised her mistake. It was only the sound of the door slamming shut, reverberating through the gallery.

By the time they had walked back round to the entrance, there was no sign on Lord Castleford's face that anything was wrong. If she had truly hurt his feelings, would he be able to brush it away so easily?

"Are you ready to go outside?" he asked, as if nothing unusual had occurred. They nodded and followed him out of the Whispering Gallery, up the steps and out onto the stone balcony where they stood, towering above the city.

Hetta looked out over London and exclaimed in delight. "Why look how small everybody is. They are no bigger than ants."

Lord Castleford pointed out all the sites of note as they walked around the viewing gallery.

"I can see the river for miles," said Georgiana, staring out across the houses to the fields beyond. "Isn't the view beautiful?"

"Very beautiful," he agreed, but she did not notice that he was looking at her rather than at the view.

They then ascended even higher to the Golden Gallery, where they admired the panorama all over again. When they had looked their fill, Lord Castleford asked them if they wanted to brave the last few steps to the ball.

Georgiana was feeling weary. "How many more steps?"

"About eighty, I believe," he replied. "A mere trifle after the hundreds you have already ascended, though somewhat more difficult to climb."

"Well, I…"

"Don't be such a killjoy, Georgie. You know I want to go right to the top."

"Very well."

Lord Castleford paid over the additional fee to the guide, who led the way up to the pinnacle of St Paul's. Georgiana was not sure she appreciated being confined in such a small space, but the experience was strangely intimate – just the three of them and a guide.

Hetta reminded Lord Castleford that he had promised to show them where Lord Nelson's bones had been laid to rest. The site was in the depths of the cathedral, directly beneath the dome up above.

The gloom of the basement matched Georgiana's melancholy reflections. "I wonder how many more men will lose their lives in the battle against Napoleon. It is right to remember the great leaders, but so many others have died. Den thinks it would be glorious to die fighting for his country, but I think war is dreadful."

"Dreadful – yes," said Lord Castleford, "but it is sometimes necessary to fight for what you believe in. To uphold freedom and keep tyrants at bay."

As they mounted the steps from the crypt, Georgiana stared up at the vastness of the building. "I would love to attend a service here and see this space filled with people worshipping God together."

"The cathedral is only full on the big occasions, such as the annual gathering of charity school children. On that day, some ten thousand children and adults assemble here. It is a truly wonderful sight. If you would like to come," he added, "I can get you a ticket."

"Can you get me a ticket too?" Hetta asked.

"Alas, the service is not until June and I fear you will be buried in the depths of Hampshire by then."

Hetta looked downcast.

"There will be other times, Hetta. When Napoleon Bonaparte is beaten, and the country is once more at peace, the King will celebrate and give his thanks to God here. I promise that I will bring you, if I have to come to Hampshire and carry you off in my carriage to do so."

That made Hetta smile. "Very well, but if the war takes too long to end, I may be married, and my husband might not like it."

"Hetta!" Georgiana exclaimed, shaking her head at her sister before turning to Lord Castleford.

"Do you think the King will live to see the peace? Father says he has been fighting madness for years. It was ill health that first took him to Weymouth. My parents have a house there where we spend several weeks every summer, but the King doesn't come anymore. Sometimes the princesses do, though. We saw the Princesses Mary and Amelia there, the year before last. Princess Amelia was not at all well, but they both seemed to be pleasant women. I cannot understand why they are not married."

"Perhaps they have not found the right man," suggested Hetta.

"More likely, the King has forbidden them to marry where they choose," Georgiana said.

"If that is the case, he must have done so because he believed that an unequal marriage would make them unhappy," Lord Castleford said. "The King is trying to prevent them from making a poor choice."

"It is right that he should protect his daughters," Georgiana agreed, "but surely part of his duty as a father is to train them to make wise decisions for themselves. Not letting them choose suggests a lack of trust."

"Sometimes an older person can see what a less experienced person cannot suspect."

Georgiana supposed he was right. Her father had forbidden her marriage to Beau, but would he have held out against the match if her affections had been truly engaged? What if she had come to London, still in love, and asked for his blessing now?

"But shouldn't the King allow his daughters to marry for love?" she said.

"Then you would advocate a love-match for happiness in marriage?" Lord Castleford asked, fixing his eyes on her face, as if he were eager to hear her opinion.

"Most definitely. My parents married for love and they are still happy together."

"Then you are at odds with most of society who believe that fortune, title and connections are the essential factors, and love just gets in the way."

"Is that what you think? Surely you would not enter a loveless marriage, to pledge yourself to someone whom you did not love? To be doomed to spend your days with one who could not sympathise with your deepest feelings about life?"

Lord Castleford was silent for a moment. "No, Miss Merry, I would not like that at all."

CHAPTER 14

Georgiana could not forget the way Lord Castleford had teased her over the Valentine, but it was not in her nature to harbour a grudge. She would have been loath to lose his friendship and appreciated that he was a much more reliable swain than Beau.

To maintain the illusion of courtship, Beau frequently drove her around Hyde Park and danced with her at balls, but he rarely took her to the theatre and refused to attend Almack's Assembly Rooms, saying it was too tedious for words.

Lord Castleford, on the other hand, was prepared to accompany her to the play as often as she wished, and far from deserting her at Almack's, he had stood up with her for the first dance.

She enjoyed their conversations, and in this respect, he surpassed all her other admirers. He treated her like a sensible person, discussing the plight of the poor and the latest news with her and not assuming that, because she was a woman, she had no interest in such things.

It was he who told her about the tragic expedition to the Walcheren where almost four thousand soldiers had died, not in the fight against Napoleon, but from a devastating fever. The account horrified her. He explained how quickly the disease had spread through the army, killing many and leaving others in a much-weakened state. She thought with a shudder it was as well that the Duke had not allowed Denmead to join up or he might even now be dead.

On a lighter note, Lord Castleford regaled her with every detail he could recall about London's most fashionable visitor, the Persian ambassador, whom he had met at Lord Radstock's house. Georgiana could not imagine anyone having such a big bushy beard and was eager to meet him for herself.

She later discovered that she had missed the chance of seeing the ambassador at the children's candlelit ball, because she had volunteered to stay home with Eliza that evening.

Hetta was excited because the Prince of Wales was opening the ball and with the date of their return to Hampshire fast approaching, she had feared that she would not see the Prince before leaving London.

Georgiana joined Eliza in the Blue Room after dinner. She drew out a letter from her reticule and dangled it in front of her sister's eyes.

"I thought the Sylph had been rather silent," Eliza said. "What words of wisdom has he written to you this time?"

Georgiana unfolded the letter and read it aloud:

"My dearest G,

What is the difference between a rose bush and a rose? One is alive and the other is not. The cut rose will die, but the bush, if well-tended, will yield roses year after year. Love is like a rose bush — romance like a rose. If you would marry for love, learn to tell the difference. A rose bush may produce many roses, but a bunch of roses cannot become a rose bush.

Growing flowers takes time. You once thought you had a rose bush, but it turned out to be only a rose that faded. Do not be deceived and make the same mistake again. Not all such stories have happy endings.

Your devoted servant,

Sylph."

Georgiana frowned. "It's not kind of Father to remind me about eloping with Beau. Does he think I failed to learn my lesson?"

"It might look like that. He doesn't know that you're only pretending. What does he mean, *not all such stories have happy endings?*"

"He is reminding me I was fortunate to escape the consequences of my foolishness. That I could have been forced into a loveless marriage or been branded a fallen woman, like the poor creatures who end up in the Magdalen," Georgiana said. "I used to think such women must be a lot wickeder than anyone I knew, but now I'm not so sure. Lord Castleford said that some of the women who ended up there were more foolish than corrupt. Not so different from me."

She sighed heavily. "I had never thought about what my fate might have been if Beau were not an honourable man."

Eliza glowed with pleasure. "Then it is well that he is an honourable man."

Georgiana supposed he was. Either that, or easily persuadable. With an inner sigh, she dismissed the recurring fear that Beau was not worthy of her sister's affections.

"I'd like to help the women in the Magdalen," she said, with sudden resolution. It seems the least I can do, given my own lucky escape. "I'll talk to Mother about it tomorrow."

*   *   *

"What an excellent idea, to donate some of your pin money to the Magdalen," Mrs Merry said when Georgiana broached the subject the next morning. "With a gentleman like Lord Castleford on the board, every penny will be put to good use. We could even attend the hospital chapel service one Sunday. Seeing as you are in a charitable mood, perhaps you would care to accompany me on a visit to the Asylum on Thursday? It is a home for destitute girls who might otherwise end up in the Magdalen."

Georgiana agreed, and to her surprise, Augusta said she would go too.

"I'm not always selfish," she said. "I do feel sorry for the poor brats in a place like the Asylum. The trouble is that most of the time, I simply forget they exist. I'm sure Helston will approve. He's almost as good as Castleford at giving his money away. Fortunately, he has plenty of it."

"Why don't you give the Asylum a donation?" Georgiana said, remembering the huge sum that Augusta had won at cards. "At least that would put your ill-gotten gains to good use."

Augusta blushed. "Maybe next month. I am a little short of funds now."

Georgiana stared at her.

"But you won a hundred pounds. Surely you haven't spent it already?"

"Don't look at me like that," Augusta said, pouting. "I lost it again. I had an unlucky evening at cards and Lady Buckinghamshire won her money back."

"You lost one hundred pounds?"

Augusta nodded. "But that is to be the end of it," she said. "I promised Helston."

Georgiana wanted to believe her.

"Mother is coming too," Augusta said, quickly changing the subject. "It does not sit well with her to appear less charitable than your mother. Of course, she has plans of her own. She wants to go to Coade and Sealy's on the way back to see their latest designs."

Georgiana looked at her blankly.

"Coade and Sealy's Gallery of Sculpture of Artificial Stone," Augusta explained. "We have to pass near the gallery to reach St George's Fields where the Asylum is. Mother will tell you that Coade's artificial stone is most superior. She's delighted with some pieces she bought a few years ago. Even the frost did not destroy them. I think she has in mind something grand for Swanmore. Maybe a lion to grace the entrance arch to our ancestral home."

Georgiana thought walking around a gallery full of bits of artificial stone sounded rather dull, but she was happy to be proved wrong. She had not expected the Tower of London or St Paul's to be exciting and she had enjoyed both visits. It did not occur to her that perhaps it was the company that had made those outings so pleasurable.

It came as no surprise that her grandmother took charge of the party she had condescended to join. Any party to which the Duchess belonged became hers. When Hetta insisted that she be allowed to go too, the Duchess decreed that they would travel in two carriages as she refused to be crushed.

The matron was standing at the entrance of the Asylum when they arrived, ready to greet the Duchess's party. The woman showed them around the institution with a deference verging on servility, which Georgiana found embarrassing.

Her grandmother, however, saw nothing amiss, and Georgiana had the nasty suspicion that she expected it as her due. She supposed the matron knew what a blessing it would be to the Asylum to have such a wealthy supporter and was doing everything she could to attract her patronage.

They watched the girls at their work, some having lessons in reading or arithmetic whilst others sat sewing or knitting.

"We take in plain needlework for our girls to do, if you should ever need our services," the matron said.

Georgiana wished she had something that needed doing.

The kitchen was bustling with activity. More girls were busy helping the cook prepare dinner for the two hundred female orphans who lived there. Georgiana noticed that many were Hetta's age or younger, but none looked as old as she was. As the matron explained how they were apprenticed to good families from the age of about fifteen, she realised how fortunate she was to have been born into a family of means. The prospect of becoming a servant was not appealing.

By the time they had inspected the dining room and the chapel, Georgiana could tell that her grandmother's interest was waning. It came as no surprise when she abruptly drew their visit to a close by announcing that the Duke would send a large subscription.

Her mother, however, refused to be hurried away. As well as promising a donation, she talked with the matron about the benefits of fresh air and the importance of words of praise to encourage good behaviour.

The Duchess was eager to be on her way to the Coade Stone Gallery and urged the rest of the party to make haste with more than a touch of impatience.

Augusta was about to join Georgiana in the second carriage when she realised that she did not have her reticule with her.

"Bother. I must have put it down when I was examining the girls' needlework. Sorry, Georgie, it won't take long. Matron will send someone to fetch it for me."

She strode back up the path and disappeared into the Asylum.

Georgiana climbed down the steps again and walked over to the other carriage to explain what had happened. Her grandmother exclaimed at Augusta's carelessness and announced that they would just have to follow on when she returned. As soon as Georgiana stepped away from the carriage, the Duchess gave the order to the coachman and they set off for the gallery.

There was nothing for Georgiana to do but wait. She sat down in the carriage again and flicked through Hetta's copy of *The Picture for London* which was lying on the seat. Nothing caught her interest until she came to the map. Although she was poor at reading maps, with the help of the index, she located the Asylum.

She noticed that the Magdalen Hospital was only a few streets away and wondered whether she could see it from the gates. Ever since she had read the last letter from the Sylph, she had not been able to get the plight of the poor souls who lived there out of her mind. Perhaps if she saw the front of the building, she wouldn't keep imagining all those destitute women who looked so like herself.

She got out of the carriage again and, guidebook in hand, walked down the path toward the gates. Down the road to the right, she could see the obelisk that was marked on the map, but the Magdalen was too far away.

As she stood at the gates, a bedraggled looking child came up to her and held out his hands. She had pitied the girls in the Asylum, but at least they had food to eat. This poor boy looked as if he had not had a good meal in weeks. If she were at home, she would have taken him to her mother, who would have made sure that he was given some bread and stew. But she was not at home, and her mother was not here to advise her.

She longed to bring a smile to the forlorn little face. She had no food to give him, but if she gave him some money, he could buy something to fill his stomach.

Her mind made up, she hurried back to the carriage to get her reticule. Purse in hand, she returned to the gates but was disappointed to discover that the boy had disappeared. She hated to think the child would go hungry when she could have prevented it and looked up and down the street, trying to see where he had gone. She was about to give up when she caught sight of him on the other side of the road.

Georgiana glanced back at the carriage. There was still no sign of Augusta. Time enough, she reasoned, to give the child some money and return to the coach before she was missed. As soon as she stepped outside the Asylum gates, an older boy appeared, broom in hand, offering to sweep a crossing for her. He must have been lurking nearby with that sole purpose in mind. With a grateful smile, she handed the boy a coin, and made her way across the dirty road on the newly swept path.

By the time she reached the other side, the bottom of her carriage dress was soiled. Georgiana looked down at the hem in dismay, wondering what her mother, or worse, her grandmother, would have to say when she arrived at the artificial stone gallery in such a dirty dress.

With a deep breath, she put such thoughts behind her. Her mother would understand when she explained that she was helping a poor boy. She needed to finish what she had set out to do and hurry back to the carriage before Augusta returned and wondered where she was.

Georgiana looked around and let out a sigh of frustration. The boy had disappeared again. She had just caught sight of him, heading down the next road, when a gentleman drove by in his gig. As he passed her, he slowed his horse and leered at her vulgarly.

Too late, she realised the picture she must be presenting, walking alone in this part of London. She feared that he took her for a woman of the street and panicked. Rather than wait for the older boy to sweep her a fresh crossing, back to the safety of the Asylum, she set off in the opposite direction, down the same road that the small boy had taken. The man called after her, jeering at her rudely for running away. She hastened along the path as fast as she could, trying to put as much distance as she could between herself and the man.

When she reached a crossroads, she glanced back. The man was nowhere to be seen. Having had his fun, he must have driven on. She heaved a sigh of relief and, abandoning her errand of mercy, she started to retrace her steps. Holding firmly to her reticule, she strode along the road with a confidence she was far from feeling.

The small boy she had been looking for stepped out in front of her, making her jump. He held out his hand and looked at her expectantly. With a smile, she opened her reticule and took out two coins which she gave to the shabby child, encouraging him to buy something to eat. Before she knew it, a group of children had surrounded her, all holding out their hands, demanding money.

One boy caught hold of her skirt. "Give us some money, Miss," he cried.

"Please, Miss, I'm hungry," wailed another.

Georgiana looked at the swarm of children. She wanted to help but even if she gave away all the money she was carrying, it wouldn't go around so many.

"I haven't got enough for you all," she said.

"Give us some money," another clamoured whilst a second child made a grab for her reticule.

Georgiana twisted away, only to find eager hands on the other side, trying to grasp her bag. Breaking free once more, she started walking along the road, in which direction, she did not know or care. All she could think of was getting away.

When she reached the end of the road, the urchins were still close behind her. Her main thought was to keep moving. She headed down the turning to the right, not knowing whether it would take her nearer or further from where she wanted to be. Some distance away, she could see a gentleman walking her way and called for help.

Only as he hurried toward her did she fear that she might be attracting the notice of someone else who would be glad to relieve her of her money – or worse. As she hesitated, unsure which way to go, a boy reached for her reticule and wrenched it out of her hand. While she was caught off balance, another tried to grab her hat.

The gentleman was rapidly approaching, waving his stick in a menacing manner. With a monumental effort, she pulled away from the children, and abandoning her reticule, she hurried back in the direction she had just come. The man called out to her to stop, but she was now thoroughly frightened and having broken away, she was not going to stop for anyone.

Glancing back, she saw that the gaggle of urchins had dispersed as the man reached them, brandishing his cane, and now he was gaining on her fast. With renewed panic, she rushed along the pavement as quickly as her skirts would allow.

She knew the man could not be far behind her when he called out again. In an instant, she realised he was not the menacing threat she feared. His voice was familiar and calling her name.

Georgiana stopped and turned and stood in a daze until he reached her. "Lord Castleford! I have never been so glad to see anyone in my life," she cried in relief, collapsing against his chest.

He put his arms around her slender body to prevent her from falling. Georgiana heaved an almighty sigh and burst into tears.

CHAPTER 15

Lord Castleford was on his way to the Magdalen when he caught sight of Georgiana, surrounded by a crowd of children. For a moment, his heart stood still as he saw the look of sheer terror on her face. He could not believe his eyes. What was she doing here, alone, being hounded by an unruly bunch of ragamuffins? They would not harm her – they were hungry, poor little wretches – but there was no doubt that they had frightened her and were eager to relieve her of anything she had on her person.

It only took him a moment to gather his wits and spring into action. Rapping his cane twice on the roof, he brought his carriage to an abrupt halt. Without waiting for the steps to be lowered, he jumped down, telling his astonished coachman that he would walk the rest of the way.

He hurried back along the road, waving his cane at the children, only to find that he had scared Georgiana away too. By the time he finally persuaded her to stop, he was almost out of breath. But then she had walked into his arms. Arms that had instinctively closed around her.

He would never forget how she looked at him in that moment. It was a look of such delight that his heart turned over. And now she was here, snuggled up against his chest, closer than she had ever been before.

He gazed down tenderly at the woman in his arms – the woman he meant to cherish for the rest of his life. It was the first time he had seen her like this – so fragile and helpless. He was aware of the desire to stroke her hair, to pull her to himself and promise to protect her forever. She was so close to him he could feel her warmth through his jacket. He realised the danger he was in. The temptation to kiss all those tears away was almost overwhelming.

Almost. Georgiana trusted him. He would not – must not – abuse that trust. Her feelings were still a mystery to him. He needed to wait. To see what she felt. It would be despicable to force her into a marriage that was not of her choosing. He had seen what that did to people. It had happened to his mother and he shuddered at the recollection of the sham that had been his parents' marriage. No. He was after something far better than that.

Reluctantly, he pulled away. He must act as if this moment of intimacy had not occurred. If he pushed his suit on her now, she might feel obliged to accept him to preserve her reputation.

He put his hand in his pocket and extracted a clean handkerchief which he offered to Georgiana. She had stopped crying and with the bravery he had come to expect, she was sniffing herself into a calmer state of mind. She accepted the handkerchief gratefully and blew her nose.

Now that the crisis was over, he wanted some answers. Why was Georgiana in this part of London, and why was she alone, with neither maid nor companion to protect her? His expression grew grim as he thought of what might have happened. By the grace of God, no one worse than a ragamuffin had accosted her. But how could she be so careless of her reputation, her personal safety?

Georgiana peeked up at his face but looked away immediately, as if she could not bear the severity she saw there. He hoped she knew that it was his deep concern for her that made him appear so stern and not disgust at her behaviour. An even more worrying thought crossed his mind. Did she think he was angry at being forced into making her an offer to protect her reputation?

He wished he could bring back that joyful look which had radiated from her face when she first realised who he was and collapsed into his arms. But perhaps that was the problem. Now that she had recovered her composure, she was embarrassed by her behaviour.

Without a word, he handed her the empty reticule that he had retrieved and offered her the crook of his arm. She took it, mumbling her thanks whilst staring into the air, unwilling to meet his eyes.

"We should walk," he said curtly, pushing down the emotion that still threatened to overcome his better judgement. He marched off down the street toward where a group of people were gathered. Georgiana almost had to run to keep up with his pace.

As they walked, he began to talk. "And now, Miss Merry," he said, with an edge to his voice brought on by his recent reflections on her narrow escape from danger, "perhaps you would care to tell me how it is that you are walking, unattended, in a far from fashionable part of London?"

Georgiana shuddered. "I was visiting the Asylum with my mother and the Duchess and Gusta…"

She glanced up at him in horror. "Gusta won't know what has happened to me. She had to go back inside the Asylum because she had left something behind, and while I was waiting, this poor little boy came to the gates. He seemed so hungry that I wished to give him some money to buy food, but when I returned with my reticule, he had gone. It was stupid. I can see that now. But I went after him. It didn't occur to me that I was putting myself in any danger. I just wanted to help."

Castleford shook his head in disbelief. He opened his mouth to speak and then shut it again, lost for words. Though deeply moved by her compassion for the poor boy, he could not believe that she had behaved so impulsively, oblivious to the risks she was taking. He hoped he would not have to wait long for the right to protect her as his wife. She clearly needed it.

* * *

Georgiana struggled to hold back the tears. Once again, she had acted without thinking about the consequences and landed herself in trouble. If it were not for Lord Castleford, the situation might well have been worse.

What did he think of her now? In her relief at being rescued, she had flung herself into his arms. She had found his embrace warm and comforting and thought he felt that intimacy too. But it seemed she had been mistaken. He could not extricate himself fast enough. Was he disgusted with the way she had behaved? He looked so stern that she barely recognised him.

"I am so grateful to you for coming to my rescue," she said when the silence between them threatened to continue indefinitely.

"Thank God that I was in the right place at the right time and that you met nothing worse than a group of hungry children."

"What are *you* doing here, in this less than fashionable neighbourhood?"

"I am on my way to the Magdalen Hospital. It is an admittance day."

As they neared the end of the street, Georgiana could see some women gathered outside one of the buildings. They turned to stare at her. There must have been about twenty of them, some on their own, others in twos. None of them appeared happy. Most seemed anxious and out of place, and they all looked at her with a degree of hostility.

Lord Castleford mounted the steps and rang the bell whilst Georgiana waited on the first step for the door to open. She could hear the women murmuring about her.

"No one could suppose this one's been on the streets. They'll take her in before the likes of us, you'll see. 'specially if the guvnor here recommends her."

"Lor' but she's a pretty one."

"Innocent too. Just look at her. Flabbergasted to be here at all, poor thing."

"All men are scoundrels, dearie. Can't trust 'em. They take what they want and leave us in the gutter. Did he deceive you with promises of marriage?"

Georgiana was relieved when the door opened and Lord Castleford ushered her into the building, closing it behind him. He led her into a small saloon.

"Do sit down, Miss Merry. If you'll excuse me, I must summon my carriage to return you to your family."

With these words, he bowed and left the room, as if the whole situation were an embarrassment to him.

Georgiana paced up and down, sighing and wringing her hands, wondering whether she would ever learn to curb her impulsiveness. If only she hadn't gone after the boy. Why, oh why, couldn't she have stayed in the carriage?

A few minutes later, a maidservant came to the door.

"Begging your pardon, Miss, but his lordship's carriage is here. Lord Castleford sends his apologies that he cannot see you returned to your friends himself but said as how I was to go with you, to make sure you reach them safely."

Georgiana gulped. She was being sent away in disgrace without another word. He must be truly disappointed in her.

The maid accompanied her out of the building to the waiting carriage, unobserved by anyone, as the group of women had disappeared. She instructed the driver and climbed in beside Georgiana.

"Don't look so dismayed, Miss," she said, with a reassuring smile. "Lord Castleford's a good man. Lots of us are truly grateful to him and the others."

There was no sign of the Duchess's carriage at the Asylum, so the maid told the coachman to drive on to Wessex House. They pulled up outside just as Lady Augusta was about to enter. Georgiana thanked the girl and hurried to join Augusta, eager not to advertise her folly to anyone else. It was bad enough that Lord Castleford knew and had been obliged to rescue her.

She grabbed Augusta's arm, and they entered the house together. As soon as they were out of earshot of the servants, Augusta demanded to know where she had disappeared to.

"When I came back outside, you were nowhere in sight. I assumed that you had gone with the others and left for Coade's Gallery. When I got there, I realised my mistake. I told Mamma we were going home and returned to the Asylum to look for you. Wilby was so apologetic that he had not seen you step down from the coach. He begged me not to say anything about it. You are fortunate that he did not have a stroke, he was so distressed."

"I'm sorry, Gusta."

"When we did not find you at the Asylum, we drove up and down the streets but could see no sign of you. Even I was getting anxious, and it takes a lot to scare me. I thought we had better come home and ask your father what we should do."

"Please don't tell him, Gusta. He will be so disappointed that I acted without thinking again."

"Have no fear. I've been discreet. No one knows apart from myself, Wilby and the footman. Mother thinks we returned home together. But I am not blind, Georgie. How did you end up coming back in Castleford's carriage?"

"I was trying to help a hungry little boy. He disappeared while I was getting my reticule and foolishly, I went after him. A group of urchins surrounded me, all wanting money. If Lord Castleford hadn't found me…"

Augusta put her arm around Georgiana's shoulders. "Enough said. I can tell you are overwrought. You're safe and that's all that matters. I won't say a word."

Georgiana gave a grateful smile and fell silent, relieved that Augusta had not pushed for the details of the embarrassing episode. There was only one person she wanted to tell what had happened. When Augusta retired to her bedchamber to change her dress, Georgiana hurried away to see Eliza and poured out the complete story.

"Please don't lecture me about acting without thinking," she said as she finished her narrative. "I know I behaved rashly and have been beating myself up about it ever since."

"You were fortunate that Lord Castleford was there to save you."

Georgiana's face clouded over. "I was, but…" She paused and sighed heavily.

"But what?"

She looked up, a dreamy look in her eyes. "It could have been so romantic. I felt so safe in his arms and he was so protective of me that for a moment I thought, maybe, we could be more than friends."

She huffed, blinking back a tear. "He soon put that idea to rest. He could not wait to escape. I must have disgusted him with my emotional outburst or my reckless behaviour or both. He sent me home in disgrace and now I don't even know if we're friends anymore."

Eliza's sympathy failed to restore her inner peace. She was on tenterhooks all afternoon and evening, wondering if anything would be said about her escapade. It was not. She went to bed believing that her secret was safe.

* * *

Georgiana slept restlessly, dreaming of hands coming out of the darkness to grab her, and running, running, running, until she collapsed onto Lord Castleford's chest. She awoke with a smile on her lips, remembering that warm feeling of peace and security before sinking into gloom at the thought of his disgust. She sighed. At least her father had not learned what had happened.

It soon became clear that her relief was premature. After breakfast, Mr Merry invited her to join him in the library.

"Are you able to explain to me, Georgiana, how my daughter ended up near the Magdalen Hospital unattended by companion or maid?"

Her first reaction was to blame the coachman for betraying her, but almost as soon as the thought had crossed her mind, she dismissed it. Wilby did not know where she had been. She knew that Augusta would not break her word, and that left only one person who could have told her father. Lord Castleford.

The colour rushed to her cheeks. She was lost for words – a circumstance so rare as to cause her father to comment.

"Have you nothing to say for yourself?" His eyes pleaded with her, longing for her to justify her actions.

Her lip quivered as she shook her head.

"It is laudable to help the poor, but how could you be so heedless as to go scampering off alone, even for such a purpose?"

"I didn't think," she said, blinking back the tears when she saw the disappointment in her father's eyes.

"Ah, the famous impetuosity," her father replied. "Lord Castleford was concerned that you were unfamiliar with London ways. It is not safe for you to walk around unprotected. Perhaps I have not impressed upon you that what is acceptable in the country where you are known is neither safe nor respectable in town. Do you wish to appear like one of those poor women at the Magdalen?"

"No, Father."

"Then be more careful, Georgiana. We are leaving you to your grandmother's care when we return to Hampshire in two weeks' time. If I hear of any more wild adventures, I will have no choice but to incur your mother's wrath and take you home with us. Do I make myself clear?"

"Yes, sir."

CHAPTER 16

Georgiana walked upstairs to her bedroom with a wooden expression on her face, hiding the emotional turmoil inside. Now even more aware of her failings than she had been the day before, she knew that if she continued to dwell on them, she would break down in tears.

She picked up a novel, hoping to channel her thoughts in a more cheerful direction, but threw it down again without reading a single word. Unable to sit still, she got up and started pacing up and down the room, her eyes blazing as she thought about Lord Castleford's treachery. How could he? Was it not enough that he had sent her home in disgrace? Did he have to tell her father too?

It would be better if she avoided him until she had conquered her resentment. Particularly today when the grievance was so raw. She had a sudden yearning to be out in the open air. A walk in the park would serve two purposes: she would not be at home if Lord Castleford called, and it would help clear her head and dispel her foul mood.

Mindful of the proprieties because of her recent indiscretion, she asked her mother's permission to go for a walk in Hyde Park. Smartly dressed in the pale blue pelisse which had just arrived from the dressmaker's and the bonnet from Mrs Wardle's millinery that had been designed to match, Georgiana set out, accompanied by her maid.

For the first ten minutes of their walk in the park, she had to endure Bessie's scolding. Her maid seemed determined to make her feel even worse about her misadventure.

"Haven't you gotten yourself in enough trouble afore today to teach you to think before you act? Oh yes. I know all about what happened. Your father made sure of that, so you mustn't blame Wilby.

Told me to keep an eye on you. Humph. Not the easiest thing to do when you go jaunting off without me. God bless Lord Castleford for coming to your rescue. The Almighty was most gracious to place that kind gentleman in your way just when you needed him."

"I appreciate that, Bessie, but he didn't have to tell Father."

"Nothing good ever came of secrets, Miss Georgiana, and so you ought to know by now. The master tells you often enough. Keep it out in the open, my dear."

Georgiana huffed and increased her pace, hoping to put a little distance between herself and her moralising maid. She was so intent on her purpose that she did not notice a carriage overtaking them until it drew up just ahead.

Observing the many-caped greatcoat that the driver was wearing, she assumed that it was Beau, come to take her for a drive around the park because her aunt had been nagging him again. She was in no mood to humour him today and intended to dismiss him as quickly as she could.

As she stood waiting for him to alight, her gaze fell on the horses and she realised to her surprise that they were not Beau's magnificent bays, but a pair of greys. She sighed. It was just like Beau to buy yet more horses.

She prepared to berate him for the extravagance, but when the driver jumped down from his curricle and handed the reins to his groom, Georgiana came face to face not with Beau, but with Sir James. She had not seen him since the night he had rescued her reticule in the theatre.

Sir James executed an extravagant bow. "Miss Merry. We meet again."

"I do not believe we have been introduced, sir," Georgiana replied brusquely, turning away.

"Yet I have discovered your name."

Georgiana resumed her walk at an increased pace while Bessie scampered along behind, trying to keep up. Sir James did not take the hint. Instead, he fell into step with her and continued to talk.

"Cruel beauty. Will you truly ignore me until I can obtain an introduction? I did not think you were so heartless. Yet even if you will not talk to me, you cannot stop me pouring out my adoration. How long I have wanted to tell you that since our one brief meeting I have not been able to get you out of my mind. Day and night your loveliness is before me, invading my thoughts and haunting my dreams. I could drown in the depths of your deep, blue eyes, if only they would look kindly on me. What wouldn't I give to hear the dulcet tones of your sweet voice again and perchance win the right to kiss your hand in humble admiration? Be kind to Your devoted servant, Won't you walk with me?" he asked, offering her his arm, a wistful expression hovering over his lips and his eyes wide and pleading like a small child begging for a treat.

Georgiana blushed at the fulsome compliments. She suspected him of flattery, but she was not immune to hearing her praises sung. The Magdalen affair had left her with such a low opinion of herself that it was balm to her soul. She felt her resolve weakening.

Sir James intrigued her. What manner of man persisted in talking to you after he had so clearly been dismissed? And speaking in such a way. It was exhilarating to be the object of such eloquent adulation.

Did she dare disregard the proprieties? She was eager to make Sir James's acquaintance, but she was still smarting from the shame that had resulted from the last time she had acted without thinking. Could she risk dispensing with the formalities?

Sir James had done her a great service in rescuing her reticule, she reasoned. Would it be so wrong to repay him with a walk in the park? What could be improper about that? Bessie was only a few steps away.

"Very well, Sir James," Georgiana said shyly, slowing her pace and taking his arm.

A look of contentment spread across his face. "Providence has smiled upon me at last. I have watched and waited, hoping for the chance to approach you, but until today, I have not dared."

He made a show of looking around. "But where are your admirers? Have they all deserted you?"

Georgiana thought guiltily of Lord Castleford who was probably calling at Wessex House at that moment. He had not deserted her; she had deserted him. She did not know how to respond, but Sir James was not expecting a reply.

"You are an angel, Miss Merry," Sir James continued. "So beautiful. So good. So far above me in every way."

"Why do you say that? You were good to me at the theatre when you retrieved my reticule."

"It is kind of you to remember such a trifling service."

"It was not trifling to me," she said. "I was delighted to get it back. For a moment, I thought I had lost it forever."

"I cannot claim as virtue what has brought me such pleasure. If I had not come to your rescue, I might never have met you."

"Even so, it was a kind act."

Sir James nodded his appreciation, but his expression was sombre.

"I fear you do not understand me when I say how far above me you are in every way, and when you do, you will have nothing more to do with me." He hesitated. "I have not led a spotless life."

"Which of us has? I am continually slipping up and paying the consequences for my folly," she said, thinking of her latest indiscretion.

"I fear that my follies have had greater repercussions."

"But thankfully, we can be forgiven and try again."

"Then you believe in second chances?"

"Yes, I do."

"When I hear you say it, I can almost believe it's true," he said, his solemn gaze not wavering from her face. "With such an angel to guide me, anything is possible. Did you understand the words I sent you?

> *O, my love's like a red, red rose,*
> *That's newly sprung in June;*
> *O, my love's like the melody,*
> *That's sweetly play'd in tune.*
>
> *As fair art thou, my bonnie lass,*
> *So deep in love am I;*
> *And I will love thee still my dear,*
> *Till a' the seas gang dry."*

Georgiana felt the colour rush to her cheeks once more as she recognised the words of her Valentine and digested the fact that it had been Sir James who had sent it.

He recited the verses slowly, each word charged with meaning and directed at her. When Lord Castleford had whispered the opening line in her ear across the Whispering Gallery, she had been quick to assume that he was not serious – that he was ridiculing her fondness for the romantic.

It did not cross her mind to consider whether Sir James was teasing her. Coming from his lips, the words sounded like a declaration of love.

Georgiana was flattered by his obvious admiration. He was some years older than Beau or Lord Castleford – a man of the world with a charm that any woman would find hard to resist. What lady did not wish to be told that she was an angel? That she was beautiful?

She pushed away the nagging doubt in the back of her mind that questioned whether someone could truly love you when they did not know you. She did not want to believe Sir James's love was only skin deep.

The remedy to her doubts was obvious. She must become better acquainted with Sir James. What, after all, did she know of him?

"Where do you live?" Georgiana asked. "My home is in the depths of rural Hampshire."

If Sir James was perturbed by this prosaic response to his words of love, he did not show it.

"My estate is in Scotland, though I am rarely there. It has too many unpleasant memories of the family I once had."

Georgiana assumed his parents must have died there. That would be a melancholy association indeed. How would she view her own home if her father and mother had departed this life and gone to heaven?

"I'm sorry," she said, coming to a halt and looking up at him with eyes that had misted over with sympathy.

"Thank you," he said, giving her arm a gentle squeeze.

* * *

Lord Castleford woke in the middle of the night in a cold sweat and sat bolt upright, the image of Georgiana's terrified face vividly before him. It took him a few minutes to gather his wits, and he sank back onto the pillows with a deep sigh. She was safe.

Closing his eyes again, he thought of those few precious moments when she had been in his arms and looked up at him as if he were everything she wanted. He felt anew the tug at his heart as he remembered the hurt look on her face as he had moved away, fearful that he would give into temptation and kiss her.

He was afraid for her. She was too trusting. It would have been so easy to compromise her reputation, so she would have been forced to marry him. He shuddered. She needed to be protected from those that would not scruple to take advantage of such a situation.

It was this fear that had motivated Castleford to tell her father what had happened. He hoped she would not feel betrayed. He wanted to look after her. To keep her safe. He would have to risk asking her to marry him, even though he was not yet sure of her feelings. And with this thought, he fell back asleep.

Castleford called at Wessex House the next morning shortly after Georgiana had left it. Politeness bade him stay and make conversation with Mrs Merry and so it was some fifteen minutes later that he left the house and remounted his horse. Armed with the information that Georgiana was walking in Hyde Park, he headed in the same direction.

It was perhaps a little optimistic of him to believe he could find her in the throng of people out walking, but he maintained a positive attitude and started to ride the circuit around the park. He had not gone far when he spotted her, talking to a gentleman whom he did not recognise. He noted with satisfaction that her maid was just a few paces behind. At least she seemed to have learned her lesson.

Georgiana was facing him as he rode toward her, but she did not seem to be aware of his approach. Her attention was focused on the conversation she was having with her companion. Even from that distance, he could see the tenderness in her eyes. Eyes that were looking up at the unknown gentleman – a gentleman who was squeezing her arm with alarming intimacy.

Castleford was not aware that his whole body had tensed up until his horse objected, tossing her head impatiently until her master responded and loosened the reins. He felt as if he had been punched in the stomach. Seeing Georgiana look up at this unknown gentleman like that was agony. He had always been a peaceable man, but he felt far from peaceable now. He wanted to throttle this gentleman, whoever he was, for evoking such an affectionate response.

He was aghast at the fierceness of his reaction. Rage was coursing through his body. Was this jealousy? If so, he needed to learn to control it. He could not approach her – not until he had conquered this overwhelming fury. Georgiana would come to no harm with her maid on the watch. He must master his emotions. With a final painful look, he dug his knees into his horse's flanks and rode by without stopping.

* * *

Georgiana was so intent on her conversation with Sir James that she did not see Lord Castleford until he was riding past. As she saw him go by out of the corner of her eye, all resentment at his interference vanished, and she was left with a deep desire for reconciliation.

His behaviour discomposed her. Had she offended him so much that he would not even stop to speak to her? Was she acting improperly, talking to Sir James like this? Why did he make her feel guilty for doing what she had convinced herself was acceptable? Did he disapprove of her conduct so greatly?

All pleasure in her conversation with Sir James evaporated, tarnished by Lord Castleford's censure. Perhaps she had lingered too long.

Before she could find an excuse for ending their walk, Sir James spoke. "I see that I have outstayed my welcome, Miss Merry. You grow uncomfortable with my company."

Although such had been her thoughts, she was quick to dissemble. "Uncomfortable? You mistake me. I was distracted. That is all."

"I noticed – the gentleman on horseback. One of your admirers."

"Whatever makes you think that?" Lord Castleford did not admire her. He disapproved of everything she did.

Sir James slapped his arm across his chest dramatically. "If looks could kill, I would be lying prostrate on the ground before you, such was the venom in the horseman's glance. Believe me when I say that I would willingly die for you, but I would much rather live for you. I bid you farewell – until we meet again."

He took her gloved hand and held it, looking into her eyes as he recited the final two verses of the poem he had quoted so eloquently:

> *"Till a' the seas gang dry, my dear,*
> *And the rocks melt wi' the sun:*
> *And I will love thee still, my dear,*
> *While the sands o' life shall run.*
>
> *And fare thee weel, my only love!*
> *And fare thee weel a while!*
> *And I will come again, my love,*
> *Though it were ten thousand mile."*

As he completed the poem, he raised her hand to his lips and kissed it. She could feel the heat of his mouth through her glove as he lingered over it, and felt her colour rising once more as the intimate moment seemed to go on and on.

At length, Sir James released her hand, bowed, and headed back toward his curricle. Georgiana stood, watching him depart, wondering whether she would meet him again, and whether she wanted to or not.

She was still thinking about him when she reached home. She did not know what to make of Sir James and was not entirely comfortable with his outrageous flattery.

And what of Lord Castleford's reaction? His behaviour made her doubt her own judgement. Had she been in error again?

She penned a brief letter to the Sylph asking for advice. In the meantime, she remembered Bessie's admonition against secrecy and told her father about the unconventional meeting. Though it was clear he was not pleased, he did his best to hide it, applauding her honesty, but urging her not to make a habit of conversing with gentlemen to whom she had not been introduced.

Despite her decision to be open about her encounter with Sir James, she found there were some parts she had no wish to share, even with Eliza. They could laugh together about Sir James refusing to take no for an answer and his well-practised flattery, and they could sympathise over the sad memories associated with his home. But Georgiana was not sure what she felt about the slow, lingering kiss on her hand, and until she did, she was not inclined to talk about it.

* * *

Georgiana did not have to wait long for a reply from the Sylph, which she read aloud to Eliza.

> *"My dearest G,*
>
> *Let me give you this warning. Beware of rogues masquerading as gentlemen who desire both your person and your wealth. Do not put yourself in the power of any gentleman who is neither husband nor father. Even the noblest of men may be tempted by your beauty. Remember the words that Evelina's guardian wrote to her: 'Nothing is so delicate as the reputation of a woman; it is at once the most beautiful and most brittle of all human things.'*
>
> *Your faithful Sylph."*

"Fancy quoting *Evelina*. I didn't even know Father had read it," Eliza said.

"He must have done. It is one of Mother's favourites."

"*Beware of rogues*," Eliza repeated. "I suppose he is warning you not to trust Sir James until you are certain what kind of man he is. It is rather strange that you have not met him at any of the balls or assemblies you have been to. Do you think he is respectable?"

"I don't know. He told me himself that he had made mistakes, but who hasn't? Surely what is more important is that he sounded in desperate need of help to do better. He called me an angel."

"Ha! If he only knew."

Georgiana glared at her sister and picked up a cushion to swat her with. Eliza held up her hands in surrender.

"I'm sorry," she squealed, trying to stifle her mirth. "Have mercy on a poor invalid."

Georgiana huffed and put the cushion down.

"What does he mean by telling you to guard yourself from *even the noblest of men*? Do you think he is referring to Lord Castleford?" Eliza said.

"I suppose so. Apart from Father, he's the noblest man I know. But Father can't know him well. I cannot imagine that he would *ever* be tempted to overstep the mark."

She recalled those brief moments, safe in Lord Castleford's arms, when he had rescued her at the Magdalen. He had given no indication of being tempted to keep her there, she thought to herself, and a wistful sigh escaped, causing her to blush as she realised what she was thinking.

CHAPTER 17

There was only a week to go before her family returned to Hampshire and losing Eliza's companionship was weighing heavily on Georgiana's mind.

"How will I survive without you?"

Eliza draped an arm around her sister's shoulders. "We can still write to each other."

"It's not the same."

"You'll have Gusta."

"I can't share the secrets of my heart with her. Anyway, since her betrothal, she has had no time for anything apart from choosing her bride clothes."

"You will be choosing your own bride clothes soon, I expect," said a voice from across the room.

Two pairs of eyes looked in amazement at their youngest sister. She had been so quiet that they had both forgotten she was there.

"Why would you say a thing like that, Hetta?" Georgiana asked.

Hetta was suddenly not so sure of herself.

"What do you know? Out with it."

"It is no big secret," Hetta said. "I mean, anyone can see…"

"See what?" her sisters asked in unison.

"That Lord Castleford wants to marry Georgie."

"Don't be ridiculous," Georgiana said, thinking of their last encounter. "Stop making things up. We're just friends." At least, she hoped they were still friends.

"I'm not. He told me."

Georgiana found that hard to believe. "Lord Castleford told you he wanted to marry me?"

"Yes," Hetta said. "I like him. If I were older, I shouldn't mind marrying him myself." With these words, she flounced out of the room.

"Do you think it's true?" asked Eliza.

Georgiana shrugged. "I suppose so. Hetta doesn't tell lies. But if he does want to marry me, he has a strange way of showing it. He doesn't pay me lavish compliments and seems to find more in me to disapprove of than admire. And remember how quickly he withdrew from my embrace when I threw myself at him when he found me near the Magdalen Hospital. Surely you would not act so coldly if you were in love with someone?"

"Maybe he is not very passionate. Not everybody is," Eliza said.

Georgiana sighed. She had reached the same conclusion as her sister, but it was surprisingly unsatisfactory. If only he were not so cold, so unfeeling, perhaps she could have loved him.

"I suppose not. There is no doubt that he is a virtuous man – a man of faith and good works – but I don't love him. Not as a wife should love a husband."

Eliza nodded wisely. "Say no more. I understand."

Georgiana suspected that she did. It was a pity Eliza had set her heart on Beau who would probably make a lousy husband if she succeeded in marrying him.

"But perhaps it would be foolish to refuse him," Georgiana said, unable to let the subject rest. "Maybe I would grow to love him."

"That sounds rather risky to me."

"I will write to the Sylph and ask for his advice about Sir James and Lord Castleford, though I won't mention any names, of course. Just to see what he says. Father will probably tell me to cast off Sir James without another thought and pursue his good and honourable lordship."

Georgiana spent a long time pondering over her words. When she had finished writing, she read out the letter to Eliza:

"To my Sylph,

I am surprised that you warn me against all men as I am quite sure that there are some gentlemen of my acquaintance whom I can trust, but if, as you say, rogues masquerade as gentlemen, and those who can be trusted look much the same as those who cannot, how am I supposed to know the difference?

If I met a gentleman whom I could trust who was good and honourable and true, but who did not make my heart sing, pray advise me, is that enough? Should I believe my heart or my head? I used to think I could rely on my heart, but my heart has let me down in the past.

Please tell me what I should do.

G."

She had just sealed the letter ready for the post when the door opened. The girls looked up, expecting to see Hetta come to apologise, but it was Charlotte.

"Grandmother says you are to go to the drawing room, Georgiana. Lord Castleford is waiting."

Georgiana cast an anxious look at Eliza. She could not meet him now, not if what Hetta said was true, and he was about to propose. Not when she felt so uncertain of her feelings.

"I can't come. Eliza needs me.".

Charlotte pulled a face and walked out of the room, shaking her head as she went. "Grandmother will not be pleased."

*   *   *

Lord Castleford entered the drawing room with a confidence he was far from feeling. It had taken him many hours to subdue the fiery jealousy that had overwhelmed him when he had seen Georgiana with that man in the park.

The rational part of his brain told him that walking with a gentleman, under the eye of a maid, was unexceptionable. That there was nothing improper taking place. But that took no account of a lover's heightened perception. Or maybe warped.

It was a gut feeling that something was not right. He had no reason to mistrust the man. He did not know anything to his discredit. In fact, he knew nothing about him at all, and that bothered him. What manner of man was he? Was it a coincidence that he had met Georgiana, or had he engineered the meeting when she had only a maid for protection?

His chest still tightened when he remembered that moment of intimacy he had observed. He could not risk waiting to make her an offer of marriage if he wanted to have a chance with Georgiana.

137

He was dismayed to find there were only two occupants in the drawing room – the Duchess and Georgiana's sister Charlotte, who was playing on the pianoforte.

Swallowing his frustration, he greeted the Duchess with his usual polished smile. For the second time, he had arrived at Wessex House to propose, only to discover that Georgiana was not there. At least she was in the house on this occasion, and he had no objection to the Duchess sending Charlotte to fetch her. Judging by the way her eyes were gleaming, he thought she had guessed his purpose.

With half an eye fixed on the door, he sat and listened to the Duchess talking of her daughter's forthcoming marriage, though he only heard one word in three. As the door reopened, he felt his heart stop beating. This was it, then. The moment of truth. His entire future hung in the balance.

His face fell as Charlotte walked back into the room alone.

"She's not coming," she said, smiling smugly up at her grandmother. "Eliza needs her."

The message was clear. Georgiana did not want to see him.

The Duchess forced a smile, but her eyes were scowling. It did not bode well for Georgiana, but he could think of no way to save her from her grandmother's wrath.

Georgiana was angry with him. It had been a risk telling her father that he had found her near the Magdalen, but he could not regret his decision. He needed to keep her safe.

Maybe it was in his best interests not to talk to her today. It was not a favourable time to propose if she was annoyed with him. He rose from his seat, intending to leave, but the Duchess was quick to recover from the setback.

"Georgiana is devoted to her sister," she said, the gleam back in her eyes. "So kind-hearted that she would forego the pleasure of your company for her sake, but we cannot allow that, can we? Come, let us go and find her."

Castleford froze where he stood. The last thing he wanted to do was to force his presence on Georgiana when she so clearly did not want to see him. He supposed he should appreciate having an ally in the Duchess, but her tactics were too direct for him and not likely to endear him to Georgiana.

"Pray excuse me. I have no wish to intrude," he said, but the Duchess brushed his reservations away.

"Nonsense. We can't have Georgiana losing her bloom, staying inside all day, can we?"

As others had done before him, he felt swept along by the Duchess. There seemed no way to refuse without being rude. A grim expression on his face, he followed her down the corridor to the Blue Room. The Duchess opened the door and glided inside. He had no option but to follow.

"I am not coming, Char…" Georgiana began.

"Tut, tut, Georgiana. As you will observe it is not your sister, but Castleford. As you could not come and see your visitor, I have brought your visitor to see you."

One look at Georgiana made him feel more hopeful than he had felt all morning. The colour had drained from her face, but her eyes were full of sympathy. She did not blame him for intruding upon her but pitied him for being caught up in her grandmother's scheming.

"I do not think you have met my second granddaughter, Elizabeth, who most unfortunately sprained her ankle the day after being presented to Her Majesty," the Duchess said with a satisfied smile. "Elizabeth, Lord Castleford."

He bowed his head. "It is a pleasure to meet you at last, Miss Elizabeth. Your sister told me you were the victim of the accident I had witnessed on the Serpentine. Please accept my commiserations for your present discomfort."

Before Eliza could make a suitable reply, the door opened and Hetta burst into the room. Paying no attention to her grandmother's frowns, she walked straight up to him.

"I thought I had missed you," she said, her big green eyes looking up into his face, "and I so particularly wanted to see you."

He smiled down at his young friend, grateful for the diversion. "What is it to be this time, Miss Hetta? Let me guess – an exhibition of waxworks or maybe a never-to-be-repeated performance at Mr Astley's theatre?"

Hetta was momentarily distracted. "I would like to visit Astley's before I go home, but that wasn't what I was going to ask you. My brother William says I am so clumsy that I shall never be able to drive my own carriage and so I was hoping you might teach me, my lord, so I can prove him wrong."

"I am flattered by the confidence you have in me," he said, "but, much as I admire your ambition, I think it is beyond my humble abilities to train you to drive in the short time left before you leave London."

Hetta looked crestfallen. "I quite understand," she said, though she looked at him as if he had betrayed her. "You believe I would damage your horses with my efforts. I suppose Will is right."

A grin stole onto his face. It was hard not to laugh. Really, she was as bad as her grandmother at getting her own way. He did not have the heart to disappoint her. Seeing a chance to please his young friend and secure him a means of escape, he grabbed it with both hands.

"I may not be able to teach you to drive, Miss Hetta, but if you will do me the honour of accompanying me to the park, I'll let you take the reins for a time and endeavour to give you your first lesson."

The Duchess pursed her lips, annoyed at the turn of events, but a moment later, her face was once more wreathed in smiles as she encouraged Hetta to change for her outing and thanked him for his kindness.

"It is rare to find a gentleman who will dedicate his time to pleasing a schoolroom miss when there is no obligation from family ties," she said. "Now if you had been an uncle or a brother, by blood or by marriage, Henrietta would have some claim on you, but as it is, I can only thank you for your kindness."

He could see Georgiana squirming at her grandmother's words, but he was not the least embarrassed by the pointed remarks. It was, after all, what he wanted.

"The pleasure is all mine."

He paused and gave Georgiana a speaking look. "I hope that Miss Hetta will always be to me the little sister I never had."

She held his gaze, neither smiling nor frowning, her eyes bright and serious. There could be no doubt that she understood what he was saying. He had made his intentions clear. Georgiana knew he was going to ask her to marry him.

* * *

Lord Castleford wondered whether he was out of his mind. He had set out that morning intending to propose to Georgiana and ended up driving around the park with her twelve-year-old sister. A wry smile crossed his lips as he thought of the picture he was presenting to the fashionable world. More than one of his acquaintances had greeted him with barely concealed surprise.

Hetta chattered away while he taught her how to hold her reins and tell the horses where she wanted them to go. She proved to be an adept pupil, listening carefully to what he told her and following his instructions to the letter. He was relieved to discover that he need not fear for his horses. Hetta had good, light hands and was soon driving the phaeton around the park with little help from himself. If they met another vehicle, he was poised, ready to intervene, but so far it had not been necessary.

He did not, however, risk taking his eyes off the path ahead. It was therefore something of a surprise when he heard himself being hailed by a familiar voice – the voice of his brother, Anthony. With a sigh, he took the reins from his young pupil and drew the carriage to a halt.

"Fallen on hard times, Cas, that you must need teach infants to drive?" Anthony Warren teased, drawing his curricle alongside.

"I am not an infant," Hetta said with a scowl. "Sir," she added reluctantly after a pause. "Or are you a 'my lord' too?"

"Just 'sir'," Anthony said, grinning at the bold response. "Are you my brother's latest flirt then?"

Her scowl vanished and she grinned back. "Of course not, sir. I'm only twelve." She paused for a moment to think. "I'm not precisely sure what a 'flirt' is, but I don't believe Lord Castleford has any."

"How perceptive of you, Miss…?" Anthony looked enquiringly at his brother.

"Miss Hetta, may I present my younger brother, Mr Warren? Anthony – my friend, Miss Henrietta Merry, one of the Duchess of Wessex's granddaughters."

Anthony's eyes danced with merriment. "She's a little young for you, don't you think? Or are you planning a long engagement?"

Castleford ignored him.

"He doesn't want to marry *me*," Hetta said, as if stating the obvious.

"Then someone else," Anthony said. "Now this is getting interesting."

"It has been remarkably quiet around here of late," Castleford said, pointedly turning the subject. "Have you been out of town?"

"Did you miss me? How touching. I got on the wrong side of Maddison and you know what he is like. It seemed like a good idea to make myself scarce until he had cooled off. Dashed hard to stop him calling me out. It probably had something to do with…"

Castleford feared that his brother might be about to utter words unfit for Hetta's ears and gave him a speaking look, nodding his head toward their young companion, urging him to mind his tongue.

"...his coat," Anthony said, as if that was what he had intended to say all along. "It was a revolting puce colour, but he took exception to being told so. I decided to take a breather and visit Mother."

Castleford's face softened. "How is she?"

"In more pain than she lets on, but always happy to see me, which is more than I can say of you. You don't seem pleased to see me at all."

"Perhaps it has something to do with your knack of disrupting the peace."

"Perhaps it has."

"I think it is time to return home, Miss Hetta," Castleford said. "Your grandmother will want to be assured that you have not over-turned my phaeton."

"Not yet," Hetta pleaded. "You see what a fast learner I am. You said you couldn't teach me before I went home but I am already an excellent driver, even though this is my first lesson. Besides, my grand-mother won't be worrying about me. I doubt whether she has given me a single thought since I walked out the door. She has little time for schoolroom misses. Too young to be married."

Anthony's nose twitched, his eyes dancing in appreciation at Hetta's frankness. "If my brother has finished his lesson for today, perhaps you would care for a turn around the park in my curricle, Miss Hetta."

"I think not, Anthony," Castleford replied. "I fear the temptation to drive your curricle would be too much for my young friend and I would like to return her to her mother in one piece."

Handing the reins to Hetta, he encouraged her to chivvy the horses into action.

"Adieu, Miss Hetta," Anthony said as he watched her drive away, making no effort to conceal his amusement.

Castleford sighed. He supposed it was inevitable that driving Hetta around the park would provoke comment amongst his contem-poraries, his brother being no exception. As the Duchess had pointed out, it gave all the appearance of a family connection. No doubt, they would be betting in the clubs how soon it would be before his engage-ment to Georgiana was announced. Not long, he hoped. He would hate to disappoint them.

CHAPTER 18

Lord Castleford wasted no time before making his third attempt to present his addresses to Georgiana. When he called the following day, he was relieved when the butler informed him that the Duchess was out, but the other ladies of the house were above stairs. As the footman took his hat and cane, Mr Merry stepped into the hall and invited him into the library. With an inner sigh, he resigned himself to delaying his mission yet again.

"I understand my daughter is enamoured with you," Mr Merry said, pouring him a glass of sherry.

Castleford's heart stood still. Was he suggesting that Georgiana returned his feelings?

"You must not let her bully you though, Castleford. She's able to wind you around her little finger and make you feel the worst wretch alive if you don't give her what she wants." He paused and his mouth twitched. "I think she inherited the ability from her mother. She has done nothing but talk about how she is learning to drive a carriage since you took her out yesterday morning."

Castleford realised his mistake at once. Mr Merry was talking of Hetta, not Georgiana. Much as he liked his young friend, he was aware of a pang of disappointment that it was she and not her sister that Mr Merry believed was smitten with him.

"I assume she has persuaded you to give her a second lesson."

Castleford looked Mr Merry in the eyes. "In truth, it was her eldest sister I was hoping to take for a drive today."

The older man met his gaze, regarding him with sudden understanding. "I see."

Castleford felt sure that he did.

"I have just finished reading this," Mr Merry said, pointing to the volumes on the table beside him.

Castleford studied the title. "*Coelebs in Search of a Wife*," he read out. "A novel?"

"Yes, but of the best kind. It is full of moral advice, cleverly disguised in short stories. My old friend Mrs More sent it to me and though she hasn't admitted it, I rather suspect she wrote it. *Coelebs* is the story of a gentleman looking for a wife. He meets many unsuitable brides before discovering the woman of his dreams. The heroine's father wants his daughter to marry an honourable man and knows the hero would make her a decent husband, but he desires something more for her."

He paused and fixed Castleford with a penetrating look. "As do I. He urges the hero to ensure he has won the heroine's heart before seeking his blessing to the marriage."

Silence hung between them as he digested Mr Merry's words. He had his blessing if, and only if, he could win Georgiana's heart.

Mr Merry ushered him out of the library and up the stairs into the Blue Room where Georgiana sat talking to Eliza. Georgiana's countenance went red with embarrassment as her father bid her run off and change, as Castleford wished to take her for a drive today, not Hetta.

With a long glance at Eliza, who lay reclining on the sofa, Georgiana withdrew to put on a carriage dress. Castleford saw the tell-tale blush and the look that passed between the sisters and concluded that Georgiana knew what he wanted to ask her.

However, once seated in his carriage, she seemed determined to act as if they were just going for a drive. To pretend that she was not aware that he was about to propose.

"How pleasant to be outside in such beautiful weather, Lord Castleford. I had expected to sit with Eliza all day, as she goes home soon, and I want to spend as much time with her as possible while I can."

"Forgive me for depriving you of your sister's company. We could have postponed our outing."

"You need not apologise," she said. "I am sure my father had his own reasons for wanting me to come out with you. Perhaps he thinks I look pale, having spent so many hours inside. No doubt a drive in the fresh air will bring the colour back to my cheeks."

Whether through nervousness or a reluctance to hear what he had to say, she chattered on, barely stopping for breath. He realised that he was going to have to make an opportunity if he wanted the chance to speak. He pulled up his horses, and the phaeton came to a halt.

"Eliza is looking forward to returning to Hampshire. She is eager to see her horse again, though I don't know how long it will be before she can ride and…"

Georgiana stopped mid-sentence as he climbed down from the phaeton. He handed the reins to his groom and turned to assist her to alight. "Let us walk a little way," he said.

"Oh, but I am not sure that we should. I mean…"

"We will not go out of sight of my groom, Miss Merry, but there are some things that a man wants to say in private."

Georgiana said nothing. She allowed him to help her climb down from the phaeton with obvious reluctance and they walked on in silence until they were out of earshot of the groom.

"Miss Merry - Georgiana," he began. "I am aware that we have not known each other long, but it is many weeks since I have valued our friendship above all others."

Georgiana sighed, but whether from pleasure or something less pleasant, he could not tell.

"Will you…"

"I still haven't seen the Persian ambassador," Georgiana interrupted.

Castleford was becoming frustrated. He had never proposed marriage before, and he had not realised it would be this hard just getting her to listen to him. She seemed determined to put him off. Was she trying to protect his feelings because she had decided to reject him, or did she not know her own heart? He could not believe that she would be so cruel if she were going to accept him.

"I do hope he will be at the Opera House tonight when the great Madame Catalani is singing. Augusta told me she is paid such an exorbitant sum of money for a single performance that she only needs to perform a few times a year. I suppose she has an excellent voice, but I have not heard her yet, and so I can only imagine."

Having got this far, Castleford was determined to finish. The uncertainty was agonising. "Miss Merry, please let me continue. You must know I have the highest regard for you, and I would be honoured if…"

"Don't."

He stopped still. Georgiana walked on a few paces and then turned toward him, but she refused to meet his gaze.

"Please do not say anything more," she said.

"But Georgiana…"

His words hung in the air. The earnestness in his voice finally forced her to look up. He had no notion of how long she stood there, looking up into his eyes. She must have seen the love he felt for her, reflected there, but he saw no answering gleam.

Castleford felt as though all the air had been knocked out of him. Georgiana did not love him. She was going to refuse him. But he had to know for sure.

"Georgiana…" he said tenderly, but she turned away before he could continue.

"No! Please do not say it. Do not ruin our friendship. If you ask, I will have to answer, and I cannot give you the reply you want."

The colour drained from his face and with it, all the emotion from his body. All his hopes and dreams were shattered in that one moment. He was a broken man.

He stood in silence, looking down at her bowed head, losing all sense of time. She would not look at him, as if she could not bear the sight of the love reflected in his face.

When at last she lifted her eyes to his again, he could see they were bright with unshed tears. "Give me time, Lord Castleford," she whispered, as if trying to soothe the open wound she had created.

Her words did not ease the pain. He did not want her sympathy; he wanted her love. A flash of frustration coursed through his body, ousting the despair and making his eyes blaze with fire.

"Very well, Miss Merry," he said in a perfectly controlled voice. "I do not want an unwilling wife." The harshness of his tone made Georgiana wince. She sniffed hard as a tear trickled down her cheek.

He was immediately contrite, and the anger went as quickly as it had come. His love for her was unchanged and he did not wish to make her cry.

"I will say no more as the subject distresses you," he said gently, his eyes full of compassion.

As they walked back to the carriage in silence, he struggled to master his emotions. He must forget his own pain and try to ease hers.

With a great effort of will, he acted as though nothing had happened. On the journey home, he gave her a detailed account of the children's ball, including a vivid description of the expression on Hetta's face when she first saw the Persian ambassador, Mirza Abdul Hassan, with his bushy black beard. He maintained the one-sided conversation all the way back to Wessex House, preventing her from the need to speak again.

* * *

When Georgiana arrived home, she could not even face Eliza. Hurrying up to her room without a word to anyone, she threw herself down onto her bed and cried as if it were her heart that was breaking, not Lord Castleford's.

What she had seen in the depths of his eyes pierced her soul. She had been so sure that he felt nothing more for her than friendship, but she had been wrong. For a few brief moments, he had revealed his heart, and she had broken it into pieces.

It grieved her to hurt Lord Castleford. She respected him, trusted him and loved him as a friend, but that was not enough for marriage. Not for her.

She wanted the same enduring love that her parents had for each other. Their love went beyond friendship. It was more than a meeting of minds. More than sharing the same faith and interests. It was a mutual desire for each other above all others that they could not hide.

You could see it in the warmth of her mother's expression as her eyes rested on her father's face. In the spontaneous kisses that her father showered on her mother, regardless of who was watching. They were like two halves of a whole. A joining of hearts and souls.

She wanted to love like that. To feel that warmth in her own heart and from the man she loved. A man who would shower her with kisses, who wanted to hold her close, who showed his love in more than words.

Perhaps she had set her expectations too high, but she could not settle for anything less. To marry without that kind of love would not be fair to either of them. She could see how intensely Lord Castleford loved her, but she did not feel the same.

What had possessed her to ask for time? She had encouraged him to think that she might change her mind, but she failed to see how that could happen. If she were going to fall in love with him, would she not have done so by now? Time would not alter anything.

It would have been so much simpler if she could have loved him. She prayed for a change of heart, but whether hers or his she did not know.

*   *   *

It was fortunate that Georgiana was engaged to hear Madame Catalani that evening or she may have been tempted to claim she had a headache and stay at home to dwell on how miserable she felt. But she could not withdraw from this engagement without causing a great deal of comment as she had been talking about her desire to see the famous opera singer for weeks.

Lord Helston had invited her and, of course, Lady Augusta, to join his party to the Opera House. Georgiana discovered that Lord Castleford had sent his apologies. She could not be sorry as she was not ready to meet him again yet.

Beau had somehow managed to secure himself an invitation, and attached himself to her, but she could not work out why he had bothered, as he made no effort to hide the fact that he would rather be elsewhere.

"I don't know how you can listen to that infernal noise and call it entertainment," Beau complained in an undertone. "It's not as if you can even understand what she's singing, because she screeches on and on in some foreign language."

"It's Italian, Beau," Georgiana whispered back. "If you hate it, why did you come?"

It only needed one word for him to explain. "Mother."

Georgiana sighed and let her gaze drift around the auditorium as she listened to the great Catalani sing. A box on the opposite side of the theatre arrested her interest. Sir James was here. She had not seen him for over a week, but he was here tonight. He was looking in her direction and nodded his head toward her, acknowledging her attention. She wondered whether he would speak to her and if he did, what he would say. His presence was just what she needed to divert her from her current state of wretchedness.

When she withdrew her gaze from Sir James's box, she was put out to find Beau staring at her, frowning.

for them. That can be tiring. Others desire kisses and – you know. They are the ones I like best."

Castleford digested this slowly.

"What is your lady like?" Anthony asked.

"Georgiana is small in stature but big in heart. She enjoys reading novels and going to the play, but I think more than anything she loves romance. She is compassionate and trusting and endearingly impulsive and doesn't always think of the consequences before she acts."

"A romantically minded girl who is likely to need rescuing. The ideal setup!"

Castleford thought of how he had rescued Georgiana outside the Magdalen. He recalled the thrill of having her in his arms and how much he had wanted to kiss her. He had been so concerned with preserving her reputation that he had probably seemed cold and distant. The intensity of his feelings must have come as a shock to her. No wonder she had hesitated to hear his proposals.

"Is she worth fighting for?" Anthony asked.

"Yes."

"Then appeal to her romantic nature before some polished rake takes advantage of her innocence and steals her away from under your nose." Anthony could see that his brother was struggling with what he was saying.

"I'm trying, Ant, but it's not easy for me. You're naturally romantic. I'm not."

He told his brother about Georgiana's reaction to his words in the Whispering Gallery. "It was so clumsy and out of character that she misunderstood and imagined I was laughing at her love of romance instead of trying to appeal to it," he said with a grimace.

"Too direct," Anthony said. "It is hardly surprising she supposed you were teasing her if you've not been in the habit of reciting poetry to her face. You should go for a more subtle approach."

"That's what I thought. More like the anonymous Valentine she received that seemed to make such an impact on her."

"Exactly. Everyone can be romantic if they put their mind to it. Try harder. If you love her, become what she needs you to be. Be a little more mysterious. Don't hang on her every word. Show her what it feels like not to have you around. Let her learn to miss you, whilst all the while communicating that you are holding back at her request, and that you are always there for her."

Castleford listened to his brother's counsel. Perhaps it was madness to take advice from a man who had never courted a woman, but Anthony's reputation for charm was unrivalled. He would try to be what she needed and prayed fervently that Georgiana would change her mind and fall in love with him.

CHAPTER 19

By the time Sunday came, Georgiana thought she would be able to face Lord Castleford again. Even if she had not felt ready, it was unlikely she could avoid him. Her family were attending worship at the Magdalen Chapel, and Lord Castleford was expected to be there in his role as one of the governors.

He *was* there. After the service, she saw him moving toward her and braced herself for the awkward conversation that she felt sure would follow. But she need not have worried. There was no awkwardness on his part as he greeted her family with obvious pleasure but did not single her out. He was open and friendly, not showing by anything he said or did that he thought the less of her, but on this occasion, he did not hover by her side as he had often done before.

Instead, he started talking to her father about the poor. He asked Mr Merry's opinion on the best ways to help the needy on his estates without encouraging laziness. Her father entered the conversation enthusiastically, and it was with obvious reluctance that he abandoned the subject when her mother gave him a speaking look, indicating that it was time to leave.

It was hard to put what she felt into words. Georgiana was aware of a sense of loss, but she could not quite place her finger on what was missing. Perhaps it was the lack of warmth that she was used to experiencing in his presence. He was there, but not there, as if she had made him unattainable. She tried to brush it off. If there was a loss of connection, she had only herself to blame.

Once the awkwardness of their first meeting was over, Georgiana looked forward to seeing Lord Castleford again. She wanted to show him she still held him in esteem and valued his friendship.

When he called the next day, she was ready to talk with him and gave him a welcoming smile. But when he came to her side, he did not sit down. It soon transpired that he had not come to see her at all; he was taking Hetta out for a driving lesson. Though he asked after her health and how Eliza was progressing, there was no time for further conversation and in a few minutes, he was gone.

The smile slipped from her lips as she watched him leave. By forestalling his proposal, she had expected they could carry on as they had done before, but such hopes now seemed naïve and foolish. He was too much a gentleman to press his suit against her wishes, and it was not fair to expect him to devote himself to her when she had all but rejected him.

Georgiana soon made her escape from the drawing room to spend the rest of the morning with Eliza. A footman reached the top of the stairs just as she was passing, and he offered her a salver bearing a letter. One glance told her who it was from, and her spirits feeling suddenly lighter, she hurried to share the contents with her sister.

"Let's see what advice the Sylph has to give me," she said to Eliza.

> *"My dearest G,*
>
> *I am honoured that you ask my advice in a matter of the heart and believe that I can do no better than recommend the words of another. As you are so fond of novels, may I suggest that you obtain a copy of 'Coelebs in Search of a Wife'? The author believes that good character is essential for happiness in marriage, but that something more is required as well. So do I.*
>
> *Beware of allowing your heart to rule your head without considering the character of the object of your affections. But likewise, your head should not ignore what your heart is saying. I have found that true love is the realisation that if that person went out of your life, the sun would never shine so brightly again. For some, that awareness comes like a bolt of lightning. For others, it grows slowly over time. Do not be in a hurry to commit yourself before you truly know your heart.*
>
> *Ever your devoted Sylph."*

"I'll see if there is a copy of the novel in Grandmama's collection, otherwise I will have to pay a visit to Hookham's Library tomorrow."

Georgiana was not surprised to find her father in the library. He was so engrossed in the book he was reading that he did not even look up when she entered. She noticed two volumes bound in red leather lying on the table next to him and grinned.

"Are these yours, Father, or does *Coelebs in Search of a Wife* belong to my grandmother?"

Mr Merry looked up. "Mine," he confessed. "Did you want to read it? I've just finished the second book, so you may borrow the complete novel if you like. You might even enjoy it. Please remember to bring both volumes home with you as they were a present from my old friend Mrs More, and I don't wish to part with them."

"I've already had *Coelebs* recommended to me," Georgiana said, taking the two volumes in her hands. She waited for some response from her father, but he had buried his head in his book again and acted as if he had not heard her. How wise, she thought. It would spoil the secret of the Sylph letters if he admitted writing them.

* * *

It was not easy to follow his brother's advice. Lord Castleford found stepping away from Georgiana as hard as he had expected. He had all but ignored her at the Magdalen Chapel and refused to be drawn into conversation when he had called to take Hetta for a driving lesson, although her eyes had invited him to do so.

Lady Harting's ball would prove an even bigger challenge. They would be together, in the same house, for the whole evening. He was aware of her presence as soon as she entered the room, but remembering his instructions, he did not gravitate to her side. It cost him a few pangs of envy to see Beau take his place beside her, but having observed them for some time, a small smile crept onto his lips and his jealousy subsided. It was clear they had an understanding, but unless he was mistaken, from the occasional look he caught between them, it was not of a romantic nature.

With a great effort of will, he kept his distance from her for half the evening, though he was fully aware of every one of her partners. When she talked, she seemed as animated as usual, but her eyes clouded over when she thought no one was looking, as if she were carrying dark thoughts within.

Could she be thinking of him? He tried to squash the hope that bubbled up inside him. He was being ridiculous. She had told him to his face she did not love him. It was more likely she was sad that her family would be going home soon. No doubt she would miss them – particularly Eliza.

At last, he allowed himself to go to her side and invite her to dance. If they did not dance, it would cause remark. He was sure she would accept, if only for the sake of appearances. It would do neither of them any good if people gossiped.

"I was beginning to think you were avoiding me," Georgiana said in a light-hearted tone that was at odds with her tentative smile. "I didn't even realise you were here until I saw you dancing with Lady Frances."

His eyes glowed, reflecting the warmth that stirred in his heart at the thought she had missed him. "It is always a pleasure to see you."

Her smile brightened, but she looked at him for only a moment before turning away, her cheeks burning. The slightest show of affection appeared to embarrass her. What had not been said hung over them, changing nothing and yet changing everything.

He needed to demonstrate he was still her friend. That she could still trust him. Putting all other considerations aside, he started talking to her in the way he had so often done before. "I hope you enjoyed your visit to the Opera House?"

It was a straightforward question, and he expected a straightforward answer. Yet Georgiana hesitated, a flurry of emotions flitting over her face. Had the evening not been as enjoyable as she had envisaged? Dare he hope that she had missed him?

Sensing her confusion, he continued. "Didn't Madame Catalani live up to your expectations?"

The worried frown disappeared as she launched into her reply. "No. I did not find her voice in any way remarkable. Whilst there is no doubt she can sing, I am not persuaded that she is superior to half a dozen other opera singers whom I am sure get paid far less for their efforts."

"There are hundreds who would disagree with you, Miss Merry."

"Do you?"

"No," he said with a satisfied smile, pleased that she still cared for his views. "Madame Catalani sings well, but it is her patrons who have brought her into celebrity. She is in fashion and therefore she commands what price she chooses."

"And if she goes out of fashion?"

"Then she will no longer be in demand and won't be able to charge such high fees for her services. I hope she is putting money aside for that day or she may dwindle into poverty like so many performers who once graced the stage."

"What a sombre thought.".

"To join your other sombre thoughts."

Georgiana's eyes darted to his face. "My other sombre thoughts?"

"Forgive me. I assumed that you would be feeling melancholy at your family's imminent departure. You will miss your sister Elizabeth particularly, I think."

"Yes, I will miss her dearly."

At the end of their dances, he returned her to her mother with no sign of the reluctance that he felt. They had started to re-establish their friendship, but it was still on shaky ground. He wanted to stay and talk with her, but Anthony had told him not to hover around her, so instead, he walked away. He hoped that his brother knew best.

CHAPTER 20

"Send my love to Lord Castleford," Hetta called, leaning out the window as the travelling coach pulled away at last.

Georgiana stood on the steps of Wessex House and watched until the carriage disappeared round the corner. She felt a lump rising in her throat and stifled a sob, feeling suddenly bereft.

Hetta's words reminded her that she had pushed away Lord Castleford, and now Eliza had gone. The Sylph letters would probably stop too as her father was no longer in London.

Her one consolation was that tonight, she would finally get to meet the Persian ambassador who was holding a reception. Even the Duke was leaving the comfort of his fireside to honour Mirzal Abul Hassan with his presence.

They arrived at the ambassador's residence in Mansfield Street shortly after nine o'clock. The street was crowded with such a huge number of carriages that Georgiana expected a crush inside.

She was right. The house was crammed with hundreds of fashionable people, all curious to meet the ambassador.

They were shown into the principal drawing room for the ceremonies of introduction, where the Persian ambassador awaited his guests with his interpreter by his side. The room had been richly furnished to form a fitting background with an abundance of scarlet-coloured Ottoman cushions decorated with gold lace.

He bowed very low to Georgiana and told her, through his translator, that she was very, very beautiful. She blushed rosily and tried not to stare at his beard, which was as big and bushy as she had heard.

The Duchess guided her husband into the card room and settled him in a comfortable seat with one of his cronies for company. She then shepherded Augusta, Denmead and Georgiana into the ballroom, though their progress was slow as acquaintances hailed her continually.

Across the room, Georgiana could see Lord Castleford and she gave him a welcoming smile that drew him to her side.

"I trust all went well with your family's departure this morning. Nothing forgotten, I hope."

"Just the opposite," she said, her eyes alight with laughter. "Mother noticed that Hetta had a book from Hookham's Library on her lap and the carriage had to stop almost as soon as it had started so she could run back to give it to me. By the way, Hetta sends her love."

Lord Castleford paused before he answered, as if reminding her it was not her sister's love that he sought. "I am honoured," he said, and went to move away.

Georgiana was disappointed that he was so ready to desert her and tried to engage him in further conversation.

"I'm so glad I've finally met the Persian ambassador. I was beginning to think I was the only person in the whole of London who still hadn't caught a glimpse of him."

He turned back in some surprise. "He was at the Opera House when Madam Catalani was singing. Didn't you see him? I was sure you were staring that way during the interval."

"How do you know in which direction I was looking? I thought you weren't there. You gave your apologies to Lord Helston."

"I assumed that under the circumstances it might be more comfortable for you if I made other arrangements."

Georgiana did not know what to say. Even in his disappointment, his concern had been for her. He had not wanted to impose his presence on her and yet he had been there and now he had inadvertently revealed that he had been watching her.

She had not given a single thought to the Persian ambassador that evening. It had not been the ambassador but Sir James she had been staring at. The recollection sent the colour rushing to her cheeks. She hoped that Lord Castleford had not observed anything unladylike in her behaviour.

He saw her embarrassment and his eyes grew tender. "Forgive me, Miss Merry. How thoughtless of me. My unguarded words have unsettled you."

Before she could think of a suitable response to keep him at her side, he excused himself and moved away as quickly as he could.

The Duchess appeared beside her just as Lord Castleford was leaving and tried to cajole him into staying, but he was intractable and would not yield to her persuasions. Her expression grew grim as she gazed after his retreating form, and then turned to face her granddaughter. She glared at Georgiana accusingly, as if asking what she had done to chase her admirer away.

Georgiana was not surprised that her grandmother was annoyed. Perhaps the Duchess thought Lord Castleford had cried off from making a declaration. It was no more than the truth, but it was her fault, not his.

With a look of determination, the Duchess scoured the crowd of other guests. Georgiana wondered with a sinking heart whether she was seeking some other poor gentleman to pounce on.

After a few moments, her grandmother's face lit up and she started across the room, ordering her to follow.

Georgiana knew better than to argue and obediently trailed behind her to where a dark and decidedly attractive gentleman was flirting with his companion. Knowing her grandmother, she dismissed the lady as unimportant and wondered who the gentleman was.

She did not have to wait long to find out.

Without ceremony, the Duchess broke in on their conversation. "Warren, my dear. How wonderful to see you. I did not know you were in town. We have seen such a lot of your brother. Indeed, he has become quite a part of our family. But he did not divulge that you were back in London."

Georgiana looked at the gentleman in a fresh light as his companion bid a hasty retreat, blowing him a saucy kiss as she went. So, this was Anthony Warren, Lord Castleford's rakish brother whom Augusta found more entertaining than the earl.

She stood a little behind her grandmother who seemed in no hurry to make the introduction, enabling her to watch and listen without drawing any attention to herself.

Anthony gave the Duchess a dazzling smile. He took her hand and raised it to his mouth, planting a kiss on each of her gloved fingers before allowing her to retrieve it.

"If I did not know that my brother never flirted with married women, then I would have no doubt in assuming that it was you that drew him to Wessex House so often."

The Duchess pursed her lips in amusement and rapped his knuckles with her fan. "You know your brother does not *flirt* with anyone."

"I, on the other hand, flirt with *all* the ladies."

"Are you not eager to meet the real reason your brother has been haunting my house?"

Georgiana blushed at the directness of her grandmother's words.

"I have already met her," Anthony said.

"You have?"

"Yes, I was introduced to his fair charmer when she was out for a drive with my brother. I invited her to take a turn round the park with me, but Castleford declined on her behalf."

Georgiana's mouth curved into a smile. Anthony must have encountered Hetta when Lord Castleford was teaching her to drive. She was grateful to him for turning her grandmother's embarrassing words into a joke.

"Possessive," her grandmother said.

"Protective, more like. I was driving my curricle and though Castleford knows I won't overturn it, he seemed to doubt whether I could withstand his companion's entreaties to take the reins. I gather that the lady is relentless."

Georgiana found it hard not to laugh at the incredulous look on her grandmother's face.

"He was afraid that my granddaughter would want to take the reins? He must have been roasting you."

"But I was assured by the lady herself that she was an excellent driver, though it was only her first lesson, because she was a quick learner," he said, his eyes sparkling with mischief.

The Duchess gave a reluctant smile. "You are not talking about Miss Georgiana Merry, are you?"

"You mean there is more than one Miss Merry?" he said, feigning a look of surprise.

"I suppose you met my youngest granddaughter, Henrietta, when your brother was so kind as to give her a few driving lessons."

"And now his fair charmer has departed, and my brother is distraught. You must have observed how out of spirits he is this evening?"

"I cannot say that I had noticed, but if he is out of spirits, perhaps my *other* granddaughter might console him for the loss of his sweetheart."

Her grandmother drew her forward at last. "Georgiana, Lord Castleford's brother, Anthony Warren."

Anthony raised her hand to his lips and kissed her glove. "I am delighted to make your acquaintance, Miss Merry. I have heard so much about you."

While Georgiana was still wondering just what Anthony had heard about her, Beau came up to them and slapped his friend on the back.

"Ant, I had no notion you were in town. Fancy a trip to Tattersall's? Templecombe gave me a tip about a hunter that might suit me…"

The Duchess cleared her throat loudly and Beau stopped mid-sentence, looking abashed.

"Beaumont, perhaps you could accompany me to find a glass of lemonade – or possibly something a little stronger," she said. It was not a question.

Georgiana smiled up at Anthony as her grandmother moved away with Beau. She was surprised she had not guessed who he was, as the likeness to Lord Castleford was pronounced when he grinned, which he frequently did. She thought Lord Castleford the taller of the two, but of a slighter build, and fair where his brother was dark.

Anthony had a physique that proclaimed the Corinthian, and like Beau, he was probably addicted to sport. But whereas Beau wore his clothes with a careless elegance, Anthony's dress suggested that he was inclined to dandyism. His neckcloth was tied in an intricate design, and his jacket was perfectly moulded to his broad shoulders.

"Your grandmother is a remarkable woman," he said, his eyes twinkling with amusement. "I can see she has put you out of countenance, but there is no need. My brother has talked of you. She told me naught that I did not already know."

"Oh." Georgiana could think of nothing else to say.

"And perhaps I know more than the Duchess," he whispered, suddenly serious, "as I know how things stand between the two of you."

Georgiana gulped hard as the ready colour flooded her cheeks. Even as she did so, his mood shifted again, and his eyes were once more alight with laughter.

He was a charming companion and soon put her at her ease, talking about her family and her home and how she liked London.

"Have you seen the sights, or have you been too busy with the demands of the season to have time for that?"

"I have visited some of London's attractions with my sister Hetta, most kindly accompanied by your brother, as I'm sure you are aware."

"Ah yes. Miss Hetta. Indeed, he is sadly cast down by her departure. I am not certain what it is about children, but they have a way of breaking through his reserve more quickly than the rest of humanity."

"Hetta's last thought before she left was for your brother. She sent him her love."

"How old is she?"

"Twelve."

"Dear me, even supposing your parents would part with her at sixteen, four years is a long wait for Castleford."

Georgiana smiled despite herself. "Hetta has always seemed older than her years so I am sure she would not mind, but what of him? He is, what, twenty-five?" Not that his age mattered to Georgiana, but it would be interesting to know, though she could have looked it up in Debrett's peerage if she had thought about it.

"Not quite that old. He is only two years my senior and I am just turned twenty-two."

"Hmm. Twelve years. Not much greater than the age gap between my grandparents, and they are happy together."

"But that is a second marriage."

"True. I take it your brother has not been married before?"

"Absolutely not."

"Then perhaps it is unreasonable to expect him to wait."

"Perhaps it is," Anthony said, holding Georgiana's gaze with his own until she looked away.

"Make haste, make haste," the Duchess said, bustling up to them at that moment. "It is close on midnight and I am sure we are not the only guests going on to the Countess of Clonmell's ball. If we hurry, we will avoid the crush of carriages when people start to leave."

"Warren, do you come?" the Duchess asked.

"It would be my pleasure."

* * *

165

The Countess of Clonmell's ball was a dreadful squeeze. Lord Castleford was nowhere to be seen, but Georgiana did not lack for partners. Half a dozen of them vied with each other for the right to take her into the first dance, a right that, until recently, Lord Castleford had claimed without any effort. Others had given way to the quiet-mannered earl, as if in reverence to a higher being.

In his absence, Georgiana was besieged by all her admirers making a push for her hand. It was a delightful feeling to be so sought after, but not altogether comfortable.

Anthony stepped up into his brother's place and claimed Georgiana for the dance that was beginning and led her off to join the set. Once or twice, Georgiana's eyes scanned the room for a sign of Lord Castleford, but it appeared that he had not come. She ought to have been grateful that he was not pressing his suit on her, but perversely, his absence irked her. She could not help thinking he had given her up rather easily.

"You seem a little distracted, Miss Merry. Are you looking for someone?" Anthony asked.

Georgiana brought her attention back to her partner. "Forgive me. I was wool gathering. It is sad to think my sister Eliza won't be there in the morning, wanting to hear how I have fared tonight. They've all gone home, and I'll miss them. Are your parents in town? Oh no – of course not. I'm sorry. Your father died some years ago, did he not?"

"Not a day too soon."

Anthony's abrupt reply came as a shock. Georgiana could hear the bitterness in his voice.

"My father's death was no loss to his family, if, indeed, it was to anyone. His permanent absence is a blessing. But let us not dwell on such melancholy subjects. My mother is not in London. She is an invalid and lives comfortably in a house that my brother built for her in Twickenham, near to where the sculptor Mrs Damer resides at Strawberry Hill. It overlooks the river and is a comfortable distance from town, allowing us to visit her often."

Georgiana was relieved to hear the affection in Anthony's voice when he talked about his mother. She wondered how it would affect a boy, growing up with a father he did not respect – perhaps did not even love. Did it explain some of Lord Castleford's reserve, having to step into the shoes of such a man? She shuddered, unable to imagine what it would be like to live without her father's love.

Beau was standing close, waiting to claim Georgiana's hand when they finished dancing. He chided her for spending so much time with his friend.

"Don't lose your heart to Ant, Georgie," he warned. "He's a heartless beast and flirts outrageously with everyone, but it doesn't mean a thing."

Anthony glared at Beau and made a great show of relinquishing Georgiana. "Adieu, *ma cherie*," he said, kissing her hand.

"Do you have to flirt with Ant so much?" Beau whispered when the dance brought them together. "If you carry on like that, no one will believe you're in love with me."

"But I'm not," Georgiana said under her breath, "and I shall flirt with whoever I choose."

They lapsed into silence, each irritated by the other's behaviour.

As they danced, Georgiana thought she glimpsed a familiar face out of the corner of her eye. Every time she turned in that direction, she looked again.

This time, she was sure. It was Sir James. She thought of their last meeting and of the adoring words he had poured out on her and comforted herself that there was at least one gentleman who was still pursuing her in earnest.

The next time she glanced his way, Sir James caught her eye and bowed his head. Beau did not seem to have noticed and she hoped her rising colour would not give her away. She did not feel able to explain how she was on such a level of intimacy with Sir James when they had not been introduced.

When she turned again, Sir James had disappeared, and she experienced a twinge of disappointment. But she need not have worried. As the dance ended, she found that he had manoeuvred himself to be in their direct path.

"My dear Beau, what a vision of loveliness you have on your arm. Pray introduce me to your partner before I expire with curiosity."

Beau looked annoyed, and Georgiana realised that he was going to refuse Sir James's request. She glared at him and, perhaps fearing that she would make a scene, he relented.

"Miss Merry, may I present Sir James Maxwell?" he said, looking none too pleased at having the introduction forced from him.

Georgiana curtseyed, and Sir James took and kissed her hand, lingering over it just a little longer than he should have done.

Beau frowned. "Miss Merry, we should return to your grandmother. The Duchess will be looking for you."

Georgiana found Beau's sudden assumption of formality amusing, but she was in no hurry to leave.

"I am sure Her Grace can spare Miss Merry for one dance," Sir James said.

"Please, Beau," Georgiana urged. "You may recollect that I am indebted to Sir James for rescuing my reticule from the clutches of the thief at the theatre."

"Very well," Beau said. "Not that I could stop you," he muttered under his breath so that only she could hear. "You never would listen to anything I said."

Sir James took her hand but did not appear in any hurry to join the dance that was forming. "I can scarcely believe that I have finally been introduced to you," he said with a warmth that made her blush. "Since the day I first saw you, I have thought of you my every waking hour. Miss Merry, you are the most beautiful girl I have ever seen."

Georgiana blushed even more. "You must not tease me, sir. I am sure you have seen plenty of girls prettier than I."

"Don't you believe me? Upon my honour, though I have seen many pretty girls, none are as lovely as you. Lord Beaumont is not much of a protector. Such a rare flower as yourself needs to be guarded. He gave you up to me without a fight. If I were your protector, I would not give you up so easily."

"Perhaps it does not suit me to be protected so assiduously," Georgiana said, disturbed by the serious tone of Sir James's voice. "I am not some poor creature who desires to be wrapped up like china."

"No matter. I can't complain that Beau has fled the field, for I have you to myself at last."

Pausing for a moment, his eyes bored into her with an intensity that made her want to look away, but somehow, she could not.

"I must surely have heard, but tell me, you are not yet engaged?"

Georgiana raised her chin in the air and gave Sir James a challenging look. "What is it to you, sir, whether I am or not?" she said, dismayed to think her *not* being engaged was a subject for gossip.

"My life breath. Pray, put me out of my misery, for though I would gladly fight for you, it would hardly forward my courtship if I needed to flee the country for having killed my rival."

"There is no need for such extreme measures," she replied in some alarm. "I am not engaged."

"I am relieved to hear it, but don't you think it romantic to fight for one's true love?"

Georgiana thought for a moment. "It would be romantic if a knight slayed a dragon and rescued his princess, but not if the knight killed all the other knights merely because they loved the same lady. The princess should be able to choose who she wants to marry. But I do not understand how it is relevant. I am not your true love. You do not know me."

"To see you is to love you, Miss Merry."

Georgiana knew he was flattering her and did not believe half of what he was saying, but as his words were accompanied by such a charming smile, the effect was overwhelming.

"I only have eyes for you, Miss Merry. Remember that," he said as they finally joined the bottom of the dance.

Sir James continued to pay her extravagant compliments every time their steps brought them together. The look of sincerity in his eyes made it increasingly hard to believe that he was merely flirting with her.

At the end of the dance, he bowed and raised her hand to his lips again. This time, he showed no sign of relinquishing it. Heat flooded her cheeks, and she pulled her hand away, embarrassed that he had held it for so long.

"I see the strength of my feelings has taken you by surprise," Sir James said with a wistful sigh. "Let me return you to your protector."

However, rather than leading Georgiana to where the Duchess was standing, Sir James moved toward Beau who had just finished dancing with Augusta.

There was a flicker of alarm in Augusta's eyes on their approach, but it quickly passed. She drew Georgiana's arm inside her own and led her away to search for her mother without a word to Georgiana's partner.

"How did you come to be dancing with Sir James?" she asked. "I did not know you were acquainted."

"Beau introduced us, but we have met before. He is the gentleman who rescued my reticule the night it was stolen at the theatre."

A line appeared on Augusta's brow. "Is he?"

She stopped walking and laid a hand on Georgiana's arm. "Sir James is an entertaining companion, but I should warn you he is not very respectable."

If she were honest, Georgiana feared that Augusta might be right, but she resented her interference. "Is that so? Then how is it you that you are acquainted with him?"

"Well, if you must know, I met him at a card party at Lady Buckinghamshire's," she said, fiddling with one of the rosebuds decorating the front of her dress. "But I haven't seen him for an age as Helston does not like me playing for such high stakes, and I promised him I wouldn't go to her card parties again."

"But what of Sir James? Why should I give him up?"

Augusta wriggled uncomfortably. "Just stay away from him, Georgie. Mama would not approve."

Georgiana felt her temper rising. Of course, the Duchess would not like it. She wanted her to marry Lord Castleford. Why should she let her grandmother dictate her actions?

She glared at Augusta, her eyes blazing. "Then do not tell her."

CHAPTER 21

Georgiana left the ball feeling fiercely defensive of Sir James. She wrote and told Eliza how unreasonable Augusta had been, warning her away from him, but not giving her any reason apart from fear of the Duchess's disapproval.

A few days later, she received another missive from the Sylph. Her father must have sent the letter to someone to put in the two-penny post for him. It was clear he thought the letters were doing some good, as he had gone to such lengths to continue writing. She soon found an excuse to escape to her room to discover what he had written.

My dearest G,

I fear there are some who might force you to promise your hand before you are ready. Do not be in a hurry to engage your affections. Consider what will truly make you happy in marriage. Decide what is necessary and what may be sacrificed, bearing in mind your character, your tastes, your family, and your faith, as well as your feelings.

Do not honour another with your trust on a brief acquaintance. Trust must be earned. Take time to discover what manner of person you are dealing with. Listen to what others say of them. Look for openness and consistency.

Your devoted Sylph.

Georgiana read the letter and read it again. There was nothing in it that implied a knowledge of her encounter with Sir James at the Countess of Clonmell's ball, and yet it was surprisingly appropriate. It warned her to get to know someone before trusting them. She knew the advice was sound and resolved to put it into practice regarding Sir James.

Not that she had any opportunity of doing so. She expected to meet him at every social gathering she went to, but the only place she saw him was across the aisle during the church service at St George's Hanover Square. It pleased her to see him there, having never noticed him in church before, but she was disappointed that he only bowed his head to her in passing, making no attempt to come over and talk to her. It did not occur to her that Sir James's reticence was in any way connected with the figure of Lord Castleford, who hovered around her like a bodyguard until she had climbed into the safety of the Duchess's carriage.

Lord Castleford continued to stand up with her at balls but paid her no more court than any other of her admirers. Despite her initial fears after forestalling his proposal of marriage, he had sunk back into the role of trusted friend. They had returned to the easy-going relationship they had shared before, but they never touched on what had happened, or not happened, between them. His feelings were a closed book. Only by the occasional long look did he betray a hint that perhaps he felt more than he said, and even now, he wanted to marry her.

In contrast, Anthony was open in his admiration. Rumours began to circulate that Lord Castleford's rakish younger brother had finally decided to settle down and had cut him out, but Georgiana was not fooled. She took Anthony no more seriously than Beau. He flirted with her as much as Sir James had done, but she knew that he meant nothing by what he said.

She had thought Sir James's attentions were genuine. That he, at least, was in love with her and not afraid to show it. He had not, however, approached her for weeks, and she feared she had been mistaken.

She played with the letter in her hands. The long-awaited season seemed unlikely to live up to her expectations. The Sylph told her not to be in a hurry to engage her affections, but there was little danger of that. She had come to London ready to fall in love, but love was passing her by.

*　*　*

Fortunately, a distraction came at just the right moment to prevent Georgiana from wallowing in self-pity. The House of Commons found Sir Francis Burdett guilty of breach of privilege and it was said he would be sentenced to imprisonment in the Tower of London the next day. There were rumours that his supporters might resort to violence to ward off his arrest. Charlotte would have been in hysterics at the prospect of a riot, but Georgiana secretly thought the possibility was thrilling, from a distance at least.

Her mind was full of questions. Would Sir Francis Burdett submit to the authorities, or would they have to call in the troops to enforce his arrest? Would there be riots in his defence? She yearned for the opportunity to discuss the situation with Lord Castleford. He might know more than the newspapers, because of his position in the House of Lords.

There was a possibility she would see him at Mrs Hope's rout that evening, but she had been to enough of these crowded assemblies to realise that her chances were slim. There were always so many people it was hard to discover anyone you knew.

As they arrived in Duchess Street, Georgiana observed the crowd swarming over the palatial forecourt in front of the Hopes' house and thought with a sigh that this rout would be no different.

Once inside, she wondered whether she had misjudged the number of people arriving as there was plenty of room to move about. As she trailed around behind her grandmother, she soon realised that her first assessment had been correct. There appeared to be fewer guests inside than she had expected because the house was so vast.

But though vast, it was not empty. The rooms were lined with paintings and shelves displaying vases and other objects from Mr Hope's collections.

She stopped to admire a portrait of Mrs Hope which she thought was an excellent likeness, but when she turned back to her grandmother to say as much, she discovered she was alone.

In dismay, she looked all around, trying to spot the Duchess, but her lack of height was a serious disadvantage. She was surrounded by strangers.

It was astonishing to think that after spending three months in London, there were still so many people she did not know. In vain, her eyes searched for the Duchess or Lord Castleford or Beau or, indeed, any familiar face.

"Miss Merry," a voice whispered in her ear.

It was Sir James.

173

She greeted him warmly, relieved to have found somebody she knew. "How glad I am to see you, Sir James. I was beginning to think you must have left London."

"How could you think that? You are still here."

"But you have not called."

"You missed me."

"I wished to further our acquaintance and was disappointed not to have the opportunity to do so."

"We have a lifetime ahead of us to get to know each other," he said, taking possession of her arm and leading her to a corner of the room where heavy drapes partly shielded them from the other guests.

Georgiana thought briefly about the proprieties. Remembering the way Sir James had behaved at Lady Clonmell's ball with a mixture of nervousness and excitement, she felt a tad uneasy about the seclusion of the spot he had chosen. But she dismissed her qualms in a flash. Why was she so concerned? It was not as if they were in a separate room alone together. Besides, no one would be watching her.

She was wrong. One person was watching her intently.

* * *

"It's that man again," Lord Castleford muttered under his breath, catching sight of Georgiana going aside with Sir James. He had seen her as soon as she entered the room. His eyes were drawn to her presence like a flower turning toward the sun.

Anthony had been enthusing about the musical programme for Mr Salomon's Annual Concert the following week, but he stopped midsentence when he realised his brother was no longer paying attention.

He sighed. "You're watching her again, aren't you?" He did not wait for a reply. "It might surprise you to learn that it is quite acceptable for ladies to talk to gentlemen at routs."

"But it is not acceptable to go apart with one."

"No need to worry about Beau," Anthony replied. "There's nothing in it. He's about as eager to get married as I am."

"Beau? It's not Beau I'm worried about," he said, a grim expression on his face.

He nodded toward the corner of the room where Sir James's back was just visible, peeking out from behind the curtain.

"I've seen her with him before, in the park. I thought then that it was suspicious. Now I'm sure. What gentleman courts a lady away from her protectors? The Duchess is supposed to be looking after her. Where is she?"

Anthony glanced across to where Georgiana was talking to Sir James and frowned.

"Do you know him?" Castleford asked.

He nodded. "Enough to know not to trust him."

Castleford's eyes darkened. "A fortune hunter?"

"Most likely."

Castleford could feel the anger welling up inside him. He looked at his brother with a murderous glint in his eye. "Then I had better intervene."

"No. Allow me," Anthony said, laying a restraining hand on his brother's arm. "I shall be able to extricate her without spilling blood."

* * *

Having dismissed her reservations about going aside with Sir James, Georgiana revelled in the prospect of having someone to talk to.

"Do you think there will be trouble in the city?" she said, asking him the question that was uppermost in her mind, her eyes shining with excitement.

Sir James looked at her blankly. "How so?"

Georgiana was surprised that she needed to explain. "They say there will be riots if Sir Francis Burdett is sentenced to imprisonment and refuses to submit to his arrest."

"It is of no moment to me."

"But who do you think is right?" she persisted, disappointed at his lack of interest. "The House of Commons or Sir Francis? Did he act dishonourably or not?"

"Miss Merry, how can you talk of politics when your ears were made for poetry?" He started to recite a poem in the same melodic tone that he had used in the park. Again, he addressed the words to her, as if each verse declared his love.

"When Delia on the plain appears,
Awed by a thousand tender fears
I would approach, but dare not move:
Tell me, my heart, if this be love?"

175

As if in a trance, she stood motionless as he took her left hand in his and trailed his right forefinger down the length of her glove with a feather-like touch.

Before the delightful tingling sensation had disappeared, she came to her senses. What was she doing? She yanked her hand away, her face suffused with colour, hoping that no one had noticed.

Her cheeks were still glowing when Sir James continued his recitation, undeterred that she had reclaimed her hand so abruptly.

> *"Whene'er she speaks, my ravish'd ear*
> *No other voice than hers can hear,*
> *No other wit but hers approve:*
> *Tell me, my heart, if this be love?*
>
> *If she some other youth commend,*
> *Though I was once his fondest friend,*
> *His instant enemy I prove:*
> *Tell me, my heart, if this be love?*
>
> *When she is absent..."*

"How glad I am to have found you, Miss Merry," Anthony said, rudely interrupting his recital.

Sir James glared at him, but quickly hid his frustration.

"Did you ever see such a vast house? It is no wonder that you got lost. The Duchess will be so relieved to hear that I have found you. Come, let me return you to your grandmother before she expires with distress," he said, offering her his arm. "Pray excuse us, Sir James."

Georgiana looked at Anthony's arm with loathing, her temper rising. His peremptory behaviour made her feel rebellious. What right had Lord Castleford's brother to dictate who she could speak to?

It was irrelevant that she had already decided to ask Sir James to return her to her grandmother as soon as he had finished the poem. Her heart was still beating wildly from the way he had touched her arm, and his words were making her feel uncomfortable. It did not seem proper for a man she knew so little to be talking of love, and whatever she had reasoned before, the fact that they were set back from the mass of people *did* make it look like a tête-à-tête.

Judging by the hard look lurking in the back of Anthony's eyes, he was not going to leave without her. But that did not mean she would hurry to submit. She turned to Sir James and gazed into his eyes.

"Until we meet again, Sir James," Georgiana said, offering him her hand, which he willingly took. He lingered over it rather longer than necessary before letting it fall.

Throwing Sir James her warmest smile, she made a show of accepting Anthony's arm and allowed him to lead her away.

Anthony was not smiling. "You should be more careful about the company you keep, Miss Merry," he said. "Sir James is beneath you."

"I know," she replied. "He told me so himself."

"There are men far more worthy of you," he said in a softer tone.

"Such as your brother?" she said, her eyes full of challenge.

Anthony did not answer.

"If he cares so very much," she continued, her anger rising, "why didn't he come and interrupt my tête-à-tête himself – if, indeed, it needed interrupting at all?"

Anthony stopped walking and gave her a piercing look. "Because, Miss Merry, I did not want Sir James to have to be carried from the room."

Georgiana looked at him in surprise. Was he suggesting that his brother would have knocked Sir James down in Mrs Hope's saloon? She found it hard to believe, but her eyes glistened at the thought. Perhaps there were depths to Lord Castleford that she was yet to discover.

CHAPTER 22

As Georgiana entered Lady Buckinghamshire's garden, dressed as the goddess Minerva, she was aware of a flutter of excitement in her stomach. She wore a long, flowing white robe, and a helmet for a bonnet, with a shield and spear in her hands, and a silver mask covering her eyes.

She had been looking forward to the breakfast masquerade for weeks. Despite their popularity, she had not attended a masquerade before. How romantic, to converse with a gentleman, disguised by a costume or mask, not knowing for certain who they were or if you had been introduced. It sounded exciting, and just a little dangerous. Her heart beat faster than usual at the delightful prospect ahead.

Nearly everyone she could see was in costume. Her grandmother was attracting a good deal of attention in her guise as Marie Antoinette and was already indulging in a light flirtation with a Roman centurion. The Duke had not yielded to his wife's persuasions and had stayed at home, using his gout as an excuse.

Lady Augusta and Lord Helston, masquerading as Queen Elizabeth and Sir Walter Raleigh, were whispering in each other's ears as lovers do. As she looked at them, something caught in Georgiana's throat. Although happy for Augusta, she was growing weary of the constant talk of weddings when her own seemed so far away. The Duchess had excelled herself, throwing them a magnificent betrothal ball, and the wedding date was fixed for the end of June. Georgiana thought it could not come around too quickly.

Lord Denmead was in high spirits. He had kept quiet about his costume until the last moment, when he had appeared, ready for the masquerade, clothed as an army officer.

The Duchess had glanced at her son and shuddered. "Please do not let your father see you in those regimentals, Denmead. I have to say they become you well, but you know how he is. One look at you dressed like that and he will imagine you lying dead on some battlefield, even though it is only make-believe."

As Denmead paraded around in his uniform in front of her, Georgiana was not certain whether to laugh or cry. He looked so proud and content, and yet this was probably the closest he would ever get to joining the army, his sole ambition in life.

The week before, Denmead had taken her to see a review of troops in the park, but he had paid her scant attention, deserting her at the earliest opportunity to talk to a group of officers. She would have been forced to spend most of the afternoon alone if Sir James had not entertained her with one of his rare appearances.

Making a lavish show of kissing Georgiana and his mother and sister, as if he were going off to war, Denmead disappeared into the crowd in search of more amenable company.

Georgiana gazed around the garden through the slits in her mask, studying the other guests. She wondered whether she could spot her friends amongst the vast array of Turks and chambermaids, pirates and kings. Not if they were dressed as Persians, she thought, and there were plenty of them, sporting the most enormous bushy beards. She doubted she could tell which one was the real Persian ambassador.

Other guests were easier to identify. She recognised Anthony at once, swaggering across the garden toward her, attired as a Spanish cavalier. He flirted with her prettily until he was distracted by a shepherdess who claimed she had lost her sheep.

"Please help me, good sir. I think they must have wandered into the wood," she said in a sweet voice. Her words were accompanied by such a saucy look of invitation in Anthony's direction that Georgiana's cheeks grew red with embarrassment.

Anthony grinned. "I am at your service," he declared. He swept off his hat and made Georgiana an elaborate bow. "Until we meet again, fair Minerva."

Georgiana stood and watched people go by. It was fun trying to identify her friends through their disguises, but she failed to spot Lord Castleford. She wanted to talk to him, to reassure herself of his continued friendship, as their last encounter had not ended well.

Lord Castleford had accompanied her to the Royal Academy exhibition at Somerset House and she had spent several happy hours examining the paintings with him, admiring the work of the exhibitors and exclaiming every time she recognised one of the people in the portraits. She wished that her brother William could have been there. He alone had inherited their grandfather's artistic abilities, and the display would have inspired him. It was a pity that he had missed out by having to return home before the exhibition opened.

Beechey's portrait of the Persian ambassador had drawn her admiration, but her favourite painting of all was Turner's *Dewy Morning at Petworth*. Without thinking, she had declared that when she had a house of her own, she would like to buy it for her drawing room. Too late, she had remembered who she was talking to. Lord Castleford. *He* had wanted to give her that home. The sadness in his eyes showed that he had not forgotten. She had sunk into silence, flushing deeply, hoping that he would forgive her for hurting him.

But perhaps she was making a mistake to search for Lord Castleford at the masquerade. From what she knew of him, she suspected that he would despise such a frivolous entertainment. If by some chance he was there, he would doubtless be one of the few guests not in costume.

Even Beau's company would have been welcome. She was ready to forgive him for embarrassing her the last time they had met. At her request, Beau had taken her to Lord Elgin's house to see his famous marbles, but the visit had been a disaster. Beau did not scruple to complain, in a loud voice, that it was a waste of time, because most of the pieces were broken. It was so mortifying that she vowed she would never go to see anything with him again. She should have asked Lord Castleford to take her instead.

Quickly tiring of holding her shield and spear, Georgiana returned to the house and resigned them to the care of a maid.

As she walked back to where the Duchess was standing, a bearded Persian accosted her, offering her his arm for a walk around the garden. Georgiana was not sure whether she should accept.

"I cannot tell who you are, sir, so I do not know if we are acquainted."

"Not near as much as I would like us to be, my fair charmer."

Georgiana recognised Sir James's voice and smiled. "Your disguise is so good that I did not realise who you were until you spoke."

"Excellent. Then no one will know who is stealing you away."

She glanced at the party she had arrived with and doubted whether any of them would even notice. Her grandmother really was a most inadequate chaperon.

Taking her arm, Sir James led her across the grass to a path leading down to a wooded area, some distance from where the tables were laden with food.

Georgiana thought of the last letter from the Sylph. He had only written once since Mrs Hope's rout, a brief missive urging her again to look for openness and consistency, but nothing further. She suspected her father was struggling to find time to write more often amid his parish duties.

It struck her as rather odd that Sir James never approached her when she was with the Duchess or called on her at Wessex House. If his attentions were honourable, why didn't he court her in the normal way?

"I have a question for you, Sir James. Why do you never call on me at home? Do you find my grandmother so frightening?"

"I have no patience with chaperons," he replied. "How can I tell you how I feel when someone is there, listening to every word I say?"

Georgiana could see that he had a point. Sir James could not whisper words of love in her ear with the Duchess breathing down his neck. She was not, however, entirely satisfied. Beau hated drawing room conversation, but he often drove her around the park. It occurred to her she had never been out driving with Sir James.

"That may be true," she conceded, "but you *never* call. Not even to take me out for a drive in your carriage. I doubt the Duchess is even aware of your existence."

Sir James dropped his gaze, as if he were too embarrassed to look her in the eyes. "She would keep you away from me," he said with a sigh. "And she would be right. I am not worthy to kiss your feet."

Georgiana's curiosity was piqued. What *had* he done to make him talk like that? Augusta had hinted that he was not respectable but had refused to tell her why. She was determined to find out.

"And why would that be?"

Sir James glanced up and met her eyes before dropping his own to the ground once again in despair. "If I explain, you'll want nothing more to do with me."

"Try me," Georgiana urged. "Everyone deserves a second chance."

"Miss Merry – Georgiana – you are too kind. I will have no secrets with you. You are so good, so unspoilt, whereas I am a sorry wretch to whom life has dealt blows from which a man may not easily recover."

"Blows? What blows?"

"When I was young, I made a poor choice. I formed an unfortunate alliance. Like so many before me, I thought money would make me happy, but I was wrong. I did not act wisely."

"What are you talking about?" Georgiana said, though she feared what he might say.

"I married the daughter of a Scottish merchant, but I soon discovered that she had no more heart than this," he said, picking up a stone and throwing it into the woods. "We had a child, a son. He died when he was just a few days old. Whilst I was still grieving, she left me."

"I'm sorry for your loss," Georgiana said. "But married?" She was unable to keep the horror out of her voice. Such a thought had never crossed her mind.

"Not now," Sir James assured her.

"Is your wife dead then?"

"No. My *loving* wife saw fit to divorce me," he replied bitterly. "I lost my child and then my wife. She resolved to cut all ties with me, and her father arranged a divorce. It is not so hard to obtain a divorce in Scotland as it is in England."

Georgiana instinctively took a step back.

"You recoil from me. Then you judge me like the rest of the world. Yet you could save me. With you, Minerva, at my side, guiding my path, I would not make the same mistakes again. Did you not say everyone deserved a second chance, or did you mean everyone but me?"

Georgiana thought of her own errors and how often she needed to be forgiven. She would, perhaps, be ruing her marriage to Beau if she had not been given a second chance.

"Everyone deserves a second chance," she repeated, "though not everyone gets one."

"You are too kind – too generous." Sir James leaned forward and placed the lightest of kisses on her forehead.

Her lips formed an 'O', but no sound came out. She did not know how to respond. These brief, intense encounters with Sir James made no sense. They set her pulse racing and her heart pounding but left her head in a whirl.

* * *

Lord Castleford *was* at the masquerade. Dressed as a beggar, with scraggly hair and a decided limp, it was hardly surprising that Georgiana had not recognised him. The disguise amused Anthony who knew how much his brother generally despised these dressing-up affairs.

Castleford's sole purpose for being there was to watch over Georgiana. The Duchess was not an effective chaperon as she was more occupied with her own flirtations than she was with looking after her young charge. Though he did not think Georgiana would deliberately step over the line of propriety, he feared that others, hiding behind a disguise, might be tempted to do so.

From a distance, he watched while she went back to the house to deposit her shield and spear, only stepping forward to deter a rather tipsy Elizabethan courtier from following her.

When he saw a Persian addressing her, his stomach tightened. Afraid that she was talking to that man again, he started to move toward her.

He was not close enough to hear their conversation, but when the Persian took Georgiana's arm and led her away from the throng of people, he decided it was time to intervene. Spurred on by a mixture of anger at the Persian and irritation at Georgiana, Castleford increased the speed of his limp.

Would she never learn? He wanted to march right over there and shake some sense into her. Didn't she realise that she was encouraging this 'gentleman' to take liberties with her person?

Not taking his gaze from the couple who were deep in conversation, Castleford limped in their direction. When the Persian leaned forward and kissed Georgiana's forehead, he halted and closed his eyes as if in pain. Only he knew that the pain was real and not some elaborate acting out of his part.

"Alms, alms," he cried plaintively as he struggled forward.

The Persian sneered. "Go away, old man. We have nothing for you."

Georgiana, however, seemed glad of the interruption and gave him an encouraging smile.

Although he could tell she did not recognise him, Castleford thought she looked uncomfortable and hoped she would take the opportunity to move away from her Persian admirer.

"Give a poor old man an arm, pretty lady," he said in a croaky voice.

"Until we meet again, Mr Persian," Georgiana said, offering the beggar her arm.

Castleford leaned heavily upon her so that their progress was slow. If he could have limped more slowly, he would have done so. Being this close to Georgiana was both torture and bliss. Ignoring the fact that she did not know who he was, he savoured every moment.

Perhaps he should have dressed as a Spanish pirate. Then he could have stolen a kiss as part of the ruse. But no, he reminded himself. He would have given himself away by his height. Besides, a stolen kiss was not enough. He was after more than that. Castleford was playing the long game. He wanted the right to shower her with kisses for the rest of her life.

Knowing he could not stay with her for much longer without revealing his identity, he surveyed the crowd for one of her family to whose care he could consign her. Though he could not spy the Duchess, he identified Beau, a little way off, also dressed as a Persian.

"Beautiful Minerva, let me leave you with this gallant Beau," he said, encouraging Georgiana to take Beau's arm. "Please protect this kind lady from your ill-mannered countryman," he urged.

Castleford's words brought a flush to Georgiana's cheeks.

Beau saw her embarrassment and guessed at the cause. "Zounds take the filly," he grumbled under his breath, tucking Georgiana's arm into his own. He nodded to the beggarly Castleford who limped slowly away.

"Why do you need protecting? What have you been up to now, Georgie?" Beau snapped. "Have you been cavorting with Sir James again?"

Castleford turned back, hearing the name of Georgiana's less than respectable admirer for the first time.

"Sir James Maxwell?" he asked in a strangled voice. But he got no answer. Beau had not heard.

Castleford hoped that he was wrong. He had never met Sir James, but he knew him by reputation. And that reputation suggested that Georgiana was being pursued by a very dangerous man.

"Be quiet, Beau," Georgiana said. "As you can see, I am perfectly safe."

"Thanks to the beggar. Who was he?"

Georgiana shook her head. "I have no idea."

Castleford smiled to himself, glad to know his disguise had worked, and continued to limp away.

For the rest of the masquerade, he kept his eye on Georgiana, but she did not drift from her party again. Though he thought it unlikely that Sir James would approach her a second time, he would not take any chances.

He need not have worried. Beau refused to leave her side until her grandmother took her home, guarding her as jealously as Castleford would have done himself.

* * *

Georgiana was in her bedchamber, changing out of her costume, when she heard an anguished scream. She looked at Bessie in alarm.

"What was that?"

She ran to the door, flung it open, and stood outside and listened. Another cry and then another echoed along the corridor. It sounded like Augusta's voice, but the howling was coming from the Duchess's apartments.

As she sped down the passageway, the screeching became louder. Georgiana's pulse was racing. Whatever could have happened?

The door to the Duchess's rooms was wide open and without hesitation, she hurried inside. She was right. The wailing *was* coming from Augusta.

"Whatever is the matter?" Georgiana asked, her face turning pale with fear.

The Duchess was sitting at her dressing table. Her maid was holding smelling salts under her nose, but her grandmother was not responding. She just sat there, as if she were a statue.

Augusta was pacing the room like a madwoman, her features contorted with rage.

"*This* is the matter," she screeched at the top of her voice, thrusting a letter into her hand.

Georgiana took the letter and scanned the lines. As she read, her mouth fell open in dismay.

Dearest Mama,

I have taken my future into my own hands. A friend has assisted me to purchase a commission in the 88th foot and I am off to Spain tonight. Do not try to stop me. You above all people should appreciate what it is to be consumed by ambition. My sole desire is to honour my family and fight for my country. Please explain to Father that I must do this. I cannot find the words – words that I realise will break his heart. And yet, I know this is what I need to do.

I will love you and Father and Augusta always.

God bless you. Denmead.

Now she understood why Augusta was in hysterics. Den had gone. The regimentals had not been a sham and he had obtained a commission in the army. How he had done so without his parents realising was a mystery. Someone must have helped him. But that was irrelevant. Den had gone and nothing was going to bring him back.

"How dare he?" Augusta yelled. "How could he throw his life away like that? Doesn't he care about us at all?"

Her screams gave way to tears and Georgiana put her arm around her, offering what little comfort she could.

Georgiana's heart went out to them. She could only imagine her grandmother's pain. The pain of losing – possibly forever – her only son. And Augusta. Losing a brother – a twin brother – must be almost as bad.

She heard a loud thud above the noise of Augusta's sobbing and looked up in horror to see the Duke crumpled in a heap on the floor, Denmead's letter beside him.

No one had seen him enter the room. They should have known that the sound would carry. He had picked up the note that Georgiana had discarded and read its poisonous message. It appeared his heart could not cope with the shock he had sustained.

The Duke's collapse shook the Duchess out of her stupor. She rushed over to where he lay and fell to her knees beside his inanimate body, beating her fists on his chest, begging him to wake up.

Georgiana sprang into action. She rang the Duchess's bell ferociously and within moments a footman appeared. He blanched at the sight before him, but Georgiana paid no attention.

"Send a man for the doctor. Tell him to come without delay. The Duke has collapsed."

The doctor did not keep them waiting long. A quick investigation established that the Duke was still alive. He banished everyone from the room whilst he examined his patient, who had been lifted onto the Duchess's bed.

Lady Augusta's maid persuaded her mistress to withdraw to her bedchamber and lie down, leaving Georgiana waiting anxiously with her grandmother for the doctor to emerge from the sickroom. When he did, he had little comfort to offer them.

"It is impossible to determine at this stage how much damage has been done. He may recover; he may not. Only time will tell."

The doctor paused. "Your Grace, the Duke is not a young man and you must prepare yourself for the worst."

The Duchess had grown unnaturally calm. "What should I do?"

"Keep him quiet. No disturbances. I will call again tomorrow, but if there is any change, do not hesitate to summon me earlier."

"Very well. Please look in on Lady Augusta before you leave. She is distraught," the Duchess said.

The doctor was shown to Lady Augusta's room where he prescribed her a sedative, and once more, Georgiana was left alone with her grandmother.

"You need to go and stay with your aunt," the Duchess said to her in a voice devoid of all emotion. "I cannot possibly look after you now. I must take care of the Duke. You heard the doctor. No excitement. No noise. The house kept completely quiet. You cannot remain here. I will send word to Lady Harting immediately."

Georgiana looked at her grandmother in horror. It would not have been her choice to stay with her cousins, but that was not what distressed her. The Duchess detested Lady Harting and must be deeply upset to suggest such a thing. It was so unnatural.

CHAPTER 23

It came as no surprise to Georgiana that Lady Harting welcomed her into her house with open arms. She feared that her aunt would use the opportunity to encourage Beau's pursuit of her hand. It seemed unlikely they could keep up the pretence for long under such scrutiny.

Georgiana did not care for the change of residence. She knew it was wrong to think ill of her aunt, but she found it hard to like her. Particularly not after she overheard her gossiping to one of her friends about the Duchess's misfortunes and blaming it all on her grandmother's bad blood. She accused the Duke of having made an error of judgement when he married 'that woman' and of perpetuating the error by overindulging his children.

Amidst all the furore of the Duke's collapse, she had found little time to think about what had happened at Lady Buckinghamshire's masquerade. Now she had too much. Sir James's confession haunted her thoughts as often as his tender kiss on her forehead. She desperately needed counsel but did not feel brave enough to write to the Sylph. She was not at all sure how her father would react. He had always preached about the sanctity of marriage and the word 'divorce' sent shivers down her spine.

But surely it was not Sir James's fault that his wife had left him? Father also preached that anyone who truly repented could be forgiven, and this was without exception. She wrote at length to Eliza, voicing all her thoughts and asking her if she was right to conclude that Sir James should be given a second chance.

She hoped for an early reply, eager to learn if her sister agreed with her line of reasoning. But it was not an answer from Eliza that arrived first, but a letter from the Sylph.

My dearest G,

You asked me once how you could tell if a gentleman is to be trusted. I urge you to examine his behaviour. Do his actions match his words? Does he behave the same way in the shadows as he does in the daylight? An honourable man will act as honourably when no one is looking as he would if your father were watching.

Do not be fooled by promises of reform. There is a world of difference between regret and repentance. It is possible to regret the consequences of your actions without being sorry for the wrong you have done. Don't forget what you have read in 'Coelebs'. Heed well the words of Miss Stanley who rejected the advances of the profligate Lord Staunton who promised to reform if she married him. She knew there would be nothing she could do if he failed to amend his ways after her marriage. 'It would be too late to repent of my folly, after my presumption had incurred its just punishment.'

I warned you once before about being alone in the company of a gentleman. No matter how honourable a man appears, do not place yourself in his power. Even the best of men may be tempted by beauty within his reach.

Ever your devoted servant,
Sylph.

Georgiana smiled to herself. She still had her father's copy of *Coelebs*. He must have borrowed the novel from the circulating library to quote a line from it. The smile faded from her lips as she thought about what he had written. She read the letter again. Its message was not amusing and one she needed to take to heart. She must be confident in the character of the man she married.

What could have prompted her father to write such things? It was as if he knew about Sir James and how she had behaved at the masquerade. But how? Eliza would not have told him. Besides, her sister did not even know exactly what had happened as there were some things she had kept to herself. Perhaps her father feared that her feelings for Beau would be reanimated whilst living under her uncle's roof.

Regardless of the Sylph's motivation for writing, the letter made her feel uncomfortable. She had been foolish to go apart with Sir James and she should not have let him kiss her, even on the forehead. He would never have done that in front of her grandmother, though she could not deny that it had caused her heart to flutter. Sir James had told her his circumstances and pleaded with her not to judge him. He said he needed her. But could she really be the means to save him? Did she want to be?

"Unbelievable ingratitude!" Lord Harting exclaimed, wandering into the drawing room and interrupting Georgiana's reflections. He thumped his newspaper down on the table. "Even sponsored one of his children and yet tried to murder the Duke in his bed."

Georgiana jumped out of her chair in horror. "The Duke?"

Lord Harting was surprised to discover that he was not alone. He shot Georgiana a weak smile and gave her a reassuring pat on the head.

"No, no, my dear, not your Duke. The King's son – the Duke of Cumberland. Attacked by one of his valets. Nasty business, but they say he will survive."

Georgiana sunk back into her chair in relief. When the Earl left the room, she picked up the *Times* and read the account of the attack. The description was rather gruesome in places. She bit her lip and thought with a smile that if Lord Castleford knew she was reading it, he would accuse her of being bloodthirsty again.

She let out a wistful sigh. There seemed little chance of him discovering it. Apart from exchanging a few words with him at the Duchess of Devonshire's music party, when she had assured him that she still wished to attend the service at St Paul's in aid of the charity children, she had not seen him since she had been staying with her aunt.

As she did not think for one moment that he would be scared away by Lady Harting, she concluded that he had finally lost interest in her. Against all reason, she felt disappointed. It was understandable that she should miss him. Nobody else talked with her the way he did, and she would have liked to discuss the attack on the Duke of Cumberland with him.

She had not seen Sir James since the breakfast masquerade. Lady Harting probably was scaring *him* away. No doubt her aunt was delighted that Beau had apparently ousted her other admirers, but

Georgiana could not help feeling that it was rather dull to be attended everywhere by a man who was only pretending to be in love with her.

Beau had accompanied her to the Duchess of Devonshire's music party, but he had not tried to amuse her and had grumbled the whole time. With considerable reluctance, he had taken her to the theatre, but when she intimated that she wanted to go again, he had refused outright, promising to take her to the opening night of Vauxhall instead.

Unfortunately, Lady Harting decided to attend as well and so, to Beau's disgust, they were forced to visit Vauxhall as a family party. Georgiana hoped she would find the evening amusing. Her fake courtship with Beau was beginning to drag. It was a real courtship she desired.

*   *   *

Vauxhall was at its most crowded, despite the exorbitant entrance fee of three and a half shillings. Not only was it the opening night, but there was a grand gala in honour of the King's birthday attended by the Prince of Wales. Georgiana had heard that Vauxhall was a magical place, and that evening, it lived up to her expectations.

When she hinted to Beau that she would like to go for a walk around the gardens while they waited for their supper to arrive, he willingly jumped up and offered his arm, eager to escape from the family party. But as they walked away from the supper booth, his mother halted their departure by suggesting – or rather, insisting – that he take his sister as well.

Beau muttered under his breath at being saddled with Frances. As soon as they were out of Lady Harting's sight, he extricated himself from his position between the two ladies and walked on ahead. Frances raised her eyebrows at this unloverlike behaviour and with a sniff and a nod which did not bode well for Beau, she linked arms with Georgiana, and they set off behind him at a leisurely pace.

Georgiana was entranced. Everywhere she looked, she saw tiny lanterns illuminating the walks which were crowded with groups of people, dressed in the height of fashion.

That did not mean, however, that the less desirable members of society were not there. She was appalled to see a gentleman of her acquaintance walking along the path accompanied by a lady with a highly painted face, and a dress cut so low that Georgiana did not know where to look. She was dismayed when the lady blew Beau a kiss as she passed and shot him such a salacious glance that his cheeks grew rather red.

"No doubt one of Beau's ladybirds," Frances whispered in her ear.

Georgiana made a point of looking in the opposite direction and tried to change the subject, but Frances was not to be deterred.

"All men have them," she continued. "You must not worry. Mama says it does not mean a thing."

Georgiana said nothing. She could not treat the matter so lightly. It upset her to hear Frances talking like that, in such an emotionless voice, as if such things were as commonplace and acceptable as she claimed.

They walked along the main path, nodding to any of their acquaintances they saw, and occasionally stopping to talk. Frances brightened when they met the unprepossessing Mr Whitlow, the only gentleman to have consistently paid court to her, coming down the path toward them.

Mr Whitlow's eyes lit up with delight. "Lady Frances," he said. "What a lucky chance."

"Indeed, it is," Frances said with an irritating titter, bowing her head and looking at her feet rather than at her suitor.

Much to Georgiana's surprise, Beau invited him to join them in their promenade – an invitation Mr Whitlow was quick to accept.

It soon became clear why. As Beau had expected, Mr Whitlow attached himself to Frances, leaving Beau to resume his walk with Georgiana in peace.

"Don't know what it is about my sister," he confided, "but half an hour in her company is enough to make my stomach turn sour."

The two couples followed the path together, but Lady Frances and her swain dawdled so much that they soon fell behind.

Georgiana was suggesting to Beau that it was time for them to return for supper when he was accosted by the buxom lady they had passed earlier. With no invitation, she took Beau's other arm, and monopolised his attention with her flirtatious talk and low-cut gown.

It seemed likely that Frances had been right, and the woman was not respectable. Georgiana could not understand why Beau did not shake her off. Perhaps he feared she would make a scene.

Trying to ignore her, Georgiana gazed in the opposite direction. It was with genuine delight and no little relief that she almost collided with Sir James as they turned the next corner.

With a surprised glance at Beau and his companion, Sir James took Georgiana's arm and walked briskly away from them.

"Pardon me, Miss Merry, but how did you come to be in such company?"

Georgiana blushed. "I hardly know. That lady seems to have some claim on Beau which has allowed her to impose on him."

"You are far too innocent to realise but, as a man of the world, I must warn you that Beau's lady friend is not what you would call respectable."

"I feared as much."

"Your innocence is not the least of your charms. I would grieve to see you brought down by associating with such a character."

Georgiana was touched by his concern.

"Forgive me," he said. "I know I have no right to intervene, but is not the desire to have that right some justification for my actions? You are my angel. The one who moves me to reform my ways and become worthy of such goodness as I see before me. Without you, I am lost."

"I cannot reform you, Sir James. I have not the power."

"Would you not give me your hand to save me from that slippery slope of ruin?"

"How could I be sure that you would not drag me down that slope with you?"

"No, my angel. It could not be. You are too good, too innocent, to be lured by evil. You are my salvation."

"I am gratified by your faith in my ability not to stray from the path of righteousness," Georgiana said gently, "but I am not your salvation. Only God can save."

"Yes, yes, of course," Sir James replied, with just a touch of impatience, "but you could be my helper – my guide. With you by my side, my soul could be reclaimed from the devil himself. I wish that I could call you my own. Say you will give me that right, Miss Merry."

While Georgiana was flattered that such a man as Sir James wanted her and believed she could transform him, this was happening too fast. She remembered the Sylph's words and questioned what she knew of Sir James and his character. Though he might be willing to marry on such a slight acquaintance, she was not. But to what depths would he fall if she denied him her help?

"Miss Merry – Georgiana – be mine," he said, raising his hand to her face and stroking it down her cheek. He leaned toward her as if he were going to kiss her when they were interrupted, and he stepped back abruptly.

A rowdy party came around the corner into the alley in which they were standing. Sir James grabbed her arm again and strode off in the opposite direction, eager to avoid the company.

"Miss Merry?" a familiar voice called after them. Abandoning his friends, Anthony ran after the retreating couple.

"The masked ball at the Argyll Rooms," Sir James whispered in her ear. "Meet me there. Do not fail."

"Well met, Miss Merry," Anthony said, taking hold of her free arm. "See, I am intent on depriving you of sole possession of so lovely a prize, Sir James."

He addressed the rest of his conversation to Georgiana as if Sir James were not there.

"I swear you did not set off in Sir James's company, Miss Merry. What happened to your party? How careless of you to mislay them. I am sure Lady Harting will be most put out if Beau returns without you. She will find it hard to forgive her son for his carelessness."

Anthony rattled on in this manner, not allowing either of his companions to interrupt him, until they were once more on the main path.

Sir James scowled at Anthony. "As you are so eager to return Miss Merry to her party, I will delegate my precious charge to you." He bowed to Georgiana and walked off in the opposite direction.

Anthony stared at her and shook his head in amazement. "What on earth were you doing walking along a solitary path, alone with Sir James? I thought my eyes must be deceiving me. Why do you ignore every warning you are given? Don't you know what manner of man you are consorting with? Sir James is a rake. He is not to be trusted."

"And you are?" Georgiana snapped. She was angry at being found in such a compromising situation, but Anthony's words redirected her anger from herself toward him.

"Miss Merry, trust me on this. He is not a good man."

"I know - he is a man who needs my help to reform."

"Reform! That's rich. Sir James is after your money. Surely you can see that?"

"I do not believe it."

"Believe it."

"How can you accuse him of design? He did not even know who I was when we first met. You are only trying to turn me against him so I can marry your brother."

The words came out like bullets from a gun – an automatic gun over which she had no control. Why had she said that? Did she want him to deny it, or was she hoping that he wouldn't? Why did it matter if Lord Castleford still wanted to marry her or not?

"I am trying to protect you," Anthony said through gritted teeth.

Georgiana had nothing left to say. Her cheeks were glowing, but the fire had gone out. She felt deflated and embarrassed that she had accused Anthony of being untrustworthy when he had always been her friend.

They returned to Lady Harting's supper box in silence. As Anthony had predicted, her aunt was giving Beau a rare trimming for losing her. He had shaken off his disreputable lady companion but was too late to discover in what direction Sir James had taken Georgiana.

Everyone was surprised when she came back on Anthony's arm.

"May I return your niece to you, Lady Harting?" Anthony said. "Miss Merry became separated from her party and was in some distress, so do not be too harsh on her. She is sorry for her mistake and I am sure she will not repeat it."

Lady Harting thanked Anthony for his assistance, but Georgiana could tell that her gratitude was forced. Her aunt did not care to be indebted to Lord Castleford's brother.

Fortunately, the incident soon sunk into the background, as Mr Whitlow and Lady Frances returned in high spirits.

Her cousin gave Mr Whitlow an encouraging smile.

"Lady Frances," he stammered, beaming from ear to ear, "has done me the great honour of agreeing to become my wife."

Lady Harting smiled her approval. "What wonderful news."

Following her aunt's cue, Georgiana was quick to add her congratulations, but she could not help wondering how big Mr Whitlow's bank balance was to tempt Frances to marry him.

CHAPTER 24

The evening at Vauxhall was not quickly forgotten. A week later, Beau was still smarting from his mother's displeasure. He was not the only sufferer. Georgiana had to put up with him following her around like a lost puppy in an attempt to convince Lady Harting that his suit was making progress.

"Do you want to come out for a drive?" he asked.

Georgiana frowned. "I would rather stay and read my book."

"Please, Georgie," he begged. "If I cannot get my mother to leave me alone, I'm going to go mad."

"Very well," she replied, marking her place and putting down her novel. "I suppose it would be pleasant to be out in the sun." She returned wearing an emerald green pelisse and a chip bonnet tied with a matching green ribbon. Beau nodded his approval, not least because she had only kept him waiting for ten minutes.

"Mother is getting suspicious," he moaned as they drove around the park. "She has not let me forget losing you at Vauxhall. It was such a relief to discover that you were safe in Ant's care. I don't believe Mother sees Ant as a rival as none of his flirtations are genuine. Funny thing, that. He's so light-hearted and Castleford's so serious. You wouldn't guess they were brothers.

"Which reminds me. That fellow Sir James. Stay away from him. I should never have introduced him to you. He made it hard for me to refuse, but I should have stood my ground and risked the unpleasantness. I never can think of what to say until it's too late. My mother would have known how to put him in his place, but I didn't. Forgive me."

"It is of no consequence," Georgiana said.

"I hope not, but there's no telling with a fellow like that what he's up to. Sir James is a clever one. I don't trust him."

Georgiana felt her temper rising. "Why are you and Mr Warren so set against him?" she snapped. "It is not even as if *you* want me for yourself."

Beau gave her a lopsided smile. "Because I like you, Georgie, and I don't wish you to get hurt. Even though I don't like my sisters, I wouldn't introduce him to them. I should have refused."

"But if you trust him so little, why is he your friend?"

"He's not my friend," Beau said, with a look of disgust. "I've shared a few bottles with him, that's all." He shifted uncomfortably in his seat.

"Thing is," he continued, with a guilty expression on his face, "when we were sharing those bottles, I may have mentioned that your grandmother has settled quite a sizeable sum on you."

So, Beau was convinced Sir James was only after her dowry as well, was he? Did he think because he was immune to her charms that no one else could fall in love with her without the lure of money?

She pushed down the feelings of rejection that his words had conjured, replacing them with an angry determination to prove him wrong. Her eyes glowed as a plan formed in her mind. She had not forgotten what Sir James had said to her at Vauxhall. He wanted to see her again. Georgiana decided to make sure that he did.

"Are you going to the masquerade ball at the Argyll Rooms tomorrow?" she asked, smiling sweetly up at Beau.

He was not fooled for a minute. "What if I am?"

"Take me with you."

Beau rolled his eyes and sighed. "It won't be the same as Lady Buckinghamshire's masquerade, Georgie. It's not a private affair. If you pay your money, you're in. The company is not select. You wouldn't enjoy it."

"So, it is acceptable for you to go to a public masquerade, but not for me?"

"Your father would not approve."

"You're making excuses."

"Darn it, Georgie. Can't a fellow go and have a bit of fun without having to do the pretty?"

"Take me with you or I'll tell your mother that our courtship is a ruse."

Beau paled at the thought. "You would not." He took one look at her resolute countenance and knew that she would.

"Your choice," she said, fixing him with a fierce stare.

"Oh, very well then. I know a place where I can hire a costume for you. You mustn't go in anything of your own. It will be much better if you're not recognised. If you stay with me and keep your mask on, I daresay we'll brush through. But when I say it's time to go, we go. No arguments."

Georgiana nodded, a huge smile on her face, delighted at having got her own way. "Agreed. No arguments."

* * *

When Lord Castleford entered White's Club that evening, he found his brother was already there. Having drunk a glass of wine with Anthony, he left him to read the newspaper while he moved to a nearby table to write a letter to his estate manager.

Castleford had written no more than a few words when Beau arrived. He gave Castleford a perfunctory nod and slumped down on the seat next to Anthony.

"It's not fair," he said, in a petulant tone, taking the glass of wine that Anthony handed him and downing it in a single gulp. "I have danced attendance on Georgie all week to appease my mother after that debacle at Vauxhall, and what must the wretched girl do but insist I take her to the Argyll Rooms tomorrow."

Castleford's pen froze in mid-air. It was not his habit to listen to other people's conversations, but the temptation to eavesdrop was too great. And if it concerned Georgiana, he needed to hear it.

"Wretched girl? That doesn't sound very loverlike," Anthony said.

Beau huffed. "Don't tease me, Ant. You know I'm not in love with her."

"Then you're not planning on marrying Miss Merry?"

"No," he said with a shudder.

"I didn't think so."

Castleford smiled to himself. Beau had confirmed what he had suspected for some time – his understanding with Georgiana was not of a romantic nature.

"We thought ourselves in love, many years ago," Beau said, "but we're just friends now. She's protecting me from my mother's matrimonial scheming. It was her idea. Trouble is, she insists I take her to this masquerade tomorrow, or she'll burst the bubble."

"She knows how to get what she wants."

"Oh yes. Somehow, she always twists me round her little finger. That's why her father said we wouldn't suit. He was right. Fortunately, my mother knew nothing about it, or she would be even more convinced of my ineptitude."

Anthony poured them both another glass of wine. "Do you think Miss Merry is hoping to meet Sir James at the masquerade?"

Beau grimaced, tossing his head from side to side. "I don't know. Possibly, but it is a chance I must take. If my mother finds out that our courtship is a ruse, she'll be furious. And if she stops my allowance, I may be forced to sell my horses, or marry some other girl. Worry not. I'll look after Georgie. She can't come to any harm if I don't let her out of my sight."

"Like you did at Vauxhall."

Beau glared at his friend. "Thanks for reminding me."

"You never told me how it was that Miss Merry found herself in a secluded alleyway with Sir James. I refuse to believe you consigned her to such a fate to have a little fun yourself."

"Fun? No. It wasn't fun at all. Out of nowhere, that actress I had under my protection last year popped up and attached herself to me like a limpet. No quiet persuasion seemed to convince her I was no longer interested and could not talk to her."

His colour deepened. "Think me a coward if you wish, but I was afraid she would cause a disturbance. I was so absorbed with trying to get rid of her peaceably that I didn't even notice Sir James was there until he was walking off with Georgie on his arm. Once I realised, I couldn't follow them quick enough. I've warned her he's not to be trusted, but she doesn't seem to want to listen."

Anthony nodded. "I've tried as well. The more I said against him, the fiercer she defended him. She told me he wanted her help to reform. From what I know of Miss Merry, that is a line that might just work with her, and Sir James is the type of man who would not scruple to use her kind-heartedness to his advantage. Let's hope we haven't sent her running into his arms in our efforts to protect her."

Castleford hoped so too. He laid his pen to rest, his letter unwritten. How could he keep Georgiana safe from Sir James? It would be simple enough to stop Beau from taking her to the masquerade, but what if she saw his interference as the action of a rival in love? Might it make her even more determined to see Sir James again? He rested his head in his hands and prayed for guidance. How could he convince her that Sir James was a scoundrel with no intention of changing his ways?

* * *

It had been far too easy to persuade Beau to take her to the masquerade. Georgiana was ashamed of the method she had used and was painfully aware of what she had not mentioned. She was sure that he would not have agreed so readily if he had known she was planning to meet Sir James.

Beau and Anthony seemed determined to set her against Sir James, but what had they said of him that he had not told her himself? It was not fair to judge a man on his past alone. If she did not give him the chance to change, it might make him desperate.

She had already written a letter to Eliza telling her about her visit to Vauxhall, but when she returned from her drive, she broke open the seal and added an extra line. *I have persuaded Beau to take me to a masquerade at the Argyll Rooms tomorrow. 'He' is going to be there. Wish me well. G.*

Georgiana was in a fever of excitement lest something should occur to prevent her from meeting Sir James at the masquerade. She excused herself from attending the theatre, saying that she felt a little unwell. Knowing how much her niece loved the play, Lady Harting became concerned and readily agreed to let her spend the evening at home.

"I am sure Beaumont will be happy to forego whatever entertainment he has planned to keep you company," her aunt said. "Perhaps a quiet game of chess or he could read to you."

Georgiana was revolted at the prospect and Beau even more so, but as the suggestion was in their interests, neither of them made the slightest complaint.

A twinge of guilt assailed her. Though she had not lied, it had been her intention to mislead Lady Harting. She had allowed her aunt to form the impression that she was ill and would spend a quiet evening at home instead of going to the theatre. At least it was true that she felt somewhat unwell. She was feeling sick with excitement.

The minutes dragged on as Lady Harting fussed over her and even offered to call a physician. Georgiana hastily declined saying that she was sure that there was nothing wrong with her that could not be put right by being allowed to do as she wanted. At last, Lady Harting's carriage was called, and the guilty pair were left alone.

Beau complained at the cavalier way that his mother had disposed of his time. She was not to know that it suited him. Putting his annoyance behind him, he urged Georgiana to hurry and get ready because he did not want to be kept waiting.

Bubbling with excitement, Georgiana returned to her room and called Bessie to help her dress in the costume that Beau had hired for her – that of the fairy queen Titania. She should have known better than to suppose that Bessie would be complaisant about her change in plans. With the freedom of a servant who had known her all her life, Bessie scolded her throughout the entire process.

"I am surprised at you, Miss Georgiana. Saying you were feeling unwell and yet all the while planning something quite different. And where might you be off to in this fancy dress? Not that you need to tell me, for I know exactly what your answer will be because I don't go around with my head in the clouds and I know full well that it is a public masquerade you are going to and no doubt without her ladyship's permission. What your father would say at this deception is fearful to imagine. I suppose young Lord Beaumont is taking you. Goodness, I don't know what mischief you're up to this time, but heed my word, no good ever came of doing things in secret and well you know it. And if you think you can pretend that you're in love with his lordship, then you can think again. I wasn't born yesterday. You've got him to do what you want, and I pray to God you won't come to any harm. Not that there is anything I can do to dissuade you from going. A more obstinate creature I never did see, but you're my darling girl and I still beg you to reconsider."

At the end of this tirade, she surprised both herself and Georgiana by bursting into tears.

"You are making too much of it, Bessie. It's only a bit of fun," Georgiana said, giving her maid a hug before fastening her mask over her face. "Lord Beaumont will take care of me. I'll come back safe and sound, you'll see."

Beau was waiting for her outside her room. "Safer to go down the backstairs," he said, grabbing her hand. "Old Tomkins tells Mother things. We'd better avoid him."

"Yes, of course," Georgiana replied, though she regretted that such furtive behaviour was necessary.

The Argyll Rooms were already full by the time they arrived. Georgiana wondered whether Sir James was there as he had promised, and if he was, how she was ever going to find him in such a large crowd of people. What would he say to her? Would he try to kiss her? And should she let him?

Everyone was in fancy dress. Some simple, some elaborate; some masked and some not. At first, they just stood there watching the glittering array of costumes.

"Dance, your majesty?" Beau asked.

Georgiana nodded. As they moved down the room with the dance, her eyes darted this way and that, searching for Sir James.

"Have you heard a word I've said?"

Georgiana stared blankly at Beau.

"You've agreed to meet him, haven't you?"

"I can't imagine who you could mean," Georgiana replied lightly, but the tell-tale blush gave lie to her words.

Beau shook his head in despair. "Dash it, Georgie. If you're here to see that fellow, I'll be sorry I brought you."

Georgiana saw that she had offended Beau and concentrated all her efforts on soothing his ruffled sensibilities. She was so absorbed in the task that she did not realise they were being watched.

When the dance finished, someone grabbed her by the hand and dragged her away while Beau's attention was momentarily diverted by the sudden appearance of the woman from Vauxhall, dressed as a pageboy, showing an indecent amount of her comely legs.

"You are more beautiful every time I see you," a voice whispered in her ear.

"It's you," Georgiana said, recognising Sir James. "How did you find me?"

"Your beauty draws me like a magnet."

"What a pretty thing to say," she said, giving him a shy smile. "But what trick did you serve on my partner? Beau promised he would not let me out of his sight. And yet, here I am, with you."

"I may have encouraged an old flame of his to distract him for a while."

Georgiana looked back to where Beau was standing. "That's the lady from Vauxhall, isn't it? The one you told me was not respectable. I fear you are right."

"There is no doubt of that. But why talk of Beau? He is happy enough and I reserve all your smiles for me."

Unanswered questions flew through Georgiana's mind as Sir James led her to the end of the Argyll Rooms furthest away from Beau. How could Sir James persuade such a woman to help him divert Beau unless he knew her himself? And if he knew her himself, was it possible that he had also sent her to attach herself to Beau at Vauxhall, enabling Sir James to 'rescue' her?

Had this woman been intimate with Beau? With Sir James? She shuddered. This line of reasoning was most disturbing. She was not as open-minded as her cousin. Frances was matter of fact about her brother's affairs, but she could not dismiss them so easily.

"My love, what troubles you?" Sir James said. "I wish you would let me kiss those frowns away."

"That is a right that I could only grant my husband," Georgiana replied.

"Then give me that right," he begged.

Georgiana fell silent. Did she want to marry a man like Sir James? Though he was exciting to be with, she was not sure that she trusted him.

While she was still trying to make sense of her feelings, Sir James leaned in toward her and stroked his fingers down her cheek and across her lips. She gulped hard at the intimacy of the gesture but could not bring herself to move away.

Georgiana felt a light tap on her shoulder. The spell was broken. Grateful for the interruption, she turned to see who it was, but not before she saw the irritated look on Sir James's face. She found herself face to face with a footman who addressed her politely.

"If you please, Miss, I was asked to deliver this letter and request that you read it immediately."

She took the letter and looked down at the direction. All that was written on it was her name, but she recognised the hand. It was the Sylph's handwriting.

Hardly daring to breathe, she broke open the seal and read the single line it contained:

I am here, watching over you.
Your Sylph.

Panic temporarily froze her senses. She was suspended in time, amid the noisy gathering, with just one thought in her mind. My father is here.

She barely registered Sir James's teasing words.

"What is this? Receiving a letter from a lover when I am before you in the flesh?"

"No, no. You have it wrong," Georgiana assured him absent-mindedly. "I have no lover." All at once, the impropriety of her situation came crashing down upon her. She would rather die than be found like this by her father. He must be furious that she was here to have travelled so far to see her.

"I need to go," she gasped, starting to move away.

"Then the letter tells you to abandon me," Sir James said as he followed her. "To what lengths will I be driven without your love to sustain me? What evil can it tell you that I have not confessed to you myself? I am a broken man, destitute of hope apart from you, my reforming angel. Will you so readily cast aside one who loves you so dearly? Do not desert me," he pleaded, grabbing hold of her arm. "I need you."

Sir James's declarations of love suddenly seemed rather hollow. What did he know of her? Was it wise to fall in love with a pretty face and the appearance of goodness? Where there was no meeting of minds, of faith, of interests?

Georgiana yanked her hand free and plunged into the crowd. She had no idea how she was going to find Beau again. All she wanted was to flee from Sir James and go home, away from the chance of discovery. The Sylph had warned her not to be alone with a man and yet again, she had ignored him. Although surrounded by people, she had behaved as if no one were watching.

Seeing her on her own, a young buck thought she was fair game. "How now, fairy princess. Weave your magic over me."

Georgiana tried to dissuade him, but he seemed oblivious to the fact that his advances were unwelcome. She panicked as the tipsy gentleman went to put his arm around her, but to her relief, he suddenly changed his mind and withdrew.

"Whoa. No offence meant," he said, holding his hands up in apology to someone who had come up behind her as he bid a hasty retreat.

In trepidation, Georgiana turned to find out who had frightened off the over-familiar reveller, hoping that she was not going to have to fight off more unwanted attentions. The colour drained from her face as she stared at the imposing figure of a Persian looming over her. The height of her protector left her in no doubt of his identity. She had received a note saying that the Sylph was watching her and here he was.

Although his bushy beard hid much of his face, she could see enough of it to judge that he was in no good humour. It was as she had feared. Her father was here, and he had come to take her home in disgrace.

"Do you know me?" the Persian asked in a gruff, slightly husky tone.

Georgiana nodded.

"Do you trust me?"

"Yes," she said in a small voice.

"Then why will you not heed my advice? God knows the love I have for you and that I have tried to guide you and protect you from yourself – your lovely, innocent, impulsive self. But to what purpose do I write if you ignore what I say? Tonight, you are Titania, Queen of the Fairies. Do not be bewitched into falling in love with an ass when you deserve a king. You do not understand what manner of man you are dealing with. I don't know what lies you told to allow your presence here, but you must have known that your father would disapprove of such conduct. Be true to yourself, Georgiana. Act in a way that does not disturb your conscience. God bless you."

He pressed a fatherly kiss on her forehead and clasped her by the hand. The Sylph led her through the crowds who instinctively parted to allow the imposing Persian through. He handed her into Beau's care.

"Take your charge home, sir, and I will try to forget you were ever so foolish as to bring her where you might have supposed she would be subject to all kinds of familiarities that can only be abhorrent to a gently bred lady."

Beau stood there with his mouth wide open, failing to think of a suitable retort before the Persian moved away into the crowd.

"Someone you know?" he said, a worried frown on his face.

Georgiana blinked back the tears and nodded. "Please take me home."

Without hesitation, Beau took her hand and headed for the door, muttering under his breath that he had been right all along.

* * *

It was many hours before Georgiana's tranquillity was restored. Bessie tutted and sighed, but she saw the woebegone look on her mistress's face and said nothing. She was too glad to see her girl home safe and sound to scold her anymore. Judging by her expression, the evening had brought punishment enough already.

Georgiana fell into an uneasy sleep, dwelling on her behaviour and how terrible she had been at following the Sylph's advice – advice which she had promised to listen to. She thanked God that he had pointed out the error of her ways and rescued her. If she had not gone off with Sir James, would her father have remained watching over her in silence? After all, he had come in disguise. If she had behaved with propriety, she might never have known he was there.

It was humbling to have been found in such a compromising situation, and she blamed herself for tempting Sir James unfairly. She had encouraged him to think she would welcome his advances by agreeing to meet him where they would both be behind masks.

Though she could not be sorry that her father had reminded her how her behaviour must appear, she was mortified that she had put him to the trouble and expense of posting up to town. She was over-come with gratitude at his gentleness in appearing in disguise thus preventing her from being subject to unbearable humiliation. It was, after all, what she deserved. Her father would have been quite within his rights to have marched into the Argyll Rooms and taken her straight back home to Hampshire like an errant schoolgirl.

To her surprise, her father was not at breakfast the next morning. Even more surprising, there was not a hint from anyone that he had ever been in London. It seemed as if she were to be given another chance and she was desperate to prove that she was worthy of such trust.

She was puzzled how he had learned of the masquerade. Eliza would not have broken her confidence, so she could only assume that Charlotte had got hold of the letter and taken it to her father as a matter of duty. It was the sort of thing she would do.

No more clandestine meetings, Georgiana vowed. If Sir James were honourable, he would court her in the proper way, and give her time to truly know her heart. If not, she needed to refuse to see him before they became irretrievably entangled.

Georgiana wrote to Eliza, giving her a full account of the dreadful evening and expressing her gratitude and amazement that their father hadn't whisked her off home immediately. She begged Eliza to be more careful with her letters in future but refused to blame her for what had happened. The mistake was hers, and hers alone.

CHAPTER 25

L ater that day, Lord Castleford drove Georgiana to St Paul's Cathedral in his phaeton for the charity children's service.

"You seem quiet, Miss Merry," he said, glancing across at her pale, drawn face. "I trust you are not ailing for something."

"I am perfectly well, thank you. Just a little tired."

"Not tired of my company, I hope," he said, trying to provoke a smile.

He succeeded. Georgiana shook her head and laughed.

"How could I be tired of your company? I have not seen you for days. Now if Beau were asking me, the answer might be different. We've been thrown together so often at my aunt's house that I think we are both a little weary of each other."

She hesitated, biting on her bottom lip as if unsure whether to continue. "I have to confess that we don't always like the same things."

"Do you mean to say he won't take you where you want to go?"

Georgiana's smile faded making him realise that his choice of words had been unfortunate. He was referring to her love of the theatre, but he had inadvertently reminded her of the masquerade.

As he had no wish to give away the fact that he knew Beau had taken her to the Argyll Rooms the previous evening, he fixed his gaze on the road ahead and appeared as if he were concentrating all his attention on his horses. He could feel her eyes upon him, studying his face for any sign that he was aware of her secret, but he did not turn.

When he was certain she no longer suspected him of any deeper meaning, he continued.

"I've noticed that Beau does not share your passion for the theatre," he said. "It must be hard to persuade him to go as often as you'd like and somewhat frustrating that his interest in discussing the play is, shall we say, limited."

Georgiana breathed out a sigh of relief and took up the theme. "I knew you would understand," she said. "How can you enjoy a concert when your companion is complaining he can't comprehend a word they're singing? Or worse," she whispered. "Snoring."

Castleford grinned. "That was too bad of him. I hope the performers did not hear."

"I dug him in the ribs until he woke up," she admitted, stifling a laugh. "He vowed he'd never take me to a concert again."

"Dear me. No music. Too little theatre. But perhaps you share a love of poetry. Has Beau been reading *The Lady of the Lake* to you?"

Georgiana giggled. "I can't imagine him ever doing so. I doubt he's aware that Scott has published a new poem if, indeed, he even knows who Scott is."

"You are right, Miss Merry. You do not like the same things. It is fortunate, then, that you are not intending to marry him."

She jerked her head round to look at him. "Why do you say that? Lady Harting is set on my becoming her daughter-in-law."

Castleford could not resist the temptation to quote two lines from *Marmion*:

> *"O what a tangled web we weave,*
> *when first we practise to deceive!"*

Georgiana's cheeks flooded with colour at his words, and she suddenly became very interested in her hands.

"Is it so obvious?" she asked in a timid voice.

"Not perhaps to the world at large, but I am a man in love."

For a full five minutes, neither of them said a word. He had hesitated to declare his love for her to throw it back in his face, but Anthony seemed to think she was looking for reassurance that he still cared for her. A glimmer of hope stirred within him that his feelings meant something to her, that speaking of them could leave her with nothing to say.

When he thought she had dwelt on his words for long enough, he broke the silence, asking for her opinion of *The Lady of the Lake* and talking about poetry until she was her normal chatty self again.

The annual gathering of the charity children of London was the magnificent spectacle that he expected. They had erected temporary galleries in St Paul's which were full of boys and girls dressed in the colours of their schools whose flags waved proudly above them.

"So many children living in poverty," Georgiana said, her eyes filling with tears as she looked around the cathedral. "It is terrifying to realise what an enormous number of poor children there are in London, but the sight here is quite beautiful. It makes me think of some lines from Blake's poem, *Holy Thursday*:

Oh, what a multitude they seemed, those flowers of London town;
Seated in companies they were, with radiance all their own."

He smiled at her. "The beauty is not in their poverty, but in their gratitude for the mercy that has brought them here. Each one is a testament to grace."

She nodded. "Every child here has been blessed by someone showing them love."

When the children sang, she closed her eyes to listen, a peaceful smile on her lips. "It sounds a bit like heaven," she whispered.

His breath caught in his throat as he studied her serene face. He thought she had never looked more beautiful.

As they drove home, Georgiana was pensive.

"Balls and concerts and routs – even the theatre. All the things that seemed so vital yesterday no longer seem important in the face of all those poor children, crying out to be loved."

Castleford nodded in agreement. It was the cry of every human heart, including his own.

* * *

During the week following the charity children's service, life in Harting House became unbearable. After the masquerade, Lady Harting interrogated Beau until she found out where he had taken Georgiana. In his own defence, he had blurted out the truth about their supposed courtship.

Beau had come to Georgiana in despair and told her the whole story. The worst of it was that his mother was not interested that they did not suit. She had been most unpleasant to him, accusing him of being as weak as his father. Still determined to have her for a daughter-in-law, Lady Harting was keeping them both so close to her that Georgiana felt like a prisoner in her aunt's home.

She was looking forward to the Duchess of Devonshire's rout. It might herald the end of the season, but she was starting to think going back to Hampshire would be preferable to the suffocating atmosphere of Harting House.

Georgiana did not care much for routs. There were always so many people crammed into such a limited space that the prospect of finding anyone you knew was uncertain. But here, at least, she would be able to escape from under Lady Harting's eye.

It seemed that the whole of the fashionable world had come to Devonshire House for the rout. Everywhere Georgiana turned, someone greeted her or stopped to talk to Lady Harting.

Lady Frances had been full of herself ever since her engagement. "How incredible that I shall be wed before you, cousin. I cannot say that I thought I would be. Maybe being the daughter of an earl has some benefits over being the daughter of a rector," she said with her annoying titter.

Perhaps you were less particular, thought Georgiana uncharitably.

"Miss Merry," a male voice called out.

Georgiana turned to see Anthony walking across the room toward her, followed by his brother.

"You are looking beautiful tonight," he said, taking her hand and lifting it to his lips and lingering over it in much the same way that Sir James did.

"Do you do that to all the ladies?" she asked curiously.

"Only the pretty ones," he replied with a roguish smile.

She turned to Lord Castleford, a slight blush on her cheeks as she remembered what he had said to her just a few days earlier. He had told her he was a man in love, yet he made no effort to take her hand. She was aware of a hollow feeling, somewhere deep inside, as she realised that he had not said he was still in love with her.

Perhaps he had been trying to break it to her that he had fallen in love with someone else. She felt an urgent need to prove herself wrong.

"Have you no wish to kiss my hand, Lord Castleford?" she said, offering him her hand and looking up into his eyes with a boldness she was far from feeling.

He stood silent for a moment, staring at her hand, and then raised his eyes to hers.

"I would be delighted, Miss Merry, but all I see is a glove."

Georgiana's mouth fell open a little as she digested his words. Was he flirting with her? But he never flirted.

"Oh yes. And I suppose that if I took my glove off to oblige you, it would seem rather fast, and so, perhaps, I had better not," she said, trying not to sound as dazed as she felt as she let her hand drop back to her side.

"Indeed," he answered in a husky voice. "I think you'd better not."

Georgiana stared at him. His voice was so unlike his own. She could not quite make it out. It was familiar, and yet she was sure he had never spoken to her in that tone before. The words coupled with the husky voice were decidedly provocative and she could feel her colour rising under his gaze.

"Pray excuse me, Miss Merry," Anthony said, drawing her attention away from Lord Castleford. "I see Lady Melbourne beckoning me, and I don't like to disappoint an old friend."

He smirked at his brother and swaggered off, leaving her alone with Lord Castleford. She was not sure whether she feared or hoped that he would resume his flirtatious manner with her. He did not.

"What is your view on the death of the Duke of Cumberland's valet?" he asked, breaking the silence before it became awkward. "Do you believe the court's verdict is fair? I have neglected to ask you before and feel sure you have formed an opinion."

The question broke the tension between them and returned things to an even keel. "I have wanted to discover what you thought ever since I read the newspaper report," she said. "Despite what anyone says, I am not convinced that Sellis killed himself."

"Why do you think that?"

"I cannot believe that he is guilty of trying to kill the Duke. If he was intent on murdering his master, why didn't he make a better job of it? He must have had ample opportunity and could have formed an escape plan. Why would he even want to murder his master? Do you suppose he owed him a sum of money that he could not repay?"

"A man may be provoked to irrational behaviour. The Duke has something of a reputation with women. If Sellis discovered his master had seduced his wife, he may have tried to kill him in the anger of a moment. It is an outrage that might push the most peaceable man to madness."

"But I thought the way you men dealt with such things was to challenge the offender to a duel?"

"The Duke would have refused to meet him if his valet had tried to call him out."

"Why? Is the Duke a coward?"

"Sellis was a servant, and duelling is only between gentlemen. It is what some of my sex call a 'gentlemanlike' means of settling a dispute, but I am not of their number. A crime of passion I have some sympathy with, though I could not condone it. But cold-bloodedly standing opposite another man, trying to kill him? How is that different from pre-meditated murder?"

"Is there nothing you think worth fighting for?" she asked.

"Yes, but how could love conquer all if I were lying dead on a duelling field for the sake of upholding my woman's honour?"

Georgiana had a fleeting vision of a bullet soaring through the air toward Lord Castleford and plunging straight into his heart, causing him to collapse, lifeless, on the ground.

She swayed a little, overwhelmed at the depth of pain she felt at such an image and tried to banish the troubling picture from her mind.

Lord Castleford reached out a hand to steady her. "Miss Merry, are you unwell?"

She opened her mouth to speak, but no words came out. All coherent thought had fled, crowded out by the awareness of his touch on her arm. Flustered, she felt the colour rushing to her cheeks and raised her eyes to his in silence.

What she saw in his expression did nothing to restore her equanimity. Concern mingled with something else. Something deeper. And that something made her feel even more flustered.

"I am quite well, thank you," she said at length. "Just momentarily overcome at such a horrid thought."

Her words seemed to deepen that other something in his eyes. She gulped hard. Although she had assured him she was quite well, he seemed in no hurry to remove his hand and she realised she did not want him to. She remembered how safe she had felt in his arms when he had rescued her outside the Magdalen and had a sudden desire to feel his arms around her again.

Lord Castleford was about to say something when Lady Augusta descended on them. He immediately withdrew his arm and Georgiana felt its loss. Never had Augusta's entrance been so ill-timed. What had he been about to say? Georgiana wanted very much to know.

With a great effort of will, she directed her thoughts toward Augusta. "How is the Duke?" she said, clasping her hands in her own.

"Father is doing well, thank you. The doctor believes the shock of Den's departure caused his heart to fail. Now that he is recovering, sea air has been recommended, and so Mama has gone down to Weymouth with him. I am staying with Lord Helston's mother. She has no daughter of her own and I think she wants to help me with my bride clothes, though I am sure Mother will have something to say to that."

Georgiana looked around. "Where is Lord Helston?"

"Out of town for a few days on business. You must keep me company," she said, taking her arm and walking off, giving Georgiana little chance to excuse her sudden departure to Lord Castleford.

"I need to talk to you," Augusta said in an urgent voice as soon as they were out of earshot.

Georgiana peered closely at her. Augusta was smiling, but her eyes looked tired and deeply troubled. "What's the matter?"

"I cannot explain. Not here. Someone might overhear." She opened the door to a side room and seeing that it was empty, she slipped inside, urging Georgiana to follow, closing the door behind them.

"I don't suppose you are beforehand with the world and have any money you can lend me, do you?" she asked nervously.

"How could you possibly be in debt? No matter how much allowance your parents give you, you always contrive to spend it."

Augusta's colour deepened. Georgiana saw the guilt on her face and let out an exasperated sigh.

"Please don't tell me you have thrown away your money on stupid games of chance. You know I hate such needless waste. Gambling destroys people's lives. Besides, I thought you had assured Lord Helston that you would not play for high stakes again."

"I did vow not to wager more than a few shillings and, despite what it looks like, I've kept my promise, truly I have. But he'll never believe me if I need to borrow money from him, and maybe he won't want to marry me anymore and…"

"For goodness' sake, Gusta, do not go into hysterics. Do you wish to draw attention to the fact that we are in a room that I am sure we should not be in? If you don't need money to pay gambling debts, what do you want it for?"

"It is for gambling," Augusta said, wiping away a tear. "But it is an old debt. I lost some money to a gentleman playing hazard. He was happy to take my note and did not seem to care about it being settled. I forgot about it, but he recently sent me a message begging me to make good his debt or he would be obliged to go to my betrothed to retrieve his money."

"If it occurred before you were engaged, I am sure Lord Helston will forgive you. He has always seemed kind, and he dotes on you. Would it be so bad if that happened?"

Augusta sniffed. "You don't understand. For a while, I was passionate about this man. He was exciting to be with. You know how I hate being bound by the rules. I saw him alone. The note is couched in terms that would make Lord Helston doubt my virtue."

She paused and let out a little sigh. "I allowed him to kiss me," she said with a blush, "but nothing more. It was a romantic diversion. That day we went ice skating, we met again, and he asked me to marry him. I had flirted a great deal with him, and I suppose he believed I would welcome his proposal. He was mistaken. I wasn't kind, Georgie and I laughed at him, telling him it was ridiculous to suppose that I would ever marry a man like him."

Her eyes flashed with anger. "The presumption makes me mad even now. To think that he, a mere baronet, imagined that he was good enough to wed the daughter of a duke!"

"Gusta, suppose you were to pay him without telling Lord Helston. Would he not retain some hold over you?"

"Surely not. When I have repaid him, I can put it behind me."

"Is it gentlemanlike behaviour to threaten you with exposure?"

"No, but…"

"Then what makes you think he would behave in a different way afterwards? You must tell Lord Helston. If you are truly sorry, I am confident he will forgive you. He trusts you. If you say you are innocent, he will believe you."

"I can't, Georgie. Please help me."

"How much do you need?"

"Five hundred pounds."

"Five hundred pounds! Do you honestly expect me to have that much money just lying around to lend to you?"

"No, I suppose not, but I'm in such a bother, I cannot think."

Georgiana shook her head. "How is a quarter of such a sum to be found? You must tell Lord Helston before this man does it for you. Don't you see? It is unlikely that your accounts would be the same. If he gives his version to Lord Helston first, it will be hard to prove your innocence."

Augusta looked unconvinced but Georgiana had no other advice to offer.

"Tell Lord Helston," she repeated. "It's the only way. Come, we had better go back before we are missed."

* * *

Their return to the ballroom had been anticipated. As Georgiana shut the door behind them, they were met by Sir James on one side, and Beau and Anthony on the other.

Augusta acknowledged Sir James's greeting with the briefest of nods and demanded Beau's assistance to discover Lady Helston as she had a slight headache and wanted to go home.

It was the first time Georgiana had seen Sir James since deserting him at the public masquerade and she expected a frosty reception, but his manner toward her was unchanged.

"What a vision of loveliness you are tonight, Miss Merry," he said, taking her hand and kissing it like Anthony had done earlier.

Georgiana gave Anthony a speaking look, showing that she knew how this action was to be interpreted. Sir James thought she was pretty, and she glowed with pleasure.

"I see you are intent on making an awkward third, Warren," Sir James said, casting Anthony a look of loathing. "Can't you go away and whisper loving words in some other beauty's ear?"

Anthony looked at her, his eyebrows raised in question.

Georgiana hesitated. Should she encourage him to leave so she could be alone with Sir James? Whilst it was delightful to be the object of such open adoration, she was not at all sure of her own heart. Perhaps if she spent more time with Sir James, all would become clear. It would be a test, she thought, remembering the Sylph's words. She would behave as if her father were watching.

She pleaded with Anthony with her eyes.

"Very well," he said, a grim expression on his face. "I can tell when my presence is not wanted."

Georgiana looked at Anthony's retreating form, sad to have caused offence, but she was in no mind to chase after him. She turned back to Sir James.

"Are you so sorry to see him go?" he teased. "I shall make a jealous husband, I assure you."

"Stop funning," Georgiana said with a frown. "He is my friend, besides being Lord Castleford's brother, and I would rather I hadn't annoyed him."

"Is Lord Castleford so important to you? You see, I am getting envious already. As soon as you mention another man, I become possessive."

"Lord Castleford is my friend too."

"Not your lover?"

"No," Georgiana assured him, a little too quickly. Was she trying to convince herself? She thought of the look in Lord Castleford's eyes when he had expressed a wish to kiss her hand and reddened. It was a side to him she had not seen before. That look hinted that he was not as passionless as she had believed.

Her thoughts were brought back to the present with a bang when Sir James reached out and grasped her hand. "I would like to strip off your glove and plant kisses all over your arm," he said, tracing a line down her glove with his other hand.

Georgiana snatched her hand away. She stood in silence, staring at it, puzzled by the way she had acted on instinct. Lord Castleford had expressed the same wish, to kiss her hand not her glove. So why had his compliment been so pleasing whereas Sir James's words sounded dangerous?

It must be about trust. She trusted Lord Castleford – with her life if need be. But she was drawn toward Sir James like a moth toward a flame. She felt the attraction, but knew, deep down, that she still did not trust him.

Sir James was frowning, discomposed by her reaction. "I am sorry. My feelings overcame me. Do not keep me waiting long, Miss Merry. I am not a patient man."

He gave her a smouldering look that Georgiana found unnerving. Despite being surrounded by people, she felt small and vulnerable and she did not like the sensation.

It was with some relief that Beau came to claim her at his mother's request. Georgiana wanted nothing more than to go home and shut herself away in her room to think.

* * *

Augusta called to see Georgiana the next day. Her face was wreathed in smiles. "I did what you suggested and confessed the truth to Lord Helston as soon as he came home. He was solemn, but he believed me when I told him that I had not given away more than a few kisses. I said I was sorry, and he forgave me, just like you said he would."

Georgiana was glad that Augusta's problems had been resolved so easily. If only hers could be. Her mind dwelt on the events of the previous evening. She had wondered if, despite his failings, she was falling in love with Sir James. Yet last night, his advances had scared her, and she had recoiled from his touch.

How could she love Sir James if she did not trust him? Perhaps it was not love she felt for him at all. Last night, it had been Lord Castleford who had left her wanting more.

She considered writing to Eliza and then remembered the result of her previous letter. It might be as well to write directly to the Sylph. She hoped that despite the fiasco at the masquerade, he would still deign to send her a reply.

> *Dear Sylph,*
>
> *I am so confused. My head and my heart are at war. I thought I was falling in love, but my head questions whether my heart has been deceived. It asks me whether it is possible to love someone that I do not trust. I do not think so. My head asks whether it is conceivable that friendship could grow into love undetected, but my heart wonders how I could be in love without realising it. If a person does not display their feelings for all to see, does it mean that they have none? Surely, I will only be happy if I am united in marriage to one whom I love with my heart and my mind?*
>
> *Could it be that infatuation masquerades as love and love masquerades as friendship?*
> *G.*

* * *

The reply came sooner than she could have hoped for.

My dearest G,

I cannot pretend that I am ignorant of those whom you refer to so obliquely and as I would very much prefer you to accept one over the other, I cannot claim that my advice is impartial. Believe me, however, that as always, I have your best interests at heart.

Do you want to be subject to your emotions or will you let your heart be guided by your mind and by your conscience? You say you do not trust this man. How then could you trust him to remain faithful to you? Could you share with him in matters of faith and learning? Would you be proud to have him as the father of your children?

Allow me to borrow the esteemed Dr Gregory's words: 'Do not give way to a sudden sally of passion and dignify it with the name of love. Genuine love is not founded in caprice; it is founded in nature, on honourable views, on virtue, on similarity of tastes and sympathy of souls.'

Plant love in a bed of trust and it will grow into a healthy plant that will last a lifetime. Infatuation may disguise itself as love for a short while, but if there is no trust, it cannot survive.

You ask whether a person may feel more than they demonstrate. The answer is unequivocally yes! If a person is unsure that their love is reciprocated, they may show far less than they feel for fear of forcing the object of their affection to feign love out of gratitude.

You question whether friendship can grow into love undetected. I believe it can. Love is not always easy to recognise. It does not always come with trumpets announcing its arrival, but you would know if it disappeared. Remember what I once told you about true love and ask yourself this question: if this man went out of your life, would the sun ever shine so brightly again?

Be true to yourself – heart, mind, and soul.

Your devoted Sylph.

She dwelt on the Sylph's words for many hours, turning them over and over in her mind. The Sylph had confirmed what she had already begun to realise. That she could not be in love with Sir James because she did not trust him.

But she trusted Lord Castleford without question. Was it possible that a tiny shoot of love was growing in that bed of trust?

CHAPTER 26

Georgiana was sitting alone in the drawing room a few days later when a footman brought a visiting card up to her. She read the name. Mrs Marchant.

It meant nothing to her. She supposed that the lady must be some acquaintance of her aunt.

"Did you tell Mrs Marchant that Lady Harting was not at home, Stevens?"

"Yes, miss. If you'll pardon my saying, she looked relieved. She asked particularly to see you."

Georgiana wondered whether someone was trying to use her to encroach upon her aunt in her absence. "You are certain that it is a *lady* who has called?"

"Quite sure, miss."

"Very well. Please send her up," Georgiana said, curious to learn why an unknown lady should want to see her. She put aside the letter from Eliza that she had been about to read and waited for her unexpected guest.

Mrs Marchant was an attractive brunette who did not look much older than she was. Georgiana invited her to sit. "I do not think we have met before, Mrs Marchant. Please tell me to what I owe the pleasure of your visit."

"No, we have not been introduced. I wanted to see you alone, to warn you."

Georgiana felt uneasy. What did she need to be warned about? And why would a stranger take that duty upon herself?

"I believe you are acquainted with Sir James Maxwell."

Georgiana blushed. "I am."

"Your blush says it all. I am here to put you on your guard against Sir James."

"And what makes you think I stand in any need of your caution?" Georgiana retorted, somewhat annoyed at the stranger's presumption.

It was Mrs Marchant's turn to colour. "I saw you at the Duchess of Devonshire's rout. I could not help myself from watching him even now." She paused. "We used to be very close."

"I am sorry if you were once fond of him, but why are you here? Out of jealousy?" Georgiana asked with a touch of irritation in her voice.

"Please believe me when I say I am not jealous for his affections anymore. I am happily married to a good man, but I am concerned he may deceive another in the same way he deceived me. May I tell you my story?"

Georgiana found it hard to accept that Mrs Marchant's motives were entirely unselfish, but she had gone to a lot of trouble to warn a stranger.

Mrs Marchant saw her hesitation. "Perhaps it would help if I acknowledged that we have a common friend. I believe you know Lord Castleford?"

Georgiana did not relish the thought of this attractive lady being Lord Castleford's friend. Were they close friends?

"I do," she said coldly.

"You need not look so fierce, Miss Merry. When I say he is my friend, I mean nothing more. I will be forever grateful to him."

Georgiana was intrigued. Mrs Marchant sounded almost reverent when she talked of Lord Castleford. What service could he have done her to provoke such admiration?

"Do continue, Mrs Marchant."

"Thank you. Last year, I turned seventeen and though my father retired from the fashionable world after my mother died, he was determined that I should have a season in London as she would have wished. He hired a respectable lady to launch me into society. Through no fault of that lady, I met Sir James.

"I was fortunate enough to receive several offers of marriage, but I would countenance none of them. I was infatuated with Sir James. He was handsome and charming and seemed to worship the ground on which I walked. We became engaged, but my father did not approve and refused to sanction the marriage. He believed Sir James was after my fortune and that his reputation was such that he could never make me happy. It was his opinion that a man bearing the shame of divorce would turn out to be the worst of husbands."

"Surely that is rather a harsh judgement on a man who was deserted by his wife?" Georgiana said.

"Is that what he told you?"

She nodded.

"I understand why you believe it, but it isn't true. Sir James deserted his wife as soon as she was with child. He squandered her money on wine and women, leaving her alone in his dilapidated house with little to live on, and he did not even deign to return home for the birth of his son. His wife left him because he was cruel and unfaithful. She only stayed as long as she did for the sake of the child, but when her son died, a few days after he was born, she took refuge in her father's house."

Georgiana said nothing. It was disturbing to discover that Sir James had manipulated the truth in his own favour.

"My father pleaded with me to give up Sir James," Mrs Marchant continued, "but I was obstinate and declared that I would stand by him. My father swore that if I continued my engagement, he would have nothing further to do with me. I am an only child and had been too much in the habit of having my own way and believed he would soon submit.

"He was so angry with me for refusing to obey him that I ran away and placed myself under Sir James's protection. Like a romantic fool, I suggested we elope to Gretna. He said it would take time to arrange and I would have to live with him until we could be married. I was so much in love that I overcame my scruples and agreed. He took me to his lodgings, in a shabby part of town. Though he told me it was to avoid detection, I now think it was because he could afford nothing better.

"One evening, a week later, he went out and never came back. The landlord demanded rent, and I had to hand over my pearls to prevent myself being thrown out onto the streets. Three days I waited before I would believe that he had deserted me. You can imagine how I felt. Ruin stared me in the face. I had no money. My virtue was gone. And I had run away from all my friends. I was so ashamed that I could not bring myself to go to my father and was not sure if he could ever forgive me.

"In desperation I thought of the Magdalen Hospital. I had been taken to visit it once as a solemn warning against becoming a fallen woman. Now I had joined their ranks. Thanks to the mercy of God, an admission day was looming, and I duly presented myself. God answered my prayers, and I was given a place. More than that, I was shown kindness. Lord Castleford met with my father. I don't know what he told him, but within a few days, I was back under his roof. My father arranged a marriage for me with a local gentleman who had formed an attachment to me before I went to London and was still willing to marry me."

"But I don't understand. Why would Sir James desert you? Did he give you no warning? If it was your fortune that he was after, as your father believed, why didn't he elope with you?"

"After he left, I tried to discover what had happened to him, thinking some accident had befallen him. The 'accident' was meeting a richer, titled lady who seemed to be falling under his spell as readily as I had done. He abandoned me because he had found a greater source of wealth, and one he believed he could get without making the arduous and expensive journey to Scotland. I think he feared my father might somehow deprive me of my fortune.

"In this lady, Sir James met his match. She kept him hanging on, and from what I have learned of her, I imagine she ridiculed his proposal, forcing him to transfer his attentions to you."

Georgiana could hardly breathe. What had Augusta said? That she had laughed at the proposal of a mere baronet. She did not dare to ask the question on the tip of her tongue. For if the lady that Mrs Marchant was talking about was Augusta, then it was Sir James who had been trying to blackmail her.

She felt almost giddy with shock. Surely Sir James, her Sir James, could not be so heartless, so dishonourable. She did not want to believe it and found herself making excuses for his actions.

This poor lady's experience was terrible, but she must be partly to blame. It showed an innate lack of morality to live with a gentleman who was not your husband.

As for Augusta, she was callous. Sir James's behaviour toward her was wicked, but no doubt it was her cruelty that had provoked such a vengeful response.

She began to question whether Mrs Marchant's story was true. Could she trust the word of a stranger?

"You could not have known Sir James was courting me from what you saw at the rout alone. Do you keep up with Sir James's progress to punish yourself? Why did you come?"

"It would go against my conscience to allow another woman to suffer what I had the means to prevent."

"But you don't know me. You have no obligation to warn me. Why should you care what happens to me?"

Mrs Marchant seemed flustered. "Lord Castleford sent me a note and urged me to visit you. As I have said, I am extremely obliged to him for intervening on my behalf. It was a small favour to ask, and I readily granted it."

Georgiana did not know how to react. She thanked her visitor mechanically for sharing her story and rang the bell for Stevens to show her out.

She was left alone with her thoughts. Lord Castleford had asked Mrs Marchant to visit her. It warmed her heart to think that he still cared what happened to her. That he wanted to protect her. But was it more than that? Was he still in love with her?

But could Sir James be so wicked? Could all she had heard be false? Georgiana gave herself a shake. What was she thinking? Lord Castleford would never have asked Mrs Marchant to lie to her. Every feeling revolted against such a suggestion. She must have been telling the truth.

This conclusion did not, however, give her the peace of mind that she had hoped for. The picture that Mrs Marchant had painted of Sir James was black indeed. It was lowering to think how foolish she had been, duped by flattery and false promises.

Georgiana was fast working herself into a melancholy when her eyes fell on Eliza's letter. She smiled. Her sister's letter was bound to cheer her up. She broke the seal, but the opening lines made her heart stand still.

I write with the utmost urgency to warn you. Father was not in London last week. Your letters have been locked away in a box in my bedroom and not seen by anyone else. How could you doubt me? I do not know who your Sylph is, but he is most definitely not our father. As to his identity, I cannot hazard a guess. What secrets have you been telling a stranger that you thought you were recounting to Father?

Georgiana let the letter drop into her lap. It was a day of surprises. This one was even more severe than the last. Desperately she tried to remember all the things she had written. Had she shared anything intimate that would embarrass her if it were known? She had talked of the struggles of her heart and asked for guidance, but her letters had always been couched in vague terms. No names had been mentioned. The advice had seemed good – like the advice her father would have given her, which is why she had never suspected her original guess was wrong.

Her mind went back to the evening at the Argyll Rooms. She had not questioned her belief that the Sylph was her father when he had appeared in person. A man may hide many things about himself, but he cannot hide his height. The Persian at the masquerade had been a tall man. So tall, in fact, that she had continued to assume that he was her father although his voice had sounded strange. It had been rather gruff, disguising the speaker's normal tone. As if the intention had been to keep the Sylph's identity a secret, even when he was before her.

It had never occurred to her how unlikely it was that her father could have discovered her plan to attend the public masquerade and reached London in time to confront her. Charlotte would have needed to purloin the letter from Eliza as soon as it had been delivered, and then her father would have had to set off immediately to reach London that evening. She had just assumed it had happened that way.

But if the Sylph was not Father, who was he? He must be a gentleman who knew her well, tall enough for her to mistake for her father, and wise enough to give advice like him.

Her jaw dropped as she realised there was only one man who fitted that description. But no. He could not be. Could he? Was it possible that Lord Castleford could be the Sylph?

She recalled their encounter at the Duchess of Devonshire's rout. Lord Castleford had been uncharacteristically flirtatious. His voice had sounded deeper, huskier, than normal, and though strange, she had thought it seemed vaguely familiar. Now she realised why. It was the same husky tone that he had used to address her as the Sylph at the masquerade. The mystery was solved.

Tears welled up in her eyes. Even when she had believed the letters were written by her father, it had felt exciting, like reliving a part of a novel. A romantic way to receive instruction.

Though she did not doubt that Lord Castleford could give her such excellent advice, that he had devised such a romantic method of giving it to her was beyond her comprehension.

She found the pile of letters the Sylph had sent and reread each one. If she were being cynical, she could say that they were designed to turn her against Sir James.

But what had he written? *Even the most honourable of men may be tempted by such beauty within his reach.* Lord Castleford was the most honourable man of her acquaintance. Was he telling her that he was tempted when he was alone with her?

Now she knew he was the writer, the letters took on a new meaning. Did he love her so much that he would warn her not to be alone with him? He had never spoken a word directly against Sir James, though he had, she thought, with a wicked smile at the recollection, called him an ass at the masquerade.

Her feelings were hard to describe. It was as if she had woken from a long, drug-induced dream. She felt…cherished. Lord Castleford had sent Mrs Marchant to her because he feared Sir James had deceived her. He wanted her to have all the facts so she could make the right choice.

In *A Midsummer Night's Dream*, Queen Titania was bewitched, so she fell in love with an ass. Georgiana realised that she had been just as bewitched. How had she been so blind? She had thought her relationship with Lord Castleford had settled into one of friendship, but all the time, he had been sending her anonymous love letters.

But if Lord Castleford were the Sylph, how could he urge her to openness when he was not so himself? It seemed that he could be secretive when it suited him. He could not know what she was going to write in those letters. She might have said something not meant for the ears of a gentleman who was no relation. Though she supposed it was not his fault that she had assumed the Sylph was her father.

It was most improper – but very romantic. Perhaps that was the place of romance – as part of a deeper, enduring love.

She bit her lip as she realised what she was thinking. Was it as simple as that? She had fallen in love with Lord Castleford without even realising it. Discovering that he was the Sylph was profoundly moving. That he would take such care of her – that he wanted to protect her from a poor alliance, even when she had all but rejected him.

But it had not caused her to fall in love with him. Rather it had made her look anew at her heart and discover the love that was already growing there.

Georgiana knew that she needed to write one more letter to the Sylph.

Dear Sylph,

It is time to follow your own advice and come out of the shadows. Do not hide behind this mask any longer. I will stay home from the theatre tonight. If the gentleman who has been masquerading as the Sylph has spoken from his heart, then let him come now and speak for himself.

G.

She hoped it was not too forward, but she could see no other way of persuading Lord Castleford to own the sentiments expressed in his letters. Should she send it to his home rather than to the White Horse where all the other communications had been directed? No. She decided it was best to keep the anonymity to the end.

What of Sir James? There was no longer any doubt in her mind. She did not love him. Had never loved him. She had been bewitched by his charm and, she had to confess, had revelled in his open adoration when Lord Castleford had seemed critical or disinterested.

It was lowering to think she had been deceived. How could she ever forgive herself for being taken in by such a man? If only Sir James were not the complete blackguard she now believed him to be.

CHAPTER 27

Georgiana went to her room and rang for Bessie. It was still more than an hour until she needed to dress for dinner, and she thought a good brisk walk would help to clear her head. She was surprised how anxious she felt. Lord Castleford would come, wouldn't he?

Bessie commented on the bloom in her cheeks. "Why, you're glowing as if you just found a pot of gold at the end of a rainbow, Miss Georgiana," she said, giving her mistress a knowing look.

"I think I have," Georgiana said with a dreamy smile. "My blue pelisse and the matching bonnet, please Bessie. And my half-boots. I'm going for a walk."

Bessie huffed. "Walking? The sun might be shining now, but it looks like rain. I hope you don't intend to go for miles. We'll get soaked."

"Far be it from me to take you out for a possible soaking. Perhaps I'll shock Stevens by taking him with me instead," she said, referring to the youngest of Lady Harting's footmen.

"Well, I suppose there's no harm in that, and I'm sure his long legs will have no problem keeping up with you. Mind you're not late back for dinner. I know what you're like when you get walking. You lose all sense of time. I don't want you having to scramble into your evening gown in five minutes flat."

"Do not fuss, Bessie," she said. "I'll be here in plenty of time. I am expecting a visitor tonight and I have no intention of missing him."

Georgiana set off at a brisk speed, smartly dressed in her pelisse of pale celestial blue, followed, at a discreet distance, by Stevens, who had not objected in the slightest to accompanying the mistress's niece on her walk.

It was only a short way to Hyde Park and as they entered the gates, she slackened her pace. She was lost in her thoughts when she heard a man's voice calling out to her. It was Sir James, driving his curricle, pulled by his beautiful greys. Could he really be as hard up as Mrs Marchant had made out if he could afford an equipage like that?

He drew his carriage to a standstill and held his horses in check whilst he spoke to her. "May I invite you up for a drive, Miss Merry? I am sure your servant will wait while we take a turn around the park."

Georgiana hesitated. She did not want to be alone with Sir James but was aware of a burning desire to hear his side of the story. Perhaps he could lighten the dark picture she now had of his character.

It would not change the way she felt about him. She did not love him. How could she when she was in love with someone else? But if she could learn that he was not quite the scoundrel she currently thought, she would not feel so wretched about having fancied herself in love with him.

"Very well," she said, deciding to take advantage of this unexpected opportunity to speak to him. What harm could come to her in an open carriage in the middle of Hyde Park? Sir James would be too busy with his horses to do more than talk.

Sir James's man jumped down and helped her climb up into the curricle. With a nod from his master, he stepped back. Sir James flicked his whip and his horses pulled away at a brisk trot.

"Fortune is smiling on me," he said. "I did not dare to hope that our paths would cross today. You look more beautiful every time I see you."

The compliments that had sounded so flattering just a few days before now seemed rather commonplace. She smiled to herself. Realising she was in love with Lord Castleford had changed everything.

"I am so glad of this chance to talk with you, Sir James," she began. "I have heard such stories about you that have forced me to think your character is past reclamation."

"Come, come, Miss Merry. I've not hidden my mistakes from you. You know what I am. That's why I need you so much. You said you believed in second chances."

"Yes, I do. But what is the point in giving you a second chance when you have not had a change of heart? How many chances do you need before you repent of your way of life and reform your ways?"

"I confessed to you from our earliest acquaintance that I had been unlucky in love."

"Indeed, you did."

"That my wife had deserted me and left me to grieve alone."

"I have since heard a different story from the one you told me. That your wife divorced you because you deserted her."

A flash of annoyance passed over Sir James's face, but it was gone as quickly as it had come and now a mournful look rested on his features.

"Pity me. Can you blame me for escaping her presence when all she did was complain that I did not love her? I discovered that I had married a shrew and I ran from the scene of my unhappiness."

Georgiana felt more anger than pity. "You promised to love her and cherish her. Did your marriage vows mean nothing to you?"

Sir James made no reply.

"There is more. What of the lady you eloped with last summer and then abandoned without a word?"

"I don't know what you are talking about."

"I have met her."

"Did she tell you I stole her away from her father's house?" he snapped. "I did not. She was obsessed with me. I could not get rid of her. What was I supposed to do?"

Georgiana was not mollified. Mrs Marchant had confessed her own silliness, but that did not excuse the part that Sir James had played. "She came to you under a false premise. You promised to marry her, but then you abandoned her."

"I could not go through with it when I discovered I was mistaken in my feelings. Would you have condemned me to another unhappy marriage?"

"You left her, not knowing or caring whether she was already carrying your child. How could you? And for what? A better prize. Do not imagine I am ignorant of who your next prey was. Did you not consider that when you threatened her, she might confide in me?"

"You have painted me black as coal," Sir James replied, "but I never knew love until I met you."

Georgiana shook her head in amazement. "Haven't you heard anything I am saying? I hoped that you would deny these accusations, not attempt to justify your wickedness. That you would try to clear your name."

"Don't you see how much I need you? With your guiding hand to reform me, I could become a new creation. Marry me and transform the life of a poor sinner."

Georgiana thought of the warning from *Coelebs* that the Sylph had reminded her of and shook her head. "I am sorry, but I am one with Miss Stanley on this point."

"Miss Stanley? Who the deuce is Miss Stanley?"

"She is the heroine of a novel I've read."

"I hate to disillusion you, but no self-respecting man wastes his time reading novels."

Georgiana thought of the Sylph letters Lord Castleford had written and smiled. "You are wrong. Respectable men are not afraid to admit reading a decent novel. Whilst undoubtedly some novels are not worth anyone's time to read, there are others which guide us in our moral journey and encourage us to walk the right path in life."

"What of this Miss Stanley?" he asked irritably.

"She refused to marry a lord based on his vow to reform, for she reasoned that if he failed to transform his lifestyle, it would be too late to change her mind. I do not choose to marry you, Sir James, despite your promise to reform. What if you never changed? I would be stuck with a dissolute husband, and I should only have myself to blame for having believed your promises."

Sir James said nothing.

* * *

Georgiana did not want to spend another minute in Sir James's company. He had failed to say a single word to improve her opinion of him.

Sir James, however, was not ready to give her up. Instead of setting her down, he raced his curricle through the gates of the park, and out onto the Kensington Road.

"Take me back at once," she ordered. "I have nothing more to say."

"But I do," he said. "I'll drive you to Richmond Park. You once told me you'd never visited and I'm sure you'll like it. I need more time to talk to you and make you understand."

"I don't want to go to Richmond Park," she snapped. "Turn your curricle around this minute. My aunt's footman is waiting for me."

"Give me another chance."

Georgiana was unmoved. "Take me back."

"I can't do that," Sir James said, slowing his curricle down as they approached a tollgate. "Not until I've had a chance to put things right between us."

Georgiana felt her anger growing as Sir James refused to take her back. But short of jumping down from the curricle while it stopped at the tollgate, risking breaking a leg or maybe even her neck, there was nothing she could do. She stared straight ahead, a stony expression on her face, refusing to give him the slightest encouragement to continue.

Despite this, he seemed determined to talk. "You have not heard how my story started," he said. "My father was a drunkard and a gambler. When he finally drank himself into an early grave, all I inherited with the baronetcy was a rundown estate, mortgaged up to the hilt. I was forced to marry for money. But I made a poor choice, and paid the price, and I've been trying to recover ever since. No one taught me how to love. You could teach me, Georgiana. Pity me. Rescue me from myself."

"I would rather entrust my future to a man who has already proved his worth – to a gentleman whom I know to be honourable and kind and reliable."

"With your help, I could be like that."

"It is no good, Sir James. I don't love you."

"You could learn to love me."

"I can't."

"Is there nothing I can do to make you change your mind?" he asked in a quiet voice. "You are my angel, my salvation. I am lost without you."

"Without me or without my fortune?"

Once more, Sir James lapsed into silence.

Georgiana cast an anxious look at the clouds which had grown ominously dark. "Please take me back before we get wet."

Even as she spoke, the first drops of rain fell.

"There is a hostelry a little further up this road where we can shelter," Sir James said. "If the weather does not ease up, I'll hire a more suitable vehicle to carry you home in. I would hate to return you soaked to the skin."

"Very well," said Georgiana, "but do let us hurry. I want to be back for dinner."

By the time they pulled in at the coaching inn, the pair of them were already uncomfortably wet. They were shown into a private parlour where Sir James encouraged her to drink something from a flask he took from inside his coat.

"This will help keep the cold out until you can dry off properly."

Judging by the smell, she presumed it was spirits and pushed it away with a shake of her head. He shrugged his shoulders and lifted it to his own lips, drinking deeply before tucking the bottle back inside his coat.

Feeling damp and cold, she sat down by the window, and watched the raindrops sliding down the glass, whilst Sir James went to hire a closed carriage to take her home.

When he returned with the news that he had hired a chaise, Georgiana noticed that his cheeks were flushed red. At first, she thought he must have been sitting too close to the fire. Then the truth dawned. He had been drinking. She hoped, for her sake, that he had not drunk much.

"Come, my dear," he urged, "or we will not get you home before they send out a search party for you."

"I hope not," Georgiana said. "I would not want my aunt to worry. Poor Stevens. He'll think I've forgotten him. I trust he is not still standing in the rain waiting for me. Surely he will realise that you will take me straight back to Harting House now that it has started pouring with rain."

They walked to the door of the inn. "A post-chaise and four?" she said, seeing the vehicle that Sir James had hired to transport her back to her aunt's house. "You are taking your responsibility of getting me back in time for dinner very seriously."

She climbed into the carriage and was somewhat surprised when Sir James climbed in after her.

"I hope you will forgive me, Miss Merry, but I am sure you would not be so uncharitable as to consign me to the elements."

"No, I suppose not," she said, a wary expression in her eyes as she shifted her position to the furthest corner of the seat. It was one thing to go out driving with a gentleman in an open carriage without a chaperon, and quite another to sit on her own with a man in an enclosed space. She had never wished for Bessie more. Being alone with Sir James made her feel decidedly uncomfortable.

The carriage headed off at a spanking pace and Georgiana was glad that she did not travel as badly as her sister Charlotte or she would be feeling most unwell.

It was ironic that she should be travelling like this with Sir James when all her hopes and dreams were centred on someone else. A few months ago, she would have treasured such an adventure. Now, she just wanted it to be over. She had no intention of making conversation with Sir James. It was disappointing that he could not say anything to redeem himself, but she was glad it was only her pride that was hurt and not her heart.

She undid the ribbon of her bonnet and slipped it off her head. It would never be the same again. The blue feather which had been the pinnacle of Mrs Wardle's beautiful creation had not taken well to the rain and was drooping rather forlornly. She laid the soggy hat on the seat beside her and steered her thoughts into more cheerful channels.

It would not do to let one ruined bonnet dull her excitement. She was on her way to see Lord Castleford. He would ask her to marry him and she was going to say 'yes'. She would have the happy ending she longed for.

It was hard to sit still. She fidgeted in her seat, counting the minutes before she could reasonably expect to be back at her aunt's house. Would Lord Castleford come as soon as he had received her message? Yes, of course he would. He would be as eager as she was to end the charade. Unless he had left town. The thought momentarily troubled her, but she dismissed it. He would not have gone out of town without taking his leave.

Would the meeting be awkward? How would she explain how she had learned that he was the Sylph? She would have to admit that she had assumed the letters were written by her father. Would he be offended by that? She hoped not. What would he say when she told him that she had suddenly discovered that her feelings for him ran far deeper than friendship? She still found it hard to believe herself. It had been a revelation.

Georgiana felt a slight uneasiness in her stomach. Whilst she did not travel as poorly as Charlotte, the speed at which they were going was beginning to make her feel unwell. It was as if they were a couple fleeing to the border to get married, the carriage was going so fast. At least it meant she would be home in time for dinner.

Absent-mindedly, Georgiana stared out of the window. The rain was lighter now. She looked over the fields and saw the sheep standing in bedraggled huddles. It was a depressing sight. Judging by how damp her pelisse felt, she imagined she did not appear much different from one of the sheep.

When they slowed down for the turnpike, Georgiana looked out the window again, expecting to see the familiar sight of Hyde Park coming into view, but instead she saw yet more fields.

She turned to Sir James in surprise. "I think the coachman must be going the wrong way. I do not recognise this place at all. Shouldn't we be back in Kensington by now?"

"I am afraid we are not going to Kensington."

"Not going? I don't understand."

"I am passionately in love with you, Georgiana, and determined to persuade you to be my wife. You must change your mind. I need you. Have pity on me and rescue me or condemn me to perdition forever."

"Only God can forgive a man and give him a fresh start, Sir James. I do not have the power to transform you and I cannot marry you."

"You must," Sir James insisted. "I need your help to reform my ways. Have mercy on me."

"I cannot," Georgiana replied in a tone that brooked no contradiction. "There is nothing on earth that you could say to me to make me change my mind. I am in love with someone else."

Leaning toward her, Sir James reached out and stroked her cheek with his finger, whispering in her ear, "Then I will have to persuade you with more than words."

Georgiana jumped as if she had been scalded and batted his hand away with her own. "Do not touch me, Sir James, or I will scream."

"You did not always find my touch so repulsive," he snarled. "Is marrying me such a dreadful prospect? I can be charming, you know. You believed you were in love with me not so long ago. I am certain you can fall in love with me again."

"Please do not talk like that. You will not make me change my mind. I would rather spend the rest of my life in a convent than marry you."

"Very well, madam," Sir James said with a scowl. "If that is how you are going to treat me, I will know how to act. Do not think you can escape me when we stop to change horses. He drew out the bottle of spirits from inside his driving coat. I will pour this whisky down your throat so that you'll be too drunk to escape."

Sir James picked up her bonnet and tossed it on the floor. Georgiana trembled as he moved along the seat toward her and pressed his body up so close to her that she could smell the alcohol on his breath. He held the bottle to her lips and gripped the back of her neck so tightly that it hurt. She had no choice but to drink.

"Ugh!" she exclaimed in revulsion. "Please don't make me swallow any more of that."

"Just a little more – for now," he said. "I don't want you falling ill from sitting in those damp clothes."

With these words, he forced her to drink again and then sank back in his seat. He smiled, but it was not a pleasant smile. It was a predatory smile, and Georgiana knew that she was the prey.

Too late, she realised that her impulsiveness had thrown her into Sir James's power. She had been looking for something to credit to his account, so that her remembrance of him was not so grim. But all she had discovered was that his heart was as black and rotten as she had been told. He had taken advantage of her generosity in not condemning him to travel outside the coach, and she had put herself in a compromising and dangerous position.

Refusing to let fear overwhelm her, she allowed it to feed her anger. "They were right, weren't they? All of them. They warned me you were a fortune hunter – that you were not to be trusted."

"Oh yes, I need your money, but believe me when I say that I am more than reconciled to taking you to wife. I am passionately in love with you."

"Love, Sir James?" She spat the words out as if they were poisonous. "What do you know of love? Love is a gift that is offered without knowing whether it will be received. You cannot make another receive that love, if love it is, and you cannot force another to love you. Love is a choice. Love does not depend on what you can get out of the other person. True love is unconditional."

"That is all very pretty, but I simply cannot afford not to marry you. I had thought I would be able to persuade your silly relation to be my wife, but Lady Augusta had the gall to laugh in my face. Revenge will be sweet when I force her to accept me as her relative once I have married you. But do not think that I am averse to it. I would never have guessed that your dowry was so substantial if Beau had not let it slip while he was in his cups. I plied him with gin hoping to fleece him at cards but found to my disgust that he didn't play. However, I saw at once that what he revealed about you was much more valuable. Poor Beau. He was so distressed at the prospect of courting you that I felt moved to cut him out."

"Then it was all planned? From our first meeting."

"The romantic rescue of your reticule?" he said with a sneer. "Of course, it was planned. Did you honestly suppose it could be a coincidence that I appeared just a moment after your bag was stolen? Your gullibility is so endearing. I can assure you I would never have caught the thief if he were not in my pay. Those child thieves are slippery devils."

Georgiana felt completely humbled. Castleford had hinted that the meeting was not a coincidence and she had dismissed his suspicion out of hand. But he had been right. They had all been right. Sir James was not to be trusted and she was a fool.

While they talked, her mind tried to come up with a solution to her problems. If she could get out of the carriage, she might find some chance to escape. She closed her eyes and prayed that God would rescue her.

As she prayed, her stomach lurched unpleasantly. The combined effects of the speed they were travelling and the liquor that Sir James had forced her to drink were making her feel queasy. Perhaps if she pretended that she was going to be sick, she could scare Sir James into stopping the chaise.

"I don't feel well," she moaned.

She did not expect Sir James's unsympathetic response. He held the bottle of vile liquid to her lips again.

"Here, take some more of this. It will help to settle your stomach."

Closing her eyes, Georgiana took a mouthful of whisky. It burned her throat so much she could scarcely breathe. She sat in silence, gazing out of the window, until she saw they were approaching a village. It was time to make her bid to escape.

"Sir James," she whimpered. "I feel sick."

Instead of stopping the carriage, he held the bottle to her lips again. "Here, have some more. It will help you sleep. We've a long journey ahead."

She had no option but to take another swig of liquor. Now she realised there was no need to pretend. She was going to be sick.

"Please stop the carriage," she said urgently, pulling her smelling salts from her reticule and holding them to her nose. "I am about to be most unwell."

Sir James cursed under his breath. Like many seemingly brave men before him, he quaked at the thought of sickness. They had slowed to go through the village of Cranford, and he rapped on the roof of the carriage to stop as they approached the Berkeley Arms.

"If you so much as squeak," he snarled, "I will pour the rest of this bottle down your throat so that you are so drunk you cannot stand up, let alone run away."

"How loverlike of you," Georgiana taunted.

The landlord hurried out to greet them. He rarely had the chance to serve the quality, who tended to stop at the White Hart, the post-house on the other side of the road. An ostler ran to the horses' heads and Sir James helped Georgiana out of the carriage.

"Pray bring help, man. My wife is most unwell."

Georgiana winced at his words and was about to argue that she was not his wife when she realised in what light she must otherwise appear, emerging from a closed carriage with no companion except Sir James.

The landlord took one glance at her pale face and urgently called his wife to take madam up to the best bedchamber and attend her.

A red-faced lady with a cheery manner bustled out of the inn and took Georgiana in hand. She led her upstairs and helped her remove her pelisse and dress and tucked her into bed.

"You'll feel better soon, my dear," she said, as she provided Georgiana with a basin. "These early months are always a bit trying. I know when I was expecting my first, I only had to travel down the street in a carriage before I felt so sick, I had to stop. Never mind, my dear. I won't let that brute of a husband of yours make you travel any further today. Anyone can see the effect this journey is having on you. What kind of man is he to force you to travel in your condition? I'll give him a piece of my mind when I go below. You're worn out and need a good night's rest."

The landlady drew the curtains and tiptoed out of the bedchamber.

Georgiana was embarrassed that the woman thought she was with child but felt too ill to care. She dozed a little but was disturbed by Sir James coming into the room. She sat bolt upright and pulled the covers up to her neck. Sitting up so quickly was a mistake. Her head began to spin again, and the nausea came back with full force.

"Come, Georgiana. Stir yourself. We must be on our way."

"Have you no sympathy?" she retorted. "If you make me move, you will regret it."

"If you prefer, we could spend the night here," he said in a menacing voice, walking over to the bed. He bent to plant a kiss on her lips, but he was forestalled by Georgiana's urgent plea.

"I need the basin. Now."

He handed her the basin and left. He could not get out of the room quick enough. Even Sir James shied away from making love to a woman who was being violently sick.

Not long after, the landlady came bustling back into the room. "You poor dear," she cooed, relieving Georgiana of the basin. She wiped her face with a damp cloth and urged her to sleep.

"I'll take some dinner to your husband and tell him to let you rest here for the night," she said.

"Dinner?" moaned Georgiana, putting her hand over her mouth as the nausea threatened to overcome her again. She had missed dinner. No one would know what had become of her or where to look for her. How was she going to get home?

Whatever would Lord Castleford think when she was not there after she had asked him to come? Would he believe that Sir James had brought her here against her will?

CHAPTER 28

Lord Castleford did not get Georgiana's note until late in the day. The letter had, as usual, been forwarded immediately from the White Horse, Fetter Lane, as per his instructions, but he was not at home to receive it. He had been kept at the Magdalen Hospital longer than normal as he had been trying to arrange a reconciliation between one of their newest inmates and her family, and he did not arrive home until just before the dinner hour.

As soon as he saw the writing, he tore open the seal and read Georgiana's brief message. He stood, motionless, staring at the letter, hardly daring to believe what he was reading. *If the gentleman who has been masquerading as the Sylph has spoken from his heart, then let him come now and speak for himself.* As the words sunk in, a smile hovered over his lips and gradually spread until his whole face was alight with joy.

His instinct was to rush to Georgiana's side, but common sense soon prevailed. He could not break in on Lady Harting's dinner table uninvited, especially since it was unlikely that she would welcome him when she learned why he had come. With a wistful sigh, he thought it was a shame that Georgiana was not still staying with her grandmother. There he would have been certain of an enthusiastic reception.

Curbing his impatience, Castleford dressed for the evening with extra care and forced himself to dine, though on this occasion, he did not do justice to his chef's culinary creations. While he ate, he considered how early he dare call on Georgiana, and then counted the minutes until the precise hour he should order his carriage so he would arrive there at the earliest possible moment.

The rain had cleared by the time he was set down outside Harting House. He ran up the steps like a schoolboy returning home for the holidays and rang the bell with considerable vigour. Mouth dry, he waited, finding it difficult to stand still, scarcely daring to hope that Georgiana had changed her mind, and yet convinced that she would not have sent him that letter if her heart did not belong to him.

The stately butler opened the door but attempted to deny him access. "Lord and Lady Harting are not at home to visitors."

"I think you will discover that Miss Merry will see me," Castleford said, pushing past the astonished Tomkins with unaccustomed zeal.

Tomkins was not used to dealing with persons of quality who would not take his 'no' for an answer. He shut the door behind him and led the way upstairs.

"You had better come up to the drawing room," he said, in a melancholy voice.

Even in his anxiety to see Georgiana, Castleford could not help wondering why anyone would employ such a gloomy butler.

"If you could just send a message in to Miss Merry," he suggested, "there is no need for me to disturb the family. I can wait for her in the library. I am sure she will come and talk to me there."

"You had better come up to the drawing room," Tomkins repeated.

Castleford was annoyed at the butler's persistence, but he had no other choice than to follow him upstairs.

Tomkins opened the drawing room door and announced in a voice of doom, "Lord Castleford."

It was doubtful whether anyone heard him.

Castleford stood on the threshold of the room and stared at its occupants in amazement. The normally robust Lady Harting was reclining on a sofa, one hand clutching her smelling salts whilst the other clasped her son's as though she were in dire need of support. Lady Frances was sitting beside her, sobbing quietly, dabbing at her eyes with a handkerchief.

Beau was in the middle of a heated conversation with his mother.

"Beaumont, you must go after her," said Lady Harting in a powerful voice that belied the pathetic appearance she was presenting. "She is young and innocent and does not know what a disastrous step she is taking."

"I'll go if you will come with me."

"Come with you? When I am prostrated with anxiety? Impossible! Besides, a woman would just slow you down. It is of paramount importance that you make all speed."

"I see what you're at, Mother. You think to turn this to your own ends by making me go alone to bring her back so I will have to marry her."

Castleford had heard enough. "Where is Miss Merry?" he asked, in a voice that cut through the furore. Three pairs of eyes looked at him in dismay.

Lady Frances promptly burst into tears again whilst her mother glared at her uninvited visitor with palpable loathing. It was Beau who came to his senses first and explained how things stood.

"Georgie – I mean, Miss Merry – has disappeared."

"Disappeared? I don't understand."

"We believe that she has eloped – with Sir James Maxwell," Beau said.

Castleford did not believe that for a moment. "No."

"No?" said Beau. "How can you say that with such conviction? You have not heard what happened."

"Enlighten me."

"Miss Merry went out for a walk this afternoon accompanied by a footman. Stevens returned alone. He said Sir James had taken her up for a drive around the park, but though he waited for her for over an hour, she never came back. As it had started to rain, he thought Sir James must have driven her straight home and returned to the house. It is well past dinner time, and she is still not here."

"What makes you think she has eloped?" Castleford asked. "Even had Sir James fooled her into thinking she was in love, she would never behave so rashly."

As he said it, he thought of her impulsiveness – the impulsiveness that had led her to elope once before. But no. She had invited him to visit her and he was sure that she had intended to be here to see him. Something had prevented it. Something beyond her control.

"It is more likely that their carriage has suffered an accident."

"If that is the case, why have we received no word?" Lady Harting said.

Castleford had to admit that he would have expected to have heard of a mishap by now. He requested that the footman be summoned so he could question him.

Stevens was soon fetched, and he stood, trembling, before Castleford's stormy face.

"The gentleman – Sir James, that is – hailed Miss Merry whilst we were walking and asked to take her up for a drive in his curricle. I hope I didn't do wrong, but I saw no harm in it, being as Miss knew the gentleman and it being usual for ladies to be driven around the park."

"Thank you, Stevens."

After the footman had left the room, Castleford turned to Beau. "It seems that Miss Merry went off with Sir James willingly enough. But in a curricle? It does not sound like an elopement to me."

"I see your point," said Beau, "but they could have changed to another vehicle later."

"Did she take any clothes with her?"

"I don't know."

"You don't know. Haven't you talked to her maid?" he asked in a patronising tone.

Beau confessed that he had not thought of talking to Georgiana's maid. He summoned Bessie to join them in the drawing room.

She stood there, wringing her hands, looking most uneasy.

"Are any of Miss Merry's clothes missing?" Beau asked.

Bessie looked at him as if he were out of his mind. "Pardon me, but my mistress should have been back over an hour ago, and you want to know if any of her clothes are missing?"

"Lady Harting seems to be under the illusion that Miss Merry has eloped," Castleford explained.

"Eloped? I think not, my lord," Bessie said gruffly. "My mistress knows better than that. And who do they think she might have eloped with, if you'll pardon my asking?"

"Sir James Maxwell."

Bessie's face clouded over. "I don't trust him. Lots of terrible stories about him and if you ask me, there is no smoke without a fire. I hope my precious girl is safe."

"As do I, Bessie," Castleford said. He turned to Beau. "What have you done so far to trace them?"

Beau blustered and mumbled and was forced to admit they had been arguing ever since they had noticed Georgiana's protracted absence and had done nothing.

Castleford's temper was rising. "So, you have assumed that Miss Merry has stayed away with Sir James of her own accord, long after you expected her home, and you are sitting here fighting rather than making any attempt to find them. Having ruled out the possibility that they are eloping, there are only two alternatives left. Either their carriage has met with an accident and word has not yet reached us, or Sir James has abducted Miss Merry and means to make her marry him."

"Come now, Lord Castleford," Lady Harting said. "You have read too many romances. Sir James could not abduct Georgiana in broad daylight. Besides, you heard from Stevens that she went with him willingly."

"Lady Harting, I know enough of Sir James to fear what he is capable of. His circumstances are straitened, and desperation may push a man to desperate measures. Miss Merry may have unwittingly put herself in his power. Have you no concern for her safety?"

"How dare you suggest that I am uncaring? I am distraught," Lady Harting wailed.

"And the woman I love is in danger," Castleford retorted in a sharp voice that took his audience by surprise. "If Georgiana had been more closely chaperoned, this could never have happened. I hold you to blame, Lady Harting, if any harm has come to your niece."

None of the occupants of the room had ever heard Castleford lose his temper before. In fact, none of them knew he had a temper to lose, as he kept it under such rigid control. Even Lady Harting withered under his contemptuous words and found nothing to say in her defence.

"Beaumont, I need a favour. Sir James has a long start on me and if I am to overtake them, I must have as much speed as possible. As your horses are quite the best in town, I believe I must beg the loan of your pride and joy. I feel sure you will be happy to lend them to me, to pursue the woman that I know you have no intention of marrying."

"At your service," Beau said. "I'll even drive them for you."

"A handsome gesture," Castleford replied, "but unnecessary."

Beau grinned. "Actually, I'm thinking of my horses."

As they headed out the door, Castleford paused and turned to address Lady Harting. "I'm going after them and I will find your niece. If Sir James has harmed her, I will make him sorry he was ever born."

The door slammed shut behind him and Lady Harting went into genuine hysterics.

*　*　*

The door shut behind the landlady, and Georgiana was left alone. She knew she must try to escape from Sir James while she had the chance.

Little by little, she sat up and was relieved to find that her head was no longer spinning, though it still ached more than she would have believed possible.

What was she going to do? The landlady seemed friendly, but if Georgiana announced that she was not Sir James's wife, she would be outraged, and might throw her out on the streets, thinking her a loose woman.

With grim determination, she slipped out of bed and pulled on her gown. She could not do up all the buttons but dared not call for help. It was easy to find her pelisse and boots, but she could not see her bonnet anywhere. Perhaps it was still in the carriage where she had taken it off. She could not waste time searching for it. The hat was ruined anyway.

Of more concern was her missing reticule. Her purse contained the small amount of money she had with her. Without it, she had nothing. Reluctantly, she concluded that it too must have been left on the seat when she was hustled out of the carriage because of her indisposition.

She opened the door and peeped out. The corridor was empty. Shutting the door behind her, as quietly as she could, she hurried along the hallway, down the stairs, and into the vestibule. As she reached the taproom, she could see Sir James's back through the open doorway. He was sitting at a table with a bottle of wine next to him and was no doubt tucking into a hearty meal.

She put her hand to her mouth. The thought of food still had an unfortunate effect on her stomach. She strode past the entrance to the taproom and through the front door.

Once out on the street, she did not know which way to go. How was she going to get back to her aunt's house without any money? She looked down at her dishevelled appearance. Her pelisse was damp, she had no bonnet, and her hair was all adrift from sleep. And she was on her own. She did not look like a lady of quality but someone who belonged in the Magdalen.

It would be dark in a few hours. What was she going to do? If she could not return to her aunt's house tonight, she was ruined. Nobody would believe in her innocence when she had left London in the company of such a man. Would they believe her anyhow? She had been alone in a bedchamber with Sir James.

She shuddered. No doubt it had been his intention to seduce her. She never thought she would thank God for making her vomit. Her sickness could not have been better timed. Even in her distress, it brought a smile to her face to recall Sir James's horror when she had announced that she was going to be very unwell.

As she walked down the road past a row of houses, she encountered a few stares from passers-by. She wrapped her arms around herself, as if she could hide her shame, mortified by the picture she was presenting.

What would Lord Castleford think of her now? The footman would tell her aunt that she had gone off willingly with Sir James. Lady Harting would be furious and would doubtless make sure that Lord Castleford knew. Her aunt would not scruple to destroy her character if she felt it was in her interests. She could not blame Lord Castleford for believing that she had changed her mind again and chosen Sir James over him.

The tears flowed, falling down her face in silence, clouding her vision. What a fool she had been. Would she never learn to think through the consequences of her actions? The effects of today's impulse could haunt her for the rest of her life. She prayed desperately for another chance. A chance to redeem herself in Lord Castleford's eyes. A chance to make a better choice.

She looked up and saw the spire of the local church in the distance. The sight made her heart feel lighter. She was certain there would be someone there who would help her. Father never turned anyone away who came to him for succour. He did not always give them what they asked for, but without exception, they were better for the encounter. The rector would help her.

Supposing he was a godly man. She knew from what her father had told her that some gentlemen entered the church as a profession and had no real conviction about what they preached. What if the rector here was like that? Or maybe he was not here at all. Maybe he was visiting London, or his sister, or his mother…

A little way up the road, she found a lane which appeared to lead toward the church. It was still muddy from the rain earlier in the day and by the time she was halfway along it, her boots were caked with mud and there were dirty splashes up her dress. Georgiana ploughed on, not daring to think what she would do if she met an unfavourable response.

When she reached the church, she found to her dismay that there was no sign of life and the front door was locked. Refusing to let her disappointment overwhelm her, she tried to stay calm. Maybe the rector was at the vicarage. She walked through the churchyard and came to a well-kept cottage which she felt sure must be the rector's home.

Georgiana's footsteps grew slower and slower. The full embarrassment of her situation impressed itself upon her mind. What right had she got to ask anyone for help? It was all her own stupid fault. By the time she reached the vicarage gate, her courage had all but deserted her. She let out a heartfelt sob and started to retrace her steps.

There was an old man still working in the vicarage garden even though the shadows were beginning to lengthen. He was so absorbed in pruning his roses that he had not been aware of Georgiana's presence until that point. Her anguished sob caught his attention. He stopped his work and turned to look at the retreating figure.

"Can I help you?" he called after her.

Georgiana turned around and walked slowly back toward the house. The old man had a kind face. She would ask him if the rector was at home. Perhaps he would be kind too.

"I need to see the rector," she blurted out.

"Hmm," said the man, nodding his head as he looked at her.

"Do you think he will see me?" she asked, nervously biting her lip. "I was wondering if…could you please tell me whether he is inside?"

He peered at her through a pair of gold-rimmed spectacles perched on the end of his nose and smiled. "No, he is not."

Georgiana let out another sob and was about to resume her flight when she was addressed by the man again.

"Forgive me, my dear. My humour was mistimed. I am Marcus Stanhope, the rector."

"Oh," she replied in surprise. "I did not realise."

"You thought because I was wearing tatty old clothes, I must be the gardener? Appearances can be deceiving, can't they?"

The rector put down his tools and gave her his full attention. Georgiana mistook his appraising look for one of contempt and felt her cheeks grow red with embarrassment.

"I know what you must be thinking," she said.

"I doubt that."

"You think I don't appear very respectable and am come to beg from you, which, I suppose I am, for I am in dire need of help and I don't know where else to turn and…"

"Indeed, my dear. I am not thinking anything of the sort," replied the rector, wiping the dirt off his hands as best he could. "I think you are a young lady who requires my assistance, and I have certainly done enough gardening for today. It was rather indulgent of me to have come out again after dinner, but my flowers require a lot of attention at this time of the year. Do come inside and tell me how I may serve you."

The man led her through the well-kept garden and in through the back door of the cottage.

"Margaret, I need some assistance here," he called.

A plump lady in a plain, Quakerish brown dress and white cap hurried through the doorway into the kitchen. With one look at Georgiana's woebegone expression, she took charge of the situation.

"Agnes, make some tea and bring it into the parlour. And plenty of scones and jam," she instructed a young girl who had entered the room behind her.

"You've come to the right place, my dear," Mrs Stanhope said. "You're safe here with us." She put a comforting arm around Georgiana and discovered that her pelisse was damp.

"You're all wet," she exclaimed. "Why don't you take off your pelisse and warm yourself by the fire? I know it's indulgent, but Marcus and I aren't as young as we once were, and we like a bit of warmth in the evening."

Georgiana looked up blankly into Mrs Stanhope's face. She had not thought beyond reaching the vicarage. She had not considered that she would need to take off her pelisse – the pelisse which was hiding the fact that her dress was only partially buttoned up. A wave of embarrassment hit her, sending the ready colour to her cheeks.

Mrs Stanhope saw the panic-stricken look on her face and shepherded her up the stairs and into a small bedroom, talking all the while.

"Caught in a shower of rain, were you? No doubt your dress is as damp as your pelisse. Let's see if we can't find something of my Sukey's for you to wear while your own things are drying. Sukey's my youngest girl and not long married, and I have a dress or two of hers here somewhere. I reckon she's a bit taller than you, but not so much as to matter. She lives along the Bath road in Longford. Her husband is the apothecary there."

As she talked, Mrs Stanhope rummaged in the wardrobe and produced a sprigged muslin dress and a shawl. "These will do," she continued. "Let's get those damp clothes off you."

Georgiana just stood there. Now that she was safe, the horror of all that she had gone through hit her with full force. She was ruined, and she had the satisfaction of knowing that it was all her own fault. The tears poured unbidden down her face.

"Why, my poor lamb," Mrs Stanhope cooed. "Whatever's made you cry like that? You sound as though your heart is breaking. No, don't try to talk. You let me do the talking right now – I can talk enough for the both of us."

Mrs Stanhope helped Georgiana out of her damp clothes and into Sukey's and then tidied her hair, all the while maintaining the flow of inconsequential chatter.

Although she was not fully aware of what the rector's wife was saying, Georgiana could feel her kindness as if it were tangible. After the strain of the previous hours, this unexpected gentleness made her weep even more.

By the time Mrs Stanhope had finished putting up her hair again, she had stopped crying. Her body still shuddered with the occasional silent sob, but the tears had been replaced by a series of violent sniffs. She accepted the fresh handkerchief that was offered her with a word of thanks and blew her nose.

"Let's go and see if the tea and scones are ready, my dear," Mrs Stanhope said. She paused. "Perhaps you would like to tell me your name?"

It did not occur to Georgiana to withhold the truth. The Stanhopes had treated her with such kindness that they had earned her trust.

"Georgiana Merry," she said, but she struggled to find the words to continue. "You must be wondering how I came to be here – what happened to me."

Mrs Stanhope forestalled her. "Not now, Miss Merry," she said, putting an arm around Georgiana's shoulders. "Food before talk. Let's join Marcus."

She led the way downstairs and Georgiana followed her into the parlour.

"Sit down, my dear," Mr Stanhope said, indicating a small armchair by the fire. "Have a scone."

Georgiana discovered that now the sickness had passed, she was ravenous. Mr Stanhope passed her a plate filled with freshly baked scones, together with a pot of home-made strawberry jam, and Mrs Stanhope poured the tea. Neither spoke whilst she ate her fill, allowing her to eat rather than talk. The commonplace business of eating helped to calm her nerves. It would not be an easy task to explain what had happened.

"Now, how may we help you?" Mr Stanhope asked.

"I don't know where to begin," Georgiana said, hoping that she would not start crying again. "I'm afraid you will not think well of me when you hear how stupid I have been."

"We are not here to judge, Miss Merry. We are here to give you what assistance we can," Mrs Stanhope assured her.

Georgiana shot her a grateful smile. "I have been very foolish. If I had listened to the advice I was given, this would never have happened." She poured out the whole story into sympathetic ears. By the time she reached the end, she was struggling to hold back the tears.

"I made the mistake of believing that he wanted to change, that I could reclaim his life, that my love could save him. But I discovered he did not want to change, but he needed my money, and that I didn't love him."

"Your only crime is to have acted unwisely," Mr Stanhope said.

"But I was happy to go with him. There was no reluctance on my part. It may have appeared that we were eloping."

"Without any baggage? In broad daylight? I don't think so," said Mrs Stanhope with a shake of her head. "And I was not aware that a curricle was the normal transport used for an elopement."

"I am ruined," Georgiana said with a sob.

"In whose eyes?" asked Mr Stanhope.

"What do you mean?" she asked. "In everybody's eyes. My reputation is shattered beyond repair. No one will believe in my innocence. Not with such a man as I have escaped from. I am a disgrace to my family and friends and…"

"All will be forgotten in time," said Mrs Stanhope.

"No, it won't," said Georgiana, almost shouting in her distress. "Only marriage could save my reputation, and I am determined not to marry Sir James under any circumstances. I would rather die!"

"Indeed, no," Mrs Stanhope agreed. "Marriage under such conditions would be a severe trial, especially when you are in love with someone else."

Georgiana coloured up immediately and tried to disclaim.

"My dear Miss Merry," said Mrs Stanhope. "The ordeal you have been through has been most distressing, but it does not, I feel, account for the level of grief you are experiencing. Those are the cries of a broken heart. You fear you've lost the man you love. Am I right?"

She nodded and the tears started falling again. "Whatever will Lord Castleford think of me? I asked him to call and he will be told that I have run off with his rival. How could I be so foolish? He will assume the worst and won't want to marry me any longer. And I did not realise how much I loved him until I knew I had put myself beyond his love."

"Listen to me, Georgiana," Mr Stanhope said with a confidence that surprised her. "If this man loves you, he will believe you innocent even if the rest of the world should find you guilty. Now, you must write to whatever friends or family will be worrying about you, telling them you are safe."

It was the most difficult letter she had ever written in her life. She bit the end of the pen she was using, wondering what she should say. She could not bear the thought of her aunt's disdain. It had seemed natural to confess the whole to two kind strangers, but she would say as little as possible to Lady Harting. Her letter was brief and to the point.

Dear Aunt,

I apologise for any distress that my unexpected departure from London has caused you. I am at Cranford vicarage with friends and will return home to Hampshire as soon as it can be arranged.

G Merry.

She decided it would have to do. Putting the letter aside, she picked up her pen again to write a brief note to her parents, begging them to send the carriage. She knew they would respond without asking why. There would be time enough for explanations when she was home.

* * *

Lord Castleford looked back at the closed door behind him and gave a wry smile. "I fear I may have upset your mother."

Beau grinned. "Think nothing of it. Wouldn't have missed it for the world. Better than going to the play."

They hurried down the stairs and into the hall. Castleford stood tapping his foot while Tomkins retrieved his hat and cane. He was anxious to be gone, but it was impossible to make the old family retainer move any faster than usual. The butler opened the door for him in his normal stately fashion, as if nothing untoward had occurred.

Castleford ran down the steps with Beau close behind him and almost collided with his brother who had just arrived to visit his friend.

"Cas? What brings you to Lord Harting's, or need I ask?" Anthony teased.

Castleford glared at his brother. "Not difficult to guess. Rest assured, I did not come to call on Lady Harting. I came to see Miss Merry, but as Miss Merry is not here, I am leaving."

"With Beau?" Anthony asked incredulously.

"I fear that my impetuous girl may require rescuing from the clutches of a scoundrel."

"A scoundrel? Sir James? Surely not? She wouldn't."

"No, she wouldn't, but Sir James would. Now please get out of my way before I remove you from my path. I'm in a hurry."

"I don't like the murderous look in your eye. Think I'd better come too. Someone needs to make sure you don't kill the man."

Castleford shrugged his shoulders. "As you wish. I assume you have your own transport?"

"Darn it. No, I walked," he replied. "I'll have to come with you."

"An admirable sentiment," Castleford said drily as Beau's curricle pulled up, "but as you can see, we have no room for a third."

Anthony was not to be put off. When Beau's groom had handed over the reins to his master, he discovered that Anthony had purloined his seat, and he was left on the side of the road as the three gentlemen drove away.

By the time the trio arrived in Cranford, the light was fading. They had quickly learned that Sir James had passed through Kensington toll-gate rather than Tyburn, but it had taken somewhat longer to trace the inn where he had abandoned his curricle.

Castleford was well known, and it had not been difficult to extract the information from a loitering stable boy.

"Oh yes, my lord. Poor lady was ever so wet like, having been caught in a heavy shower of rain which is why the gen'leman was hiring a carriage to take 'em home again. Least that's what he said, but if that was so, why did they go off in the opposite direction from where they came from? Havy cavy if you ask me."

"Did the lady seem in any distress?"

"Nah! Just cross 'cos she was wet and terrible worried about being late for dinner. As for 'im, I think he had other things on his mind, if you know what I mean."

Castleford smiled grimly. Then she was expecting to see him tonight. It was as he had always thought. This was no elopement. Sir James had abducted Georgiana.

They stopped at every post house along the road trying to find news, but no one could help. Sir James had not changed horses at any of them.

"It doesn't make sense. He must have picked up a fresh team somewhere or we would have overtaken him," Beau said.

"I wonder," Castleford mused. "It is taking a risk, but I think it is worth losing an hour to retrace our steps. We only enquired at posting houses. What if Sir James did not change horses, but was forced to stop earlier than he had planned?"

Anthony looked at his brother's pale, drawn face. "If there had been an accident, we would have seen some evidence of it on the road."

Beau turned the carriage with consummate ease and headed back along the way they had come. They drew a blank at the first two inns they stopped at, but at the third, they were more successful.

"Well, blow me down!" a stable lad exclaimed. "As if one lot of fancy coves in a day weren't enough, here's another."

Castleford alighted from the carriage and greased the boy's hand with a coin. "I don't suppose those 'fancy coves' are still here?"

"Lor' yes. Lady wasn't well and went to lie down in the best bed-chamber the moment they arrived."

Anthony gave a worried glance at Beau and jumped down after his brother. He put a steadying arm onto Castleford's shoulder.

"Easy."

"Easy? No, Anthony. This won't be easy. It will take all the strength I have not to break every bone in Sir James's body."

Beau's mouth fell open in wonder.

Castleford strode into the inn and accosted the landlord who bowed and scraped and shook in his boots when he demanded where

Sir James was. He pointed to where the baronet sat, in the otherwise deserted taproom, nursing a glass of brandy.

Castleford turned to the landlord. "I have private business with this gentleman," he said, dismissing him with a nod.

The landlord took one glance at the harsh look on Castleford's face and wiped the sweat off his brow, begging him not to make it a killing matter or he would ruin him.

Anthony reassured the man that his brother had everything under control. "At least, I hope he has," he muttered under his breath.

Castleford walked over to where Sir James was sitting, warming a glass of brandy in his hands, with the half-empty bottle standing on the table next to him.

"Give me one good reason why I shouldn't run you through with my sword and rid the world of such a pestilent being."

Sir James was in the act of lifting his glass to his lips and Castleford's voice made him jump so much that he spilt some of the brandy over his waistcoat. He leered up at his adversary.

"Lord Castleford. What a pleasant surprise. Now I wonder what can have hastened you to my side at this outlandish place. You have a bad habit of involving yourself in my affairs that I must deplore."

Without any warning, Castleford picked up the glass and threw the contents full in Sir James's face. He spluttered and rose to his feet, staggering backwards slightly and knocking his chair over in his rage.

"Brave action for a coward. You've never met anyone in your life, Castleford. Shooting wafers at Manton's is not the same as putting a bullet in a man, you know? Name your friends. Maddison will second me. You will meet me for this."

"Where is Miss Merry?" Castleford asked.

"Lady Maxwell is in our bedroom," Sir James said with malicious satisfaction.

"You are mistaken. Miss Merry is not your wife and never will be."

"Oh, I think it is you who are in error. Miss Merry will be glad to change her name for mine after this evening's work. She is quite a treasure. What lovelier woman could I have chosen to warm my bed?"

Castleford felt a keen desire to throttle Sir James, but years of rigid control somehow enabled him to restrain the impulse.

"Where is Miss Merry?" he repeated, without raising his voice.

"Upstairs – in my bed. I had to make sure she would not come running back to you," he boasted. "Think what you're doing. The best you can do for her is to leave us well alone. In time, an elopement will be lived down but take her away from the protection of my name and your beloved Georgiana will never be received into society again. Unless, of course, you intend to offer her your name instead, but I wouldn't have thought a man in your position would be interested in second-hand goods."

Castleford had been pushed beyond what he could bear. He discovered a primitive urge to bash Sir James's brains out. Before he could stop himself, his right fist whacked Sir James on the jawbone, wiping the smile from his face. Sir James reached a hand up to his bleeding chin and winced. Before he could respond, Castleford struck out again, hitting his nose and sending him sprawling across the floor.

Anthony and Beau stood in the doorway, watching in silent approval.

Much as he was enjoying the satisfaction of pummelling Sir James's face, Castleford knew that boxing was not his forte and his style was most undignified. He thought, yes, he really thought, that he needed time to cool off. His anger was out of control. If he continued to wreak vengeance now, he was in danger of killing his adversary. Besides, he had a mind to punish Sir James.

"My brother will second me," Castleford said in a deceptively calm voice. "He will await your challenge, Sir James."

Anthony looked aghast. He had never expected to hear such words from his brother's lips.

"You're in trouble, Sir James," he said. "Can't walk off with another man's woman and expect him to take it quietly. Apologise, man, or you could find yourself laid up for months. Castleford won't kill you, you can be sure of that, but – well, he's a man in love, or can't you tell? No, I don't suppose you can. I sympathise. I've never been in love either, but believe me, I have known him all my life and I have never, ever seen him this angry. Of course, I could just let him beat you up now. In fact, I might even help him. You really are a poor excuse of a man, aren't you?"

Sir James wilted under such a verbal onslaught. For all his bravado, Castleford concluded that he had succeeded in frightening him. He had threatened a challenge as a taunt, never expecting for one moment that Castleford, renowned for his peaceable ways, would accept.

Sir James staggered to his feet and tried to reach the door, but Beau barred his way, causing him to stumble and fall to the floor again.

"Tut, tut. You can't run away like that. Castleford asked you a question. Where is Miss Merry?"

Even from his ignominious position, Sir James could not resist a poisonous retort. "I've already told you. Upstairs – but she was not dressed for visitors when I left her. I would think she would be too embarrassed to see you before she has my ring on her finger."

Castleford hauled Sir James to his feet by the scruff of his neck and propelled him through the doorway where he tripped over the landlord who was hovering outside.

"Just a minor disagreement," quipped Anthony, following his brother up the stairs. "Nothing to worry about. Sir James took something of my brother's and once he has got it back, we'll be on our way."

The landlord looked aghast when he saw the blood pouring from Sir James's nose, but Beau continued to reassure him it was just a little misunderstanding.

Reluctantly, Sir James led the way to the bedchamber where he had left Georgiana and pushed open the door. The room was empty.

Castleford raised his eyebrows in enquiry. "It would appear that you have mislaid Miss Merry," he said with a sweetness of tone that did not match his expression. "Are you sure she was ever here?"

"Of course, she was here," Sir James retorted, snatching his caped driving coat from the chair as if he expected to discover her hiding underneath. The sodden wreck of a hat that Georgiana could not find fell to the ground. Castleford recognised the bonnet and bent over to pick it up.

As he did so, he noticed something else that had been knocked on the floor and pushed under the chair. Reaching out his hand, he pulled out Georgiana's reticule. He stared at the small bag for a moment, his concern growing as he realised the implications.

"It is time we went," he said to his brother.

Castleford turned to Sir James. "I will not require your assistance in finding Miss Merry, but you had better pray that I find her unharmed," he said in a voice of uncompromising severity.

He opened the door to leave but hesitated for a moment on the threshold and twisted to face Sir James once more.

Looking him directly in the eye, he added with icy politeness, "I trust you will not forget to send your second to wait on my brother?"

Anthony went to follow, but he also turned back at the doorway to address Sir James. "Inadvisable," he muttered, shaking his head.

"Master swordsman. Fencing champion. Doesn't boast about it, but it's the one sport he's rather good at. I wouldn't put it to the test if I were you," he added as he shut the door in Sir James's face.

The two brothers hurried downstairs to where Beau was waiting. He had appeased the landlord who had muttered about the vagaries of the quality and gone off to serve his regular customers. It seemed unlikely that he would ever express a desire for the custom of the gentry again.

"Our bird has flown," Anthony said in answer to Beau's enquiring look.

"To where?" asked Beau. "Back to town?"

Castleford held up the reticule. "No money."

"Ah, I see. Hang it, you can't walk around carrying a woman's hat and reticule, Castleford," Beau said, taking possession of the soggy hat and bag. "I'll put them in my curricle."

Whilst they were alone, Anthony placed a comforting hand on his brother's shoulder. "Don't worry, Cas. We'll find her."

Castleford nodded. The thought of Georgiana being out in the open, in the dark, with no money and no one to protect her filled him with dread. He closed his eyes and prayed that God would keep her safe.

CHAPTER 29

"What's the plan?" Beau asked as he returned from the stables.

"Go into the village and find out if anyone has seen her," Castleford said. "We'll meet back here in an hour."

"Where are you heading?" asked Anthony.

"To the church."

"Of course. Rector's daughter. Obvious place to seek help. Why didn't I think of that?"

"Because, dear Anthony, I have the brains in the family."

Anthony pulled a face. "I have brains enough to see that you might be right. I hope she's there."

They set off in different directions, hoping and praying that their search would be successful.

Castleford appreciated being left alone with his thoughts. Georgiana was a remarkable woman. She had escaped from Sir James's clutches without any assistance from him. Not the dramatic rescue he had anticipated, but if she was safe, he did not care.

Despite his concern for her current whereabouts, he could not help smiling at the thought of the ludicrous look on Sir James's face when he had opened the door on an empty room.

An anxious spirit spurred Castleford on his way, and his long legs reached the church in half the time it had taken Georgiana. He walked across the churchyard to the vicarage and rang the bell, trying hard to resist the temptation not to rap the knocker as well while he waited for an answer.

He was shown into the parlour where the rector sat alone, but the empty cups showed that until recently, he had entertained company.

"Lord Castleford. I've been expecting you."

"Is she here?"

Mr Stanhope nodded. "Assuming 'she' is Miss Merry – yes, she is here."

Castleford's brow cleared and he let out a sigh of relief. "Thank God! May I see her?"

"Please sit down."

Castleford recollected his manners, which had temporarily deserted him in the face of his fears for Georgiana's safety. "Thank you, Mr…?"

"Marcus Stanhope," the rector replied, holding out his hand. Castleford shook it and then, somewhat reluctantly, took the chair that was offered to him.

"Miss Merry came here some hours ago in great distress. We promised to help her, and she chose, of her own volition, to honour us with her confidence. She believes, with good reason, that her reputation is in shatters – that she is ruined in the eyes of the world. What do you say to that, my lord?"

Castleford grimaced as a wave of intense pain coursed through his body at the thought of Georgiana being at Sir James's mercy.

"I do not care what the world says, Mr Stanhope. She is not ruined in my eyes. I want to marry her – to give her the protection of my name against anything the world may throw at her."

"Is that all?"

"All?"

"Just your name, Lord Castleford?"

"It will be a marriage in name alone if that is what she wishes after all that has happened."

Mr Stanhope shook his head, frowning. "That would be no marriage at all, for either of you. If you offer her your name without your heart, I do not believe that she will have you. You arrived on my doorstep tonight as a man in love. Do not make a proposal of marriage which she might deem to be made in pity. Give her your love – a love that will last a lifetime."

Castleford saw at once that the rector was right. A marriage in name alone was not what he wanted at all. This was not a time to hold back his ardour out of gentlemanly scruples. Georgiana needed to know how much he loved her. That he still wanted her, whatever had happened with Sir James.

"You are perfectly right. I don't know what I was thinking. Perhaps I could see Miss Merry now, that I might offer her my hand *and* my heart?"

Mr Stanhope nodded and led the way out of the parlour and across the hall. He opened the door of the room opposite, encouraging Castleford to enter.

"I have a visitor for you, Miss Merry," the rector said from the doorway before leaving Castleford alone with Georgiana.

"Oh no, please, I cannot see anyone…"

"Miss Merry."

Castleford spoke gently, trying not to startle her. Georgiana recognised his voice and jumped up from her seat, turning to face him. She started forward, hands outstretched, but having taken a few paces, she stepped away again, letting her hands drop to her sides, her eyes fixed on the floor.

"Lord Castleford. What are you doing here?"

"I believe you wanted to see me."

"I did," she said, raising her eyes nervously to his face. "At least, I asked the Sylph to visit me, and I was certain he was you. Whatever must you have thought of me, finding me gone when I had requested you to come?"

"I assumed, Georgiana, that something or someone had prevented you from being there. And I was determined to make sure you kept your appointment."

"Oh," she said, taking in his words. "What did you think when you received my letter? Were you surprised that I had penetrated your disguise?"

"Surprised? No. I expected you to discover the identity of the Sylph more quickly. If not before, I supposed you would guess after my appearance at the Argyll Rooms. I could hide my face and my voice, but not my height. The beggarly old man at Lady Buckinghamshire's was a better disguise. Bending over I could conceal how tall I was, but I thought I might need to move faster at the Argyll Rooms – and I was right."

"That was you too? I never guessed. Until today, I believed the Sylph was my father," Georgiana confessed. "So much of your advice seemed to be what he would have said. It didn't occur to me that the Sylph could be anyone else until Eliza wrote that father had not been in town the night of the masquerade. I soon deduced that it must be you. Why did you do it?"

"It was your own words that put the idea into my head. I wanted to protect you, but I had no right to tell you what to do. I hoped by this means I could influence you for good. To keep you safe. I was – and still am – in love with you, and I had reason to think your impulsive nature might get you into trouble."

Georgiana blushed as he confessed his love for her, but the mention of her impulsiveness made her shudder. "That day at the Magdalen? Please don't remind me."

He paused. "It was long before that. The first time we met."

"I don't understand."

"It was almost three years ago, at a posting inn just south of Reading."

He watched her eyes grow wide with horror as realisation dawned.

"It was you. You and your mother," she whispered.

He nodded. A whole variety of emotions flitted across her face – dismay, wonder, gratitude – but any pleasant feelings seemed to be ousted by distress.

Seeing her anguish, Castleford's assurance dissipated. Had he kept quiet for too long? Had his secrecy destroyed her trust in him? Was this last revelation too much for her to bear?

Castleford sank to his knees. "Can you forgive me?"

* * *

Georgiana could not believe what she was hearing.

"Forgive you? For what?" she said, falling on her knees beside Lord Castleford. "Rescuing me from an imprudent marriage? Saving me from the ragamuffins near the Magdalen? Or for coming to my rescue today when my impulsiveness has ruined me? I feel so ashamed, I can hardly bear it, but the fault is mine and mine alone. Why do you ask for my forgiveness?"

"For my subterfuge. For urging you to be open and honest while I hid behind the mask of the Sylph."

"I forgive you if there is anything to forgive. Perhaps it was wrong of you, but it was very romantic," she said with a shy smile.

"Thank you," Lord Castleford said, getting to his feet and pulling her up beside him.

But Georgiana could not forget the events of the day and would not allow herself to stay close to him. It would be too tempting to throw herself in his arms as she had done once before, and she could not bear the thought of him pushing her away from him with disgust when he heard what had happened.

"I wasn't thinking of romance when I started writing. I just wanted to look after you. When you rejected me, I was consumed by despair. You have Anthony to thank that I did not give up. He asked me whether you were worth fighting for and encouraged me to become what you needed. As you were not interested in giving me the right to care for you as my wife, I continued to masquerade as the Sylph, trying to protect you from a distance."

"It is hard to explain how I felt when I realised that you were my Sylph," Georgiana said. "The revelation changed everything. It was fun when I thought my father was writing the letters, but when I discovered it was you, I became aware of just how much you cared about me. It was as if scales fell from my eyes. All at once, I knew it was you I was in love with. I felt that if you went out of my life, the sun would never shine so brightly again."

The worry melted from Lord Castleford's face as she quoted his own words back to him. He closed the distance between them and with one hand, he gently raised her chin, so she had to look at him.

"Do you still feel like that?" he asked huskily.

Georgiana stifled a sob. "You don't understand," she said, pulling herself away from him and refusing to meet his eyes. "I've been such a fool. For a time, I thought I was falling in love with Sir James. He flattered me into thinking I could be his salvation. I am not certain when the doubts started to creep in. Perhaps they were there all along, but I ignored them. The things you wrote made me question whether I could be in love with someone I didn't trust. Even when I didn't want to marry you," she said, stealing a timid look at Lord Castleford's face, "I would have trusted you with my life."

He took her hands and squeezed them encouragingly.

"The comparison between you and Sir James was too stark. You were everything good that he was not. Once the seed of doubt was planted, it grew with great speed. When Mrs Marchant came to visit me at your request, I did not want to hear. It was no longer a matter of the heart, but it hurt my pride to learn that I had been such a poor judge of character. Without thinking, I stupidly put myself in Sir

James's power, all for the sake of proving that he was not as wicked as people said he was. But I discovered to my cost that he was every bit as bad as I had been told. When I declared I wouldn't marry him, he forced whisky down my throat to make me drunk so I couldn't resist him. He took me to an inn and pretended I was his wife. No one will believe that I am innocent now. I'm ruined."

"I believe you."

"You do? But I was in the bedroom with him – alone."

"I know."

"You know? Then you've been to the inn? Did you…did you see Sir James?"

"I did."

"Oh."

"He was not well when I left him."

Georgiana looked up at him in surprise. "Not well? He was in perfect health when he ran from the bedchamber."

Now it was Lord Castleford's turn to look surprised. "When he ran from the bedchamber? What did you do to him?"

Georgiana squeezed her lips together, but she could not keep back her smile. "I told you already that he forced me to drink liquor. Unfortunately – or as it turned out, fortunately – the whisky made me nauseous. When I announced that I was going to be sick, he stopped trying to kiss me and fled from the room with such a look on his face that it almost made up for the sickness that followed."

They looked at each other and burst out laughing. It felt good to share the joke with Lord Castleford.

"You said that Sir James was unwell when you left him," Georgiana reminded him when their laughter had subsided.

Lord Castleford's countenance became serious, but his eyes still laughed. "Sir James's indisposition was rather sudden. He was suffering from a bloody nose."

"You hit him!" she exclaimed, clapping her hands together in delight.

He shook his head in mock despair. "You are bloodthirsty, aren't you? I'm afraid I took unfair advantage of his befuddled state. If Anthony and Beau had not been there to restrain me, I might have left him in an even worse condition."

At these words, the smile vanished, and she became quiet again. "I suppose they both know what happened?"

"They would have joined in, but three against one seemed a little unfair. They were almost as anxious as I was to uphold your honour."

"How did you find me?"

"Divine inspiration. When I discovered you were not at the inn, I decided that the church was the most obvious place for you to come for help. And now that I have found you," he said, lifting her chin again with one hand, so he could see into her eyes, and clasping both her hands with the other, "I have a question to ask you. Miss Merry – Georgiana – will you marry me, my dearest, most precious love?"

Georgiana tried to pull away, but he held her hands in a firm grip. "But you can't want me now after I have behaved so badly."

"I want you more than words can express," he said, his voice husky with longing.

Georgiana closed her eyes as he lowered his mouth to hers. Their lips met in a gentle kiss, sending shivers down her back and legs. But he did not pull away. He kissed her again. On the forehead. On the nose. And then on the lips. This time, his kiss was not gentle. It was passionate and demanding, awakening a longing deep inside her.

He released her hands so he could stroke her hair and draw her closer to him. Of their own accord, her hands reached up around his neck whilst her mouth returned his embrace with a passion as fierce as his own.

At length, they drew apart, both somewhat out of breath.

"Oh! I thought you didn't want to kiss me," she exclaimed.

"I have wanted to kiss you ever since you first cajoled me into dancing with you. I did not love you until at least a day later and it must have been a full week before I liked you."

"That is outrageous. How could you want to…?"

He cut off her words in a most satisfactory manner.

Georgiana persisted. "But you cannot still wish to marry me after what has happened?"

"You cannot know what agony I have been through, Georgiana, not knowing where you were and whether you were safe. Whatever occurred is past. I want your present and your future."

She peeked up at him through her eyelashes. "I suppose I could be convinced…"

Lord Castleford took great pleasure in convincing her. His eyes glowed with desire as he lowered his mouth to hers again and kissed her until she was breathless.

"Will you marry me, Georgiana?" he repeated when they finally drew apart.

"Yes, Lord Castleford. I will marry you."

"Lord Castleford? That sounds too formal a way to address your future husband. Call me Frederick, or Cas like my brother does if you prefer."

Georgiana considered his suggestions. Somehow Frederick sounded unapproachable and she could not imagine *ever* calling him Fred. She rather liked the idea of using his nickname. With a sigh of contentment, she rested her head against his broad shoulder.

"I do love you, Cas."

* * *

The door creaked open and Georgiana jerked away from Lord Castleford, her cheeks turning a becoming shade of pink. Castleford turned as Mr Stanhope entered the room. The rector did not try to hide his satisfied smile when he saw them draw hastily apart.

"Whilst I hate to interrupt," he said, addressing Castleford, "there are two gentlemen here, one of whom claims to be your brother. They seem most eager to see you. May I show them in?"

"By all means," he replied.

Mr Stanhope went to fetch them.

"They will want to know that you are safe. I was supposed to meet them back at the inn some while ago, but I was rather distracted," he said, kissing Georgiana, "and forgot."

He pulled out his watch and looked at the time and then walked to the window to see if the sun had set. "If we can hire a suitable carriage, there should be enough light left for us to drive to Fairview – my mother's house in Twickenham. We can't be more than seven or eight miles away. Unless you would rather go back to your aunt's," he added with a wicked grin.

"No!"

"I didn't think so."

At the mention of Lady Harting, Georgiana's face clouded over. "My aunt – I sent her a note. She will know of my disgrace. It is very lowering."

"Lady Harting will not expect you to return," he said, with a harsh edge to his voice. "I told her she was to blame for not taking proper care of you."

"Oh. You saw my aunt."

"You invited me to come and see you."

"Yes, of course. I was forgetting. It all seems so long ago."

A few moments later, Anthony burst into the room. He glanced from Castleford to Georgiana and back again and grinned.

"No need to say a word, Cas. The contentment written all over your face says it all. May I be the first to congratulate you, Miss Merry? I'm afraid you get my disreputable self as your new brother, but on balance, I think you have a good bargain."

Georgiana smiled up at him as he took her hand and kissed it, lingering over it provocatively until Castleford coughed loudly.

"You may welcome your future sister in an appropriate fashion, Anthony. I would request that you leave the lingering kisses to me from now on."

Anthony laughed and planted a chaste salute on Georgiana's cheek. "I will have to remember that I'm under strict orders not to flirt with you."

"My, what a merry chase you've led us on tonight, Georgie," quipped Beau, following Anthony into the room. "I wouldn't have missed it for the world. Worth the whole thing to see the look on Sir James's face when Castleford accepted his challenge."

Castleford grimaced. Now that the danger had passed, he was horrified at how he had behaved and regretted yielding to the impulse to punish Sir James. It was bad enough that he had hit him, but worse that he had taunted him by hinting that he would accept his challenge. If only he had remembered in time that vengeance belonged to the Lord, not to him.

Hoping to protect Georgiana from unnecessary distress, he had not planned to tell her about the challenge until after he had paid the price for his reckless words.

"Thank you, Beau," he said, frowning. "I think you have said enough."

But it was too late. The damage was done. All the colour drained out of Georgiana's face as she stared up at him, eyes wide with horror.

"You're going to fight Sir James?" she whispered. "Because of me?"

"A momentary lapse of judgement," Castleford apologised.

"I don't understand. You told me you didn't believe that fighting duels was the way to solve disputes. Please tell me you haven't changed your mind. You won't meet him, will you?"

He placed a comforting arm around her. "There is no need to fret, my love. I assure you, Sir James will not put an end to my existence. You cannot suppose that I would jeopardise our future happiness by fighting a scoundrel like Sir James? There will be no meeting. An apology will be made, and it will come to nothing. Trust me."

Georgiana gave a weak smile, and the colour slowly returned to her face. "I believe you."

She might believe him, but Anthony and Beau did not. Castleford caught the look of sheer disbelief that passed between them and glared, hoping that Georgiana had not noticed. They knew as well as he did that Sir James would make no apology. He had struck Sir James. A duel was the only honourable recourse.

Lacking confidence in Beau's discretion, Castleford gave him no opportunity to talk to Georgiana, dispatching him to hire a carriage to carry them to Fairview.

He dashed off a few lines to Georgiana's father to counter the letter that had already been posted and to invite the family to join them for their wedding, which he hoped would take place at his mother's home the following week.

It took him no more than a moment to decide not to write to Lady Harting. Georgiana had sent a message to say she was safe. Her aunt deserved nothing more. Beau would tell her soon enough.

A few words with Mr Stanhope secured their maid Agnes as a companion for Georgiana on the drive to Twickenham. With hot bricks to keep their feet warm, the two ladies ensconced themselves in the old-fashioned travelling coach that Beau had hired.

Having promised to come to Fairview for the wedding, Beau said his farewells and returned to the Berkeley Arms, intending to rest his horses and drive his curricle back to town the next day. He hoped that the landlord would not refuse him a room for his share in the day's irregular proceedings.

Castleford and Anthony climbed into the coach, and it pulled away, driven at a sedate pace in the fading light.

Georgiana dozed, exhausted, and Castleford watched her sleep. He was still watching when she awoke with a jump, unsure of where she was. She looked around, afraid, as if remembering the trials of her last journey. But when he met her troubled gaze and smiled, the worry disappeared from her face and, with a look of contentment, she drifted asleep again.

The house was in darkness when they arrived at Fairview, but Castleford was not dismayed. Being an invalid, his mother kept early hours and must have already retired for the night. Anthony jumped down from the carriage and battered on the door until he heard the bolts being drawn back.

"Mr Anthony. My lord," the surprised butler exclaimed. "How can I apologise enough for not being ready to receive you?"

"Think nothing of it, Newcombe," Castleford assured the distressed servant. "How could you be ready when we sent no word? Please, could you summon Mrs Newcombe? I have need of her."

Newcombe bustled away to fetch his wife whilst Castleford helped a sleepy Georgiana out of the coach. By the time she entered the hall, Mrs Newcombe was there to welcome her.

"The best guest bedchamber for Miss Merry, who has done me the great honour of agreeing to be my wife," Castleford said to the housekeeper.

The redoubtable Mrs Newcombe did not show by as much as a blink of an eyelid that she thought his words in any way remarkable.

"Very good, my lord. May I wish you joy? Please follow me, Miss Merry."

Castleford bent and kissed Georgiana's forehead before Mrs Newcombe whisked her away and into bed.

269

CHAPTER 30

The two brothers retired to the library where they discovered that Newcombe, with welcome foresight, had already deposited a decanter of brandy and glasses.

Castleford slumped in a chair and contemplated his future with a heavy heart. It should have been a time for celebration. Georgiana was safe and had agreed to be his wife, but there was still the matter of the duel to resolve. He had saved his beloved from the results of her impulsiveness, but there was no one to save him.

In the anger of a moment, he had hit Sir James and recklessly accepted his challenge, and he could not turn the clock back. He knew God had forgiven him for his desire for vengeance, but it did not free him from the consequences of his lapse of judgement.

In silence, he sipped his brandy, listening to Anthony rattle on.

"I'm for an early meeting – tomorrow if we can manage it. Don't want this hanging over your head when you'd rather be thinking of more pleasant matters. I'll make all the arrangements. You'll choose swords, of course. I don't think much of Sir James's choice of second. Maddison is an unreliable fellow and somewhat inclined to violence when he's in his cups. I'll keep a close eye on them both and ensure they play fair. You can be confident that I won't let you be killed by your opponent's tricks."

"I appreciate your concern, but it will not be necessary," Castleford said.

Anthony glanced across at him in surprise. "I don't understand."

"I intend to apologise."

"You intend to what?"

"Apologise. I have no intention of meeting Sir James."

"How could you even think of apologising to that scoundrel?" Anthony said in an exasperated voice. "He deserved everything he got. Besides, you hit him. You know the rules of etiquette as well as I do. The only way he could be persuaded to accept your apology would be to offer him your whip and let him strike you. You must meet him, Cas. There is no honourable alternative."

"I will not fight."

Anthony looked aghast. "Think what you are saying. What of your honour?"

"What is honourable about fighting a dishonourable man?"

"But Cas, how can you permit that scoundrel to get away with it?"

Castleford longed to make his brother understand. "What would you have me do? Pink Sir James with a sword and have him swear his revenge on me? Or perhaps you envisage me ridding this world of his vile being? A tempting idea, I grant you, but not one that my conscience allows, or the law supports. I must do what I believe to be right."

"And what will you do if he refuses to accept your apology?"

"I will not fight."

"Once it becomes known that you have withdrawn from the engagement," Anthony said in a quiet voice, "and you can be sure that Sir James will make it known, you won't be able to hold up your head in polite society. You will be ridiculed. Blackballed. Branded a coward."

"It won't come to that. I will make certain Sir James accepts my apology."

Castleford met his brother's gaze and watched the colour drain from Anthony's face as he realised what he was proposing.

"Cas, no. Think about what you're saying. You cannot hand him your whip and invite him to take his revenge on you for punching him. You would be putting yourself at his mercy."

"As you have said, there is no honourable alternative."

"But he can't be trusted. You've humiliated him and he won't forgive that. Abducting Georgiana was a desperate move. By rescuing her, you've probably ruined him. He has every reason to hate you. What's to stop him taking out all his anger on you?"

"Nothing."

"But you haven't thought this through," Anthony said, his features contorted with agony. "Given the chance, he might kill you."

Castleford gave a wry smile. "I'm relying on you to make sure he doesn't."

"You won't defend yourself?"

"I will not. This way, I face humiliation, but I'll have a clear conscience before God. Will you still act for me?"

Castleford stared into his brother's eyes, hoping for a glimmer of understanding, but he saw nothing but distress.

Anthony drained his glass and with a resigned look, he gave Castleford a brief nod. "You can rely on me. I'll arrange everything."

* * *

Georgiana awoke in a strange bed, a stranger in her future mother-in-law's house. Last night, she had felt secure in Lord Castleford's love and that had been all that mattered. The morning was full of uncertainties. Would his mother like her? Would her father forgive her? What would her aunt say?

Deep down, there was another uncertainty that nagged at her peace that she did not want to give voice to. That despite Castleford's assurances, he would be forced to fight a duel to uphold her honour.

A maid brought her a cup of chocolate and helped her out of her borrowed nightdress and into the gown that had received such a soaking the day before, transformed by some unseen power into a wearable garment again.

A footman directed her to the breakfast parlour where Castleford was already waiting. Overcome with sudden shyness, she hovered in the doorway until he looked up. Abandoning his newspaper, he was soon at her side, taking her hand and leading her to the table to sit by him. It warmed her heart to have him act in such a possessive manner. She returned his welcoming smile, a smile which said so much.

As Lady Castleford kept to her room and Anthony had sent word that he would not be joining them, breakfast was served immediately. The sight of food reminded Georgiana that she had missed yesterday's dinner and, realising how hungry she was, she tucked into a substantial meal.

After they had eaten, Castleford took her to meet his mother. The Countess beckoned her to come and sit with her and shooed her son away.

"Georgiana and I need time to become acquainted and we do not require your assistance, Frederick."

"Then I will take my leave of you both as I have pressing matters of business to attend to in town."

Georgiana's eyes shot to his face, the nagging fear that he would not come back again bubbling to the surface of her thoughts. Despite his assurances that the duel would not take place, she could not believe that Sir James would apologise.

"Don't look so distressed, love. I'll be back tomorrow."

"Promise me you won't fight Sir James," Georgiana said, holding onto his arm as if she could prevent him leaving. "Even if he will not apologise."

"I don't expect him to. It is I who need to apologise, not him."

"You?"

"I struck him and must make amends."

"But how will you insist that he accept your apology? Won't people say you are not brave enough to fight?"

Castleford paused, a tight expression on his mouth. "There is an honourable way to oblige him to accept my apology."

"How?"

He seemed reluctant to say more and would have dismissed her curiosity, but Georgiana was not satisfied. His reluctance exacerbated her need for an explanation.

"Tell me," she said in a voice that brooked no argument.

He turned away from her in some distress. "I must offer him my whip and allow him to exact penance for the offence."

Lady Castleford had been listening in silence, but at this she cried out, and Georgiana exclaimed, "No!"

Castleford glanced at his mother and then turned back to Georgiana and sighed. "It is the only way."

"But Sir James is not to be trusted," Georgiana wailed. "He will have no mercy on you. I would rather you fight than allow him to beat you when you are defenceless to resist."

"I do not choose to stare down the barrel of Sir James's gun, and I refuse to engage in a sword fight and risk killing him. This is hard, but it is the right thing to do. God will protect me. Now, you must let me go," he said, removing her hand from his arm.

Georgiana could not hide her dismay. Doing what was honourable and right came with a high price.

"Besides," he continued, adopting a brighter tone, "I am impatient to make you my bride and must return to London to get a special licence so we can marry as soon as possible. If you do not object, I thought we could be married here, in my mother's house, away from the public eye. I confess that I relish the prospect of presenting you to society as my countess unannounced. It is good to surprise people occasionally."

Georgiana followed Castleford's lead, and brushing aside the dreadful image of Sir James taking a whip to his back, she hastened to approve of his plan. To be wed at Fairview, with minimal delay, sounded perfect. She was as impatient as he was to be married and after all that had happened, returning to London unwed was not an option.

He walked over to his mother and gave her a peck on the cheek before turning to Georgiana. Ignoring the fact that his mother was watching, he took her in his arms and kissed her full on the lips. Georgiana's face turned pink with embarrassment, but Lady Castleford seemed to see nothing amiss and smiled indulgently on the engaged couple.

With considerable reluctance, she released Castleford, but he made no move to leave.

"Be off with you," Lady Castleford said, waving her son away with her hand.

"I would be happy to oblige, but I'm still waiting for Anthony." With a last kiss on Georgiana's cheek, he headed for the door. "It looks as if I will have to drag him from his bed if I want to reach London today."

At that moment, the door opened and Newcombe entered, carrying a letter.

"One of the maids found this in Mr Anthony's room, my lord," the butler said, offering Castleford the note. "Thinking it might be of some import, I took the liberty of bringing it to you without delay."

Castleford took the letter and broke open the seal. Georgiana watched his brow pucker with concern as he read its contents.

"Foolish boy," he muttered under his breath.

"Well?" Georgiana asked.

"It appears that Anthony shares your distrust of Sir James and has taken it upon himself to resolve my challenge by fighting the duel in my place," he said in a voice full of barely suppressed emotion. "For the sake of my honour and my future happiness with you."

His words filled Georgiana with horror. She could not bear it if Anthony were killed in a duel fought in her defence. What was more, she knew Castleford would not be able to bear it either.

He started pacing up and down the room. "I must go after him at once and save him from his misguided heroism. This is my fight, not his, and I can't allow him to risk his life on my behalf. Sir James's quarrel is with me. I will make him accept my apology."

Castleford gave Georgiana's hands a quick squeeze and dropped a kiss on her forehead before pulling away. In a moment, he was gone.

Georgiana watched the door shut behind him and tried not to allow the emptiness to overwhelm her.

"Come here, child," Lady Castleford said, patting the seat beside her. Georgiana did as she was bid.

"You look so like your father. He was good to me when I needed a friend. It was about twenty years ago, when my sons were very young. My husband took me to London, for the sake of appearances, but then ignored me. I was so miserable and alone. Your father danced with me at the Duchess of Devonshire's ball and listened to me chattering on about my boys. I've never forgotten his kindness."

Her words distracted Georgiana from her worries and confirmed her suspicions that the Countess's marriage had not been happy.

"Those boys of mine were always getting up to mischief. Or rather, Anthony got himself into trouble and relied on Frederick to come to his rescue."

"He's still good at coming to the rescue," Georgiana said.

With a little encouragement, she shared her story, and confided her fears for both Castleford and Anthony.

"Hush," said Lady Castleford, trying to reassure her. "You must trust Frederick and trust God. All will be well."

Georgiana hoped rather than believed that she was right. She could not help fearing that Castleford or Anthony or both of them would fight and be killed. And if they died, she would know it was all because of her folly in being duped by Sir James.

Lady Castleford channelled Georgiana's thoughts into a more positive direction by telling stories about her sons. As she talked, her face glowed with affection. It did not take Georgiana long to realise that Castleford and Anthony were her pride and joy.

Part the way through the afternoon, Lady Castleford's dressmaker arrived, and their conversation became centred on designs for a wedding gown fit for a countess. It should have been a delightful experience, but Georgiana found it hard to enthuse about a dress which she feared she might never wear.

She ate little at dinner and was relieved that the Countess made no comment. If only Eliza could have been there to comfort her. She felt sure her sister would understand.

Lady Castleford kept early hours, and they retired soon after ten o'clock. But it was long before Georgiana fell asleep. She tossed and turned, trying not to think about the duel, eventually falling into an uneasy slumber. Nothing short of seeing Castleford again would put her fears to rest.

* * *

When Georgiana awoke the next morning, she was as tired as when she had gone to sleep. It felt as if she had dreamed of Anthony and Castleford fighting Sir James all night long.

Too restless to stay in bed, she rang for help to dress and was soon walking through the garden, trying not to watch for the arrival of a carriage as it was not yet nine o'clock.

Every time she thought she heard a noise, she hurried to where she could see the drive, only to be disappointed that no vehicle was approaching. After half an hour of flitting backward and forward, she gave up the pretence of walking through the gardens and took up a position by a raised stone seat which commanded a view of the drive.

At last, she saw what she had been waiting for – a carriage coming through the entrance gates. She picked up her skirts and hurried down the path that led round the front of the house.

Castleford's travelling chariot had just drawn up. Hardly able to breathe, she watched the footman lower the steps and open the carriage door.

Anthony appeared in the opening and climbed down. He looked weary, but otherwise unharmed, and a wave of relief passed over Georgiana. Castleford had reached him in time. But where was his brother?

"Cas?" she squeaked at Anthony.

"Right here, my love," Castleford said, hopping down from the carriage after his brother.

Georgiana threw herself into his arms, overcome with joy at seeing him again and still in one piece.

"I told you all would be well," he said, holding her close.

"I know, but I feared you would not reach Anthony in time to stop the duel and if you did, that Sir James would not accept your apology without hurting you terribly."

"He didn't."

"He didn't? Then you're hurt? Or you were forced to fight?"

"There was no duel," Castleford reassured her.

"As it happens," Anthony said, following them through the front door that Newcombe was holding open, "no apology was required."

Georgiana's head jerked up, and she looked enquiringly at Anthony, but it was Castleford who spoke.

"Sir James has decided this country does not offer enough opportunities for a man of his talents."

"He's fled to France," Anthony said, "regretted only by his creditors. Maddison informed me when I tried to arrange the duel. Sir James's lodgings were empty and his landlady none too pleased as he scarpered without paying his rent. Abducting you must have been his last hope. So, my sacrifice was not required after all. No duel and no apology necessary. He's gone."

"But why did you do it?" Georgiana said, turning to Anthony. "Why would you risk your life taking your brother's place when you knew he intended to apologise?"

Anthony looked down at his feet in a rare moment of embarrassment. "I'll never have a love like yours and I wanted to protect your happiness. And I couldn't bear the thought of Cas being humiliated, putting himself in the hands of that scoundrel, when he is the most honourable man I know."

Georgiana reached out and gave Anthony's hand a grateful squeeze.

Her action seemed to break him out of his serious mood. He looked up, with a wicked smile on his face. "And I couldn't risk him being killed. Think of all the responsibility I'd inherit. Not to mention the need to get married. No, thank you!"

"Some of us are looking forward to getting married," Castleford said with a light-hearted smile, though Georgiana could tell he was moved by his brother's words.

"And this," he said, brandishing the special licence he had procured in front of her, "means that we can set the day when I claim you for my own and make my promises in the sight of God and our family to love and cherish you forever."

"Oh Cas, I do love you," Georgiana said, gazing up at him.

He replied in a most satisfactory manner. Lowering his lips to her upturned face, he gave his betrothed a long, lingering kiss under the gaze of two interested pairs of eyes.

Newcombe stifled the smile unbecoming to his station and returned to his work. Anthony let out a rather wistful sigh and, as the kiss showed no sign of abating, he sauntered off to find his mother, whistling as he went.

EPILOGUE

"I Frederick Warren take thee Georgiana Merry to be my wedded wife, to have and to hold, from this day forward, for better for worse, for richer for poorer, in sickness and in health, to love and to cherish, till death us do part, according to God's holy ordinance; and thereto I plight thee my troth."

Georgiana stole a glance to her left as Lord Castleford spoke his promises. It was not the wedding she had always imagined, in her home church, surrounded by the friends and neighbours who had watched her grow up, but it was perfect, or very nearly so.

The chapel of Fairview exuded a serenity that reflected Lady Castleford's godly character, and though not in his parish church, her father was still taking the marriage service. She wished her grandmother could have been there, and the Duke and Denmead, but apart from them, all those they loved best were here to celebrate their wedding.

She was aware of Castleford's eyes glancing across at her as she said her promises, repeating the words after her father.

"I Georgiana Merry take thee Frederick Warren to be my wedded husband, to have and to hold from this day forward, for better for worse, for richer for poorer, in sickness and in health, to love, cherish and to obey, till death us do part, according to God's holy ordinance; and thereto I give thee my troth."

As Castleford slipped the ring on her finger, the reality sank in. This band of gold proved it. And then her father spoke the words that confirmed it:

"I pronounce that they be Man and Wife together, In the Name of the Father, and of the Son, and of the Holy Ghost. Amen."

A huge smile spread across her face. She was married. She was actually married. As if in a dream, Georgiana listened to her father reading a Psalm and giving a short sermon.

Castleford took her hand and led her out of the chapel and into the hallway where the servants were lined up before them. The butler stepped forward and offered them congratulations on behalf of all the staff.

"Thank you, Newcombe. My wife and I are most grateful."

Georgiana glowed with happiness. My wife. How she revelled in the sound of those words.

They proceeded into the saloon where they stood, side by side, ready to greet the rest of the family. Castleford took advantage of them being alone for a moment and leaned down and stole a kiss. He had just pulled away from her when Newcombe opened the door again to let in the guests.

Lady Augusta came through first, accompanied by Lord Helston. A flicker of surprise crossed Georgiana's face before she understood. The members of their family were being ushered in according to rank. Augusta was the daughter of a duke and took precedence over Georgiana's parents, her aunt and uncle, and even over her mother-in-law. With a gulp, she realised that she was a countess now and must get used to such things.

"Mother was mortified that she could not come," Augusta said, "but it would have been impossible for Father to travel and Mother won't leave him. She is in alt, if a trifle put out that you have beaten me to the altar. Still, this meagre affair would not have done for her, and I would hate to deprive Mother of the big society wedding she craves. I do hope she won't keep us waiting much longer. Waiting is so tedious."

As Lord Helston finished shaking Castleford's hand, Lady Augusta took possession of her future husband's arm. Helston threw his friend a wry smile and allowed his intended to steer their path toward some chairs at the far end of the room.

"She will keep his hands full," Castleford whispered to Georgiana as his mother approached, leaning on Anthony for support.

"I think you may be right," she whispered back.

"Lord Castleford, Lady Castleford," his mother said with a twinkle in her eye as she leaned forward to kiss her son and then her new daughter.

Georgiana's brow clouded over as a thought occurred to her.

"I suppose you will be the Dowager Countess now," she said with an apologetic look. "Do you mind very much?"

The new Dowager Countess laughed. "Why would I want to keep a name that means so little to me?" she said. "I am perfectly content. You hold my Frederick's heart. I could not pass over the title or the care of my son to a worthier woman."

Anthony grinned and kissed Georgiana on the cheek. "Welcome to the family, sister," he said before taking his mother to her chair.

Lord Harting shook hands with Castleford while his wife gave a weak smile and muttered some words of congratulation, which sounded more genuine than Georgiana had expected. With barely a look at Castleford, Lady Harting moved away.

"I don't think she's got over the way your husband raked her down," Beau whispered in her ear as he leaned forward to kiss her on the cheek. "Won't say a word about it, but I believe Mother's relieved I didn't marry you. She's finally realised that I can't control you."

"Is that what she wants? A woman you can control?" Georgiana asked.

Beau shrugged. "More like one she can keep under *her* control. Thinks she could manage my wife the same way she manages me. But I don't intend her to dictate my life once the purse strings are in my hands at last. There are sacrifices I've made for the sake of my horses, but it won't be forever."

Georgiana thought there was a glimmer of hope that his mother would not always manipulate him.

Beau cast a sidelong glance of respect at Castleford. "He'll make you a far better husband than I," he said with a grin. "You'll listen to him."

Georgiana sighed as Beau moved away. She had already shared Eliza's secret with Castleford. "Do you think there's any hope he might prove to be a good husband?" she asked, looking up into Castleford's face with all the uncertainty she felt.

"Don't despair. Stranger things have happened. Beau may yet surprise you."

At last, her mother and father approached, followed by her brother and sisters.

Mrs Merry took hold of one of Castleford's hands and one of Georgiana's. She looked at them both and said: "Don't forget. Love is a choice. Choose to keep loving each other, no matter what. Forgive quickly. Keep talking. And trust God to give you strength for whatever life throws at you."

"Good advice," said Mr Merry. "She's a wise woman, your mother. Listen to her."

"The sort of advice the Sylph would offer," Georgiana whispered as her parents moved away, glowing warmly up at her husband as she remembered the part the letters had played in bringing them together.

There was no time for him to reply as her siblings were approaching, but words were unnecessary. He gave her hand a quick squeeze, his eyes reflecting the glow in her own.

Hetta came right up to Castleford and without any inhibitions, she threw her arms around him. "I said I'd like to have you for a brother," she said, her face buried in his coat. "I'm so happy I could burst."

"Well, don't burst in here," Castleford replied. "Mrs Newcombe would not enjoy cleaning up the mess."

Hetta giggled. "Perhaps we could have a game of chess later, Cas?" she asked, readily adopting his pet name and looking up at him with the expression that had won her so many favourable replies in the past.

"Not tonight," he said, his eyes twinkling. "I can't neglect your sister when I've just married her. I don't think she'd like that."

"Oh yes. I see," said Hetta, nodding as if she were a wise old woman. "Best not to upset Georgie. She is your wife now."

Eliza offered them her congratulations and then hovered by her sister's side. "If I stay with you, perhaps I can avoid my aunt," she said. "Lady Harting puts me in a quake before she even opens her mouth and I feel sure she will interrogate me if she gets the chance."

Seeming to know that his bride would appreciate some time with her sister, Castleford left them alone and went to talk to his mother.

The sisters were still talking when Beau drifted back over to them. Eliza's face turned white as he approached.

"I seem to remember that Georgie told me you are a fine horse-woman," he said, addressing Eliza. "Come to think of it, didn't you used to pester me to let you ride my black stallion when I visited the parsonage when you were just a girl."

Eliza nodded but seemed incapable of speech. She sent her sister a desperate plea for help with her eyes.

Georgiana sighed. How was Eliza ever going to get to know Beau when she was paralysed with shyness whenever he was near?

"Beau wants to breed racehorses," she said, trying to be helpful.

"Racehorses?" Eliza squeaked.

Beau needed no further encouragement. Georgiana left Beau expanding on his dreams to the only woman in the room who wanted to listen to him.

For a few moments, Georgiana was alone, but not for long. Lady Harting saw her opportunity and approached. Her aunt glanced across to where Beau was engaged in animated conversation with Eliza. Her sister was smiling up at him but saying little.

"Elizabeth seems to be a prettily behaved young lady," she said to her with a sickly-sweet smile. Georgiana was too happy to let the words upset her, but the implication was clear. Her aunt did not think *she* was so prettily behaved, though she would not dare to say it to her face, especially not if her husband were nearby.

"Yes, aunt," she said, with an equally sweet smile, hoping it would win Eliza some approval with Beau's mother. Georgiana knew her aunt was being fooled by Eliza's current docility. Lady Harting was not to know that just now, Eliza was overcome with shyness, but she behaved with far less constraint in other circumstances.

The conversation continued in a stilted manner. Every word that her aunt spoke seemed designed to provoke, but before Georgiana was stung into saying something that she would later regret, her husband was back at her side. Lady Harting immediately made her excuses and moved away. Perhaps Beau was right, and Castleford had scared his mother so much that she now shunned his company.

Georgiana glanced around the room. To her surprise, Charlotte was having a heated discussion with Anthony. "What can they be arguing about, Cas?" she asked. "They only met yesterday."

"I expect they're talking about music."

"Music? I know it is the subject closest to Charlotte's heart, but Anthony?"

"My brother has some hidden talents."

"As do you," Georgiana replied. "I understand you were a fencing champion at Cambridge. Don't let Eliza find out or she'll be pestering you for lessons."

"Has Anthony been making trouble again?"

"Not at all. It was your mother who told me."

"What else has she been telling you?"

"Well, there was the time when…"

Georgiana stopped mid-sentence as her brother approached them. He thrust a piece of paper into her hand.

"It's only a rough sketch," William said, "but if you wish, I could paint it for you. I mean, you need not put it up anywhere if the finished painting is not to your liking, but…"

Castleford looked over her shoulder as Georgiana examined the drawing. It was a picture of their wedding. They were standing at the altar, looking sideways at each other, with her father beyond, dressed in his robes, with his prayer book open.

"I'm impressed," said Castleford. "You've caught Georgiana's expression exactly. You should go to the Royal Academy and study under West."

William's eyes lit up at the unexpected praise, but then the fire went out again. "Thank you for the thought," he said, "but I paint merely for amusement. My path lies in a different direction. I go up to Father's college at Cambridge later this year. But I'll finish the painting before I leave, I promise."

Castleford looked after him as he moved away. "The boy's got talent. Won't your father consider an alternative to Cambridge?"

"I don't think my brother will ask."

Castleford waited for her to explain.

"He is the only son. The only one who can follow in Father's footsteps."

"You mean he's destined for the church?"

Georgiana shook her head. "No, but he's the only one who can go to university. You must see. Lord Harting has only daughters. As things stand, William will inherit the earldom one day. He perceives it as his duty to go up to Cambridge like his father and uncle before him."

"But does he love studying like your father does?"

Georgiana hesitated. "He is more than able, but no, he does not love it."

Castleford looked at her, a serious expression on his face. "He should do what he loves, not what he thinks his father wants him to do."

"Try telling William that," Georgiana said with a sigh.

She noticed that Anthony had moved away from Charlotte who was left sitting by herself in the corner looking somewhat melancholy. Georgiana took her husband's hand, and they walked over to her.

"Aren't you going to wish me joy, Charlotte?" she said. "It's a wedding, not a funeral. Why the long face? Don't you like my husband?"

Charlotte blushed. "I hardly know him," she said, "but I can see you're happy. That you love him."

"But?"

"I'm afraid for you."

"Afraid for me? Surely you don't believe Castleford will beat me?" she said with a laugh, trying to make Charlotte smile.

She failed. Her sister said nothing, but Georgiana could tell she was fighting with some deep emotions.

"Come on. What is it?"

"Now you're married, you'll soon be with child and I fear you will die."

Georgiana blinked. That was rather a melancholy thought for her wedding day. She sat down beside her sister and put her arm around her shoulders.

"My life is no less in God's hands now than it was before. No one knows how long they will live on this earth. What is important is that we live in faith and hope that this life is not the end. Yes, I might die in childbirth. But equally well, I might be thrown from a horse or inflicted with consumption. Love is always a risk, but it is worth it when your love is returned. I would not give up this love, whatever the cost. I hope you'll feel that way too one day."

"Well, I won't," Charlotte replied in a firm voice. "I have no intention of ever falling in love. With the money grandmama has settled on me, I shan't dwindle into poverty as a single woman. I don't need a husband and I shall never marry."

"Then we'll have to keep each other company in our old age," chipped in Anthony, who had sauntered up in time to hear Charlotte's words. "One woman for the rest of my life? Perish the thought. I would be ruing my marriage before the year was out."

Georgiana looked at each of them in turn and gave a knowing smile. "It will be fascinating to see which of you caves in first."

Anthony and Charlotte both exclaimed, declaring that they would never marry in a most determined fashion.

Georgiana and Castleford left them to it.

* * *

At last, the day was done, and they were alone. Soon, her family would return home to the parsonage, back to the busy life of the parish, and Georgiana would not be going with them. She would be treading an alternative path now, at the side of her husband.

They walked along the corridor arm in arm until they came to Castleford's rooms. He opened the door, and she paused uncertainly, looking down at the floor, feeling suddenly shy.

He put one finger under her chin and tilted it upward until she was gazing into his eyes, which glowed with an intensity she had not seen before.

"And now, Lady Castleford," he whispered, standing so close to her that she could feel the warmth of his breath on her neck, "you are all mine."

"I do believe you have been hiding your true colours, my love," she said, her heart beating faster as the heat rushed to her cheeks. "Those are the most romantic words I have ever heard."

With the glimmer of a smile, Castleford pulled her into the room after him and shut the door.

AUTHOR'S NOTE

A Reason for Romance is a work of fiction, inspired in part by my own story. Like Lord Castleford, my husband Andrew became convinced that I was his 'one woman' long before I came round to the idea. He wanted to marry me; I just wanted to be friends. As committed Christians, we prayed together that one of us would change our minds. I never expected it to be me! Over thirty years later, Andrew and I are still living out our happy ever after.

The historical detail and language used in the novel are as accurate as I could make them. The only exception that I am aware of is the words of the wedding service. I added the word 'be' to the vows as written in the 1662 *Book of Common Prayer* to make them easier to read.

To find out more about the history behind the story, take a look at the historical notes included in this book. Further information is available on my website: regencyhistory.net.

My thanks go to my friends and family who have encouraged and supported me. Special thanks to fellow author Philippa Jane Keyworth for her invaluable feedback and help with the covers. Thanks also to my editors Abigail Flynn and my husband Andrew, and to Mirabelle Knowles for the final cover design.

If you enjoyed reading this book, please consider leaving a review on Goodreads or Amazon to help others to find it.

HISTORICAL NOTES

TIMELINE FOR 1810

18 January: Queen Charlotte's birthday drawing room held at St James's Palace.

18 January: The attempted robbery of Mr Brown of Ark Hall near Coventry - reported in *La Belle Assemblée* for January 1810.

19 January: The *Morning Post* published a report of skating on the Serpentine River, including a reference to a lady skater.

27 January: *The Merchant of Venice* was performed at the Covent Garden Theatre with the pantomime, the *Harlequin Pedlar*.

2 February: The House of Commons resolved to enquire into the disastrous military expedition to the Walcheren.

5 February: *Othello* was performed at the Covent Garden Theatre with the pantomime, the *Harlequin Pedlar*.

14 February: Valentine's Day. The Persian ambassador recorded in his journal that it was an English tradition for lovers to send anonymous letters and love poems to their sweethearts on Valentine's Day.

26 February: A children's candlelit ball was held at Lord Darnley's house in Berkeley Square, opened by the Prince of Wales.

1 March: An admission day was held at the Magdalen Hospital.

10 March: Madame Catalani performed at the Opera House.

16 March: The Persian ambassador entertained around 500 people. About half of them left at midnight to go to the Countess of Clonmell's ball in Portman Square, and their carriages caused a traffic jam.

5 April: The House of Commons found Sir Francis Burdett guilty of libel upon its best rights and privileges.

5 April: Mrs Hope held a rout at her house in Duchess Street.

6 April: Sir Francis Burdett was sentenced to imprisonment in the Tower of London. A mob gathered to prevent his arrest.

9 April: Sir Francis Burdett was arrested and conveyed to the Tower, escorted by the military.

9 April: Mr Salomon's annual concert was held at the New Rooms, Hanover Square. The musical programme was advertised in the *Times* on 6 April.

16 April: A review of troops was held in Hyde Park.

22 April: Easter Sunday.

30 April to 16 June: The Royal Academy exhibition was held at Somerset House. The exhibition guide listed J M W Turner's *Dewy Morning at Petworth* and William Beechey's portrait of the Persian ambassador.

22 May: Lady Buckinghamshire held a breakfast masquerade. Sources suggest that it was held at the house of the Dowager Countess of Buckinghamshire and not the current Countess, her daughter-in-law Eleanor.

28 May: Music party held at the Duchess of Devonshire's house.

31 May: The Duke of Cumberland was attacked in his bed and his valet, Sellis, was found dead.

4 June: Vauxhall Gardens opened for the season with a splendid gala in honour of His Majesty's birthday.

6 June: A masked ball was held at the Argyll Rooms.

7 June: The annual gathering of the charity children of the metropolis took place in St Paul's Cathedral. Admission was by ticket only and a charity sermon was preached, and a collection made in aid of the work of the charity schools.

12 June: The Duchess of Devonshire held her last grand rout of the season.

GLOSSARY

Bandbox: A lightweight box made of pasteboard or thin wood used to hold light articles of attire.

Blackballed: In White's and other gentlemen's clubs, members were elected by existing members voting using a system of white balls for 'yes' and black balls for 'no'. A prospective member was 'blackballed' if anyone voted against them.

Chaise: A carriage, typically with a single seat for two people.

Chaperon: A female companion for an unmarried lady. She was typically a married lady or a widow, though she could be of any age.

Charity school: A school funded by voluntary contributions to teach poor children to read and write. They were usually run by religious groups who provided the education and uniform free or at very low cost.

Corinthian set: A group of fashionable gentlemen who excelled in sport.

Curricle: A light carriage with two wheels driven by its owner. The most fashionable curricles were pulled by a pair of carefully matched horses.

Drawing room: Short for withdrawing room. Ladies retired to the drawing room after dinner, leaving the gentlemen at the table to imbibe stronger drinks, such as port. The gentry received visitors here.

Drawing room, the Queen's: The Queen held special receptions at St James's Palace which were called drawing rooms. A young lady, wearing full court dress, was presented to Queen Charlotte on her entrance into London society.

Duel: A planned combat between two gentlemen because one of them had offended the other. The weapons used were duelling pistols or swords. It was viewed as cowardly not to give satisfaction for an offence by refusing another gentleman's challenge. A gentleman could, however, decline to meet an inferior person, such as a servant, with no slur on his courage. Duels were illegal, so often took place early in the morning at remote locations. A duel could be averted by making an apology, but once blows had been exchanged, any apology had to be accompanied by the offer of a whip with which to punish the offender.

Gig: A two-wheeled carriage, driven by its owner, and usually pulled by a single horse.

Hazard: A game of chance played with two dice, often for high stakes.

Introduction: An introduction was more than just getting to know someone's name. A gentleman would be presented to a lady by a third party – a chaperon or friend who could vouch for the gentleman being a desirable acquaintance for the lady. Until formally introduced, a lady and gentleman were not supposed to talk to each other.

Ladybird: Originally a term for a sweetheart, but in vulgar usage, it referred to a light or lewd woman.

Pelisse: A long fitted coat.

Phaeton: A light, four-wheeled carriage that was driven by its owner rather than by a coachman. Depending on its design, it was pulled by a single horse or a pair.

Post-chaise and four: A hired travelling chariot pulled by four horses. It was driven by postilions who were hired with the chaise.

Postilion: A person who rode one of the horses pulling a carriage. A postilion-driven carriage had no coachman but was guided by one or more postilions riding the nearside horses. A postilion was also known as a post-boy.

Post road: A road used by those delivering the post. There was a system of posting inns or post houses at stages along a post road where horses and postilions could be hired and replaced. This enabled travel to take place at the highest possible speed by continually refreshing the horses.

Regency: The Regency period was the nine years from 1811 to 1820 when the Prince of Wales, the future George IV, ruled as Prince Regent during the final illness of his father, George III.

Reticule: A lady's purse or small bag designed to carry around personal items that used to be kept in a pocket. Pockets became impractical when dresses became more streamlined and so a reticule acted like a portable pocket.

Rout: An assembly or 'at home' on a large scale. The measure of success seemed to be that it was a squeeze rather than anything else. The guests did not sit, but moved from room to room, often with no entertainment provided. They usually began at 10pm or even later and lasted into the early hours of the morning.

Season: The season was the time of year when the upper classes went to London to socialise with each other. It was the best opportunity to meet a suitable marriage partner. During the Regency period, it typically ran from November or January through to June or July, roughly coinciding with the sitting of Parliament.

Second: A friend who stood by each combatant in a duel. Seconds planned the meeting and ensured fair play. They were responsible for trying to effect a reconciliation without resort to violence.

Set-down: A snub, often by a person of some importance to someone of inferior social standing.

Spencer jacket: A short-waisted jacket that ended just under the bosom.

Sweetmeats: Items of confectionery; fruits preserved with sugar.

Tête-à-tête: A private conversation between two people.

Travelling chariot: A four-wheeled, postilion-driven carriage used for long journeys with a single forward-facing internal seat for two people. It was driven by one or more postilions rather than by a coachman sitting on a coach box which would obscure the travellers' view. Fresh horses could be hired at inns along the post road.

Turnpike: A toll gate or a road with a toll gate. Turnpike Trusts were set up by Acts of Parliaments during the 18th and 19th centuries in order to improve the state of the roads. Trusts maintained individual stretches of road and had the right to levy tolls on road users to finance this. A turnpike gate blocked the way to travellers to make them stop and pay the toll for the stretch of road that they were using.

Two-penny post: A postal system that operated within a limited area of London and its suburbs, allowing for the fast delivery of letters. There were six deliveries a day, so it was possible to receive a letter and send a reply that would be received the same day. It was like a Georgian courier service!

Watchmen: Men who patrolled the streets at night, looking out for crime and fire. Every hour, they called out the time and described the weather.

Whig: One of the two main political parties during the Georgian period. The Whigs believed in the power of the people and favoured economic and political reform.

HISTORICAL CHARACTERS

Amelia, Princess: Princess Amelia (1783–1810) was the youngest daughter of George III and Queen Charlotte. She visited Weymouth in 1808 with her sister Mary to try sea bathing for her health.

Blake: William Blake (1757–1827) was an English Romantic poet.

Buckinghamshire, Lady: Albinia Hobart, Dowager Countess of Buckinghamshire (c1737–1816) was recklessly extravagant, gambled heavily, and organised lavish parties. At one time, she ran an illegal gambling concern in her house, allowing play for high stakes.

Burdett, Sir Francis: Sir Francis Burdett (1770–1844) was a radical Whig politician who wrote a letter published in *The Political Register* on 24 March 1810 accusing the House of Commons of abuse of privilege by excluding non-politicians, including the press, from the debates on the disastrous Walcheren expedition. The letter was found libellous and on 5 April, Sir Francis was judged guilty of breach of privilege by the House of Commons. On 6 April, he was sentenced to imprisonment in the Tower of London, but a mob gathered outside his house to prevent his arrest. He was successfully arrested on 9 April and incarcerated in the Tower until the end of the parliamentary session on 21 June when he was released.

Burns: Robert Burns (1759–1796) was a Scottish Romantic poet and song lyricist.

Catalani, Madame: Angelica Catalani (1780–1849) was a popular Italian opera singer.

Charlotte, Princess: Princess Charlotte of Wales (1796–1817) was the only child of George, Prince of Wales, the future George IV, and Caroline of Brunswick.

Charlotte, Queen: Queen Charlotte (1744–1818) married George III in 1761, just a few hours after meeting him for the first time. The marriage was a happy one and produced 15 children but was overshadowed by the King's mental illness in later years.

Clonmell, Countess of: Henrietta Louisa Scott, Countess of Clonmell (1785–1858), was the daughter of George Greville, 2nd Earl of Warwick. Her husband Thomas Scott (1783–1838) was 2nd Earl of Clonmell in the Irish peerage.

Cumberland, Duke of: Ernest, Duke of Cumberland (1771–1851) was the 5th son of George III and Queen Charlotte. He became King of Hanover in 1837 on the death of his brother William IV as only men could inherit the Hanoverian throne. On 31 May 1810, the Duke of Cumberland was attacked in his bed and his valet, Sellis, was later found dead. On the testimony of the Duke and his staff, it was believed that Sellis had attacked his master and then committed suicide, but there were some who questioned the verdict.

Derby, Earl of: Edward Smith Stanley, 12th Earl of Derby (1752–1834) after whom the Epsom Derby was named. The Epsom Oaks was named after his hunting lodge in Carshalton, Surrey, and his mare Bridget was the first winner.

Devonshire, Duchess of: Elizabeth Cavendish, (née Hervey, previous married name Foster) (1758–1824) was the second wife of William Cavendish, 5th Duke of Devonshire. She had previously been his mistress.

Devonshire, Duchess of: Georgiana Cavendish (née Spencer), Duchess of Devonshire (1757–1806) was the first wife of William Cavendish, 5th Duke of Devonshire. She is attributed with writing *The Sylph*, a novel published anonymously in 1778.

Devonshire, Duke of: William Cavendish, 5th Duke of Devonshire (1748–1811) was a wealthy Whig politician and nobleman.

Egremont, Lord: George Wyndham, 3rd Earl of Egremont (1751–1837) and owner of Petworth, bred racehorses at a stud near Lewes including five Derby winners.

Elgin, Lord: Thomas Bruce, 7th Earl of Elgin (1766–1841), controversially collected the Elgin marbles while he was Ambassador to Constantinople (1799–1803). They were part of the temple of the Parthenon and other ancient buildings in Athens. He shipped them back to England at great cost so they could be studied. The Persian Ambassador was not impressed when he visited them in April 1810. The British Museum bought the marbles from Lord Elgin in 1816.

Gregory, Dr: John Gregory (1724–1773) was a Scottish doctor and moralist. He wrote *A Father's Legacy to his Daughters*, published posthumously in 1774.

Hamilton, Lady: Emma, Lady Hamilton (1765–1815), was the second wife of Sir William Hamilton (1730–1803), who served as the British ambassador to Naples from 1764 to 1800. She became Lord Nelson's mistress in 1798 and bore him a daughter, Horatia, in 1801.

Hart: William Cavendish, Marquess of Hartington (1790–1858), known to his intimates as Hart, was the only son of Georgiana, Duchess of Devonshire, and her husband William Cavendish, 5th Duke of Devonshire. He became 6th Duke of Devonshire in 1811 and inherited eight houses, including Chatsworth, Devonshire House, Hardwick Hall and Chiswick, and around 200,000 acres of land.

Hope, Thomas: Thomas Hope (1769–1831) was an art collector, interior designer and author. His wife was Louisa Beresford, an acclaimed Irish beauty. Their house in Duchess Street was described as 'magnificent' by the Persian ambassador.

King: George III (1738–1820) was King of Great Britain 1760–1820. He suffered from mental instability which may have been caused by the hereditary condition of porphyria. This forced the Regency period of 1811 to 1820 when the future George IV ruled as Regent.

Lamb, Lady Caro: Lady Caro Lamb (1785–1828) was the only daughter of Georgiana, Duchess of Devonshire's sister Henrietta and her husband Frederick Ponsonby, Earl of Bessborough. She married William Lamb, the future Viscount Melbourne, in 1805.

Leeds, Dowager Duchess of: Catherine Osborne, Duchess of Leeds (1764–1837) was the second wife of Francis Osborne, 5th Duke of Leeds (1751–1799). After her husband's death, she was known as the Dowager Duchess of Leeds. She is included in the list of nobility at the Queen's birthday drawing room in January 1810 in *La Belle Assemblée*.

Leveson-Gower: Granville Leveson-Gower, 1st Earl Granville (1773–1846), was known as Lord Granville Leveson-Gower before being made Viscount Granville in 1815 and then Earl Granville in 1833. He had a long-term relationship with Henrietta Ponsonby, Countess of Bessborough, but in December 1809, he married her niece, Lady Henrietta Cavendish (1785–1862), the younger daughter of her sister, Georgiana Cavendish, Duchess of Devonshire.

Manton: Joseph Manton (1766–1835) was a British gunmaker who had a shop in Davies Street, Berkeley Square. In his reminiscences, Captain Gronow recorded that he was amongst those who often visited Manton's shooting gallery and shot at the wafer. Gentlemen bet considerable sums of money on a shooter's success in hitting the small target.

Mary, Princess: Princess Mary, (1776–1857), later Duchess of Gloucester, was the eleventh child of George III and Queen Charlotte.

Melbourne, Lady: Elizabeth Lamb, Viscountess Melbourne (1751–1818) was a leading Whig hostess and mother of William Lamb, Viscount Melbourne, the future British Prime Minister.

More, Mrs: Hannah More (1745–1833) was an evangelical Christian writer whose moral works were highly influential in her time. She was the author of *Coelebs in Search of a Wife* (1808).

Nelson, Lord: Admiral Horatio Lord Nelson (1758–1805) was a British naval hero. After he died at the Battle of Trafalgar on 21 October 1805, his body lay in state in the Painted Chamber at the Royal Naval Hospital, Greenwich. He was buried in the crypt of St Paul's Cathedral in January 1806, but it was not until 1808 that the sculptor John Flaxman started work on the monument in his memory and it took ten years for him to complete it.

Persian ambassador: Mirza Abul Hassan (1776–1845) was the Persian ambassador to Britain. He was London's most celebrated visitor during his stay in 1809–10. He kept a journal which is a useful source for the history of this period. His presence prompted Persian-inspired fashions and it became popular to dress as a Persian at masquerades. During his visit to London, he stayed in Mansfield Street.

Radstock, Lord: Admiral William Waldegrave, 1st Baron Radstock (1753–1825), became friends with the Persian ambassador and entertained him at his home – 10 Portland Place.

Salomon, Mr: Johann Peter Salomon (1745–1815) was a German violinist, composer and conductor.

Siddons, Mrs: Sarah Siddons (1755–1831) was probably the greatest tragic actress of her time. Her most famous roles were as Shakespearean characters such as Lady Macbeth.

Wales, Prince of: George, Prince of Wales (1762–1830), the future George IV, was the eldest son of George III and Queen Charlotte. He ruled as Prince Regent (1811–20) during his father's last illness.

Wales, Princess of: Princess Caroline of Brunswick (1768–1821) was the estranged wife of George, Prince of Wales, the future George IV.

West: Benjamin West (1738–1820) was a Pennsylvanian-born artist, famous for his history paintings like *The Death of General Wolfe* (1770) and *The Death of Nelson* (1806). He was President of the Royal Academy of Arts 1792–1805 and 1806–20.

HISTORICAL PLACES

Almack's Assembly Rooms were in King Street, St James's. During the Regency era, the rooms were governed by lady patronesses who restricted entry to those members of the gentry and aristocracy who gained their approval, and it was necessary to have a voucher issued by one of these ladies to buy tickets to attend. Here, a young lady demonstrated her suitability as a marriage partner to prospective husbands, giving Almacks the nickname of the *Marriage Mart*.

The **Argyll Rooms** were a fashionable venue for concerts, masquerades and other entertainment (1806–30). The spelling of Argyll varied.

Astley's Amphitheatre was a well-established arena for equestrian spectacles but was only open during the summer. During the winter season of 1810, Mr Astley's troupe gave equestrian performances in his newly built Olympic Pavilion in Newcastle Street, Strand.

The **Asylum** was situated in St George's Fields and was a refuge for female orphans who might otherwise be drawn into prostitution. They were given a basic education and then apprenticed, usually as domestic servants. The Asylum was in St George's Fields.

Barker's Egyptian Panorama was in Leicester Square and was advertised in the *Times* on 5 February 1810. It was a panoramic view of Cairo and the pyramids that gave the spectator the illusion of actually being there.

Coade and Sealy's Gallery of Sculpture of Artificial Stone was situated at the south bank end of Westminster Bridge and was the showcase for Eleanor Coade's artificial stone factory. She even supplied guidebooks to the gallery. Coade successfully developed a durable artificial stone that was cheaper than stone itself. During this period, she was in partnership with her cousin John Sealy.

Covent Garden Theatre was one of the two theatres in Georgian London licensed to perform plays during the winter season. The other was the Drury Lane Theatre. The Covent Garden Theatre was burned down on 20 September 1808 and rebuilt in record time, reopening on 18 September 1809. The manager raised the prices to recoup some of the rebuilding costs, but it was an unpopular move, and performances were disrupted by the Old Price riots or OP war, for around six weeks until the management agreed to reduce prices. The disrupted opening night performance was of *Macbeth* with Mrs Siddons in her most famous role of Lady Macbeth.

Hookham's Library was one of the main circulating libraries in London. It was situated in Old Bond Street.

Hyde Park was a popular place to promenade on foot, ride on horseback, or drive a carriage in the afternoon.

Kensington Gardens were originally part of Hyde Park, created when Kensington Palace became a royal residence. During the Regency era, they were a fashionable place to promenade, particularly on Sunday afternoons between two and five o'clock, between February and June. Many people followed a path across Hyde Park from Hyde Park Corner to reach Kensington Gardens.

The **Lyceum Theatre** on the Strand was built as an exhibition space but was later converted into a theatre. From 1809 to 1812, the Drury Lane Theatre company performed at the Lyceum under their own licence whilst their theatre was being rebuilt after a fire.

The **Magdalen Hospital** was a home for prostitutes who wished to reform and to provide an asylum for young women who had been seduced and might otherwise be forced into prostitution. In 1810, it was situated on the east side of the road leading from Blackfriars Bridge to the obelisk in St George's Fields. Applications for admittance had to be made in person and were considered on the first Thursday of every month.

Miss Linwood's Exhibition of Pictures in Needlework was in Leicester Square and was advertised in the *Times* on 5 February 1810. It comprised around sixty needlework copies of works of art.

Pidcock's Museum was a menagerie situated over the Exeter Exchange in the Strand. *The Picture of London for 1810* gave a list of the animals that were housed in the apartments on the first floor.

Richmond Park in Surrey is a royal park open to the public about eight miles from Hyde Park.

The **Royal Academy** was founded in 1768 and was the first body in Britain to provide professional art training. Every year since 1769, the Royal Academy has run an art exhibition. From 1780 to 1838, it was based at New Somerset House.

St George's Hanover Square is the parish church of Mayfair, making it the most fashionable church in London during the Regency.

St James's Palace is a royal residence on Pall Mall in London. A fire in 1809 destroyed much of the palace, but the state apartments survived, and were still used by the court for holding drawing rooms.

St Paul's Cathedral was open to tourists in 1810. Visitor attractions, including the Whispering Gallery, were described in *The Picture of London for 1810*.

The **Serpentine** or Serpentine River is an artificial lake in Hyde Park. When it froze, it was a popular place for skating during the Regency era. The Humane Society was given some land on its banks to build a house to receive people who had been rescued from falling through the ice. This is mentioned in Feltham's *The Picture of London for 1810*.

Strawberry Hill is a Gothic castle in Twickenham, London, built for the brilliant letter writer and Whig politician Horace Walpole (1717–1797). On his death, he left the house to his cousin, the sculptor Anne Seymour Damer (1749–1828) who lived there until 1811.

Tattersall's Repository was situated near Hyde Park corner and was the premier venue for the sale of horses and carriages by auction. There was also a subscribers' room where horse racing bets were settled.

The **Tower of London** is a historic royal fortress on the north bank of the River Thames. Although it was a tourist attraction, it was still used occasionally as a prison. Sir Francis Burdett was incarcerated here in 1810. *The Picture of London for 1810* described what could be seen and how much it cost. There was no list of animals kept in the menagerie in that year, but the previous year's edition gave a full list. The story about why the monkeys were banished was quoted in the 1802 edition.

Vauxhall Gardens were pleasure gardens situated in Lambeth, Surrey, south of the River Thames. They were a fashionable venue for outdoor entertainment throughout the Georgian period. Typically, they were open from May to August, but it depended on the weather. The amusements included a concert, dancing, promenading along the walks lit by thousands of lamps, fireworks, and an artificial cascade.

White's Club was an exclusive club for gentlemen based in St James's Street where gentlemen could discuss business or politics, meet with friends for conversation or cards, and have a meal. White's had a famous betting book that has been preserved.

MILITARY REFERENCES

(in chronological order)

The **Battle of Valencia de Alcántara** in August 1762 was a successful Anglo Portuguese attack on the Spanish town of Valencia de Alcántara during the Seven Years' War, led by John Burgoyne.

The **Battle of Tournay** on 22 May 1794 was fought over the Belgian village of Pont-à-Chin during the Flanders Campaign between the French and the Coalition forces of Austria, Britain, and Hanover. The Coalition forces were ultimately victorious but with heavy casualties.

The **Treaty of Amiens** was signed on 27 March 1802 and provided a temporary break from the war between France and Great Britain. It ended in May 1803 when the British declared war on France. Many wealthy members of the gentry and aristocracy visited Paris while the treaty was in force.

The **Walcheren Campaign** was a disastrous British military action in 1809. The aim was to destroy the French fleet and the first action was to seal the mouth of the River Scheldt to stop Antwerp being used against them. John Pitt, 2nd Earl of Chatham, led thousands of British troops to take the Dutch island of Walcheren at the mouth of the river, but the swampy conditions led to widespread fever – probably a combination of malaria, typhus, typhoid and dysentery. Around 4,000 men died of the fever and thousands more never fully recovered. The campaign was hotly debated in parliament.

The **88th Regiment of Foot**, known as the Connaught Rangers, served in the Peninsular War from 1809. After joining the regiment, Denmead would have served under Lieutenant-Colonel John Wallace in the Battle of Bussaco in September 1810.

LITERARY REFERENCES

A Father's Legacy to his Daughters was written by Dr John Gregory in 1761 after the death of his wife to instruct his daughters in matters of religion, conduct and love. It was published posthumously by his son in 1774. It is quoted in one of the Sylph letters.

A Red, Red Rose is a 1794 song in Scottish dialect by Robert Burns which is often published as a poem.

Coelebs in Search of a Wife is a novel by evangelical Christian and moralist Hannah More published in 1808. Lucilla Stanley is the heroine of the book and she rejects the proposals of the profligate Lord Staunton, later accepting the hero, Charles.

Debrett's peerage: *The Peerage of the United Kingdom of Great Britain and Ireland* by John Debrett is a guide to the peerage, first published in 1802.

Evelina, or the history of a young lady's entrance into the world, is a novel by Frances Burney published in 1778.

Holy Thursday is a poem by William Blake published in 1789, which describes the annual service in St Paul's Cathedral for the poor children of the London charity schools.

Lady of the Lake is a poem by Sir Walter Scott, which was published in London on 16 May 1810.

Marmion is a poem by Sir Walter Scott published in 1808. Lord Castleford quotes two lines from the poem to Georgiana:

> *Oh, what a tangled web we weave,*
> *When first we practise to deceive!*

Tell me, my heart, if this be love is a song by George Lyttelton, Lord Lyttelton, written in 1732. Sir James recites verses of this to Georgiana.

The Picture of London was a London guidebook by John Feltham published annually.

The Sylph is a novel attributed to Georgiana Cavendish, Duchess of Devonshire, published anonymously in December 1778.

MARRIAGE AND DIVORCE

In the early 1800s, marriages in England were governed by Hardwicke's Marriage Act of 1753. This required couples to be married in the parish church of the parish where at least one of them lived, either after banns had been read or by common licence. A couple needed parental consent to marry if they were underage.

As no such consent was necessary in Scotland, couples who wanted to marry without parental consent fled north and eloped across the border, to places like Gretna Green, to get married.

In England, the only way to be married more quickly or in a place other than a parish church was by special licence. This could only be issued by the Archbishop of Canterbury and was expensive. But it meant that a couple could be married at any time and in any place, such as in the private chapel of their home.

Before the Matrimonial Causes Act of 1857, the only way to obtain a divorce in England and Wales was by a private Act of Parliament. It was only granted for cases of adultery. 322 private divorce Acts were passed between 1700 and 1857 and of these, only four were initiated by women, because for a wife to bring a case, the adultery had to be compounded by something worse, such as life-threatening cruelty or incest.

In Scotland, divorce was available in common law, and was granted by the Commissary Courts. A case for divorce could be brought for adultery or desertion by either party of a marriage.

DISCUSSION QUESTIONS

1. Which character in the book did you like best? What was it that attracted you to them?

2. Lord Castleford asks Georgiana whether she would deprive the poor of help for fear that they might prove less deserving than she believed. Are you challenged by his words?

3. Lord Castleford and Anthony both hate their father's infidelity but react to it in different ways. Castleford is determined to be different whilst Anthony fears he is too much like his father. What faults have you seen in your parents and how have you reacted to them? Which brother are you more like?

4. It is Georgiana's fondness for the novel *The Sylph* that gives Lord Castleford the idea of writing her anonymous letters of advice. What books have you read that have influenced your life?

5. There is a strong sibling relationship between Georgiana and Eliza. The bond between Lord Castleford and Anthony is less obvious but comes out strongly when Castleford is in trouble. How do your sibling relationships or those of your children compare?

6. Georgiana pretends to allow Beau to court her for her sister's sake. How did their deception make you feel? Do you think the ruse was justified?

7. Lord Castleford strikes Sir James in his anger and has to deal with the consequences. Have you ever been in a similar situation where you have had to deal with the repercussions of acting rashly?

8. A duel was considered a more gentlemanlike way of settling a dispute than fist fighting. Do you agree? Do you think Lord Castleford is right to refuse to fight? Why or why not?

9. Were you shocked to learn of the etiquette attached to making an apology after a blow had been given? Do you think offering the offended party your whip to strike you was a reasonable way to make recompense? Did anything else in the book shock you?

10. In the Sylph letters, Lord Castleford describes being in love as feeling *that if you went out of my life, the sun would never shine so brightly again.* How would you describe true love?

ABOUT THE AUTHOR

Rachel Knowles loves happy endings. She first read Jane Austen's *Pride and Prejudice* at the age of thirteen and fell in love, not only with Mr Darcy, but with the entire Regency period.

Since 2011, Rachel has been researching late Georgian and Regency history and blogging about her research on her website: regencyhistory.net.

Rachel lives in the beautiful Georgian seaside town of Weymouth, Dorset, with her husband, Andrew. They have four daughters and a growing number of grandchildren.

Sign up to Rachel's newsletter to follow her writing and research journey on regencyhistory.net

Lightning Source UK Ltd.
Milton Keynes UK
UKHW041248210521
384126UK00001B/12